The Greek House

Dinah Jefferies began her career with *The Separation*, followed by the No.1 *Sunday Times* and Richard and Judy bestseller, *The Tea Planter's Wife*. Born in Malaysia, she moved to England at the age of nine, and went on to study fashion design in London, work in Tuscany as an au pair for an Italian countess, and live with a rock band in a commune in Suffolk.

A personal tragedy in her past changed her life, and she now draws on the experience in her page-turning novels of love, dark family secrets and mystery set in stunning locations, worlds where readers can escape and lose themselves. She is published in 29 languages in over 30 countries and lives in Gloucestershire. *The Greek House* is her eleventh novel.

To find out more about Dinah Jefferies:

www.dinahjefferies.com
/DinahJefferiesBooks
@DinahJefferies
/dinah_jefferies_author

Also by Dinah Jefferies

The Daughters of War Trilogy
Daughters of War
The Hidden Palace
Night Train to Marrakech

The Separation
The Tea Planter's Wife
The Silk Merchant's Daughter
Before the Rains
The Sapphire Widow
The Missing Sister
The Tuscan Contessa

DINAH JEFFERIES

The Greek House

HarperCollins*Publishers*

HarperCollins*Publishers* Ltd
1 London Bridge Street,
London SE1 9GF
www.harpercollins.co.uk

HarperCollins*Publishers*
Macken House, 39/40 Mayor Street Upper
Dublin 1, D01 C9W8, Ireland

First published by HarperCollins*Publishers* Ltd 2025
1

A catalogue record for this book is available from the British Library

ISBN: 978-0-00-861204-7 (PBO)
ISBN: 978-0-00-870276-2 (TPB, AU, NZ-only)

Typeset in Dante MT by HarperCollins*Publishers* India

Printed and bound in the UK using 100%
Renewable Electricity at CPI Group (UK) Ltd

MIX
Paper | Supporting
responsible forestry
FSC™ C007454

This book contains FSC™ certified paper and other controlled
sources to ensure responsible forest management.

For more information visit: www.harpercollins.co.uk/green

*For my husband, my daughter, my son-in-law,
and my grandchildren.
Thank you for all the wonderful
Ionian Island holidays we've shared.*

'Among all peoples, Greeks have dreamt life's dream most beautifully'

Johann Wolfgang von Goethe

PART ONE

Corfu

AUGUST 1923

CHAPTER 1

Dulcie

Dulcie narrowed her eyes at the bright light streaming in through half-open curtains, then glanced at her bedside clock. Still early, but the familiar tightness in her chest and the sense of foreboding were already there. She shivered, though not from the cold. It was August, and this was Corfu. She wasn't having a heart attack either, not at the age of thirty-eight, but the presentiment that had gripped her yesterday was deepening. She caught her breath and for a moment or two could not seem to exhale.

She left her bed, slipped on her lilac kimono, and unwrapped a mint from the glass bowl on her dressing table, popping it into her mouth and sucking the cool of it, on what was already becoming a warm day. She wiped her brow, picked up her silver hairbrush and, lifting the weight of her strawberry-blonde hair from the back of her neck, brushed it, then twisted and pinned it into an elegant low chignon.

Thoughts tumbled in her mind, but she picked up her pen, took a sheet of writing paper out of the desk, and began to write. After a moment and hearing the *huoh-huoh-huoh* of the gulls she looked up, sitting completely still, listening, considering.

Everything is going to fall apart.

The words were not pencilled into her mind, but rather as indelible as the little teardrop stain blooming on the cuff of her kimono. The drip of blue ink a constant irritation – a mark on the tip of her nose or maybe her chin where she'd absentmindedly touched the skin – the writer's curse, an editor's curse too. She put down her pen to gaze out of the window, inhaling the scent of rosemary from the bushes in their courtyard garden.

After too long Dulcie sighed, shook herself mentally. There was no point dwelling on what she could not change. Whatever was going on in the rest of Corfu, she could only focus on *her* life, on *her* family. That was what mattered. Right now, she had only to wash and get on with the day – for there was plenty to be getting on with. Later, she would answer some work letters, though it was much harder to concentrate with the children around.

After bathing, she sat at her dressing table in her underwear and applied a dark red Guerlain lipstick, adding a dab of rouge to her cheeks, while wondering what the mood in town would be. Yesterday, when she and her family had arrived from Merchant's House – their summer home in the north – there had been a general air of unease. News of the murders had only recently broken. Would reality have sunk in, now?

Dulcie stood, spraying her wrists with Tabac Blond – a daring scent she'd fallen in love with – then slipped into a green Madeleine Vionnet dress that clung to her curves. The impractical silk dress made her feel immensely desirable. She knew what happened as women grew older, and she was determined to remain visible for as long as she could.

She straightened her back, left her bedroom, and went downstairs to fetch the children, for she'd arranged to meet Odel at the café that morning. Dulcie hadn't wanted to leave Merchant's for the tall narrow town house where her husband, Captain Piers Caruthers, director of the British police school, lived during the working week. But there were undeniable advantages to being in town – and proximity to a good friend was certainly one of them.

With Billy's hand clasped in one of hers, Thirza following closely behind, and Dulcie's cousin Columbine, along with her daughter, eleven-year-old Ianthe, dawdling a little way back, they stepped out onto the street to find people fizzing with excitement. It was a dazzling Corfu day. The intense purple bougainvillea shone like satin against the elegant pale buildings, while the golden light had diamonds dancing upon the sea, and the windows of a perfectly ordinary jewellery shop sparkling and glittering like an Aladdin's cave. Dulcie drew in a breath. The sea with its indigo depths and changing moods made everything feel better. Made her feel better. That was what she wanted.

But Dulcie's calm was not shared by the people they passed as they negotiated the steps down to Dimarchiou Square, then cut down the Avenue to eventually emerge at the southern end of the Liston.

Her Greek wasn't too bad and, as she glanced over at the fountain in the Spianada Square, she knew enough to catch words and fragments as she passed by: whispers of *'murder'* and muttered asides about *'those* Italians'.

Those Italians were the murdered men: Enrico Tellini, an Italian general, his two Italian aides, plus an interpreter and a chauffeur, ambushed and assassinated near the town of Ioannina on Greek territory. The men had been there to help resolve a border dispute between Albania and Greece and now Italy blamed Greece for the murders and was demanding retribution.

Dulcie drew Billy closer to her at the thought of more trouble but resisted the urge to reach for Thirza, too – for Thirza, at sixteen, was far less likely to indulge her. It was easier, at Merchant's, to pretend all was well, but here, one could not ignore the agitation in the air.

Odel was already seated beneath the striped awning of their favourite café watching a cricket match on the huge green. A tall, imposing woman with lustrous chestnut hair and eyes like dark melted chocolate flecked with gold, Odel was very Greek, very beautiful, and Dulcie's closest and oldest friend.

Dulcie twisted round to Thirza, 'Darling, I think an ice cream is in order, don't you? Why not slip around the corner with Billy and Ianthe?'

'Where is Ianthe?'

'Look, just over there. She's on her way.'

'Such a slowcoach,' Thirza complained.

'Be kind.'

Thirza gave her a resigned look, waved at Ianthe, and set off with Billy.

'Have you seen?' Odel asked, reaching into the capacious brown bag at the side of her chair, and pulling out a few folded newspapers. Dulcie glanced nervously over the headlines as Odel spread them out. Only one was an English language paper.

ALBANIAN GOVERNMENT STILL DENIES MURDERS

MORTIFICATION FOR GREECE ON THE CARDS

'And what about this?' Odel said, picking up one of the papers from Athens and translating as she read. '"The Italian demands for reparation for the murders is disproportionate, and not driven by craving for justice at all but designed to inflict the bitterest humiliation upon Greece."'

Odel caught Dulcie's eye and grimaced – and Dulcie felt her own unease rise, too. It took a lot to worry Odel, after all. Even as children, at school together in England, Odel had seemed unflappable. As grown women, they had travelled the world together. Odel, a brilliant linguist, had often acted as Dulcie's translator; she'd been a steadfast companion. If Odel, who was Greek herself and married to a Greek administrator in the Prefect's office in Corfu, was worried, then everyone ought to be.

'It's tripe,' Columbine said, as she fell into the chair opposite. 'We all know the murderers were Albanian bandits. Not Greeks at all. No argument.'

'We don't know anything for sure,' Odel said and sighed. 'And none of the victims were robbed.'

'That's as may be. But you only have to look at those dark brooding mountains to imagine what goes on over there,' Columbine argued, flapping a clumsy hand at the flies hovering around the table.

'I think Odel knows what she's talking about,' Dulcie said, irritated, gesturing to the waiter to bring coffee.

'And I don't?'

'I didn't say that.'

'Didn't have to.' Columbine pointed a trembling finger at her, knocking over a glass of water. 'I know what you meant.'

'Oh, for God's sake,' Dulcie muttered as she mopped the mess up with a napkin.

Columbine narrowed her eyes then added in a singsong voice, *'Dulcie the golden girl,'* before returning to her normal aggrieved tone. 'Just remember I've spent as many summers in Corfu as you have. I know as much as you do.'

There was a moment's uneasy silence. Dulcie knew Columbine resented what she believed was Dulcie's easy life. But really her cousin knew nothing, nothing at all.

'What about wine?' Columbine said. 'I rather fancy a cool white.'

'Don't be ridiculous,' Dulcie said sharply. 'It's not even eleven.'

Columbine flushed in embarrassment, and Dulcie felt a twinge of guilt.

The children returned, Ianthe immediately leaning against Columbine, and Billy making for Dulcie's lap.

'I've got chocolate, Mummy,' he said, holding up what remained of his cornet. 'Double!'

Dulcie laughed. 'Good for you. But please don't get it on my dress.'

'Oh,' Thirza said. 'Nearly forgot. A kid handed me this. Said to give it to you.'

'What kid?'

'How would I know? Just some kid.' She reached into her pocket, drew out an envelope, and handed it to Dulcie.

'Can we have lemonade?' Billy pleaded.

Dulcie shook her head. 'Not after double chocolate ice cream.'

'Aren't you going to open it?' Thirza said.

Dulcie turned the envelope over then shrugged.

'Give it to me. I'll open it,' Columbine said, her face still flushed. 'Are you sure it wasn't for me? Someone wanting money. I do have a few . . . well, you know, a few unpaid bills.'

'I'll open it myself,' Dulcie said as she threw some coins on the table then rose from her seat. 'First I need to powder my nose.'

In the upstairs ladies' room, Dulcie glanced out of the window, from where she could observe her family collecting their belongings and then slowly meandering away.

She slid a fingernail under the flap of the envelope and pulled it open to reveal just nine words on a single sheet of white paper. Not handwritten, nor typed either, but instead, each word made up from individual letters cut from newspapers or magazines. She read the line twice.

YoU are GOing TO Pay FOR wHaT YOu did

CHAPTER 2

Ten minutes later Odel had returned home, and the rest of them were now ambling along the elegant colonnaded arcade of the Liston, Thirza, Billy, and Ianthe chattering and exclaiming at shop windows, while Columbine followed a little unsteadily. The Liston was the best place to see and be seen and reminded Dulcie of St Mark's Square in Venice. Even in the aftermath of the recent shocking events, people were out walking and going about their business, and Dulcie tried to allow the familiar sights and scents to soothe her, to dissipate a little of her foreboding. She thought about the unnerving note. What could it mean? Surely it must be a mistake. Perhaps it really had been intended for Columbine after all, because *she* was the one constantly getting into scrapes, and Dulcie was the one constantly rescuing her, and not just with money. Anyway, the only true secret Dulcie had was . . . and then she shook the thought away. She had learnt long ago that she had to stay in the present, put her past in a box, close the lid, and never, ever, look at it.

Whatever the future held, today was very fine indeed. In a little while, they would return home for lunch. Fresh lobster, her favourite, accompanied by salad, followed by a *Sicomada*, a luscious Corfiot cake of dried figs, almonds, orange peel, pepper, cinnamon, wine, and ouzo. Then, afterwards, Dulcie would visit the refugee children housed up at the fortress. The poor things had been brought over from Asia Minor, often known as Anatolia, when they had been made homeless by the recent Greco-Turkish war and Dulcie had taken on responsibility for them.

After that she really needed to request that her general manager post over a list of recent non-fiction acquisitions. The publishing house hadn't branched into fiction yet, though it was on the cards for the future. How she missed her younger days of travelling and writing. Impossible with two growing children and, although being desk-bound had its moments, it wasn't nearly as much fun.

Through the milling shoppers, Dulcie spotted her husband striding towards her, face set, and jaw clenched.

'Can you take the children, Columbine?' she called out, feeling instinctively that she did not wish them to hear whatever Piers had to tell her – but as soon as she had spoken, Billy was pulling away from the others and racing back to throw his arms round Dulcie's waist.

'I want to go with Mummy,' he insisted, just as Piers reached her side.

'You're turning the boy into a cissy,' Piers said, frowning down at Billy. 'Should have been sent off to England to board by now.'

As Dulcie stroked her son's curly hair, he looked up at her, his hazel eyes pleading to stay with her.

'He's too young,' she said.

Piers twisted his mouth in irritation. 'I was sent away at eight. Did me no harm. And Billy is already nine.'

Piers had been the one to insist he wanted a family. *She* had been the one to hesitate, at first. She thought of that conversation now.

'Don't all women want children?' he'd said.

Did they? She didn't know.

'I do have a career,' she'd replied.

'Your little books?' And he had laughed at her.

She had bristled. 'I own a publishing house,' she said, although back then she only owned one half of it.

A business that makes us more than ten times what you do, she stopped herself from saying.

In the end, she'd given in. And now, it was *she* fighting to keep the children by her side, and he was the one wishing to send one of them away.

'Now Billy,' she said. 'Go with Thirza, there's a good boy. I promise I won't be long.'

The children and Columbine wandered off, Billy declaring to anyone who would listen that his preferred ice cream flavour was pistachio, not chocolate after all.

'I like this dress,' Piers said, reaching out to lay a hand upon her waist.

Dulcie forced herself not to pull away from him.

'Thank you,' she said.

'Good last night, wasn't it?' he said, in a lower voice. 'All I've thought of this morning is your naked body and I long to ravish you right now.'

'Before lunch?' she quipped, blinking back her surprise. Much as her husband liked to *do* it, he rarely *spoke* of sex. She didn't know if she liked it. This talking.

'What time is it?' he asked, oblivious of the look on her face.

She glanced at her wristwatch. 'Half past twelve – *are* you joining us for lunch today?'

Piers shook his head, expression turning serious.

'That's why I came to find you. Lunch is off. I've just been told that all British foreign nationals need to report to the consul, and I have to spread the news around. It's pretty serious.'

Dulcie's heart sank.

'A number of Italian warships are looking to drop anchor not far from the city,' Piers said, lowering his voice. 'We don't know why, exactly, but the top brass are worried.'

'Do I really need to come too?' Dulcie said.

'Darling, I don't want to scare you,' he said, and reached out to drape an arm around her shoulders. Dulcie stepped away from him, his protective arm feeling more oppressive than reassuring.

She wanted, suddenly and with a pressing intensity she could feel in her bones, to go home – properly home to Merchant's, not the town house. She pictured the journey in her mind's eye. Their large motor boat easing them around the east coast of the island all the way back home to Merchant's House, in the north-east. The fresh sea breezes cooling them down and with things the way they were, heaven knows they needed that. And the boat – with its beautifully varnished wooden hull and two helm positions, one for her at the bow, and one for the crew at the rear – was Dulcie's pride and joy. It was always nice to travel by sea, especially after a sweltering day, and the sandy tracks that masqueraded as roads, almost impassable as soon as the rains began, were never Dulcie's first choice.

At Merchant's, she felt the rest of the world didn't exist. No politics, no strange notes, nothing to worry about – only the sound of the sea upon the shore, and the smell of salt and pine in the air.

'Dulcie?' Piers said impatiently. 'Are you listening? You have to come now.'

'I need to collect my new hat,' she protested, though really she wanted a moment alone to calm herself, slow down the too-fast beat of her heart, maintain a tight grip, without Piers noticing.

He gave her an annoyed narrow-eyed look then glanced at his watch. 'We only have half an hour.'

She sighed. 'Very well, I'll meet you there.'

Piers shrugged. 'Make sure you are *all* there. Including that drunken cousin of yours.'

Dulcie wiped her brow with a fresh handkerchief then spun around to hurry towards the hat shop a little further down the street. A rickety old place, but the milliner had been designing for the Caruthers family for decades and was still the best in town.

Dulcie climbed the stairs and found Thalia in a room fragranced with lavender.

The older woman, dressed entirely in black, pointed at the window. She was usually the chatty kind, though

Dulcie could only ever catch a few words of the extremely rapid Greek she spoke. Now she registered the mixture of excitement and anxiety in the woman's voice.

As she walked over to join Thalia, the woman passed her the binoculars.

Dulcie could see beyond the nearby street and across to the Port Square gardens. To the left stood the Venetian port where the police training school was based and where Piers spent most of his days. She moved the binoculars up a little to reveal the port harbour where beyond the outer harbour walls – *oh my Lord!* – Piers had been right. A mass of black ships, their masts and rigging resembling the antennae of giant water-boatmen insects, were anchoring outside their beautiful city.

As Dulcie focused the lenses more clearly on one of them, a thundering blast shook the building. She leapt in shock, dropping the binoculars to the floor. The women stared at each other, then back at the sea, where a huge plume of black smoke was now rising from one of the ships.

The blasts came again, and Dulcie shuddered as a vast wall of thunder battered the island.

Boom! Boom! Boom!

Again and again and again the building shook. Dulcie's heart pounded so hard from the shock of it, she was certain it would fly from her chest. Could this be what she had sensed might be coming? Was this it?

Thalia clutched her arm.

'Dear God!' Dulcie muttered, sweat prickling her hairline. 'The Italian navy is shelling us.'

Why the hell were they doing this? Then she saw the flames and columns of smoke towering above the old fortress! Bloody idiots. There were still armaments stored up there! And they would almost certainly explode.

And then her thoughts were tumbling, scattering, colliding. 'I have to find my children,' she said.

Thalia clung on to her sleeve and issued a strict warning in Greek. All Dulcie heard was, 'Not safe, madam.'

She shook herself free and without another word took the stairs two at a time, going over on her ankle just as she reached the bottom. Cursing, she limped into the street. A sickening acrid smell caught in her throat, as the ear-splitting *boom, boom, boom* repeated and repeated. She felt dizzy, disorientated. The band around her head tightened. She closed her eyes, wanting to make it all go away, but when she opened them again, she spotted Columbine dragging the children back along the street towards her. Billy with tears and dirt staining his dear little cheeks, Thirza and Ianthe clinging to each other, their faces pinched white with fear.

'Run to the British consul and stay there,' Dulcie shouted above the noise. 'Thirza, look after Billy.'

'It's all right, I can do it,' Columbine said.

'I don't think so! Thirza will do it.'

Columbine frowned. 'Why do you always try to make me look foolish?'

'Oh, for God's sake! This isn't the time for one of your complaints, Columbine.'

'I promise to look after him.'

'I'm perfectly capable of looking after my own brother,' Thirza muttered. 'I'll do it.'

Dulcie took a deep breath. 'Look, I don't care who looks after him so long as someone does. You can both do it.'

'But where are you going, Mummy?'

'I have to see to the children.'

'The refugees?' Columbine gasped, clearly cottoning on.

Thirza clutched hold of her arm. 'Mummy. No!'

The sharp sweet smell of the explosives filled the air. *Cordite*, she thought, acrid, smelling of pear drops, followed by the musky smell of TNT. Dulcie unhooked herself from her daughter and began limping towards the eastern edge of Spianada Square.

Piers was out on the street again too and when Dulcie realised he was coming after her she picked up her speed and, despite her painful ankle, began weaving through the hordes of startled, confused people spewing onto the streets.

'For God's sake, woman, it isn't safe,' Piers yelled after her.

She staggered on but he quickly caught up and held her back by the elbow.

She wrenched herself free, but coughed, choking on the thickening air, and the suffocating smell of burning rubber. Her throat felt raw, but she managed to swallow.

'The shelling is aimed at the fortress,' she said. 'Has anything hit the town yet?'

'Not so far but you *must* come with me. We have to go.'

A shell exploded somewhere further up the hill. A pungent red plumed cloud of smoke obliterated everything, but Dulcie could hear the screams and the shouts of the terrified crowd.

The shouting reached a crescendo as men and women pushed and pulled, desperate to flee the harbour and the fort. Piers held Dulcie in his grip and shouted in her ear, 'Keep back. If they carry on like this people will be trampled.'

'I have to help the refugees,' she shouted, holding back tears.

'You can't, Dulcie. Not until this is over and we have to get to the consul now.'

'But why?'

As the crowd surged, bursting outwards and away from the square, the noise abated enough for him to lower his voice a little. 'The Italians will need a record of who is here and who is not. It'll be all-out war if they kill any British citizens.'

'But the refugees? They're only children.'

Before he could answer, the bombardment started up again. Hands over her ears and hunched into herself, her ankle finally gave way and Dulcie sank down onto the road, ripping her beautiful silk dress. Unable to see, she wiped her smarting eyes with the back of her hand. She still couldn't see. Smoke. Tears. People running. Pounding footsteps. Another surge of screaming people surrounding her. *Make it stop! Make it stop!* The Great War had only ended five years before so how could Italy be doing this now? Hadn't they had enough of fighting? Weren't they sick of death and damage, injury, and loss? So much loss. So many young lives.

Her eyes were not so raw now – and with the smoke clearing a bit she scanned the sky. Were those aeroplanes?

CHAPTER 3

The British consul's office

Piers helped Dulcie climb the steps and enter the building. Nobody noticed them. Men jostled each other as they attempted to join the throng in the main assembly room, women with clipboards tried to squeeze through non-existent gaps, and from somewhere close by a baby screamed. The mother, squashed against the wall, cradled the baby in her arms and looked utterly exhausted. Dulcie craned her neck to see over the crowd and spotted Columbine's back as her cousin headed towards one of the lounges. Thank goodness the children were safe. She clapped her hands over her ears as an immense uproar reached her from the assembly room. Through the open door she glimpsed plump red-faced men thumping desks and threatening retaliation, and their poor wives reaching out their hands to placate them.

'Please,' the consul was shouting. 'Please can we show some restraint? We *are* British.'

Nobody took any notice at first but gradually the hubbub died down and people turned towards him and all you could hear then were the sound of ambulance bells and sirens in the distance.

Oh God, she thought. *Why did this have to happen?*

'Look,' the consul continued. 'I'm given to understand this is not an act of war.'

There was a roar of disbelief. 'Not an act of war?' someone called out. 'Last time I looked, one country shelling another bloody well was an act of war.'

'What is it then? Eh, consul, a children's tea party?' some bright spark shouted from the back.

'Mussolini issued an ultimatum,' the consul continued. 'The demand for reparation for the murdered Italians, you may have read about it. As the Greeks refused to meet those demands, this is the Italian response. They will occupy the island until the Greek government pays up.'

A loud muttering swept around the room. 'Bloody Mussolini,' and, 'Who the devil does he think he is?' and, 'Bomb the buggers back!'

The consul held up a hand. 'Gentlemen please. I need a list of everyone present and also a list of any British who may currently be on the island but up in the country and not in town.'

The man liked the sound of his own voice and, as he droned on, Dulcie stopped listening. She smoothed down her torn dress and rubbed her heel where the new high-heeled court shoes had caused a blister. She would never have worn them, had she known what the Italians were planning. She closed her eyes, and just as she always did when she needed to escape, found herself drifting back to the summer of 1913, ten years before, when she had been in her late twenties.

It had been a dazzling moonlit night, and they were guests at the Achilleion, the fairy tale palace built by the Empress Elisabeth of Austria and only finished twenty years before.

At the edge of the pillared colonnade, she'd found a spot where she couldn't be seen, or so she thought. Under cascading purple bougainvillea, she'd gazed across the garden's silvery trees, and listened to the sound of crickets, with not the slightest hint that she might be about to throw everything up in the air and change her life forever.

But *he* had seen her. Oh yes. And she had seen *him*. Would she go back in time and change that starlit night in 1913? No. Because . . .

She gulped back her sadness. No. Because it had meant everything.

A breath of cool air was all she had been after. She had believed she was alone leaning against a stone pillar in her carefully chosen Lucile of London black silk evening dress but then, as an owl hooted, a man spoke up.

'You are too hot,' he said.

'Pardon?' She only partially turned towards him.

'You are too hot.'

It wasn't a question but of course he was right.

He gave a little bow as she turned directly towards him.

He stepped forward into the light and she took in the deepest eyes she had ever seen, and a lion's mane of honey-brown hair. Younger than she, his teeth shone white against his tan, his smile disarming as he gazed at her. He was a beautiful young man.

'Dulcie Caruthers,' she said.

'The travel writer?'

'I suppose I am.' She couldn't admit how wonderful it felt to be referred to as a writer again and not just a mother and wife. Sometimes she felt as if the most creative part of herself had been forever squashed.

'Pleased to make your acquaintance. I too love travelling and have the heart of a vagabond.'

He tilted his head and studied her.

No more was said but she could not look away. She'd wanted to come back with a smart remark but as they stared at each other for far too long, there was only silence. In those moments during which everything was about to change forever, or nothing was, she was aware that neither of them could possibly tell which it would be. She wasn't a great believer in fate, preferring to think that humans made their own fate, and yet. *And yet.* She felt as if she already knew every cell in his body, every thought in his head, every word he might ever speak. Impossible. Completely impossible. But still. And she felt that he could read her mind too. *Was* reading her mind.

Then she remembered her husband, blinked rapidly, and took a step back, breaking the spell. She mumbled an excuse and almost *ran* back inside.

And she had thought that might have been the end of it.

But, of course, it hadn't been.

She felt the crinkle of the horrible anonymous note, now in her dress pocket. Could this possibly be what it was referring to?

Someone coughed and then cleared his throat behind her, and she came back to the present with a start, glancing around the consulate in dismay. She must prevent what had happened in the past from haunting her. She didn't belong back there. His breath on her neck, his fingers in her hair. Her heart beating too fast. She bowed her head.

She did not trust herself to speak but forced herself to nudge Piers.

'What?' he muttered under his breath.

And now she found her voice again. 'Do you think there will be an assault from the air too?'

'Not from what the consul is saying, but you never know. If things escalate . . .' He raised his hands and shrugged. 'You'd all best get back to Merchant's and make haste.'

'Yes,' she said, longing for the dappled sunshine of her orchards at Merchant's House, with the fair-weather mistral shifting the leafy canopy overhead, and the joyful sound of her children's voices reaching her from the garden.

'What about you?' she added, feeling a moment of genuine warmth for him and glad he was there beside her.

He puffed out his chest, in his element. 'I'll be needed here in town.'

'All right. But please be careful. I'm going to collect the children now. They'll be in one of the lounges at the back with Columbine.'

He nodded and she struggled through the crowd into the hall where a leering, heavily whiskered man with whisky-soaked breath put a warm hand on her bottom. She dashed his hand away, cursed him, then hurried along a corridor to a room at the back where she knew there were sofas and comfy armchairs. Columbine would have taken the children there. But when she finally made it, she could only see Thirza with little Ianthe, both slumped on a chair, arms around each other.

With startling, blue-green speckled eyes like the egg of a blackbird and skin the colour of porcelain, Thirza did not resemble her little brother Billy. Her wild red corkscrew curls – a brighter and deeper shade of Dulcie's own strawberry-blonde – made Thirza stand out and people always thought she must be Irish.

'Mummy,' she called. 'Over here.'

Dulcie crossed the room and knelt in front of them. 'Are you all right? Where's Billy?'

'Columbine went to look. He was with us so he must be around here somewhere.'

Dulcie winced as she tried to get up and Thirza shot her a worried look.

'It's just my ankle. I think I'm going to need to bandage it.'

'Sit here, Mummy. We'll go on the rug. You didn't get hit by anything, did you?'

'No.'

The relief as Dulcie sat and took the weight off almost made her cry. She flexed her ankle, and it seemed to help.

A woman she vaguely knew was distributing lemonade and cups of tea. Receiving hers gratefully, Dulcie rested the cup and saucer on her knees, and glanced around, her eyes settling on Thirza. With a sinking feeling she recognised the determined look now spreading across her daughter's face.

'I'm going to look for Billy,' Thirza said, jumping up again. 'Coming, Ianthe?'

Dulcie recalled Odel's summing up of Thirza when she was only two years old. 'Sharp, bold, and she already knows that if she's determined enough, she'll get away with anything.'

It was true. Thirza had been a different kind of trouble from the start. She'd wanted to change her own napkins at eighteen months, declaring, 'Thirza do it.'

And although christened Theresa, Thirza became her nickname, and it had stuck.

'I'm going,' her daughter repeated, adamant now. Already too tall at sixteen, the lanky long-legged kind, she towered over Dulcie.

'No, Thirza. You are not. We're going to wait for Columbine. She's probably only taken him to the lavatory. I don't want two of you on the loose.'

'On the loose, Mummy? We're not wild animals.'

'Please no argument. Look after Ianthe.'

Thirza gave an exaggerated sigh but did as she was told.

The mood in the room had changed from unease to indignation with people demanding to know if they were to be locked in, but then Dulcie spotted a consul secretary entering the room with a clipboard. She watched as names were added to the list and saw that once identified, people were allowed to leave.

She struggled to her feet when it was their turn and added all of them including Columbine and Billy.

'Come on, girls,' she said. 'I think I see Columbine now.'

But as Columbine approached, Dulcie saw her face was red and blotchy, and her eyes appeared to be darting everywhere. In Piers' words, her cousin had gone to seed, but she looked a mess even by her standards.

'Billy?' Dulcie asked, looking around expecting to see her dark-haired darling. But Billy wasn't there. A stab of anxiety made her gulp.

Columbine shook her head. 'Hasn't he come back to you all?'

'You didn't find him?'

Visibly trembling, Columbine reached for a chair. Her voice when she spoke again sounded high and unsteady. 'I . . . I . . . I feel terribly sick,' she said.

'What about Billy?' Dulcie demanded, wanting to shake her. The bloody woman was drunk again! At a time like this.

'I don't know.'

'What do you mean?'

'He's gone. In the blink of an eye, he just vanished.'

'Where?'

Columbine shook her head.

'Stay with the girls. I'm going to look myself.'

'But—'

Whatever Columbine had been going to say Dulcie did not hear.

CHAPTER 4

When Dulcie and Piers rushed outside to look for Billy, she gasped in horror at the demonstration of Italian military power that met their eyes. Hundreds of Italian sailors and dark-helmeted soldiers, rifles and bayonets resting on shoulders, thundering down the street, marching in unison, their leader proudly carrying the Italian flag. It completely put an end to any hope of Corfiot opposition. Some locals, repeatedly throwing their hats into the air and raising their hands in surrender, had already given in, while others stood watching sullenly, their rebellious muttering dark and furious. Further away fighting had broken out.

'Bastards have seized the fucking island,' Piers stuttered.

Back at the consul, she had struggled to find Piers at first, but once she had, they had hastily searched the building together before going outside.

'What now?' he said as they gazed around. There was still no sign of Billy, and she had no idea . . . what now?

Her throat tightened and, hovering at the edge of her mind, pictures of Billy played on a loop. Grasping for the right words and with a fear-fuelled icy calm she managed to say, 'He may have gone to watch the boats come in. You know how he loves boats.'

'Good idea. How's your ankle?'

'Easing up.'

They made haste to the harbour as best they could where more and more long wide boats were docking – barges carrying more helmeted men from the gunboats and warships. They wore dark, heavily buttoned Italian uniforms and were presided over by officers in white. An invasion of insects. Thousands upon thousands of them.

'Jesus!' Piers muttered under his breath.

She heard her husband's groan, felt him reach for her hand. But Dulcie could only think of her son. *Billy. Billy. Where are you*, she continued to repeat silently as she scanned the faces. Surely, he had to be here somewhere.

There, she thought, her heart flipping over, but when the child turned it was not him. They walked on.

'That's Billy,' she said a moment later, grabbing her husband's hand. It was, wasn't it? She felt sure it was.

Her husband shook his head.

'*Non potete stare qui!* Halt. Go back. You cannot be here.' The shout had come from an Italian officer.

She didn't obey and began to stride towards the boy. Piers was wrong. The child was Billy.

'Come on,' Piers said, catching up and dragging her back. 'Don't be an idiot. It isn't Billy, and we have to go.'

The Italian glared and pointed his rifle at them – and now she saw the child was just another boy with dark curly hair. Not tall enough, she clung to Piers for leverage and rose up on the tips of her toes, arching her neck to see over the increasingly deep throng of people. But no matter how many small boys she saw, not one of them was Billy.

That was when her hands began to shake and she knew this was what she had feared, this was what had woken her, had caused the sense of foreboding that had tightened her chest and stopped her breath – not the shelling of the island at all.

And now all she could do was spin on the spot, looking around and around and feeling more and more frantic with every minute.

'Think, Piers. Think for God's sake. Where could he be?'

He put a hand on her arm. 'Stop Dulcie. He'll be around here somewhere. Don't panic. He's nine, not four or five.'

'The water. What if he's—'

'You can't think like that,' he said, interrupting her. 'Take a breath and calm yourself.'

She strained to do what he said. But the breath wouldn't come.

'Dulcie. Look at me. You know he likes to wander off. That's what has happened.'

He sounded calm but when she looked in his eyes all she could see was the same anxiety that she was feeling reflected back at her.

She managed to gain a breath. 'I suppose he could have gone up to see the refugee children.'

'Trouble is it looks like the Italians have barred the way.'

'He's so small, he might have slipped through.'

She bit her lip, thinking of the refugee children. Some of them surely must have died up there during the shelling. Somebody had to go to them, but she had to find Billy first.

'I don't believe it,' Piers said, shocked. 'Look!'

A number of Greek officers and officials were being frog-marched down to one of the waiting boats, among them Corfu's Prefect, Petros Evripaios, who had been taken from the prefecture against his will. Dulcie held her breath. Odel's husband worked in the Prefect's office. What would happen to him if the Italians were in control of absolutely everything on the island?

'The Italians won't care about us,' she moaned. 'They won't help us find Billy. Let's go.'

They dodged the main crowds and the motor vehicles and tried the smaller lanes of the town, but fights were still breaking out there and people were running and scattering in every direction. Dulcie took off her heels and stumbled barefoot, careless of what people might think, snagging her silk stockings, grazing the soles of her feet, scanning and scanning the people for just a glimpse of her son.

Still no sign.

By the time they turned to go back to their town house, her dress was soaked in sweat, her hair had come loose from its pins, and a violet wash had spread across the sky. It was almost the twilight hour.

Piers had said very little for the past hour. Now, he took hold of her hand and squeezed it. 'He'll be at home, darling. You'll see. Thirza's gone back just in case.'

Dulcie nodded. 'He loves roaming around on his own, like you said. Maybe he has just gone for a walk.'

Who am I fooling, she thought but didn't say. And the voice in her head said: *Yes, he does go off, but never for this long. Never ever for this long.*

As they arrived at their town house near the port, she rushed forward, spotting that someone had left the front door wide open, barely registering Thirza leaning against the wall, head bowed in silent devastation and Columbine and Ianthe looking white and worried.

CHAPTER 5

'There you are, what did I tell you?' Piers said. 'Billy has let himself in and left the door open.'

'Billy,' Dulcie called out as she dashed inside, her ankle protesting at the sudden movement. She stood in the dark entrance hall and yelled again, 'Billy!'

Nothing.

'Why hasn't anyone switched on the lamps?' Piers muttered and then he called out, 'Come inside, Thirza.'

'Billy. This isn't funny. You're scaring Mummy.' Dulcie's voice shook and not knowing if he was hurt or too scared to come out, she felt sick. Was he all right or was he all alone somewhere and frightened? Or something even worse. Trembling, she waited.

Still nothing.

'He'll be hiding. Don't worry,' Piers said, his voice tense. 'We'll find him.'

At that moment they heard sobbing. Dulcie listened but shook her head. Not the sobs of a child.

'Nobody move. Wait here,' Piers ordered as he lit one of the oil lamps. 'There. That's better.'

Dulcie gasped. 'Oh no! Piers, look! Look at the walls.'

He lifted the lamp to see that all the framed original illustrations she'd drawn for her travel books were gone.

'I should have kept them at Merchant's,' Dulcie whispered.

'Bastards!' he muttered.

'It gets even worse,' Thirza said, finally speaking up. 'That's why I couldn't stay in the house, and anyway Billy isn't here.'

'He may be hiding, love,' Piers said without conviction.

Cautiously they stepped further inside, lighting more lamps as they went.

Dulcie could hardly breathe, shocked at the state of their home. Furniture upended. Cushions ripped open, feathers everywhere. Anything of value stolen and the acrid smell of urine filling the air.

Their cook, Camille, met them in the drawing room, looking dazed and exhausted and dabbing her eyes with her apron.

'I am sorry,' she said. 'I could not stop them.'

'Italians?' Piers asked and she nodded. He rested a hand briefly on the older woman's shoulder.

'Is Billy here? Have you seen Billy?' Dulcie asked, her voice shaking.

The woman shook her head.

As they hurried from room to room looking for Billy, Columbine trailed after them, pale and shaken. Hot tears pricked the backs of Dulcie's eyelids as she called for her child, throwing open the doors of storage cupboards and huge old-fashioned wardrobes. She kept on calling his name to come out from wherever he was hiding.

It became clear that their entire house had been looted. Every single room on the ground and first floors.

'Could the Italians have taken him?' she asked Piers.

'Why would they?'

In their bedroom Dulcie discovered her mother of pearl jewellery box lying smashed on the floor, her precious jewels gone – a diamond necklace once belonging to her mother, jade earrings Piers had given her when they became engaged, and a sweet little sapphire bracelet her father had presented to her on her twenty-first birthday. She stared in horror then fell onto the bed pounding the pale satin cover with her fists, until eventually, gasping for breath, she lay still, utterly spent. Piers patted her back.

'Look,' he said. 'We can't sleep here tonight. There's broken glass everywhere.'

'I'm not leaving.'

'Dulcie, your feet are bleeding. Go to St George's Hotel, and I'll take a torch and look for Billy.'

'I'm coming too,' Thirza said.

'No. You are to look after your mother.'

Thirza gazed back at him stubbornly then muttered, 'The Italian officers will have taken all the hotel rooms.'

Columbine who had been silent through all of this suddenly spoke up. 'She's right. I have the keys to my friend Lucie's house. She's in England. It's small but we can go there. She won't mind.'

'No,' Dulcie insisted. 'I'm staying here. What happens if Billy comes back?'

'Fair point.'

'You bloody well should have looked after your brother,' Dulcie hissed at Thirza. 'This is your fault. Why don't you ever do what you're told? I asked you to look after him.'

She heard her own shrill voice and the dreadful edge to it. The edge that must not be reached. *Step back. Step back*, she told herself. But she could not. 'It's your fault,' she repeated. 'Your fault.'

Thirza stared at her. Didn't defend herself, just looked pale, shocked, and terribly hurt.

Piers said, 'Thirza and Ianthe, go and check if the attic rooms are habitable. There's nothing to steal up there so they should be.'

'I'll help them,' Columbine said.

Dulcie grabbed her by the elbow. 'No, you will not. You are damn well going to tell me exactly what happened when Billy disappeared.'

Columbine bit her lip.

'You were drunk, weren't you? Instead of looking after Billy, as you promised, you slipped out for another gin and left him in the street.'

'No.'

'What then?'

'It wasn't my fault.'

Dulcie clenched her jaw and only just managed to hold on to her temper. 'What wasn't? Tell me!'

Columbine's voice was small and choked when she spoke, so weak Dulcie could barely hear her.

'Say that again.'

This time Columbine screamed at her. 'He wanted to go back for his bloody hat.'

'Go back where?'

'Here. To the house.'

Dulcie gasped. 'You let him go on his own? Are you insane?'

'I tried to tell him no.'

'He's nine years old, Columbine. You should have stopped him.'

Columbine hung her head and Dulcie wanted to kill her. An uncontrollable heat was rushing through her body, making her feel dizzy.

She glared at her cousin. 'The Italians were bombarding the island, and everyone was running in fear for their lives and you, what . . . *you* just let him go?'

CHAPTER 6

It was still early but already bright when Dulcie woke. She hadn't slept – not just because of the lumpy attic bed – and was so paralysed by a growing sense of dread she didn't know where to turn. What if Billy was lying lifeless in some awful place? And as she allowed the thought into her mind, a crack opened up inside her, so wide she felt her entire world might fall right through it. She'd spin and sink right into the horror of whatever hell she could imagine might be lying in wait. But if she were to find Billy there, she'd willingly throw herself in, allow the emptiness to swallow her until she saw his dear face again. Feeling utterly ragged, she squeezed her eyes shut for a moment. No. He could not be gone. She had to believe she would find him alive and well. Picturing his smiling hazel eyes, his cheeky grin, she roused and dressed herself before any of the others and went out to look for her son. Her little boy.

She had to find him.

The new fortress – an austere group of buildings dominating one of two hill peaks – had been built in the sixteenth century. From the new fort there were rumoured to be connecting tunnels linking it to the old fortress though no one had ever found them. The fortified island of Vido protected the sea, not that it had been any use on this occasion. She couldn't help thinking something must have gone terribly wrong. Something high-level. Because if this Italian invasion was not war, then what was it? She swept the hair from her eyes and made her way up to the older fortress built on a promontory and separated from the city by the Contrafossa, a wide Venetian-built moat, a brilliant defensive tactic which meant the fortress on its artificial island became an absolute citadel with, back in the day, a drawbridge. She usually admired the stunning views over the town, the sea, the Greek mainland, and much of Corfu island itself, but not today.

She crossed the bridge of the Contrafossa, passed beneath the huge gate, then headed for the two big bastions left and right of the central entrance. The Italian soldiers guarding the way to the fortress stared at her unbrushed hair and wild look but let her pass. Her ankle felt better, thank God, but she knew she probably looked mad as she demanded to know if they'd seen an English boy with dark curly hair.

The fortress included a Venetian prison, two English barracks, and a military hospital. She headed for the barracks where most of the Greek refugee children made homeless by the recent Greco-Turkish war were living. Once there she tried to find out how many had been killed or injured, but the Italian soldiers weren't saying. They shuffled their feet, avoided her eyes, and, shaking their heads, muttered to each other. Then as she turned a corner, two soldiers carrying a child stopped when they saw her. A thin little boy lay on the stretcher very clearly close to death. She knew him. Leandros was his name, and he was all alone in the world.

Eyes blurred with tears, she reached out to stroke his cheek, say a brief prayer, and then carried on. After searching for an hour among the burning embers, the scattered shrapnel, the bodies still awaiting removal, the smell of scorched wood and burnt flesh had become unbearable. Dulcie walked slowly back down the hill with a heavy heart. She had put so much energy into ensuring the refugees were properly looked after, fed, and kept warm. And still no Billy.

But where was she supposed to report Billy's disappearance? The town was in utter turmoil so who would mount a search party in these conditions? The Greeks? The Italians? The British?

She hurried back to the house to join the others and found Ianthe standing in the open doorway.

'Mummy says the Italians are going to announce something in the main square,' she said excitedly.

Dulcie ignored her, went inside, and saw Columbine on her way down the stairs carrying a bag full of rubbish. For such a large woman she looked utterly haggard.

'We've been clearing up,' her cousin said.

Dulcie just stared at her.

'Have you got Billy?' Columbine asked, but she didn't look Dulcie in the eye and instead just stared over her shoulder at the open door as if Billy might be standing there.

'No.'

'Has anyone seen him?'

'Oh, for God's sake!' Dulcie snapped. 'It's bit late for you to be worrying about Billy now!'

Columbine almost crumpled in front of her.

Dulcie stalked off and came across Piers smoking in the drawing room.

'I've informed the consul,' he said grimly as soon as he saw her. 'He's going to organise a British search party. Suggested we go to the police station to make a formal report but when I checked just now it was all locked up.'

'Don't we have to be in the square or something?' she asked him, barely taking it in. 'Maybe it will open after that?'

'I'll make enquiries as soon as it finishes. The Italians won't want a missing English boy on their casualty list. Try not to worry. We will find him.'

Not worry? She shook her head.

A little later, still shocked to see the extent of the damage in the house, which looked so much worse in the sharp light of day, Dulcie felt overwhelmed. Their cook and their cleaner were still sweeping up broken glass and wiping the precious Persian rugs where the Italians had stomped their dusty booted feet. Not normally inclined to rage, her rising anger was taking over from fear and Dulcie would willingly have stuck a knife into one of the bastards if she'd had the chance. It was their fault Billy had gone missing, in all the terror and confusion of the shelling. Though she would never forgive Columbine either.

A little later, when she and Piers were searching again, and Thirza had stayed back at the house in case Billy came home, they stopped to hear the proclamation in the main square.

'I am Rear Admiral Bellini,' the Italian in charge said in heavily accented Greek and then again in English. 'I am in command, and I declare the island is now under martial law. This is not an annexation but an occupation of the island until Greece makes the required amends to Italy for the murders that took place on Greek soil.'

A ripple of outrage ran through the crowd, but Dulcie's own dark thoughts were crowding out the man's words. What if Billy had gone too close to the water? It wouldn't have taken much and in all the chaos anything could have happened. Her heart lurched. *No. Please, not that.*

'Amends, my arse,' she heard Piers hiss. 'They have no proof it was Greeks who carried out the attacks. If you ask me, it's just an excuse for a permanent occupation of the island.'

Dulcie felt sorry for the murdered men. To have died over a simple boundary issue was insane. But that was men for you, and because General Tellini, chairman of the commission sent to resolve the dispute, and four others had been killed, they were now in this mess. She wondered if the culprits *had* escaped into Albania, a wild and dangerous country, just as Columbine had inferred, a place of semi-anarchy ruled by bandits and outlaws. Could that actually be true?

As the crowd hushed, the admiral continued speaking. 'I have ordered the Greek fleet to retire to the Gulf of Volos and to stay away from all Italian shipping.'

A loud gasp erupted from the crowd already angered at the Italian flag flying at governmental headquarters instead of the Greek one.

'We have closed the Straits of Otranto to Greece's ships,' he continued. 'And all activity by Greek shipping companies is prohibited. All military arms, munitions, arms depots, and other military equipment and barracks on the island must be surrendered.'

Dulcie felt herself growing terribly hot. 'I can't stand here listening to this. Piers, I can't. I have to look for Billy.'

'Please wait. It'll be over soon. And we can't get anywhere in this crowd.'

The Italian continued speaking. 'All wire, wireless, postal, and telephone communication is suspended.'

'We'll soon see about that,' she said, biting back her fear and muttering under her breath.

Dulcie had contacts in England, and personally knew Lord Curzon, Secretary of State for Foreign Affairs at the Foreign Office. Paralysed by overwhelming worry about Billy, she vowed to do everything she could, maybe even contact Lord Curzon to ask him to help.

'Whatever it takes,' she whispered with very little idea of what that might actually mean.

But suddenly the admiral had finished, and the crowd was moving around her but too slowly, much too slowly, people's faces grotesque, their mouths gaping black holes, their eyes wide and staring, their voices slow and long-drawn-out. Peals of maniacal laughter hurt her head. *It isn't real. It isn't real.* She felt dizzy, blinking rapidly, her eyes darting about. This couldn't be happening. Not Billy vanishing. Not the Italians. Not this feeling that she was about to die. And yet it was.

She reached for her husband. 'Piers, I feel as if I'm going to faint.'

CHAPTER 7

The afternoon was already sizzling hot, and the town felt oppressive and unsafe as if, just beneath the surface, the voice of resistance was brewing. Piers had caught Dulcie just before she blacked out. Now she was waiting for him and, in a moment, they would go to the police station. She was just closing her bedroom window when she spotted a friend down in the street below.

'Have you seen Billy anywhere?' she called, trying to keep the panic from her voice but failing.

Her friend's eyes widened. 'Oh no! He hasn't wandered off at a time like this?'

'Worse than that. Much worse.' Dulcie gulped back tears but couldn't stop her voice from catching. 'We haven't seen him since yesterday afternoon.'

'Oh, darling. That's terrible.'

Dulcie nodded.

'You must be going out of your mind. I'll let everyone know. We'll find him.'

'Thank you.'

'What about the consul?'

'Piers has been. They'll do what they can.'

She didn't say but, in her heart, she feared that one little boy – her little boy – would be a low priority while all this was going on. The thought devastated her.

A little later Dulcie was already sweating as she and Piers approached police headquarters where two Italians were in the process of lowering the Greek flag and arguing about how to do it. Across the road a knot of Greek men and women, who had gathered either to watch or to shout insults, were resisting attempts by Italian soldiers to move them on.

'What the devil!' Piers protested at the sight of the flag at half-mast.

'Don't harass them,' she said. 'We may need their help.'

He conceded the point but expressed his disgust with a loud clearing of the throat then, shoulders exaggeratedly drawn back, he led her inside. 'Wouldn't be surprised if Mussolini himself was behind the killings and the occupation of Corfu was planned all along,' he muttered.

'Shhhh,' she whispered. 'You can't say that out loud. And at least the place is open now.'

At the front desk an Italian, with not a Greek in sight, manned the reception desk.

Piers told the man who he was and explained he needed to see the chief of police, who also happened to be Piers' own superior commander. He spoke first in Greek and then in English.

The Italian shook his head and, shrugging, turned away.

Dulcie tried out her Italian on him.

Instantly his eyes lit up and he let them pass. When they reached the police commander's office, they found another Italian installed. The room smelt of stale cigarettes and fried fish, the walls painted a nauseating institutional green, but at least this man did speak some English. Dulcie sat on a hard upright chair, crossed her ankles, picked at the loose skin around one of her nails, and allowed Piers to explain.

'A nine-year-old,' the man repeated. 'My deepest regret.'

She was aware of the man's eyes on her chest and glanced down, suddenly aware she'd worn the wrong dress, a smart yellow one she kept here in town, and, owing to a summer of indulgence, the fabric was now stretched too tightly across her breasts. She felt her colour rising beneath his shameless gaze.

'A nine-year-old *English* boy,' Piers reiterated. 'My son.'

'Not that we aren't upset about the refugee children,' Dulcie quickly added. 'I'm on the committee that organises their welfare.'

Dulcie was here only to request a search party to find Billy, but she couldn't help adding, 'How many refugees died, sir? Just for my records.'

'The bodies are in the morgue.'

Piers glanced at Dulcie then spoke. 'You are certain my son is not among them?'

The Italian looked uneasy, and Dulcie remembered Piers saying the Italians would not want to have killed any British people for fear of an all-out war. But it was the only card they had to play so she said, 'I think we'd better see the children, just to be safe.'

'Darling,' Piers said. 'Are you sure? I can go on my own.'

'Unsuitable for a woman,' the Italian added grimly.

Dulcie rose to her feet. 'Don't be ridiculous. I'm going with you.'

The Italian nodded. 'Very well. I will send one of my men along. It is important to make haste in finding your son. If the child is not found within three days, the chances become very slim.'

'Three days!' Dulcie repeated, shocked. 'That's only seventy-two hours.'

'Be sure to look for him in any small spaces where a child might hide. Does he have favourite places he likes to go?'

'The harbour, but we've already searched there,' Piers said.

'The British Cemetery,' she said. 'He loves it there.'

'Note down everywhere you go. Keep a record. And,' he said, hesitating for a moment. 'I have to ask this, you understand, but could he have run away?'

'No!' Dulcie replied aghast. 'Of course not. He was a happy child. We're a happy family.'

The bodies had been taken to the morgue at the new fort where another Italian flag was being raised, and Dulcie was slippery with sweat inside her dress by the time they'd walked there. Even then it took some waiting before they were finally led inside the building and along a corridor to a few steps down to a semi basement where the smell almost made Dulcie pass out again.

'Handkerchief over your mouth. Here. Take mine. It's clean,' Piers said, but as they entered the room, even he faltered. Sixteen bodies were laid out on the floor, each one covered by a grey blanket.

'They're so small,' she whispered.

'You do realise some will not,' Piers said. 'You know. Not be intact.'

She bit her lip and nodded.

Piers and the Italian spoke for a few minutes, but Dulcie wasn't listening. She was picturing Billy, and praying, begging, that he would not be among these poor children.

Piers took hold of her hand and squeezed it. 'He says there are three times this number seriously injured and in hospital. But he's certain those in the hospital are only refugees.'

She flinched at the word *only*.

He sighed and they took a few steps towards the first child. The Italian pulled back the blanket. Her eyes filled with tears as she leant over him. It was the little boy she'd seen being carried on the stretcher, Leandros, his cheeks and forehead blackened with dust and the smell of smoke lingering in his hair. She reached out, longing to wipe away the dirt and stroke his face one last time, but with the two men watching she felt foolish and withdrew her hand. This poor little boy had already lost his home and his family. Now he had lost his life too.

They continued along the line. She felt hot and sick and at that moment hated Mussolini for allowing this carnage to happen. So many young lives taken senselessly over a minor border dispute. It was unforgivable.

'The next one has no . . . I am not sure you should look. You cannot identify.'

Piers took her elbow. 'He means—'

'I know what he means,' she interrupted and turned her face away, trying to remember what her son had been wearing. Her scalp prickled as she quickly searched her memory. Thirza had on her favourite red-and-white-striped dress, Ianthe was in blue, but Billy. What the hell had Billy been wearing? It was so hard to remember with boys. She recalled cream shorts and a white shirt. Was that it?

'Look at the clothes, Piers,' she said. 'See if they're Billy's. White shirt. Cream shorts.'

Was she right? She heard a few shuffles and then her husband's gasp. Her blood ran cold, and she felt herself sway.

'No,' he said, catching hold of her. 'Not Billy.'

Doubling over, she steadied herself and then, looking up at Piers, she shook her head.

'You go on without me. I have to breathe. Fresh air. I . . .' and then she ran up the steps, along the corridor, and finally, once outside again, she leant against the stone exterior wall coughing and heaving. The men raising the Italian flag, which was almost done now, stared at her but she didn't care.

After a moment she straightened up, for in her mind's eye she'd seen Billy wearing his hat pulled down low the way he liked it. His favourite raggedy straw hat. Had he been wearing that too?

She pictured him at Merchant's barrelling through the trees at breakneck speed. Billy, his eyes bright and shiny, his arms held out wide, a ball of energy shouting, 'I'm an eagle, Mummy. An eagle. Watch me.'

But she couldn't remember if he'd been wearing the hat when she last saw him just before he disappeared.

Disappeared.

Columbine had said he went back to get the hat.

And Dulcie gulped back a sob because she now knew that if they didn't find Billy within the next day or two, nothing about their lives would ever be the same again.

CHAPTER 8

Birdsong woke her. How could the birds still be singing when she didn't know where her little boy was? After lying awake for hours she had finally fallen asleep at some point. Now, she gazed at the sunshine streaming in and saw the dust motes dancing in the air. So much dust. At least they were back in their own bedroom with a comfy double bed. Piers was not there beside her and she was surprised by how much she wanted him to be with her, but he'd woken her at dawn to say he wanted to speak to someone at the consulate. He hoped that by leaving so early he might have better luck at getting things moving more quickly and he told her to go back to sleep. It had already been two days, and they were getting nowhere.

Dulcie could smell coffee and toast and heard the low rumble of conversation and movement rising from the ground floor. Were Columbine, Thirza, and Ianthe at the breakfast table already? She swung her legs over the edge of the bed, rose to her feet, and in the bathroom splashed her face and stretched. Then she flung on her robe and hurried downstairs.

She was already seated with the others by the time the Caruthers' cook Camille came into the dining room carrying a dish of scrambled eggs, sausages, and fried tomatoes. As she put the dish down, she haltingly told of some gossip she'd heard about an English child who had been seen in the Jewish district recently.

'I do not know if this true,' she added.

But Dulcie could barely contain the hope that drowned out everything else. She would find Billy today. She would!

'I could come with you,' Columbine offered.

'*You've* done enough already!' snapped Dulcie.

Columbine had never been good in a crisis, even when they were younger. Raised almost as sisters, it had been Dulcie who'd had to be the grown-up one, the one who'd always had to take the lead.

Without telling Piers, who was still with the British consul, and leaving Thirza to stay at the house just in case, she headed off to search the district of the city that was threaded with a maze of narrow alleyways and lined with tall, softly coloured houses

As she walked, she prayed fate would be on her side and take her in the right direction. When people smiled at her as she passed, she wanted to shout:

Don't look at me. Don't speak to me.

As she walked, she thought about the Jewish district. Napoleon had seized Corfu in 1797 and had given the Jewish population certain rights, but when the island had become a British protectorate in 1815, the Jews lost their right to vote. It saddened her as she had never really understood why. And then less than thirty years after the British had left there had been a month-long pogrom, resulting in the departure of many Jewish families.

Turning a corner, she spotted her friend Odel just in front of her and called out.

'Darling,' the other woman said. 'It's been a bit frantic but as soon as I heard about Billy, I called at your house. Thirza said you'd be here. How are you coping?'

Dulcie shook her head and Odel opened her arms. Dulcie hesitated but then fell into them, swallowing her reply.

'How can I help?' Odel asked after a minute. 'I haven't got long. It's my husband.'

'Thaddeus?'

'He has not been arrested, thank God, and is still working. On purely administrative detail, but I don't know how long that will last. He's going to move to our summer house in a couple of hours and I need to pack his effects. Sensitive documents and so on. I don't know how safe he'll be now that the Prefect has been taken.'

'What about you?'

'It's all rather ghastly. I'm going with him for a few days then I'll be back here keeping my ear to the ground.'

'Oh, Odel!'

'I know. Don't worry, I'll be all right. But tell me, how can I help you?'

'Honestly, I'm trying so hard not to simply cry all day long, but I'd love you to come with me if you have time.'

The streets were eerily quiet, so they knocked on doors calling on everyone they knew and those they didn't know too. After a couple of hours, Dulcie stood on the corner of a street with the beginning of another headache and feeling damp with sweat. After a few moments, she rolled her shoulders to release the tension, and Odel led her to a café where she ordered them both a cool lemonade.

When the drink arrived, Dulcie questioned the owner about Billy.

A small man with a thatch of dark hair, he scratched the top of his head, narrowing his eyes as he reflected, then said, 'An American child was staying in my street.'

'Oh? A boy?'

He nodded. 'Nice kid.'

'You're certain he was American, not British?'

He gave a shrug. 'I think so. But it was before the Italians came and I'm sure the family had left before the bombardment happened. Maybe the day before.'

'Thank you,' Dulcie said though her heart was sinking.

'Gossip spreads rapidly in a small town like Corfu,' Odel said. 'Distorting in the process. Try not to worry. We *will* find Billy. I'll talk to my husband before he leaves.'

Dulcie wanted to stand in the street, tear her hair out, and scream at the top of her voice, *What have you done with my son?*

'I'll have to go back now,' Odel said.

They hugged and Dulcie whispered, 'Be safe, my friend. Be safe.'

A little later, although they had been told there were no English children in the hospital, she and Piers went there to see for themselves but once again there was no sign of Billy. As they walked out, Dulcie's eyes filled with tears when Piers said, 'I think you should go home to Merchant's, with Columbine, Thirza, and Ianthe.'

'But—'

He held up his hand. 'No buts. I, meanwhile, will speak to the police again, take part in the search parties, navigate the hospital as often as I need to, and deal with the Italians.'

She sighed deeply. 'I can't leave here. Not while he's still missing.'

'If you stay, you're going to end up ill. It will put my mind at rest knowing you're safe at home.'

She reached up and touched his cheek, surprised by how considerate he was being and, unhinged as she was by Billy's disappearance, she knew there was sense in what he said. 'Thank you,' she said. 'But I won't go to Merchant's. Not yet anyway. I want to go to the British Cemetery.'

A little later she found herself alone in the oasis that was the British Cemetery. She called for Billy as she walked up the yellowing grass alleyway lined with tall cypress trees and then turned into the narrower paths that rambled through magnolias, roses, wisteria, and, further on, more trees. The peace and cool of the cemetery was her favourite place to think. She used to come with her father and loved every part of it. Today was different. She felt tired and weary but just as she was about to call it quits, she spotted the cemetery cat and bent down to stroke him. And there, half hidden in the bushes, something yellow caught her attention.

What was it?

Down on her hands and knees now, she reached in and tugged at it, eventually pulling out a teddy bear looking the worse for wear. Modelled on a real-life bear, it was a German Steiff bear, exactly like the one Billy took with him everywhere. Her German friend Ingrid had given it to him for his sixth birthday. Had he been here recently? He hadn't told her that he'd lost it, but he might have been worried that she'd be angry with him. She struggled to recall when they last came here together. Or, and her heart hammered at the thought, had someone snatched him and brought him here the day he disappeared? There were buildings all around. Places where a child might hide. *Or be kept.* Then another thought hit her. Billy could easily have been taken by boat and that was why they hadn't found him anywhere on land. He'd been taken by boat to some isolated cove where there were caves. Heart pounding, skin clammy, and dripping with sweat, she cradled the bear to her chest and wept. Billy had not been seen for two whole days.

CHAPTER 9

The next morning the sound of voices woke Dulcie. For a moment her heart didn't pound with anxiety, and she felt normal, but then in an instant, it all came crashing back and she groaned.

She heard the voices again and realised that not all of them belonged in her home.

'Yes, officer, of course,' she heard Piers saying. 'We can speak in here.'

The police.

Dulcie threw off the bedcovers and reached hastily for yesterday's clothes, dressing herself as swiftly as she could, before hurrying from the room – not even sparing a moment to put a comb through her hair or look for her shoes.

She recoiled as she entered the room barefoot. And although sunlight streamed in through the French windows of their drawing room, showing off its elegant furniture and beautiful proportions, all she could think was that there were too many people. Columbine and Ianthe were positioned by the windows overlooking the courtyard garden, Piers had an arm around Thirza as they stood close to one of the sofas, and two men were standing stiffly either side of the fireplace.

'Have you found my son? Is he—' Dulcie blurted out, not stopping to greet the officers.

But the uniformed men were shaking their heads.

'They want to ask you some questions,' Piers explained, voice uncharacteristically gentle. 'Why don't you sit down?'

He moved away from Thirza and ushered Dulcie towards a chair, then introduced the gentlemen: one officer was Italian, and the other was a Greek Piers already knew.

'My name is D'Agostino,' the Italian officer said, in reasonable English but in a sharp, cold tone of voice. 'We have mounted two separate search parties. One yesterday evening and one early this morning. *Mi dispiace*, but so far there has been no sign of your son. This is now the third day since your son disappeared!'

Three days.

Her heart almost stopped but she listened as D'Agostino continued to take charge. The Greek policeman fidgeted and by the look of the muscles tightening around his eyes, he seemed annoyed, his nose clearly out of joint.

'What about the cemetery?' she said. She had given the bear to Piers, and he'd promised to organise a thorough search of the cemetery and gardens nearby, hopefully with dogs who might be able to follow the correct scent now that they had the teddy bear. A second Steiff bear on the island was unlikely, although not impossible.

'Yes. Yes.'

'You took dogs?'

'Yes.'

'And?'

'Nothing. I am sorry.'

'Then why are you here?' she demanded, feeling fury rise up within her. What good were they if they could not find Billy? What was the point in all this?

The Greek took the opportunity to speak. 'Can you tell us exactly what happened when you last saw your son?'

She sighed. 'My husband must have told you everything.'

'All the same. It would help to hear it from you too.'

He spoke gently, clearly understanding how hard this must be for her. Perhaps Piers had asked him to go easy on her.

'The searches you mentioned. I take it you mean in Corfu Town itself?' she asked.

'We thought it wise to start here,' the Italian said, taking control of the interview again. 'So?'

She explained everything and when she'd finished, he narrowed his eyes and gazed at her. 'You did not take care of the child yourself?'

'My daughter was looking after him,' she said, feeling defensive.

'As I understand it your daughter is only sixteen.'

'Quite old enough,' she snapped. 'And anyway, my cousin Columbine was there too.'

The officers turned to regard Columbine, and Dulcie did, too. The woman looked awful; certainly not someone you'd choose to look after a child. Nails bitten and raw at the edges, huge bags under her eyes, blotchy red cheeks, and badly applied, too-bright orange lipstick.

Dulcie couldn't help asking herself how it was possible that her cousin could have let Billy go at a time like that. Could he have shrugged her off – he hated being treated like a baby – and maybe he'd become separated from the others when the shelling began and not gone back for his hat at all? Even so he knew how to get to the consul, could have found his way there on his own, blindfolded. So, what had happened?

'He just vanished,' Columbine said, picking at the skin around her nails. 'We were on our way to the consul's office. I was further ahead, or maybe behind Ianthe and Thirza. I can't quite remember. It's bit of a blur . . . I . . . I . . . I'm not sure.' Her words were slurred. She hid it well, but the men could tell she'd been drinking. They all could.

'What else can you tell us?' the Greek officer asked.

'Billy wanted to get his hat. He wouldn't stop going on and on about it. I told him he couldn't go, ordered him not to go, but when I looked round, he wasn't there, at least I think so.' Columbine began to cry.

'He disappeared before the shelling?' the Italian officer asked. 'Or after?'

'Before . . . No . . . I don't know. When the terrible noise began or maybe after. It's all muddled up. I . . .'

Dulcie could see the scorn in their faces.

Thirza frowned. 'The shelling had already begun, Columbine. Don't you remember?'

Columbine stuttered but gave up with whatever she'd been going to say.

'Anyway, it's my fault,' Thirza continued. 'I didn't look after Billy when Mummy asked me to, but Columbine was with him, you see, so I thought . . . Well, I thought he was all right.'

Dulcie could hear so much pain beneath her daughter's apparently calm words and felt her heart twist with guilt. It had been she herself who had first blamed Thirza with her sharp accusation.

'It was *not* your fault,' she said – but sharply rather than kindly, for her anger was spilling over. She glared at the officers. How *dare* they.

'Columbine and my daughter were perfectly capable of shepherding the other children to the consul's office. We did not know *you* were going to shell Corfu at that precise time, or we might have, might have . . .'

She paused, swallowing, too upset and too angry to finish.

'Might have?'

'Might done things differently. Might have got the hell out of the way. Might have run for our lives. Might have escaped to our house before it was *looted* by Italian seamen, *officer.*'

There was a short silence until the man continued in a tightly controlled voice.

'And yet your boy went missing in those few minutes and your cousin did not notice. Did your son have reason to run away? Was he scared of something? Or someone? Had he been in trouble?'

A picture arose in her mind. A beautiful sunlit day. Billy racing into the sea, waving like a mad thing when the water came up to his chest. Grinning wildly.

'He is a well-behaved, very happy, much-loved child,' she said, narrowing her eyes and trying to contain her sorrow. 'He did not run away. There was no reason for him to run away. No reason at all.'

He nodded slowly, stroking his chin. 'I ask because there has been no ransom demand.'

Thirza gasped. 'You think he might have been kidnapped?'

'You come from a wealthy family,' the Italian said. 'But we would have expected to hear by now, in that case.'

Dulcie didn't speak but the white envelope came into her mind. She thought about fetching it now but, feeling certain it had nothing to do with Billy, she didn't want these men to even set eyes on it. She hesitated for a moment, glancing at Piers. No. She really didn't want Piers asking awkward questions either, and the note did not mention a ransom demand, nor did it suggest kidnap.

'So, if he did not run away and has not been kidnapped, we might have to assume he has met with an accident.'

Or something worse, Dulcie thought. *Something much worse*.

From what felt like a long distance away, Dulcie heard Thirza asking the police what they thought had happened and it was the Greek officer who replied with genuine pity in his voice.

'I am so sorry, miss, we just do not know.'

'We may have to assume the worst,' D'Agostino said.

The Greek stepped in. 'But we are not at that stage yet. We still have hopes of finding him.'

'You are planning to search the rest of the island?' Piers said. 'The island really isn't so large, and he might even have been taken across to Paxos. It would be easy enough.'

'Naturally, we hope to look into everything, but you will understand that my men are very occupied at present.'

Piers nodded, and Dulcie bit back a scream of frustration. It wasn't good enough.

'Surely there are still lots of places to search *here*,' she insisted, her voice sounding tighter and higher. 'Abandoned buildings, farms, barns. You can't have searched everywhere. And what about the coast, the beaches, the isolated coves? He might well have been taken by boat and not even as far as Paxos.'

'Needle in a haystack, madam. And I understand there's a storm on the way, so it would be too dangerous to send small boats out now.'

She glanced at the windows. The sun had gone in and there were dark clouds already gathering.

'So, you'll just let my son rot. Is that it?'

The Greek officer shook his head but D'Agostino ignored her comment completely. 'We will need to take a look at your son's bedroom,' he said, 'but first I have one more question for you.'

Dulcie noticed the Greek officer shifting about. She tried to catch his eye, but he looked away.

'Go ahead,' she said curtly, returning her gaze to the Italian officer.

'Do you *know* where your son is, Mrs Moreland?' he said.

So, it had come to this. They actually suspected her of having something to do with it! She could not help herself as she rose to her feet and took several steps away. At the door she clenched her jaw and spoke in a clipped voice. 'It is Caruthers-Moreland actually. I am a Caruthers. My husband is Moreland. My son's bedroom is upstairs, first on the right. Do see yourselves out.'

She stumbled up the stairs, threw open her bedroom door, and as she looked at the darkening sky, she spotted her abandoned shoes. She picked one up, and then the other, before hurling them both at the empty wall space between the two sash windows. They landed, most unsatisfactorily, in the wastepaper basket, and a near hysterical laugh burst from her. But in that moment, she knew what she was going to do. Oh yes. To hell with them and their half-hearted efforts! If they were not going to search the beaches and the coves, she was going to do it herself.

CHAPTER 10

In the middle of the night Dulcie tiptoed to the largest spare bedroom carrying an oil lamp and arguing with herself. Was this too risky? Probably, but she still had to do it, didn't she? She opened the door, wincing as it creaked, and then waited for a moment praying she had not woken anyone. She lifted the lamp, peered in, and faltered. She hadn't expected to see Columbine sitting by the dark window, fully dressed, with her hands in her lap. Dulcie moved closer and couldn't fail to see the hollow, lost look in her cousin's eyes. As Columbine fluttered a hand towards her, Dulcie felt a stab of pity and wondered if there was anything she could do to help, but then dismissed the thought. *What to do about Columbine* had been a conversation she'd been having for years – with herself and anyone else who would listen. Finding Billy was her priority now and, in any case, Columbine was to blame for his disappearance.

Anxious to find what she needed quickly and make her escape, she turned away, opening the large wardrobe doors, reaching inside and taking out a leather satchel. She patted it down and checked it was empty. Columbine was the last person she wanted to witness all this, but it couldn't be helped.

'What are you doing?' the woman asked.

Dulcie didn't turn round but muttered something meaningless.

'What?'

'I just need the satchel. Is that all right with you?'

'Of course. Are you going somewhere?'

Dulcie sighed.

'At this hour?'

'Columbine,' Dulcie snapped, turning to gaze at her. 'I'd rather not have an interrogation.'

'Sorry. I just thought . . .'

Dulcie saw a glimmer of something like hope in her cousin's eyes. 'You thought?'

'I could come. If you're going to search for Billy, that is. I could come too.'

'I don't think so. Odel will help me.'

The look of hope in Columbine's eyes faded.

But then Dulcie remembered Odel had already gone. She'd need someone to help her, although Columbine had to be the world's worst sailor. But if Dulcie steered the boat, her cousin could help tug it into the sandy coves she wanted to search.

Cook had spoken to an uncle who owned a small motor boat he rarely used, and he'd agreed to lend it for a price. So, just as long as the police were wrong about a coming storm, they'd be fine, and maybe Columbine needed to feel useful for once.

'All right,' Dulcie said, and she couldn't quite identify the look on Columbine's face. A kind of yearning, she thought, or maybe even courage. Was her cousin trying to make amends? Was that it?

'You'll need waterproofs,' she said and tapped the wardrobe door. 'Spare jackets in here. Spare lives in here too.'

'What?'

'Nothing. Just that who we've ever been, and every bit of detritus we've ever owned, is stuffed in there. Jigsaws, board games, dried-up tubes of paint. Old clothes. Even my wedding dress, I think. They all end up in there.'

Columbine laughed. 'No dead bodies?' Then she paused and looked mortified. 'Oh my God, sorry, I didn't mean—'

Dulcie raised her brows and sighed. 'No bodies, so far, but any more comments like that . . .'

'Sorry, again.'

'Billy's alive, Columbine. We just have to find him.'

'Of course. Of course. Are you going to tell me where we're going?'

'You'll see soon enough.'

In the early hours just before dawn they quietly passed along the narrow colonnaded alleys between the tall Venetian houses and quickly arrived at the port. It was only then that Columbine cottoned on. 'Oh,' she said, looking crestfallen.

Her cousin might well say '*Oh*' – for this was not going to be easy. But Billy was Dulcie's love and if he was never found his loss would become the wound that would never heal. She was scared; scared of the sea turning too rough for a small boat, scared of the armed Italian soldiers on the lookout everywhere, but most of all she was scared of never finding her son. She had to do this, whatever the danger. She ached for her boy, at times so deeply that she didn't know how her body and soul could keep going. And yet keeping going was all she could do.

'What about the Italians?' Columbine said, voicing Dulcie's own fears. 'Won't they be patrolling the waters?'

'Yes, but that's why we're leaving now. They'll be expecting to see small fishing boats. We'll go unnoticed among them.'

They both wore dark sou'wester hats, trousers, and waterproof jackets not too dissimilar from those worn by fishermen. Columbine was visibly shaking but they could easily have been taken for men with their hair tucked away and their hats pulled low.

Dulcie fixed a carbide lamp to the prow, just as the fishermen did, and once settled in the boat she held her breath as they left the port right under the eyes of the Italian guard.

When they were far enough away from the port and her heart had stopped thumping, she smiled sadly and said, 'See, we're fishermen now.'

Columbine gave her a weak smile in return.

The boat smelt of fish but now Dulcie caught the traces of smoke drifting over from the glowing fires from across the water in Albania, and she felt better. Connected. Less alone.

As they headed north the clouds melted away and the sun – a huge crimson ball – rose from behind the Albanian mountains, turning the sky pink and the sea a transparent silvery lilac. There would not be a storm. The police had been wrong.

At first, with the sun dancing on the surface of the water above purple and yellow rocks, it felt like a bit of a jaunt. Two women out for a little fishing, or for a pleasure trip around the island. Delicious crab sandwiches, white wine, and individual pastry parcels of *Bougatsa*, smothered in sugar and cinnamon and filled with custard – all wrapped in greaseproof paper and packed away in a hamper. But this was no jaunt and there were no crab sandwiches. Only the bottle of water Dulcie had furtively slipped into the satchel to replace the wine Columbine had brought along, and some very basic cheese sandwiches Cook had rustled up.

She hadn't told Piers what she was doing. Just left a note saying she and Columbine were undertaking their own search and wouldn't be too long. Cook had been sworn to secrecy.

The good weather continued to hold. In fact, Dulcie felt warm enough to take off her jacket and a little while later they passed the spot where she'd normally dock at her own little jetty at Merchant's. She gazed up at the verdant landscape: the cypress trees, the Jerusalem pines, and the olive groves carpeting the hills. Just the scent of it made her heart skip a beat. How she longed to be back in her normal everyday life there with Thirza and Billy complaining that she was always working. It was true. She didn't have enough time to be a good mother *and* get on with her work as well. And now something about being on the water so close to home meant Billy was there with her, in her dream world, leaping in and out of her mind as she ran through the years, Billy calling her, the word *mother* echoing in her ears. *Where are you*, she called back, wanting to breathe him in. *Where are you?* But there was no reply.

She saw Columbine looking pale and wondered what was going on in her mind. She'd been too quiet.

They carried on past Merchant's, and the ilex and the agapanthus close to the diving ledges so beloved of her children.

But then as they sailed past the small beaches on their way to Kassiopi, Columbine said, 'Might they have brought him somewhere close to Merchant's?'

'Who?'

'You know. The men. If they were planning to extract a ransom.'

'I don't know, Columbine. I don't know anything.'

'I'm sorry.'

Dulcie shook her head and didn't speak. The day remained relatively calm with just a slight breeze tapping her cheeks and ruffling her hair, but Dulcie's heart was breaking, and she barely noticed the blue of the sea or the sound of the seabirds following in their wake. She thought of the fish swimming beneath them instead – the big fish eating the little fish – and she felt very little indeed.

'Should we dock at Kassiopi?' Columbine asked. 'Try Paralia Mpataria or Kerasia Beach? I feel a bit sick.'

'Take some deep breaths. You'll be fine. And no, I'm going to head west. To the hidden beaches and small coves between Paleokastritsa and the south.'

'You know there are more than fifty beaches on Corfu, not to mention the tiny coves. We'll never search all of them.'

'You're right. Any ideas?'

Columbine shook her head. 'I like sunbathing on a beach, and I don't really like the sea.'

Dulcie sighed and suddenly the sky darkened. Columbine really was right. This was a monumental task and now it looked like rain. As the wind began to rise, the boat rocked and Columbine, attempting to get to her feet, shrieked and wobbled precariously.

'For the love of God, sit down,' Dulcie commanded as the boat rocked again and she saw that Columbine had turned a sickly shade of acid green.

In that moment Dulcie felt wretchedly sorry for her cousin. Columbine's life had been such a mess, the walls of loss and disappointment leaning in on her until all she really had was her desperate need for alcohol and her daughter Ianthe.

Columbine suddenly doubled over, twisted round, and, leaning right over the side of the boat, she heaved and retched repeatedly until she was spent.

Watching this, Dulcie felt lost and alone. And now the glowering black clouds were scaring her.

Perhaps there really was a storm coming after all, for the island weather could turn on a sixpence.

'All right?' she asked as Columbine straightened up.

'I need a cigarette,' her cousin said, the colour returning to her face.

'In this wind?'

Columbine's face crumpled as with shaking hands she reached for the satchel. She felt inside it and lifted out the bottle of water. 'Oh!' she said.

'Exactly. What were you thinking?'

Tears slid down her cousin's cheeks. 'I'm sorry. I'm so sorry.'

It was terrible to see Columbine like this and it was clear she really needed a doctor or maybe a psychiatrist. Someone who could help her to help herself, because propping up Columbine every time she fell was not working.

Dulcie softened her voice. 'It's only drizzling and everything will be all right once we're heading down the west coast.'

But would it ever be all right again? Feeling the salt spray on her bare arms and the salty tears stinging her cheeks, she wasn't sure.

She wasn't sure at all.

CHAPTER 11

As they reached Cape Drastis, Dulcie realised there would not be enough cover to hide a child there and, as they passed by, a memory shook her, so clear and bright that her eyes watered and she blinked rapidly. She hadn't expected the recollection of her first visit to this part of Corfu to affect her.

The white cliffs, small caves, and tiny strips of sand, accessible only by boat, had meant they could be alone. She'd come with Piers before they married and of course before Thirza was born. That was the day he tried to persuade her to give up her travels and her writing, saying there was so much beauty here, in Corfu, why did she need to go away. They'd watched the pinks and golds and crimson of the sunset together, their hands entwined. She had felt the pulse of him throughout her own body, and it had seemed like a sign that she was in the right place with the right man after all. Hermes, the great messenger of the gods, turned messenger in their shared pulse, in their shared heartbeat.

Swept away by the magic, she'd been tempted, contemplating his suggestion for a week or two, but that hadn't lasted, and the subject became a bone of contention between them. Did resentment always herald the death of love? The matter was only fully resolved after Billy was born and then she had willingly stayed at home.

'What about Porto Timoni?' Columbine was asking, having recovered her equilibrium.

'Maybe. But I'd like to get to Rovinia.'

The drizzle had stopped, and the sun was breaking through again by the time they reached Rovinia. They pulled the boat up through turquoise waters, the ochres and greens of the rocky surfaces beneath their feet clear as day, and then onto the narrow beach of tiny white pebbles and fine grey sand.

'This is more like it,' Dulcie said, gazing at the high rocks behind the beach then, slipping and sliding on the pebbles, she headed for the cave at the end of the beach.

'Nature calls,' Columbine said and went the other way.

Dulcie began her search but after an hour or more she hadn't found a single sign to indicate that Billy might have been brought there. She'd once heard of a trail leading up to the mountain from here. Could they have taken Billy that way? She didn't begin to ask herself who *they* could be.

She walked a little further and found an opening. The track, a narrow, dusty route, steep with loose rocks and lined with enormous thistles, brambles and other spiky bushes, would not be an easy climb. As she scrambled up the incline, frequently losing her footing, and holding out her hands to save herself, thorns scratched her face, her hands, her ankles. Her eyes stung from the clouds of dust she was kicking up and her head ached. Hot, sweating, and discouraged she glanced around. So far, they'd seen no sign of Italian guards patrolling the coastal waters, although she knew they were keeping an eye on small vessels, as well as being on the lookout for forbidden naval and merchant ships. She wouldn't want to get all the way to the top of the track and end up face to face with an Italian land patrol either.

Back on the beach she saw Columbine sitting hunched up by the boat. *What now*, she wondered.

But Columbine, hearing her footsteps, turned round, a broad smile lifting the misery previously etched on her face. 'Silly me,' she said. 'I slipped on the rocks and hurt my back, but I found this.' She held up a child's faded red ball and then handed it to Dulcie. 'Could it be Billy's?' she asked.

Dulcie gazed at the ball.

'You don't look very pleased.'

'No. It's not that. You've done well to find it and it could be Billy's, though these balls are everywhere. Every child on the island has one.'

'Oh.'

'But we'll see,' Dulcie added.

'Could we go home now? Let the police know we found it and then they could come with dogs.'

'Just one more stop. I'd like to get to Glyko while the weather holds, and then we'll go home. I promise.'

Columbine glanced up at the sky and looked nervous. 'Are you sure? It's a bit blowy.'

Dulcie sighed. She had harboured a hope that this quest might, with the discovery of Billy, bring about a healing of the troubles between her and her cousin. But too much water had passed under that bridge. Too many wrongs.

Too many resentments. On both sides. Dulcie was guilty too. If she'd done just one thing differently, how might things have turned out? She thought of the anonymous note. Her constant reminder.

Back in the boat she considered what to do and kept close to the coast, but as they approached the Glyko headland she moved further out to avoid the rocky shore.

The wind started up again, this time whipping her hair into her eyes – was this day never going to decide what it wanted to do? – and while she tried to snatch the hair from her face, the boat began to sway. As she was looking up to get a better view of the land, she failed to notice how far the boat was being driven back in the direction of the rocks.

Where the wind had only blustered before, now it erupted, chopping the sea. She struggled to control their direction, but they were still being dragged backwards. Again she tried to navigate them further from the dangerous edges of the coast, but the now wildly rocking boat had developed a life of its own. The wind was stronger too, slicing up the water, lifting up the boat, bouncing it back down, and sending sprays ten feet into the air.

'What's happening?' Columbine shrieked.

Dulcie felt the slam of it through her entire body as the rough sea hurled the boat against the rocks as if ordered by the will of Poseidon. Time slowed while all about her frantic crashing motion unfurled. She felt oddly distanced from herself as she remembered her classics. Poseidon, one of the twelve Olympians in ancient Greek mythology, presiding over the sea, storms, earthquakes and, strangely, horses.

Columbine screamed and Dulcie instantly switched back to life, seizing the tiller, her heart banging against her ribs. The clouds turned black, the wind bellowed, and Columbine screamed again. And again.

Dulcie yelled at her, 'Shut up! For God's sake shut up! I need to think.'

Their only hope would be to negotiate back around the headland and drag the boat onto the rocky Glyko beach. Then they could walk the coastal path to Liapades. But the boat was trapped on the rocks, so how would she even get them to the beach? The heavens opened, and rain hammered the sea, the boat, and the two women in it. Dulcie could barely see through the deluge and the white spray exploding from the churning water. It was far too dangerous to try to reach the beach.

'Grab a bucket,' she shouted. 'Grab a bucket from under the bench and start bailing out the water.'

Dulcie grasped hold of an oar from beneath her seat and, pushing with all her strength, she managed to eventually release them from the grip of the rocks. Praying there wasn't any serious damage to the boat, she made her decision. She couldn't aim for the beach but instead she'd head south and then work her way up the east coast to Corfu Town.

'I'm going to get us home and quickly,' she muttered.

But the boat began to drift, the engine stalling. They weren't sinking so the rocks hadn't fractured the wooden hull, but could they have run out of fuel? Or had the fuel line been broken in the storm? Something else might have broken, the prop shaft bent, the propeller? She just didn't know.

What she did know was that they had no power and were being carried out to sea. 'Oh Jesus,' she moaned, as she tried again and again to get the engine to spring to life, but the motor had completely ceased its thrum. 'Not this. Please, not this!' she pleaded.

But nothing she could say or do was going to help, for the engine had failed. They were alone at sea in a storm and nobody knew they were there.

CHAPTER 12

Dulcie was silent as she listened to their horses' hooves and stared ahead at unmade sandy roads lined with dusty Judas trees. They passed grassy verges dried to gold, the air full of the scents of aromatic plants, thyme, mint, oregano, marjoram, and the tiny yellow flowers of feathery dark green giant fennel.

She could feel Piers seething by her side. 'For God's sake Dulcie, you could have been killed.'

'I wish I had been.'

'Dulcie!'

'Would you care?'

'Of course,' he spluttered, but did not look at her, keeping his eyes on the winding road ahead. 'If that Italian patrol hadn't spotted you . . . well it doesn't bear thinking about.'

'I knew what I was doing,' she retorted. 'It's my job to know.'

'Your job *was* writing books, not risking your bloody life!'

'I had to go. It was perfectly sensible.'

'No. It was not. It was as about as far from sensible as I've ever seen you. And as for taking Columbine. Did you lose hold of your wits?'

'Probably,' she said.

They were silent as they began to ascend the pitted and rocky tracks with nothing but laurel and myrtle at their sides.

Piers was right. All they'd found was a red ball and Dulcie hadn't had the heart to tell Columbine that Billy had never owned a red ball. But, at last, she was going home to Merchant's, and there was a very slight chance Billy might have been brought this way. Slight because this was now the sixth day since her darling boy had gone.

Once the Italians had deposited her and Columbine at the town house the day before yesterday, and after Piers had finished berating her, he told her there had been a report of a young boy matching Billy's description seen leaving town and heading north in a horse and cart with two men. Dulcie had wanted to leave right away but the police had insisted on talking to her. Now she felt a wave of determination seizing her. She would hunt that cart down.

They slowly snaked past gnarled olive trees as the carriage rose up the steep hill, the track turning in on itself at the top and then winding down the main approach to the house where stately cypresses marched towards a high wall. There Venetian stone gateposts and wrought-iron gates protected the entrance to the Caruthers estate, preserving the house in lonely seclusion clinging to its position above the sea.

'How is Thirza?' she asked.

Thirza had gone ahead by boat along with Ianthe the day before.

'Honestly Dulcie, how do you think she's been?'

She would find out soon enough, for they were drawing up to the house now.

Dulcie gazed up at the mottled rose-coloured Venetian façade, the Roman roof tiles, and the green shutters of their Corfu summer home. She'd always loved this house, standing romantic and magnificent, holding court over a perfumed garden with wild rose bushes and oleanders spilling down to their own rocky cove, its beach, tiny harbour, and her beloved Ionian Sea. But the house was unnaturally silent, brooding, as though it shared their pain.

When they entered their hallway the mutinous look in her daughter's eyes almost floored her. Thirza had run down the stairs looking red-faced and now stood hands on hips accusing her, eyes blazing.

'Mummy! How could you?'

'I didn't—'

'You didn't think. You never do. All you ever care about is Billy. Not me.'

Piers put out his hand to halt her in her tracks. 'Come on, Theresa. Stop this.'

'No. She is selfish. She always has been.' And with that Thirza strode right past them and out through the open front door.

Dulcie could tell her daughter's gait was stiff as she stalked along the first terrace of the garden, her shoulders rigid with anger, but she knew that inside, her beautiful girl was hurting terribly. And it was her fault.

'I'll—' she said, feeling her eyes grow warm with unshed tears, as she started to go after her.

Piers caught her elbow, holding her back. 'Give her time. She doesn't mean it. Let her calm down in her own way.'

Dulcie gazed at the sunlight streaming across the tiled floor and sighed. 'Columbine is here too?'

'Where else? She came with the girls.'

'Piers, I couldn't stand by and do nothing,' she said. 'You don't understand—'

'Don't I?' His hand tightened on her arm. 'He's my son, too.'

Dulcie forced herself to soften.

'I know,' she said. 'I'm sorry.'

She wasn't. But Piers softened, too, just as she had known he would.

'I'll return to Corfu Town directly,' he said, more gently. 'I want to be there, in case . . .'

'What's happening with the Italians?' she asked. 'Are they actually doing anything to help us?'

'Other than rescuing you and Columbine?'

She sighed audibly.

'Sorry. Cheap shot. They're searching more widely across the island now. And they have put up posters. It's got them rattled for sure and I've been in touch with Scotland Yard.'

'Thank goodness. Will they send someone?'

'They might.'

'I was going to suggest where they could look.'

'Good, I'll pass your ideas on,' he said.

She nodded. A lump had formed in her throat, and she was struggling not to cry.

'Politically, the whole situation is still a mess,' Piers went on. 'The Italians are still insisting that the murders were committed by armed bands in the pay of Greece. The Greek government denies this, of course. My view is that Mussolini believes that Corfu, once occupied by Venetians, should be part of Italy again.'

Dulcie forced herself to maintain an interest, while inside, she wanted to scream. Scream that time was running out, scream that she did not care about anything, anything that was not Billy.

'Yes,' he continued. 'We have to hope the diplomatic moves going on behind the scenes bear fruit but there are plenty who believe the fascist regime is the only thing saving Italy from communism.'

Dulcie nodded.

'I'll just get a few things together and then head south. Try and rest,' he said in a genuinely kind voice, his arm draped around her shoulders. 'I promise we'll find our son. I miss him too.'

He kissed the top of her head, but that only made her feel even more guilty for the things she had withheld from him. For the thing that she would always withhold from him.

Like a wraith, Dulcie wandered the house in the dark, candle in hand. She ended up in Billy's bedroom, of course, where she lay on his bed and breathed in the familiar smell of her child. The traces of the boy who had been rolling in the newly mown grass. The salty scent of the boy who had been swimming in the sea. The hair washing powder also given to her by her friend Ingrid, with a violet-scented fragrance that Billy hated, and the mildly spicy Pears transparent soap. Her mind raced with images of him throughout his life, as a baby, a toddler, a chubby four-year-old, and now as a skinny nine-year-old. The boy who was never still. She longed for each and every incarnation of him and grieved them all.

'Billy,' she murmured, her voice almost swallowed by her fear. She missed her funny, clowning boy so much. His big smile. Gangly legs. She adored him, and though a mother was not supposed to have favourites she loved him the most. Loved him more than life itself. He always responded to the feelings of others, so unusual in a boy, and so unlike his sister who had many good qualities, but worrying what other people were feeling was not top of the list.

She went to his window and gazed out, listening to the land whispering the secrets of its many conquerors, the sea sighing and singing. Control of Corfu at the mouth of the Adriatic Sea led to control of trade and military routes between east and west and north and south. The Greeks, the Romans, the Goths, the Byzantines, the Normans, the Neapolitan Angevins, the Venetians, the French, and the British all had known this. And the land still told its tales of Venetian settlers and the surviving Venetian aristocracy even now living in crumbling stately splendour hidden from the ordinary folk behind forests of cypress trees and umbrella pines.

So many years of losses and gains. And now Mussolini's naval and military forces. But why, if this enchanted land would tell her all this, why would it not tell the story of what had happened to her darling boy?

As she left his room, she heard muffled sobs and listened carefully. Thirza. She walked quietly along the corridor to her daughter's room, hesitating before she went in. After a few minutes she pushed open the door and slid into bed with her girl.

'We will find him,' she whispered as she gently stroked Thirza's hair. 'He is alive, my love, and we will find him.'

'You really believe that?'

'I *must* believe that. I'm so sorry I worried you. And I'm sorry I was angry with you. It wasn't your fault. Not at all. Tomorrow we'll look for him all over the estate and in the surrounding land. A boy was seen coming this way. He may have been brought here and left somewhere.'

'And we will find him, won't we?'

Dulcie felt her chest tighten but had to try to believe it. For her fear of exposure, her fear of the old wounds ripping open and revealing the wrongs of the past, were as nothing compared to the fear that she might never see her son again.

CHAPTER 13

The Merchant's House, north-east Corfu, seven days after Billy disappeared

It was a cool, quiet morning, save for the cockerel crowing. Dulcie stood barefoot on the tiled hall floor and listened. Everyone was up. She could hear their low murmurs and footsteps above her as they searched the entire house once again, while waiting for the silky curtain of mist in the garden to melt away. Hermes, the wild wing-eared dog, would be following them into every room, tail between his legs. He must also miss Billy. Just as soon as the bright shafts of sunshine broke through and revealed the blur of the blue sea and sky, she went outside, the scent of rosemary strong in the air.

As she tramped across the garden's hard sun-baked ground, Thirza joined her and said, 'We already looked everywhere before you came.'

'It won't hurt to try again,' Columbine said, coming up behind them and assuming the unlikely role of peacekeeper.

They all went off in groups to search different areas, agreeing to loop back at lunch time. Columbine and Dulcie to the orchards and extensive gardens. Their housekeeper Eleni and her adult son, Spiro, to the barns and stables. Thirza and Ianthe to their cove and the natural harbour protected by land on three sides. With cypress trees growing almost to the edge of the pale blue water, it was barely a harbour really, just a little stone landing jetty with moorings and a boathouse where the boats were repaired. But a favourite of all of them. If Billy were anywhere, he'd be there.

Dulcie forced herself to put one foot in front of the other, ordering herself not to cry, all the time scanning, inspecting, examining every single inch of the grounds.

She found plenty of Billy's things lying about the place – his bicycle, the tin soldiers he'd left outside in May when the blue scabious and yellow marigold grew wild, his lost swimmers, a half-eaten sandwich, plus jumpers and socks he must have cast off. All of it broke Dulcie's heart. She wanted to weep and tear the hair from her skull but instead she forced herself to stay calm.

She had not found his hat but stood on the veranda beside one of two huge ancient terracotta urns and looked inside its depths, still desperate to find it. Not there either. He always wore that hat here – she had to prise it off his head when he came indoors – but he wasn't usually allowed to wear it in Corfu Town, so why had he gone back for it?

'You look like a hillbilly in that,' she'd say, and he'd fall about laughing.

'I am Billy. I am a hilly Billy.'

She glanced up as a burst of song came from the large overgrown bay tree where so many little birds had made their home and then she carried on looking for Billy's hat.

Piers had searched their town house for it but with no luck, so either it had to be here or, if she really couldn't find it, that must mean Billy had managed to get back to their town house and, having found the hat, had been wearing it when he went missing.

When the girls came back up, Ianthe kicked her heels in the dirt and Thirza looked red-faced and close to tears.

'Oh Mummy, there was no sign of Billy,' she said and gulped back a sob. 'What has happened to him?'

Dulcie squeezed her daughter's shoulder. But she could not answer. She had no answers. Unable to bear making conversation, even with Thirza, and desperate to be on her own, Dulcie suggested the girls help out in the kitchen and then she retired to her study.

With its grand oak table and marble fireplace – fabulous during the iron-grey Christmases, when they burnt cedar wood and currents of cold air gusted through this large, draughty house – it had always been her sanctuary as well as her place of work. But no more.

And now it had been nearly seven whole days. She could not bear to even think about Billy and yet it was all she did. Think of him and jot down everything they'd done since the moment he vanished. Anything to distract herself from the pain that had lodged in her chest and from which there was no relief. Writing had always been her escape but now, while her mind was in turmoil, and fear ran rampant through her days and her nights, what could she say that made any sense other than – *Where are you, Billy? Where are you?* They had to find him, they had to, for what was it all for, without him?

She looked at the shelves stretching to the ceiling along one entire wall, where hundreds of books jostled for space, including her own travel books. Although it felt like another lifetime, at least she had achieved that, hard won though her success had been.

The Caruthers publishing house, her father's publishing house, had not agreed to take her work on, and she'd felt shamed when, on their final holiday as a family, her father and his brother had laughed at her ideas.

'You can't write travel books. You're a girl,' Columbine's father had sneeringly said, his breath smelling of whisky.

But after he died so *tragically*, if that was even the right word, she had persuaded her father to agree, and her first book was published the following year. Once she inherited her uncle's half share of the company two years later when she was twenty-one, there was no stopping her. Her father had shrunk after his brother died, the fight gone out of him, so once she became partner and equal shareholder with her father, four books, written and illustrated by her, were published under the titles: *Travel Guides for Ladies*. They had sold well, and she had been vindicated. Her father had been impressed and had even admitted he'd been wrong. Now he was gone too. Despite everything, she had loved him, and she missed him, but at least the business was all hers now. But what did all that matter!?

She rose to her feet and with one furious movement she swept all the papers to the floor, her recent scribblings along with the white envelope. Fearful of opening it again, she wanted to scream. Scream out the pain. Scream and scream until her voice cracked. But Dulcie Caruthers was not a screamer. Dulcie Caruthers was softly spoken, well organised, with a carefully hidden side to her character. She knew people admired her elegance and grace, but inside she was every bit as outspoken and passionate as her daughter Thirza. Growing up with a dominant father had taught her there were quieter, some might say more underhand, ways of getting what she wanted.

Her family did not really know her. Not her daughter, nor her husband. They didn't know what she was capable of, didn't know how she frequently felt trapped in her role as wife and mother, didn't know there was a snarling frustration within her that she fought to control every day. They only knew who she pretended to be, who she'd made herself become, when she married Piers. Who she'd wanted to become, for when she and Piers married, he had genuinely become her world.

Until he wasn't.

But before that, before 1913, she had done everything to please him. In whatever way he wanted her, he'd had her. And after 1913 . . . She had tried then too. She had tried to be the person he wanted, every day, but every day it had become more and more difficult.

Her marriage might appear perfect, but in truth, it was unsteady, like an old red-brick wall in an English country garden. Lopsided, overrun with ivy, and home to hedgehogs. This house had always stood firm though, had belonged to Dulcie's extended family from the early nineteenth century when the British ruled the Ionian Islands. Many, many decades before Piers came on the scene, and was posted to Corfu where she had met him.

She glanced down.

The polished floorboards of her study gleamed. Their Greek housekeeper Eleni – a widow of fifty who offered hope to everyone around her and was rumoured to have the gift of clairvoyance – took pride in seeing to that. The gold-framed portraits of Dulcie's ancestors glinted in the sunlight and photographs of her family filled the dark pink walls. In the mornings her study windows, bordered with multi-coloured stained glass, threw kaleidoscopic patterns of light across the room. Now the windows were wide open onto the garden, and the scent of late roses drifted in on the breeze. The doors throughout the house were painted palest ochre and looked as if they had been dusted with early morning sunshine, but nothing helped her feel better today. Dulcie had always seen her home here as a refuge – and had not minded slowing down with her family, as long as she could do so here.

She reached down to the floor and, picking up the envelope, slid the note out once again.

YoU are GOing TO Pay FOR wHaT YOu did

Should she tell someone about the note – the police? Piers? If it was linked, somehow, to Billy, she should not have hidden it. Could it even be why Billy had been taken in the first place? She felt such a surge of guilt charge through her that she clutched her chest in pain. Yet it did not look like a ransom demand. Not at all. It was sheer poison. And cruel. She glanced around her room wildly then folded the note again and retrieved her little camphor wood box from its hiding place. She'd hide the note in there along with her old personal letters and photographs, where no one would ever know to look. From the box she took out her only photo of the man she'd loved so passionately and deeply. In the picture, she was there beside him and he was holding her hand. She kissed his face and thought of destroying the photo. But she couldn't. It was all she had of him now. Instead, she carefully tore the photo in two, slipped the image of the man into her handbag and returned her own image to the box. Last of all she slid the white envelope and its horrible contents into the box too.

'Cousin Dulcie!' she heard Ianthe call out. 'Thirza! Lunch!'

Columbine downed the first glass of wine almost before Dulcie had finished pouring it. Her cousin was, as usual, eating and drinking her way through this terrible crisis. Dulcie had already found her stuffing herself with chocolate right after breakfast. Devastatingly pretty in youth, she was carrying far too much weight now, and Dulcie wasn't sure, but had she imagined the trace of gin on her cousin's breath at ten that morning?

Piers always called her 'your dipsomaniac cousin'.

'It's good to be back at Merchant's,' Dulcie said, pushing her food around her plate. Already slim, she was fast becoming all angles, her stomach heaving every time she attempted to swallow food.

'Huh!' Columbine muttered and made a sour face then poured herself another glass of wine. 'It's fine for you.'

Dulcie took a sharp breath in. 'You do recall my child is missing? Nothing is fine for me.'

But Dulcie knew there was the other thing, the thing Columbine's father had done, that no one ever mentioned, and that had not helped the woman at all.

'You know very well what I mean.'

'If you're referring to your father—'

'I wasn't. Not exactly.'

'Well either way I'm truly sorry he died here and in such,' she paused, unsure. 'Umm . . . circumstances.'

'Merchant's was the right place. It should have been his. I'm not surprised he did what he did.'

Ianthe began to cry.

'Look,' Thirza said. 'This isn't the time to bring up old accusations. We need to focus on finding Billy.'

'Sorry,' Columbine said.

Ianthe stopped crying and they finished the meal in near silence save for, 'Pass the salt please' and 'Anyone for more bread' and 'Is there any pudding?'

'Come on everyone,' Columbine said, and pushed back her chair. 'Let's think of the things that Billy loves, to cheer ourselves up.'

Dulcie frowned, wishing that they had agreed not to mention Billy over lunch. Eating was hard enough without feeling she had been punched in the stomach. Even the pudding – an almond, lemon, and apple tart – tasted like ash in her mouth.

Thirza said, 'Remember how much he loves the smugglers' latch?'

'Yes,' Columbine said rather dismissively. 'He was obsessed with smugglers. Such a boy!'

'Especially the thought of emptying a chamber pot on a bad man's head,' Ianthe added.

But Dulcie wasn't listening and rising to her feet she said, 'I've had an idea.'

While the others were talking, she had been remembering how from the end of 1914 to 1918 the Allies had used the island as a naval and military base and what had once been the Empress Elizabeth's dream – the Achilleion – had become a French military hospital. Confiscated now by the Greek government, and lying completely unprotected, it remained a source of loot for any smuggler who fancied a foray into the strange world of collectible *objet d'art*. But maybe, just maybe, it was the perfect place to hide a child too.

'Time to go on a wider search this afternoon,' she continued. 'Come on! There's no time to waste. We'll take the horses. Who wants to ride with me?'

CHAPTER 14

Later when the day had ended in bitter disappointment, and everyone was asleep, Dulcie opened her window. Their search had yielded nothing with no sign of Billy anywhere. No cart. No child. No kidnappers. No ransom note. Nothing. She heard the wind hissing in the trees and stared into the night air and then out over the blackness to the sea, invisible beneath a moonless sky. Then, lying in bed, she listened to the first crash of thunder and pictured Zeus, huge and angry wielding a thunderbolt in the vast emptiness. The sea would be wild, rolling, unforgiving, and in the garden torrents of water would be dragging her beloved plants down to the sea. A flash of lightning sliced the sky apart and transformed her room. For a moment it glowed, an eerie electric blue. Rain pounded on the roof, the walls, the trees, splattering onto the pergola above the terrace, onto the tables, onto the chairs, echoing the torment crashing inside her.

After *he* left, the man she had loved, she had thought she'd known how it felt to be empty but – compared to this – that had been nothing. How was she going to live if they didn't find Billy? How could she bear to breathe if they didn't find him?

Back in the days before Billy, for there was a *before*, even though it didn't feel like it, love had made her feel full of herself without the need to be someone special. Her husband had done the opposite. But she had never truly known how it felt to be utterly empty – a living husk – until now, when only habit kept her going. Like a machine, she staggered through each day, one hour at a time, cleaning her teeth, washing her face, bathing, dressing, drinking tea, speaking when spoken to. Little by little she was not only losing her son but losing herself too. Her mind was going. Nothing else explained this feeling.

What would happen when she completely lost herself?

She had been a forthright woman liberal in her views, and that did not chime well with her husband nor with her own upbringing. She admired the Bloomsbury group and their rejection of bourgeois habits and the rigid old-fashioned conventions of Victorian life. She'd even met Leonard and Virginia Woolf at Monk's House, their home in the village of Rodmell, a few miles south of Lewes in East Sussex, but Piers had fiercely discouraged the acquaintance.

She had loved him once, admired his good looks and determined nature. He had offered her a different life, an escape in a way, and in her naivety she'd closed her eyes to the warning signs. Only too late did she realise that sex alone did not a marriage make, and they were not at all well suited. He had lovers, she knew that, though she didn't know how many. She'd had just the one and for such a terribly brief time.

Even if Piers had accepted that she would never be the perfect housewife, there had been an effervescence in her that, try as he might, he could not subdue. Yet she had resigned herself to her marriage, though maybe not quite as cheerfully as she'd pretended.

The man she had loved had been quite different . . .

Waiting for the oblivion that never came, she must have been awake for hours when Piers, smelling of whisky and horse, climbed into bed beside her.

'I rode through the night,' he whispered. 'Are you all right?'

She didn't answer, feigning sleep while his hand smoothed her inner thighs. Papering over the cracks in their marriage seemed pointless now Billy was gone. She did not want Piers, did not long for him, yet he had the ability to somehow make her yield. Something to do with the physical power he had, the knowledge that even if she resisted, he could still do exactly what he wanted. It most certainly was not love and she despised herself for her weakness. No, it was more than that. She despised herself for sometimes actually enjoying being subdued by him in the only way he could, turning her over, pinning her down, making her moan. There was something strangely satisfying in surrendering to this. Were women always destined to be so? She wondered if it were wrong but as long as it didn't happen too often, she would let him overpower her, take her, just as he always had done. In the beginning she had thought it was just what men did.

But the man she had truly loved, with his gentle touch and light-hearted humour, had taught her something very different and she had struggled to go on without him.

Even with his own issues he had taught her passion. Not taking but giving, touching her where she had never been touched before, physically, and emotionally. He had been the key to unlocking everything she had protected herself from, everything she had kept hidden. She had not realised that along with feeling so alive came an increased awareness of death. Of endings. But he had opened her up and there had been no turning back. How she'd gloried in his body, or rather her body and how it felt when she was close to his. You never got over how someone made you feel.

As she felt her orgasm build, she pictured him, his body, his eyes, the way he made love to her, and that was all it took to finish. Of course, Piers thought it had been all his doing, and after he too was done moments later, he promptly began to snore.

CHAPTER 15

Eight days after Billy disappeared

As dawn edged round her bedroom, Dulcie slid from the bed, dressed quietly, and made her way outside in search of Piers. The garden was her joy, with two long straight terraces her father had built, their supporting walls made from roughly hewn local limestone and, as she wandered, she felt the cool of the smooth-cut stone paving beneath her feet. Followed by the ever-faithful Hermes, she walked to the stone balustrade that marked the boundary of the terrace and leant against it to gaze out at the wet grass, the shrubs, and the trees sparkling under the morning sun. The sea was glassy, peaceful now, and apart from fallen branches in the garden and some missing plants there was no great sign that the north-west wind had whistled through the land and a late summer storm had rocked the night. The western side of the island was windier, although the best sandy beaches were there too. Early in the morning a dense fog could make it hard to see on this, the east side, but the sun soon burnt it off. Today, however, it was clear.

She gazed further down the steep slopes of the garden, where the terraced areas had been left to grow wild with roses and oleander. She slipped around to the side of the house where cherry, citrus, apricot, orange, fig, and pear trees provided leafy shade – the place she usually loved to sit and read. Nothing, no sign of her boy, nor her husband.

Determined to hunt through the orchards and the olive grove again, she went in search of her gardener Spiro, their housekeeper's son, who was always up early. Rich with the hum of insects, the orchards were well into bearing fruit now, but she preferred them earlier in the year carpeted in frothy white Queen Anne's lace and bright blue borage flowers. She reached up to pick an apricot but didn't even take a bite. They had already searched there before, but this time she wanted to spot if the ground had been badly disturbed anywhere. She hadn't told the others what she was going to do and when Spiro asked why she was obsessed by unsettled ground she had looked at him, unable to voice the reason. Then she had seen the way his eyes widened as he understood.

She heard the sound of a diesel outboard motor slowing down as it reached their tiny harbour, and her heart quickened, hoping the caique that brought their newspapers and daily supplies had also brought good news. They didn't need milk or cheese, which came from their nanny goats, nor vegetables, nor the eggs which came from their hens. Fruit was plentiful, and water gushed from their mountain springs. But the caiques brought everything else and importantly it brought news from Corfu Town. All she longed for was a letter telling her Billy had been found.

It wasn't the caique.

The rising wind carried the sound of men's voices up the sandy, boulder-strewn path – voices Dulcie recognised.

She hastened round to the front of the house where an ashen-faced Piers was marshalling in the same two policemen who had interviewed her before.

'Piers?' she said, hearing alarm in her own voice. 'I didn't know where you were.'

'I woke early, but listen darling, they have news. We all need to sit down.'

'Just tell me.'

'Madam, your husband is right,' the kindly Greek officer said.

Eleni entered the hall. 'Coffee in the drawing room, sir?'

Piers nodded, with a glance back at the police to indicate they should follow as he guided Dulcie through to a sofa in their drawing room.

Once they were all seated, she stared at the Italian officer. 'Well?'

'Mrs Moreland.'

She didn't bother correcting him this time.

'We now have reason to believe your son was abducted, possibly with the sole intent of kidnap and ransom, but with the island in, shall we say . . . confusion, something must have gone seriously wrong.'

She chewed her cheek, tasting the iron-like flavour of her own blood, her mind somersaulting, out of control. *Please don't let this be the end. Please.*

'A child's clothing has been found.'

She inhaled sharply, digging a nail hard into the fleshy part of her right hand and forcing herself to stay silent and not scream and scream at them to stop.

'It was discovered by a shepherd near a small estate at the old village of Perithia on Mount Pantokrator.'

She couldn't speak. Wouldn't speak.

'We found cream shorts, dirty of course, and a white shirt, also dirty.'

'They could have been anyone's,' Dulcie said at last, her voice thin and much too high.

'Darling,' Piers said. 'They have Billy's hat too, in their boat. I've just seen it.'

Oh God. Oh God. Oh God.

'A man has been arrested for your son's murder,' the Greek officer said.

She doubled over. 'No! No!'

'I'm so sorry.'

She glanced up at him and then at the Italian. 'But that's just the clothes. You haven't found his body.' Her voice was rasping now, her breath coming way too fast, and a pain, a tearing pain was crushing her chest. 'Billy might still be alive.'

'We think it unlikely.'

She sat upright again. 'Why?'

'There was blood on the shirt.'

Dulcie gasped and felt herself crumple.

'They found Billy's Swiss army penknife,' Piers said, trying to wrap an arm around her. 'An officer's knife, Dulcie.'

She pushed him off. 'Where? Where was it found?'

'In a house nearby.'

'Billy might have dropped it. Anything could have happened.'

'Maybe,' the officer said, 'but there were bloodstains on the knife too.'

Dulcie bent her head for a moment, not wanting to see the expressions on the men's faces. Those smug policemen with their fake sorrow and their fucking murder. How they must be loving this.

'How do you know it was his penknife?' she asked gruffly, still not looking at them.

'The initials, darling,' Piers said, his own voice cracking. 'Your father's initials carved into the wooden handle.'

The Italian policeman cleared his throat, but nobody spoke.

Dulcie struggled with the thoughts crashing around in her head. He couldn't be dead. He couldn't be. Wouldn't she feel it somehow if her child was gone forever? Wouldn't her own heart stop beating? Instead, she just felt numb. Cold as ice. Her beautiful, smiling, living boy, could not be dead. And yet they were saying he was. That somebody had hurt him. That there was blood on his clothes. She closed her eyes and screwed up her face against this knowledge. This awful, awful, knowledge.

A piercing scream broke the silence followed by a deafening crash. Dulcie looked up, swivelled round, and saw Thirza standing white-faced in the doorway, along with Eleni who had dropped the coffee tray, and was now using her apron to dab her eyes. How long had they been standing there? Had they heard everything?

While Piers showed the policemen out and talked to Eleni, Thirza rushed to be with Dulcie, crying and choking as her mother sat in numb immobilised shock. Eventually Thirza shook her mother and Dulcie blinked as if awakening from something or somewhere so dark, so godforsaken, that no one could ever follow.

'Oh, my darling girl,' she said.

And in that moment the spell that Corfu had cast upon them had finally been broken.

PART TWO

Corfu, seven years later

Spring 1930

CHAPTER 16

Thirza

Winter's rain had cloaked the island in fresh green growth and, lit by the sun, the countryside sparkled and shone. As they travelled, Thirza thrilled to see the land so alive with wildflowers – pinkish-purple honesty, the magenta blossom of Judas trees, swathes of white chamomile, and crimson anemones too – all nodding their heads to the sunny sky. As sheep and goats wandered among the trees of the ancient olive groves, and across the remote meadows and uncultivated hills, she was glad the fierce summer heat was yet to arrive.

Exhausted by the long sea journey from England all the way to Naples, staying just one night at the Grand Hotel Parker's, and then by train to Brindisi and eventually the overnight ferry to Corfu, her heart nonetheless had soared to see the joyful colours of spring once they were on the island.

None of them had felt able to return since Billy died, and it was challenging coming back after seven long years away. Yet from the moment they arrived at Merchant's, Thirza was gripped by nostalgia so strong it brought tears to her eyes. Home. At twenty-three she was finally home again in their little corner of paradise, their haven. Could there be anything better? And yet. She struggled to contain the overwhelming pressure in her chest and her longing for times past. This had once been the happiest place you could ever imagine. What was it now?

She stood on the edge of the top terrace, stretched her arms out wide, and breathed in the salt and seaweed.

'Thirza!' Ianthe called out, sounding exasperated. 'The trunks haven't arrived.'

She glanced back at Ianthe, noticing the wisteria covering the wrought-iron pergola was crammed with gorgeous hanging flowers, just as if they'd never been away. 'Though it needs cutting back,' she muttered.

'They were supposed to be ready for us, here in the porch,' Ianthe said, standing by the front door. 'And look, everything is dirty.'

'What were you expecting?' Thirza replied. 'We've come to clean the old place up before Ma arrives.'

Perhaps Ianthe hadn't been the best choice of companion on this mission. Her cousin might be pretty – with golden hair that tumbled gracefully almost to her waist and enormous blue eyes – but resilient she was not. Already, Thirza could tell whatever work needed to be done to bring Merchant's back to its former glory was going to be down to her. But she could not regret it. It had taken a whole month of persuading, for her mother to agree to come back too, and Thirza was determined that by the time she joined them, everything would be perfect.

'The trunks will probably arrive later,' she added, turning away, running past the native turpentine tree with its fresh coppery leaves, then down the steps to the second terrace. The garden wasn't quite as overgrown as she'd expected.

'Probably?' Ianthe shrieked. 'I need my dresses now. What if Walter were to arrive early?'

'Try on some of Columbine's dresses, you know, from back . . .' She paused briefly, then carried on down the paths that led to the lower levels of the garden, where the pink-and-white oleanders had gone completely wild. She raised her voice. 'Back then. Wear one of those.'

'Those frumpy, old-fashioned frocks?' Ianthe said, outraged. 'With Walter just about to arrive?'

Thirza rolled her eyes. Walter Brown was Ianthe's dapper beau, an American, and he was due to join them, too, perhaps with Columbine. Seven years after they had left, and the family was coming back to Merchant's – hopefully not for the last time.

'Does your frock matter?' she said. 'We're going to be cleaning most of the time, anyway.'

'Don't remind me,' Ianthe groaned. 'And why can't we pay for some cleaners? Cleaning will ruin my nails.'

Thirza took a deep, calming breath. She could not have this conversation with Ianthe, again – had the girl been paying any attention, these past years? After the Wall Street Crash the year before, the Caruthers publishing house had suffered significant financial losses. And since the entire family relied on Dulcie's business to fund their lifestyles, their situation was now far more precarious – not that Ianthe seemed to understand.

'We have to save money to pay for any building work,' she told Ianthe. 'You know that. And you can paint the walls if you don't want to clean.'

'No chance. Firstly, I can't go into Corfu Town with Walter in one of Mother's frumpy old-fashioned frocks – and secondly, he would not be impressed to see me painting walls.'

Thirza had stopped listening.

'Where are you going?' Ianthe demanded, stamping her foot like a girl of five or six, despite her eighteen years.

'For a swim of course,' Thirza yelled over her shoulder, peeling off her dress in relief.

She removed her sandals as soon as she reached the rocks just above their little harbour, protected by land on three sides, and cradled within a larger bay. A bit more carefully now that she was barefoot, she picked her way over the sharp rocks and barnacles, passed the small stone landing jetty and the boathouse, then arrived at the secluded sandy cove. Nobody could see her except from their garden and, even so, cypresses grew like a curtain almost to the edge of the water. In only her knickers and vest she hurled herself into the ocean, gasping at the cold. Here she could stretch and be herself, unconfined by London life where, as the daughter of Dulcie Caruthers, she had struggled to find her own niche.

It was only at Merchant's that she could remember being happy. Her family happy, too, because Dulcie had not been the same after Billy died. *Was murdered*, she corrected herself, still with a blast of the old rage that had never truly faded. Her mother had grown even thinner, paler, colder. The man had been arrested and tried, but the shock when he got off! It had been something to do with the only evidence being circumstantial, and the police not finding Billy's body.

Now, she swam right round past the rocks to another much smaller cove where she could be seen by no one at all. Although, as she glanced up, she noticed the old house, standing on a promontory just north of their own, was gleaming, as if only recently painted cream. And was that smoke rising from the garden? A bonfire? It could just be a trick of the light. Corfu light was ineffable, full of shivery tricks that made you see what could not be there, made you unable to see what *was* there, with an enchantment that meant you heard things too.

When she was younger, Thirza had tried so many times to capture the colours of the sea as they shifted from blue to green to purple, but the resultant paintings usually ended up in the bin, torn to shreds. She would capture it one day, she told herself. She was an artist now and, as well as being here to clean the house, she was going to concentrate on her latest commission – a series of paintings for a children's story book.

As she swam, she was constantly aware of Billy's presence. Swimming beside her, demanding they race.

Thizzy. Thizzy.

Beat you to the cove and back.

Turning somersaults in the water and not coming up for ages, just to scare her. Then, hair plastered to his forehead, pink-faced, and grinning like a Cheshire cat, exploding from the water.

She finished her swim and shook herself on the beach. He would be absolutely everywhere, of course, and she sighed, for the memories of him when he was little were intense. How he'd insisted she read to him, laughing and giggling, his eyes so full of light and love, so tangible now that it knocked her out of herself. Gasping for breath, her eyes began to water.

'It's just the salt in the sea,' she muttered crossly. But it wasn't. It was the terrible absence they were all having to learn to live with. What else was there? She'd been sixteen when he disappeared, and it had changed their lives forever.

After her swim, Thirza could not put off going inside the house any longer. In her wet underclothes she glanced up at the blushing Venetian façade, mottled pink by age, where cream-coloured roses spilled unfettered. The house was showing a few signs of damp now, and the faded green shutters were crying out for a fresh coat of paint, though the Roman roof tiles still looked fine. She'd always loved this romantic house. They had all loved it.

Ianthe had not let herself in and was sitting on a stone step outside with their suitcases next to a tub of long-neglected plants and looking red-faced and cross.

'About bloody time,' her cousin muttered.

'Why didn't you go inside? It would have been cooler.'

'You know I'm scared of spiders.'

Thirza laughed. 'Honestly Ianthe! Come on. I'll unlock.'

'You need to put some clothes on.'

'I will.'

The brass doorknob and handle were discoloured, green and mottled. It took a few minutes to even move the key a tiny fraction in the lock. For a moment Thirza worried that the mechanism might have rusted, and they wouldn't be able to enter the house without breaking a window. After several attempts it finally turned, and she heaved the stiff door open with her shoulder. It creaked noisily and they went inside.

'God, it smells awful,' Ianthe said, her hand covering her mouth and nose.

'You're right. More than just musty. Something must have died in here – a bird or . . .'

She stopped herself from saying 'rat', knowing Ianthe wouldn't be able to cope.

'Yuk.'

'What we need is light and air. Let's leave the front door open, throw back all the shutters and open the windows. Do you want to do downstairs or upstairs?'

'Downstairs,' Ianthe said with a grimace. 'But why isn't Eleni here? Didn't your mother ask her to return?'

'She wrote. Yes. And she kept her on a retainer but maybe Eleni doesn't want to work here again . . . after Billy.'

Thirza marched up the stairs to the gloom of the first floor and went into her old bedroom that, like her mother's room, faced the front garden and the sea. So many memories. Not just Billy's ghost but the ghosts of their former selves too. As if multiple versions of themselves might have continued living there while they had all been in England. The house teeming with their voices as if they had gone on in lonely isolation for the past seven years.

Mummy, where are my bathers?

Billy, I told you already.

God Lord Dulcie, can't you keep them under control.
You can't catch me. Can't catch me.
I give up. Where are you hiding?

Childhood tears. Laughter. Her mother's admonishments when their games got out of hand, and their father's irritable complaints when he fell over the toy-strewn rugs.

Her earliest memories were all from here. Stalking the garden, seeking out insects and small animals to draw – often trailed by Billy. She smiled at the memory of being sixteen, dancing naked on the beach and lighting an enormous fire for a barbecue, her mother's whistle warning her to whip on her clothes just before her father arrived on the beach. Dulcie didn't mind her swimming naked, sometimes even did the same. Now Thirza wriggled out of her wet underwear and slipped into a dry housecoat of her mother's.

She opened the shutters and, as the bright sunshine streamed in, she could see the true state of the place. There were cobwebs. Great black clouds of them, and the dust of the last seven years lay thick on her dressing table, her bedside table, the floorboards. She dragged a finger through some of the dust on one of the interior windowsills and wrote her name, then she took a deep breath, shrugged, and raised her head to look at the view of the sea. Blue and so beautifully luminous with the line between sky and water blurring and the shadowy mountains of Albania looming in the distance.

The Corfu incident of 1923, as it was now called, was long over. After much wrangling the Italian demands had been met by Greece, and the Italian soldiers had departed the island after staying only one month in total. Since

Thirza and her mother had left Corfu, her father had remained for work as he always did, only visiting England occasionally. She sighed deeply. In more ways than one, their family had been destroyed by Billy's disappearance. But here, it was easier to remember how they used to be. And, as strange as it was to be here, after all these years, she knew she'd been right to come. She only wished it hadn't taken her so long to return, but now she planned to make the old place look as beautiful as it had been years earlier. For her mother as well as herself.

CHAPTER 17

A week later, Thirza glanced across at the hall clock.

'Damn, damn, damn!' she muttered as she put her paintbrush down on the top rung of the ladder. 'What now?'

Although it was still early and not yet hot, she already felt weary, and the sound of angry voices coming from the garden seemed like trouble. Had she forgotten to pay someone?

She'd expected this summer to be different and it was. How could it not be?

The housekeeper's son Spiro had arrived yesterday, all smiles and apologies, and told her Eleni would return to work for them just as soon as she came back from visiting her sister in Athens. He promised to bring his gang of odd-job men, and they would paint the exterior of the house and take down the shutters for sanding and repainting, but not until he finished the job he was currently working on. The interior work would be up to Thirza and Ianthe and, when the painting was done, they'd mend and adapt the soft furnishings. For now, it was clear Thirza was still on her own, paintbrush in hand.

She heard Ianthe's annoyed voice followed by a man protesting in a foreign accent.

'I promise I was not spying,' he repeated.

Thirza climbed down the ladder and made her way outside where she found a red-faced, sundress-clad Ianthe berating a bespectacled man who had a camera hanging from his neck and looked a little as if he had nowhere special to be.

'*Buongiorno,*' he said with a little bow.

'Hello. Are you lost?'

'Not really,' he said in English and then pointed at the house on the promontory which she'd noticed earlier. 'I am staying at that house over there for the summer. I saw signs of life and so I came to introduce myself.'

'Well there's only me and Ianthe here and we are rather busy.'

'I see. If you can spare the time, it would give me great pleasure to invite you both for drinks this evening.'

'Ianthe?' Thirza said.

'I don't understand Italian,' she muttered, looking sulky and ignoring the man's excellent command of English. 'Anyway, I can't go. Walter must surely be arriving today.'

Thirza doubted Walter would show his face until the place was spick and span, but she turned to the Italian. He was older than her, sophisticated, in his thirties she thought, but very good-looking, and she noticed how smartly dressed he was, with medium brown hair cut well in the way of Italian men and, behind the spectacles, the most amazing dark eyes ringed with gold.

'Well, it's nice to meet you,' she said, suddenly aware she'd been staring at him, and that she was wearing old dungarees splattered with white paint and might even have some of it in her hair too. 'I'm Theresa, Thirza for short.'

He held out his hand. 'You have an unusual Christian name.'

'Yes. I suppose.'

He seemed a little awkward for the briefest moment and then he said, 'Well, people call me Emilio, Emilio Bellini. Would six o'clock suit you?'

Ianthe looked shocked. 'You can't go on your own.'

'Of course I can. Thank you, Signor Bellini.'

'Emilio, please.'

Thirza walked alone to the house on the promontory that evening, the land glowing golden all around her. Emilio ushered her into a simply furnished but recently painted drawing room, where she now stood at an open window and was in danger of losing herself in the most beautiful view on God's earth. Almost the same view Thirza could see from her own bedroom. The view that had, at times, been the only thing left that she had been able to cling to.

'I'm sorry your friend couldn't come,' he said.

'Friend? Oh, you mean Ianthe. She's my cousin, second removed or something. I can never remember.'

'There are many cousins of differing status in my family too.'

'Yet you are here alone,' she replied, having wondered what he was doing here on his own, especially as he had looked a little forlorn earlier that day.

'They would not be interested.'

116

'That's a shame. It's a terrific island, or it used to be.'

'Used to be?'

'Oh,' she said, as he stood there as if waiting for clarification, and in that moment, she knew she could not tell this man the truth. 'I just mean there's more political turmoil than there used to be. My father works in Corfu Town but we don't often see each other. I live in England.'

Thirza paused and didn't even mention her mother as she had originally intended to do. After living in Dulcie's shadow for so long, this was a chance for someone new to see her as a person in her own right. As she thought of her mother, she recalled the sorrow in their London home and how her own yearning for Billy had only been assuaged by the thought of Merchant's, assuaged as much as anything could be when your little brother was gone forever.

'You look rather sad,' the Italian said.

'Not at all,' she said, knowing her smile was insincere, and she thought she noticed a hint of sadness about him too.

Then, as if reading her mind, he said, 'I wondered if you knew anything about the family that used to live around here?'

Surprised, she muttered something noncommittal.

'Or about the little boy who went missing?'

'No,' she said, turning away as Billy ran around her mind like a puppy chasing its tail. 'I don't know anything about that.'

How could she talk about Billy with a stranger? It would feel like a betrayal and would hurt far too much.

'The story seems to be well known on the island.'

'I've heard that,' she said, and then changing the subject added, 'Don't you just love the colour of the sea?'

'Yes indeed.'

There was a brief silence. Then he said, 'So, you and your cousin are just working here on the island, sprucing up the house for the owners?'

She circled back to look at him and laughed. 'That's me.'

'What may I offer you? I have champagne.'

'That will do nicely.'

'You're an artist,' he added as if appraising her.

'How can you tell?'

'I too stand at the window staring at the sea.'

'Oh,' she said, not really understanding. 'I love the sea but I didn't take you for a kindred spirit.'

He smiled. 'I am not bohemian enough?'

She felt embarrassed, and wanted to hide her burning cheeks, as that was exactly what she'd thought.

'You, however, have the most marvellously abandoned hair.'

She blushed again despite herself and felt annoyed that she had. Over the years her hair had darkened and now fell about her shoulders in deep auburn-red ringlets, some of which flew out around her head as she moved. 'My father calls it my crowning glory, and you're right. I think I must be almost entirely bohemian.'

He smiled and his dark eyes lit up with amusement, the gold rings around his irises flaring even more brightly.

She couldn't speak, turned away and drew in slow breaths, then she said, 'Emilio, do you ever wonder about the depths of the sea? The deepest darkest places where nobody has ever been or even seen.'

'Does the thought of that scare you?'

She smiled. 'A little.'

'Did you know,' he said, changing the subject. 'Bitters were added to gin as they were thought to combat seasickness?'

'I did not.'

'Are you hungry?'

She thought about it. 'I think I'm always hungry.'

He smiled again and she felt really drawn to him. 'As an Italian I like food. And I like a woman who eats. I hope that is not too forward a thing to say to an Englishwoman.'

'Of course not, especially as we have already ascertained my bohemian credentials. You are free to say whatever you like, Signor Bellini.'

He laughed an open, friendly laugh.

'Well, I am touring the Ionian Islands this spring and summer in preparation for a book. *An Italian in Greece* sort of thing, a combination of travel writing and history.'

'How fascinating.'

'I wonder, would you be prepared to tell me about the island, maybe show me some key locations? Perithia on Mount Pantokrator for example.'

She felt herself blanch, and quickly turned to face the view again. 'I am rather busy,' she eventually managed to say.

'Painting and decorating?'

Having regained her equilibrium, she said, 'Not only that. I'm an illustrator and I have a commission to complete while I'm here.'

'There! I said you were an artist.'

She turned to smile at him, unable to hide how excited she was to be paid to do what she loved, and, leaving out the fact that her mother's contacts in the world of publishing had initially helped her gain a foothold, she told him how determined she was to make a name for herself.

'My aim is to be totally self-supporting,' she said, aware that she was still living at home and, although she could support herself now in a day-to-day way, it would be much harder if she had to buy somewhere to live or needed to pay rent.

Then realising she had lapsed into silence she added, 'Anyway, you might like to visit the island of Paxos. I've heard there are other writers and artists living there.'

He walked her back to Merchant's though it wasn't far, and Thirza was not the least bit afraid of the dark. In the cool night air, she caught the tangy sharp fragrance of lime and something woody too. His cologne maybe?

'I will take my leave,' he said as they approached the house. 'Thank you for a pleasant evening.'

'Thank you for inviting me.'

'How very correct we both sound,' he said.

'Do you not like correctness?'

He reached out his hand and she shook it.

She knew she was flirting, and with an older man too. Thrilled that he didn't know anything about her, that he was attracted to her just for herself, and she could be anyone she wanted to be, she allowed a tiny smile to escape. She was done with pretending to be what people wanted her to be. This summer, whatever else happened, she was going to be herself, and if she didn't quite know what that meant she was going to find out.

'I think you are not such a formal person,' he said. 'Not really.'

'You are right. I am not, Signor Bellini,' she replied, taking a step away and hiding her widening smile as she turned to face the door.

CHAPTER 18

The next morning, Thirza awoke refreshed. Raring to go, she slipped into her paint-splattered dungarees and tied back her hair. She ate a round of toast and drank a mug of very sweet hot chocolate. Today she would get the boathouse ready. Take down a can of distemper and all her artists' paints and also her drawing materials in a large brown box. She loved working to the sound of the sea, and you couldn't get any closer to the sea than the boathouse. It was the constant movement, the background sounds, and the smell of it that gave life to her drawing and seamlessly stitched her into the natural world, the only place where she truly belonged.

Ianthe came down to the kitchen just as Thirza was getting up from the table.

'I want to hear about last night!' Ianthe demanded. 'What's he like?'

'Who?'

'Your Mister Bellini.'

'He's not *my* Mister Bellini,' Thirza said. 'But . . . he's nice. Wants me to show him around.'

'Really? He must be twice your age. What would your mother say?'

'She knows an awful lot of writers.'

'Not what I meant, and you know it.'

'I'm twenty-three,' Thirza said, heading for the door. 'Not twelve.'

'Where are you going?' Ianthe asked.

'Sorting out the boathouse today,' Thirza replied.

'Oh God,' Ianthe groaned. 'Don't you ever stop? Why do you care so much?'

'You wouldn't understand,' Thirza said. 'This place – it's a part of me.'

'It's ours by rights, you know,' Ianthe muttered under her breath.

'What? What did you say?' Thirza twisted round to look at Ianthe.

'Nothing.'

'No. Come on.'

Ianthe shrugged. 'Just something my mother said.'

'What?'

'Only that Merchant's actually belonged to my grandfather, not yours.'

Thirza tried to hide an eye roll, but Ianthe spotted it and scowled. 'I know you think Columbine is mad. But she isn't, you know.'

Thirza hardly knew what to say. Columbine was not like the rest of them, and she could be unstable.

'I don't blame you, but she is different now. Doesn't drink at all. Yet she's terribly thin . . .' Ianthe's voice caught. 'And terribly unhappy.'

'Oh Ianthe, I'm sorry. Do you know why she's taken a turn for the worst?'

'She won't tell me anything. But I think she blames herself for what happened to Billy.'

Thirza thought back to that terrible day and remembered Columbine's neglect of the little boy she had promised to look after. It was no wonder that she felt guilty. Thirza felt guilty too.

'All I know is that she sees a psychiatrist every fortnight. Has done for the last year. He's called Franklin and he's an American, like Walter.'

'How can she afford it? Aren't such doctors terribly expensive?'

'Your mother is paying.'

'Of course she is,' Thirza muttered. Dulcie didn't seem to mind bankrolling their entire family, and Thirza could hardly feel too indignant on her behalf – for she certainly had accepted enough money from her mother, too. But at least she was trying to be self-sufficient – not like Ianthe who would leap straight from Dulcie's pocket to Walter's.

'What was that you said?' Ianthe demanded.

'Nothing!' Thirza replied, already regretting the slip of her tongue. She didn't know why she was being so sharp with Ianthe, who hardly deserved it – and truly, wasn't it admirable that Columbine was seeking help? Even if it was seven years too bloody late. Thirza's complex mix of emotions to do with Columbine were usually kept hidden, but she couldn't understand why her mother still kept the woman afloat, considering she had just let Billy walk off at such a dangerous time.

Before Thirza went down to the boathouse, she tried the door to her mother's study. There had always been cash kept in there and she'd need the back-up money to pay the workers when they finished the job. The funds her mother had given her would not last forever.

She turned the handle, but the door would not open.

She fetched the bunch of keys they kept on a hook in the kitchen, then methodically tried each one.

Nothing worked.

Possibly it had been secured because of the cash, though Thirza could not remember it ever being locked before.

Her mother was still something of a closed book to her, and there was so much she didn't know about her past. As a young child Thirza had loved curling up on the sofa in there, listening to the clackety clack of the typewriter keys and smelling her mother's French cigarettes and the endless cups of coffee. Being in there had always comforted her, made her feel that no matter what, all was right with her world. Just as long as the keys went clackety clack.

The rituals that hadn't seemed especially important at the time had turned out to be the things that actually held a family together. Made them, *them*. They were the glue. Later, after what happened to Billy, the glue had dissolved, and they were left free floating in their own separate ways.

A memory arose of their old black-and-white dog hurtling through the house chasing a squealing Billy. The dog's ears so large that they flew out like wings, and so they had called him Hermes.

'What message is he delivering today?' It was their father's standing joke.

'That it's time for cake,' Billy shouted out and then giggled.

Thirza tried once more to open the door, but it remained stubbornly closed, so she made her way down to the boathouse instead, still feeling perplexed about the locked study. Why had Dulcie locked it before she left for England seven years ago? She hadn't locked anything else.

Thirza thought again about Ianthe's assertion. Could there really be truth in it? Should Merchant's have been Columbine's and not Dulcie's? She'd heard it whispered before and had dismissed it as one of Columbine's drunken delusions. One of many in her chaotically messy life.

Now she wondered what other small, previously unnoticed, unremarked-upon details about Dulcie's life might add up to something much bigger. Everyone had secrets, didn't they? Were there documents in the study that might reveal the history of Merchant's? Could her mother be hiding something in there, something she didn't want anyone to know about, and that was why she'd taken the key with her? Or was it simply because of the cash?

Thirza unlocked the blue peeling boathouse door and went inside. It smelt musty and damp, but she put the distemper and brushes on the bare floorboards and then opened all the windows. The sea and the sky and the colour of blue rushed in and for a moment she felt dazzled, as if the little house was submerged in shimmering water, blinding her.

When she recovered, she took in the state of the place. The floor needed cleaning and painting, but she'd see to that last of all. First, the walls. She planned to mix some yellow pigment into the distemper she'd found in one of the sheds. She could arrange for more to arrive with the caique and, when the walls were done, she'd touch up the woodwork with linseed oil and finally deal with the floor. She'd love to paint it blue. It would take her a week or so, she supposed, for so much of the wood needed sanding.

A little later she was back up at the house filling a pail with water when Ianthe came out to the scullery looking for milk.

'I could help you in the boathouse,' the girl said, leaning against the door jamb in a desultory way and scuffing her foot back and forth in the dust on the hard concrete floor. 'If you like?'

Thirza didn't answer for a moment.

'Thirza?'

'Oh, you don't need to. There's still plenty needs doing in the house.'

'Please. I get lonely. And the house feels . . .' She shrugged. 'I don't know.'

But Thirza knew. Sometimes she felt as if the house were waiting for Billy. Just like she was, even though she knew it was impossible.

Thirza straightened up. She'd heard the tears in Ianthe's voice. 'It's all right, you know. There's only us.'

'I know.'

'All right. If you can carry this down, you can start by cleaning the walls. Grab a cloth and I'll bring down another pail.'

Ianthe clapped her hands like a little girl. 'Oh good. It'll be fun.'

But try as Thirza might, she could not regain the refreshing calm of the morning. It felt as if every time she found herself happy here, she was beset by memories.

Down in the boathouse Ianthe prattled cheerfully on, but Thirza felt herself sinking deeper and deeper into melancholy – until a new voice interrupted their work.

'I hope I'm not trespassing,' a man called out.

With a start Thirza looked down through the open window. Bellini smiled up at her and she was startled when her heart skipped a beat.

Ianthe came to join her at the window. 'Hello. You can walk there, no problem.'

He gave her a little bow and she grinned. Thirza felt a tiny spike of jealousy. Of course, he would flirt with Ianthe. So fresh and pink and pretty. Everyone did.

He held out a Thermos flask. 'I have coffee.'

'That's nice,' Thirza said, wilfully misunderstanding him.

He laughed. 'Would you like some? Shall I come up?'

'No,' she said. 'It's either dirty or smells of paint in here. We'll come down.'

They descended the outside staircase and then the three of them sat on the rocks together. Thirza wanted Ianthe to leave but then, seconds later, wanted her to stay.

'I'm going to paint and draw in the boathouse when it's ready,' she said, trying not to show how flustered she felt by her reaction to the man's proximity.

'Your commission?'

'Yes.'

Ianthe chattered away and Emilio was the soul of politeness, talking and listening, asking questions. Thirza just wanted to get up and leave. Or stay. She wasn't sure.

After a while Ianthe rose to her feet and, saying she needed the loo, hurried up to the house. Emilio's eyes followed her, and the moment he knew Ianthe could not see them anymore, he gazed at Thirza and said, 'I am so pleased to have met you both.'

She detected the same shadow of sadness she'd noticed before, though it didn't linger.

Up until now only one man had touched her deeply. She had vowed never to let it happen again and, so far, it had not. But this! She had a firm strong body, but felt vulnerable as if sitting on unsteady ground that might give way and swallow her if she allowed him to come any closer.

'Are you all right?' he said.

'Of course.' She had answered rather sharply but didn't know what to do about it.

'You look a little lost today.'

How could he tell? She *was* feeling lost. Had felt it every single day since Billy's death, though nobody had come close to mentioning it before, as if the wall of silence kept everyone out, and so her loss had grown, brick by brick, until it had become impenetrable.

'Well, if you must know, I am feeling a bit out of sorts today.'

'Too much work?'

'Maybe.'

'Can I help?'

She shook her head. She wished she *could* talk to him, but nobody could help. Nobody could bring Billy back from the dead. She still saw him though, hiding in air thrumming with flying insects, his body half in and half out of the fringes of the undergrowth further down the garden where it was wild.

You can't see me.

You can't see me.

How could she tell Emilio that being at Merchant's was both a joy and a crippling pain at the same time, when she had already denied all knowledge of the child?

'What is it you do?' she asked, unused to this close kind of attention, and feeling awkward.

'I am a writer, as I told you. But also, a businessman.'

She glanced down at his hands. Elegant hands.

'I think you may need curtains.' He was looking at her, and she felt naked before his gaze, as if he could see right through her.

'What?'

'The light is too bright this close to the sea. You will need curtains.'

She nodded.

'For when you are painting.'

She felt herself turning red but managed not to drop her gaze. All she said was, 'Yes.'

There was a short silence then he said, 'How long?'

'Sorry.'

'How long before you're ready?'

I'll never be ready, she really ought to say.

'I mean, how long until the boathouse is ready?' he clarified.

'Ah. A week, I think,' she said. 'Maybe more.'

He glanced away then back at her and, putting a hand to his heart in mock sorrow, he said, 'And soon I have to go away on business for a week or so, but how shall I manage to leave this gorgeous place?'

She looked at him as he laughed and then she joined in too.

After a moment he rose to his feet, so she stood and took a step away from him.

'So,' he said. 'I hope to see you again before long. Now I have work to do and photographs to take.'

She inclined her head.

'For my book. Remember?'

'Oh yes. Of course.'

'Something tells me we shall become firm friends,' he said, touching her hand briefly before stepping away.

CHAPTER 19

Spiro arrived a couple of days later, along with his gang of odd-job men who turned up mostly on bicycles or donkeys. They carried ladders and tools, all the paraphernalia needed to take down the shutters for sanding and repainting, and to paint the exterior. They were a jolly lot, cracking jokes and laughing in the way men did, putting down one tool or another, wrenches and screwdrivers, rulers, hammers, and checking who needed what to do what. Thirza smiled at their antics, left them to it, and went in search of their housekeeper Eleni who had arrived with them.

She found her in the kitchen taking off her coat.

'Am I pleased to see you,' Thirza said with a grin.

Eleni scrutinised her. 'Young Theresa, all grown up,' she said, then held out her arms.

Thirza fell into them, and their hug was prolonged.

When they finally drew apart, Eleni smiled knowingly. '*And* you look like a woman with a secret.'

Thirza thought of Emilio Bellini and recalling his last comment to her, and that touch on her hand, she had to fight a smile.

'I'm not that kind of woman,' Thirza replied, feeling the heat rising, though her voice was almost steady.

Eleni raised her brows. 'If you say so.'

'Well, I'm so happy you're here, but now I must get on,' she said, and quickly made her escape.

'Something tells me we shall become firm friends,' he had said.

If only she could recall his exact tone of voice. Had it been teasing; had he been making fun of her? Or was there a promise? A suggestion of more. Then again, maybe he was just being polite. Or just being Italian.

Thirza had been looking forward to visiting all the places she loved along the coastline, so for a break from the house, she set off on horseback, taking the rough tracks that led away from Merchant's down to the sea. But almost without realising it, she began heading in a different direction – had felt the pull of it ever since Emilio had mentioned it several days before. Billy had been talking to her in her dreams too, and all at once she knew she *had* to go there. The place where Billy's clothes had been found – Perithia on Mount Pantokrator – but not with Bellini. So after turning away from the coast, she eventually rode further uphill into the mountain. The sun, beating down on her head, neck, and shoulders, was stronger than she'd expected and even before she was halfway there her head was thumping, and she felt a little sick.

The walk up from Perithia to the Pantokrator summit where you were met with breath-taking views of the island and of Albania was easy enough if you were young. But she didn't need to get to the summit, only the village, and in any case, she'd seen the view before. She passed orchards of cherry trees, fig trees, pear and apple trees, the air sweet, fragranced with wild sage and thyme, and when she finally arrived, she dismounted and tied the horse up in the shade, then stood gazing around at the rocky landscape that surrounded the village of Perithia. She could believe the stone houses had been built in pre-Christian times as some claimed they had been. It was a terribly sad place, for part of it was in ruins, and as she walked down narrow cobbled streets and listened to the birds in this quiet spot it felt so reminiscent of a time gone by.

She came across an old woman dressed from head to toe in black and carrying a giant marrow.

'Morning,' the woman said in Greek.

'Lovely day.'

'You not from here?'

'Not exactly.'

'Well, you be careful as you go. You know a little boy died here some years ago.'

'I heard about it.'

'A bad day,' the woman said, and a complicated mix of emotions seemed to move across her face, before settling on resignation.

'Did you know the man they arrested?'

The woman stood there and stared as if still weighing something up. 'It was a bad day,' she finally said again. 'A bad day.'

'Yes.'

'He left. The man and his family. Athens. People say they changed their name.' She pointed at a house with its roof fallen in, didn't say another word, just nodded and then walked away.

Any unsettled ground was now long grown over, but Thirza found a patch that looked a little different, a little rougher. She knelt down and touched the earth with her fingertips, as if Billy might be lying there below and she might feel a presence. His energy . . . but there was nothing. Not a shiver. Not a tremble. She felt certain Billy was not buried in this place, but also she did not have any sense that Billy had even been there. Did not feel that he had *ever* been there. She felt nothing of him at all. No echoes of his smile, his laugh . . . his terror. He could not have died alone on the mountain, nor in this old village. She was sure of it. The police had never found his body and his clothing could have been brought here by anyone. Same went for the penknife. There had been wild suggestions about what had happened to Billy. Her darling mother had been accused. Her father too. But that had all been lies. Cruel vicious lies.

On her way back home she looked about at the lonely landscape and the empty tracks, trying to make sense of it all, and felt some relief when she finally reached the blue of the sea again.

As she reached Merchant's the sun still shone down from a perfect sky. She felt a bit strange after her trip, and finding Spiro building a fire she went to help. Luckily, they had not left the stuff they wanted to burn outside, or it would have been too damp. Now they dragged out all the broken furniture that had previously been dumped in one of the outhouses, found the old curtains Thirza had already jettisoned, and added any other unwanted bits and pieces, until they had accumulated quite a little mountain. Spiro put a match to the lot and for a moment it didn't seem to take.

'Perhaps it's too damp after all,' she said.

'Just wait. I placed some old dry rosemary cuttings at the bottom and some of the furniture is only pine, so it will catch.'

She watched the fire splutter, wondering if he was right, then said, 'Spiro, do you have a sweetheart?'

He smiled. 'Funny you should ask.'

Thirza clapped her hands. 'You do! You do! Tell me.'

His eyes shone and his cheeks reddened. 'Magdalena is a girl from a good family in Athens. I am saving to be married.'

'I am so happy for you but goodness, how will she cope with living here?'

He shrugged. 'I may move to Athens.'

'Oh! What about your mother?'

'Eleni will come too of course.'

'Of course. You know we would all miss you very much.'

He sighed. 'I would prefer to stay. My wife might come to live here. Nothing has been decided.'

Then the flames suddenly burst into life and the whole thing began to blaze and the smell of rosemary and pine filled the air making Thirza think of Christmas. But that was months away and she didn't even know where she would be, but the changes in Spiro's life had Thirza thinking about Emilio again – everyone else was moving on with their lives, so why not her too?

So, in the evening Thirza slipped into a cotton dress and, once Ianthe had gone to bed with a headache, she walked to Emilio Bellini's house feeling frightfully modern and hoping he had not yet left to do whatever business he had talked about. People frowned on a woman having sex before marriage, but Thirza thought that was very unfair.

She thought of Emilio, an actual grown-up man. Her exploits had only been with young men her own age, two of them, and she hadn't really cared for either. And the artist of course, whom she had yearned for. 'He who shall not be named,' she muttered.

As for the other two, well, Philip had been a fumbling Eton-educated young man without a clue about women, and Gregory had been a Cambridge bore who read medieval poetry to her when all she'd wanted was a kiss. But the artist . . . that had been unrequited and upsetting. Emilio Bellini was as different from them all as she could possibly imagine.

But there were no lights in any of the windows when she arrived, and she realised he must have already left after all. She was surprised to feel disappointed and wondered what business he was seeing to. But it was nothing much. Just a touch of disappointment, she told herself, as she marched home swinging her arms in the way of a woman without a care in the world. A young woman who was hardly disappointed at all.

Back home Eleni held up a lantern on the doorstep when she heard Thirza's footsteps. 'I was about to lock up,' she said.

'No need. I just went for a walk. I'll lock up from now on.'

But Eleni looked at her in such a way she felt sure the older woman understood what she was up to and wasn't happy about it at all. Eleni could see right through you and visiting a man on one's own at night meant a girl was no better than a harlot.

CHAPTER 20

In the cool of the kitchen a few days later, Thirza, pencil in hand, sat down to make a list of everything she still needed to do. The kitchen hadn't been painted yet, although over the last week she had washed the walls and scrubbed the floor on her hands and knees, so at least you could actually *see* the tiles now. Lovely handmade encaustic tiles in repeating patterns of sea green, powder blue and pale grey, the same ones that were in the hall. Cleaning them had been a labour of love.

She began her list.

One: Mend wobbly chairs.
Two: Paint any kitchen chairs that are still sturdy.
Three: Empty out cupboards.
Four: Beat rugs.
Five: Carry on painting.

Ianthe, sitting there watching her, tossed her curls about and asserted her intention to paint her mother Columbine's bedroom a lovely soft creamy colour.

'It will be nice for her,' she said, 'especially if she arrives with Dulcie.'

'I don't think Dulcie will be keen to travel with Columbine. They've barely spoken these last seven years.'

'That's not my mother's fault.'

'Isn't it?'

Ianthe instantly looked close to tears.

Thirza ignored them and said, 'Anyway, I don't expect Dulcie will want to be here at the same time as your mother.'

'She'll be here soon, won't she – Dulcie, I mean?'

'In about two weeks, I imagine. Maybe more. No one has even said if Columbine is definitely coming.'

'Well, she *might* arrive with Walter, and anyway I don't care. My mother has more of a right to be here than anyone. It isn't fair. It's always about *your* mother, isn't it?'

Thirza sighed. 'Oh Ianthe, not this again.'

'Well, it's true. You know that as much as I do. Everyone knows, even though nobody ever acknowledges it.'

'You know it's all lies.'

'No. I don't. And my mother says—'

'Anyway I was saving that can of distemper for my mother's study,' Thirza muttered, interrupting her.

'You can't even get inside Dulcie's study to paint it.'

'All right, take the paint. Anything to stop you whinging on and on about the past. I'll ask Spiro to bring you a ladder. You'll need it for the ceiling and the top of the walls.'

Ianthe smiled suddenly, looking fresh, pink, and triumphant, the suggestion of tears gone in a flash.

'You can't paint in that dress, mind you,' Thirza said, accepting that the girl had been more helpful recently, getting into the swing of things at last.

But Ianthe was wearing a pretty blue-and-white sprigged dress in finest cotton lawn with puffed sleeves and a nipped-in waist. Thirza glanced down at the old canvas shorts and fraying shirt she herself was wearing. 'Haven't you got anything older to wear? You'll ruin that. And what about Walter?'

'Blow Walter. I'm cross with him. Not even a note to explain why he still hasn't come. The caique has been, hasn't it?'

'A couple of times this week. And it's due today.'

'There you are then. Blow Walter,' Ianthe said, flouncing up the stairs.

Eleni came in from the pantry and flapped a dishcloth at them. 'I have lunch to prepare, and you just sit here writing lists! Now shoo! Shoo!'

Despite adding 'beat the rugs' to her list, Thirza had already beaten the beautiful Persian rugs in the drawing room, very gently of course, and they had dried out on the terrace. She glanced around as she went into the room, freshly painted and only lacking new curtains.

A little later, along with their food and fuel order, a letter arrived with the caique. Thirza tore the envelope open and read that her father wanted her to come to lunch the very next day. There was, *someone he wanted her to meet.* Someone?

She felt torn between staying at home to carry on with the boathouse, and her curiosity. Of course, she wanted to see her father too.

She still needed to tackle Dulcie's bedroom, then her own bedroom, and the dining room. Other rooms too, of course, but maybe she could ask for Spiro's help inside the house, because she had neglected the boathouse, and it wasn't anywhere near finished. One week, Bellini had said, and that had almost passed. She hummed to herself and went to check the hall, paintings wiped down and rehung, the whole place looking wonderful and smelling of the spring flowers Eleni had arranged in a heavy cut glass vase, their scent drifting in the air.

Intrigued by her father's invitation, she sat down on her bed and calculated how much distemper she needed to finish the boathouse *and* the interior of the house. Then she went to the shed to see how much was actually left, where it quickly became evident they would need more. And that alone was a good enough reason to have to go to Corfu Town. 'Two birds, one stone,' she muttered to herself. But who was this *someone*?

CHAPTER 21

Corfu Town was exactly the same as it had always been and yet the atmosphere could not have been more different from those days back in 1923. The fear, the rumbling anxiety, was gone. In spite of the Italian invasion, and the terrible loss of Billy, Thirza had always felt more herself in Corfu Town than she had in London, and not only because the marvellous weather offered the kind of freedom that meant you could wear fewer clothes.

It was a heavenly place of blue and gold, colour and light, Venetian mansions and flowers, and whenever she'd been away the town had lived in her heart. Even during the last seven years *and* despite the awful reminder that she had seen Billy for the very last time right here. You never knew that something would be the last time until the moment had passed. Had she known she would have held him so tightly that he could never have let go.

She still felt a little uneasy, however, and avoided the café they'd all been to on that fateful day. Instead, she found a small place she didn't know hidden away in the maze of alleyways.

As she took her seat outside, she ordered a *tsitsibira* – ginger beer – a relic and reminder of nineteenth-century British rule when Corfu was a protectorate. She watched the cheerful faces of the people passing by and thought of her mother who rarely looked cheerful anymore. Their relationship had changed since 1923 and not just because she, Thirza, was an adult now. In some ways Dulcie was more distant with everyone, and Thirza felt herself mourning the innocent days of her childhood, the halcyon days, when none of them had known what lay ahead, nor had any inkling of how dramatically it would change their lives.

After her coffee she wandered about the little squares, and up and down the steps, finally coming across the builders' supply store almost by accident. She went inside, ordered what she wanted from the smiling owner, who had the widest moustache she'd ever seen, and asked for the distemper to be delivered by caique. To her surprise, and just as she was leaving, she spotted Odel coming in.

She waved, Odel rushed over, and the two women embraced.

'Oh, my goodness!' Odel said, letting her go. 'What a joy to see you. I heard you were back.'

'From my father?'

Odel frowned. 'No. I don't think so. Anyway, how are you? Shall we walk down to the esplanade, sit on a bench and talk?'

'You don't have shopping to do?'

'Nothing that can't wait. I want to hear all about you, and Dulcie of course. How is she?'

Thirza shrugged. 'Honestly? It's hard to tell. She's quiet.' She paused. 'What about you? Do you still have an apartment in the Condi Terrace?'

'We do, though not for much longer. My husband, Thaddeus, is retiring soon.'

'Oh?'

'I'm afraid the incident of 1923, the occupation by the Italians I mean, it knocked him back. He has a few years on me, and his health suffered. Plus, I hope you don't mind me saying, but what happened to your brother Billy left us all sadder and older.'

Thirza shook her head and said, 'It's fine.' She didn't want Odel to think that any mention of her brother was forbidden, but neither did she want to reveal the gulf that had opened between herself and Dulcie.

'Personally,' she said. 'I prefer people to speak about my brother. When we don't talk about him at home in London, I feel as if he didn't even exist, as if his life didn't matter.'

'Oh darling,' Odel said, placing a reassuring hand on her arm.

Thirza sighed. 'We still don't really know what happened to him, do we? How he died, I mean.'

'No.'

'Did you go to the trial?'

Odel nodded slowly.

'And?'

'Well, your father must have told you.'

'He wrote that the evidence was deemed circumstantial, not enough for a conviction. That it might have been different had they found Billy's body.'

'Yes.'

'Was it awful?'

Odel nodded.

'I wanted to come back for it. Mother wouldn't let me.'

'She was right, I think.'

As a nearby clock struck one, Thirza rose to her feet. 'I'm afraid I have to go, but it was just like old times seeing you. Father has summoned me to lunch. Says he has someone he wants me to meet.'

Odel winked and gave her a conspiratorial look.

Thirza narrowed her eyes. 'You know, don't you? You know who it is.'

Odel smiled. 'Not in my gift to say.'

Thirza bent down and kissed her on the cheeks. 'Come and see us at Merchant's. I hope Mother will be coming soon.'

Thirza arrived at her father's house a little late. Before she had a chance to consider how she felt about being there, the door opened, and a woman was standing there beside her father, smiling. Bottle blonde, heavily made-up with cupid's bow lips and so curvaceous that her dress stretched too tightly over her bosom.

'Hello,' the woman said, her voice light and tinkly. 'I'm so pleased to finally meet you.'

'Penelope,' her father said. 'Let me introduce you to my daughter, Thirza.'

Thirza felt prickly. The woman could only be three years older than her at most.

Penelope stretched out her hand and Thirza reluctantly took it.

'Penelope is my,' her father said, then paused before continuing uncertainly, 'my new secretary.'

The woman raised her brows and gave him a look.

'What happened to Mrs Rawlins?' Thirza asked.

'She retired. She wasn't young.'

She might be doing her father a disservice, maybe this woman was his secretary and only that, but by the look of her, Thirza was willing to bet she couldn't even type. And, she thought, had her father *not* wanted her to know about this Penelope woman, why had he invited her, Thirza, to lunch? Why couldn't he just be honest instead of fobbing her off with a lie? Was he simply embarrassed?

Now he asked if she would stay the night and Penelope looked at her directly for her answer.

Thirza muttered a reply. She didn't want to be rude, but her hackles were up, and she had to be loyal to her mother.

'Shall we go to the dining room?' Penelope said and immediately turned to lead the way. 'Luncheon is ready.'

'I'm afraid I have to dash,' her father said, and gave her a peck on the cheek.

'Nothing like giving me some warning, Pa!'

It raised a smile and, before she could object any further, he said, 'I'll see you at Merchant's soon.'

And then he was gone. Had her father and Penelope planned this together? This little tête-à-tête between women.

The dining room had been redecorated since Thirza was last there. The wallpaper shone as vines and grapes in gold and purple snaked their way across the walls and the polished floor tiles gleamed in the light cast from a gold-plated crystal chandelier. The whole room glittered and as Thirza gazed at the carved leaves and flowers of the ostentatious chandelier, she tried to hide her smile.

'Do you like the new décor?' Penelope asked, smiling too, though the challenge on her face was clear to see.

'It's different, I suppose.'

'It is, isn't it. Now look, I know what you're thinking,' Penelope was saying.

I doubt it, Thirza thought. Also, she couldn't avoid the irony of her father having a secret 'mistress' while at the same time she was hiding the truth about how much she was longing to see Emilio Bellini.

She realised Penelope had continued speaking and now stood there waiting for Thirza's response.

'Sorry,' Thirza said.

'So, you don't mind?' Penelope eventually asked, at the same time as indicating they should sit.

'What?'

The woman gave her an exasperated look and it soon became clear that she was definitely more than her father's secretary.

'As I was saying, you're right, of course. In fact, your father and I have been together for almost five years.'

Thirza gasped. She didn't want to hear it. This woman's defence of her relationship with Piers, but it seemed to be coming whether she liked it or not.

Penelope shrugged. 'Your mother never comes here. Do you really expect him to remain celibate all this time?'

'My mother never comes because her heart is broken.'

Suddenly serious, Penelope said, 'I'm very sorry about your brother.'

Thirza nodded, looked at the floor, and there was a brief pause. Then she said, 'Father *has* visited London during that time.'

'Once a year is not enough. We've been discreet. I love your father, Theresa, and I believe he loves me. I was hoping you and I might become friends.'

Thirza suddenly felt helpless in the presence of this woman and her glittering dining room. It was Penelope's work, of course it was. Piers would never have strayed so far from the soft neutrals Dulcie favoured. Her mother's approach oozed good taste, class, a sense of refinement, though Thirza couldn't help admiring Penelope for daring to be different.

As the new housekeeper brought in the first course, Thirza glanced around at the dining room again and spotted that the new chairs were reproduction Louis XVI, gilded, and with their seats and backs covered in pink, striped silk. She couldn't deny it was a bold choice, but goodness, if Dulcie ever came back, how much would she loathe this room?

CHAPTER 22

The day after Thirza arrived back at Merchant's was also when blond-haired Walter was due. After the surprise of meeting with her father's 'mistress', she was not looking forward to seeing Walter, whom she didn't know well or particularly like. She wondered what the attraction was. Money, she suspected. Nobody knew what had happened to Ianthe's father, or even who he had been. Her mother used to say that the poor girl had been whispered about for years as one story after another was invented to explain the man's absence, until the day came when the subject was eventually dropped altogether. But Ianthe had always wanted somewhere to belong and someone reliable to belong to. Hence the imminent arrival of Walter.

And what if Columbine turned up with him? The thought was enough to make Thirza want to throw something. Dulcie had not forgiven the woman her carelessness over Billy, her recklessness, her part in his disappearance and subsequent death, and neither had Thirza.

She was chewing on the end of her pencil and thinking about the order of her list again, when she heard creaking sounds coming from her mother's bedroom up above her. Old houses meant odd noises. Everyone knew that. She'd read that some people believed houses held the echo of past tragedies in the fabric of their walls. Was the loss of Billy imprinted here?

Whatever the case, she marched up the stairs, stalked along the corridor, and flung open her mother's door.

Only silence met her.

What had she expected? Dulcie still hadn't confirmed an arrival date, and Billy? Well, Billy was gone. Never again would he turn a somersault on her mother's precious silk rug. Never again would he be reprimanded for attempting a cartwheel, legs thrashing wildly, their mother's combs and brushes flying from her dressing table into the air as he landed awkwardly. Only she, Thirza, could execute the perfect cartwheel and never indoors. It had not occurred to her to be jealous of how much her mother loved Billy, except for that one time when Dulcie had risked her life looking for him during a storm at sea.

The room was dark but for shards of light piercing through the shutters. She opened them and then the windows too, enjoying the scent of wild honeysuckle drifting in. Then she fingered Dulcie's delicate silk dresses hanging in the wardrobe, drawing out one in a gorgeous shade of peacock blue, a colour that shifted between blue and green as she swirled it around.

When she held the dress against her own body and gazed into her mother's full-length mirror, she instantly looked different. Although shorter on her than Dulcie, it set off the red of her hair and made her blue-green eyes shine. She had little interest in fashion, no idea about clothes at all really, but decided to borrow it – her mother wouldn't mind – and perhaps she'd save it to wear when she next saw Bellini.

Then she opened the bottom drawer of Dulcie's dressing table where a jewellery box housed her mother's items of 'daily' wear. Trinkets, she called them. Thirza lifted out the box, opened the lid, and touched the earrings, necklaces, and bracelets. She glanced inside the drawer again and saw a photograph tucked away at the back. Curious, she slid it out, and held her breath, for there was Billy, grinning his toothy smile, preserved forever. Her heart jolted. Was he *really* dead? It seemed impossible and she still could not quite believe it. She allowed the tears to fall for a few moments, then wiped them away, held the photograph to her lips, then slipped it into her pocket and prayed for her little brother.

Dulcie had simply abandoned everything when they'd left right after his clothes had been found and before the intrusive newspaper coverage of the trial could destroy them. She must have forgotten about this photo.

When Walter and Columbine arrived, Thirza stood in the hall and gazed at the older woman, struggling to hide her shock. Columbine wore a badly altered summer dress and was leaning against the doorframe, as if without the strength to hold herself up. Far too thin, the skin on her neck hung loosely, sagging in folds.

'Hello,' Thirza said. She had expected to feel a stab of resentment, but it was impossible not to feel some sympathy.

Columbine took a step forward but didn't smile. She was unsteady on her feet but with no trace of alcohol on her breath.

'How are you?' Thirza asked.

'You know. Fine.'

Clearly, Columbine was not fine. Despite heavy make-up, you could see her colour was all wrong, and the haunted look and purple shadows around her eyes told a different story.

Thirza turned to the smiling American, Walter. The epitome of good health and clean living, with startling white teeth, he could have been considered handsome but for his protruding ears which rather spoilt things. As long as he was good to Ianthe and *she* didn't care about the ears, Thirza wished him well.

Ianthe flew down the stairs, embracing her mother first and then Walter. She clung to Walter as if to a life raft and Thirza felt a bit sorry for her.

She fed them cream cheese and cucumber sandwiches with a good dollop of pickle and a bottle of local wine, which Columbine pointedly ignored. Thirza then made her excuses, telling them she had business to attend to.

'Oh,' she added from the doorway. 'Feel free to help yourself to fruit, ginger biscuits, cake if there's any left, tea. Anything you want. Eleni has a day off today so we're fending for ourselves. Ianthe knows where everything is.'

Thirza was hoping to see Bellini, but as the hours drew on and dusk fell, there had been no sign of him at all. Back at the house she glanced out of the windows and repeatedly escaped to the boathouse to check for a note or some sign of him having been waiting there. There was nothing. How stupid she was for even being the least bit bothered. And she wasn't really, just a little bit irritated, that was all. But she preferred it when people kept their word, because if a person did not care about a small commitment, how would they behave over a larger one? Although the truth was he'd only said he would *hope* to see her in a week or so.

In the morning Thirza glanced around the kitchen to check if Eleni was there, but found only Columbine.

'Hanging out the washing,' Columbine said flatly. 'Eleni. There's coffee.'

'Toast?' Thirza offered.

'Not hungry.'

'Well, I am. Could eat a horse. I'll toast a couple of slices for you in case you change your mind. We do have *the* most delicious homemade marmalade.'

Columbine didn't speak, just gazed at the table with blank eyes. Now that she'd scraped off yesterday's make-up, she looked ghostly.

'Honestly Columbine, you need to eat. You hardly had any supper.'

'Don't fuss, Thirza. I'm fine.'

Thirza made the toast and pulled out a chair. As she liberally spread butter and then the marmalade, she kept glancing at Columbine. 'Have you seen my mother at all?' she eventually asked.

Columbine shook her head, the sadness on her face clearly visible. 'I tried twice, but she wouldn't answer the door.'

'Maybe she was out.'

'I saw her at an upstairs window.'

'Did you want to talk to her about Billy?'

'Maybe. That . . . and other things.'

Looking back, it was hard to remember what Columbine had actually said when Billy vanished. Hadn't she claimed that he'd gone for his hat before she had a chance to tell him not to? Or was it that she had said no, and he had defied her? That had always seemed so odd to Thirza. It sounded plausible enough but Billy was not a naughty child. He might have argued but he wouldn't have run off. She wanted to ask Columbine what had really happened, but what would be the point after all this time?

'So, what are your plans?' Thirza asked instead.

Columbine gave her a strange sort of smile as if entertained by her question and reluctant to answer, then she said, 'Plans?' as if Thirza had asked when she was thinking of travelling to the moon and back.

'Right,' Thirza replied, realising she was not going to get an answer. 'I'm off down to the boathouse. Have a nice morning. Get some sun.'

She left the kitchen, grabbed two blue cushions from the snug, a couple of orange and white throws, and ran down to the boathouse where she opened all the windows to get rid of the smell of paint. The window frames still needed painting, or oiling, as did the floor, but she made up the daybed and hung the curtains she'd run up earlier. The fabric had never been used – a cheery blue-and-white-striped cotton – and as the poles and rings were still in place, rather splattered with paint, they would have to suffice for now. After that she raced back up to the house, rolled up a navy-blue rug from a spare bedroom, and then carried that down too, not once questioning why she was doing all this before the boathouse had even been finished.

She was kneeling on the floor setting the rug in place, slightly out of breath and dishevelled, her hair a mess, when she heard his voice.

'Thirza?'

Oh no. Not right now.

She attempted to smooth down her hair – always a pointless exercise – then looked out of the window, knowing she'd be red-faced from the exertion of running back and forth from the house. She motioned him to come up but as he pushed open the door and entered the room a minute or two later, she felt tongue-tied and stupid.

'I apologise for being late,' he said, giving her a quizzical look.

'Late?'

'I was held up. My business in Italy took longer than expected.'

'Ah,' she said, so he had been counting too. 'I hadn't noticed.'

'Are you all right?'

She nodded.

He narrowed his eyes and tilted his head slightly.

She nodded again. 'I'm fine.'

'You were expecting me?'

She was about to nod a third time but caught herself and said, 'Maybe,' her voice too high-pitched. *You're bloody well squeaking*, she chastised herself.

'You seem . . . I don't know. Different. Do you want me to leave?' He motioned to the unfinished room. 'You're obviously busy.'

154

She shook her head and then the words tumbled out in a rush. 'I had to go to Corfu Town and now I'm a bit behind. The boathouse isn't finished. I couldn't be in two places at once, you see. The house isn't finished either.' And she ended with a lame sigh.

He glanced around. 'The boathouse looks charming. And anyway, I've come to talk to you, not to inspect your decorating skills.'

Thirza didn't know what to do. She felt too tall, too awkward, and clumsy, and she hadn't even put on a dress. What must he think of her in her paint-splattered dungarees?

'Would you like to close the curtains?' he asked. 'The glare from the sea is rather bright. Or we could just go for a walk.'

She shook her head but couldn't say any of the words she had planned. Nothing would come out. Embarrassed, she listened to the sound of the sea and gazed at the floor, taking in the unpainted wooden boards. Could never remember being so bashful before. She was Thirza Caruthers-Moreland, not some snivelling girl. She was self-possessed, and resourceful, someone who coped with life and all its challenges.

And yet.

'Thirza,' he said. 'We can do anything you wish to do. Walk, talk, swim.'

'Cycle,' she asked, and swallowed hard. 'I like to cycle. It might be a good way to see the island.'

He reached out and then his hand dropped. 'I don't have a bicycle.'

'We have several. You can borrow one.'

155

He nodded and once again she noticed that sad lost look he'd had when she first met him.

'How about you? How are you?'

'There have been some troubles in my life lately. But let us not talk of those.'

He lifted his hand and touched her arm, and she sensed something passing between them, but then she jolted away.

'I should go,' he said.

'I feel a bit light-headed, that's all,' she said, wanting him to stay and feeling like a silly girl. 'I just need to sit down.'

He led her to the daybed and sat beside her in silence. She really wanted to tell him the truth about who she was but could not get the words out. When a tear slid down her cheek, he wiped it away so tenderly she thought she might weep.

'I'm sorry,' she said. 'It's just, well, I don't really know. But please don't go.'

'I could tell you about why I was in Italy, if you like?'

'Oh, yes, do.'

He smiled at her, his eyes scanning hers. 'I'm opening a hotel in Naples with my sister. Bellini's, it will be called. We both received a legacy from our uncle, so have given up our jobs to work on this new project together.'

'How marvellous.'

'It takes a great deal of time and money, and in the meantime, I have been contracted to write the book I told you about. When that's done, I will be free to focus entirely on the hotel.'

She nodded, wanted to ask more about his family. *His wife.* Oh Lord. She hadn't really thought of that before. Did he have a wife?

She opened her mouth, but now other words wouldn't come out because without being told she knew that this acquaintance, for want of a better word, would only exist in the here and now. His past, her past – for what they were worth – were not a part of this. Nor was his current situation. Or hers.

She turned to look at him, holding her breath, until he smiled so warmly she was completely mesmerised and could no longer fight what she really wanted.

He put an arm around her, and something electrifying passed between them. Without a pause, they both fell back onto the bed. And that was it. He was kissing her while undressing her and she was undressing him until they both lay semi-naked half on and half off the bed.

'Come on, let's lie further up,' he said, and gently pulled her and himself up so that their heads rested on the cushions at the top. She felt him touching her breasts, stroking them, circling the nipples with his fingertips, and then he put his palm on her flat stomach, and she felt the heat burning into her. He ran a hand over her outer thigh and then between her legs and again she felt the heat of him and an irresistible pull in her pelvis.

She desired him with an almost primitive longing but was still too self-conscious to be comfortable.

'Is this all right?' he asked.

'Yes,' she whispered. 'But I need a drink.'

He sprang up and she saw he was already firm. She liked that even though there was something faintly ridiculous about a naked man with an erection uncorking a bottle of champagne and both of them watching the spume spurting in an arc across the room. He noticed the expression on her face, caught her trying not to laugh, then he laughed too. And in that moment the ice, whatever was left of it, was completely broken.

She drank her champagne in one gulp and then smiled and said, 'I think I'm all right now.'

He grinned at her. 'Thank goodness for that. I'd better come prepared with more champagne next time.'

And then he made love to her and she to him, though perhaps the more appropriate word was fucking because *oh my God* this was an entirely new experience. And, all doubt gone, she wanted more. Lots more.

CHAPTER 23

With him, it was wild. Without him, all she thought about was when she would be with him again. What had happened to independent, strong, wilful, Thirza? The Thirza who didn't need anyone? Now, she actually *hurt* when Emilio wasn't there. She had exploded into a new version of herself. A woman who raised her legs around the shoulders of a man, feeling utterly wanton as he made almost violent love to her. Almost, but not quite, leaving her flushed with pleasure and shaking from head to toe. This was a new way to be a woman and it had taken her by surprise, shocked her even. But she was happier than she had been in a long time.

One evening about a week later it rained, really rained. She'd been out walking, thinking she had plenty of time to get back and change before going down to the boathouse – where they now met every evening, to drink champagne, and eat snacks of cheese, olives, and local bread. But now rivulets of water were pouring from her hair, and her skirt and blouse were completely drenched. She sheltered beneath a tree for a while, but the rain didn't hold off.

In the boathouse she dried herself with an old towel she used when sitting on the rocks, rubbing her hair as best she could, but it still hung limply around her shoulders. She pulled off her wet clothes and when she heard the door opening, she wrapped herself in the already damp towel.

Emilio came in wearing a mackintosh and carrying an umbrella.

'Filthy weather,' he said. 'Isn't that what people say in England?'

She laughed. 'I suppose it is.'

'I thought you might show me your work.'

'You want to see my paintings while I'm dressed in a wet towel?'

'Why not?'

So, she showed him her latest watercolour paintings for the children's story book. It was about a family of field mice who were going to be evicted from their home when the threshing began.

'But they're charming,' he said lifting one, then another. He had long slender fingers, a pianist's fingers. Beautiful hands in fact.

'You're good,' he said.

'It's just bread and butter really,' she said, but she was pleased. She turned to look at him, taking in her work with such care, and had to bite back a sigh.

There could be no future for them, she knew that. The age gap, for a start, and the fact that he'd said nothing about his circumstances. And yet she adored his charm, his intensity when he gazed at her, the serious way he listened to everything she said. And it was difficult, in moments as perfect as these, to imagine ever being happier.

'What do you really want to do?' he asked.

'Paint landscapes and portraits too. I love looking at faces.'

There was a short silence as he turned and then held the back of her neck, drawing her to him. The towel fell to the floor and her hair dripped onto his fingers. He held her like that, gently digging his fingertips into the soft flesh beneath the spot where her skull began, driving her all the way to the bed, where she lay down on her back.

'I'm still wet,' she complained.

He removed his wire-framed spectacles. 'Then I shall kiss you dry.'

She opened her legs, and he began by kissing her ankles, the undersides of her knees, and then the insides of her thighs.

'Have you done this before?' she managed to say, though her voice came out oddly for the sensations going on down below had affected her ability to speak.

He looked up and she looked down, noticing how long and thick his eyelashes were from this angle. 'Had sex?' he asked.

'No. Have you had sex with younger women?'

He frowned. 'Younger? No.'

'Older?'

'Maybe. Do you ask the age of all your lovers?'

'All,' she muttered, not wanting to say it had been so few.

It thrilled her to be with him, especially when she anticipated what might be coming next and, thrusting her pelvis up, she managed to stifle the urge to scream as he began kissing her where she had never been kissed before. She was not used to this. Had read about cunnilingus of course, had giggled over it with her schoolfriends, but

Jesus when it first happened, she felt she was going out of her mind. He knew exactly what to do with his mouth. Oral sex was like going to heaven in almost agony and wanting to shriek until she couldn't take it anymore, the stimulation so intense she felt she might die until she finally orgasmed and fell back exhausted. She lay there gasping for breath and laughing, at the same time dying to ask where he had learnt to do that so proficiently. Then just as she was recovering her ability to breathe, to speak, she heard a voice and leapt to her feet.

'Theresa. Thirza. Are you in there?'

She hadn't realised the rain had stopped and it flashed in her mind that she might not have drawn all the curtains and twisted around to check. She hadn't closed the ones hanging at the window facing the sea because nobody could see them from the water. The rest of the curtains were closed, thank goodness. Emilio reached up for her wrist, his eyes questioning her.

'Your employer?'

'Stay until he's gone,' she whispered, remembering her lie, and feeling guilty as she pushed him away.

'When will I see you again?' he asked, as she pulled on her wet skirt and blouse. 'Tonight?'

'I'll try to get away,' she promised, flattening her hair a bit.

Then she went out to greet her father who had begun to walk away.

'Sorry,' she said. 'I was sleeping.'

'You look awfully red-faced and rather wet.'

'It does get warm in the boathouse.'

He looked rather puzzled. 'It's actually quite cool, Thirza. It's been raining, you know.'

162

'I was sheltering in there and must have fallen asleep. I like working this close to the sea.'

Had she screamed? Had he heard her? The embarrassment and awkwardness if he had was too much to bear. His anger too. But he seemed to accept what she'd said and, appearing distracted, he took her by the elbow and led her up to the house.

After she had dried herself and put on a clean pair of shorts and a fresh blouse, they sat outside on the terrace and Eleni brought them homemade lemonade. At last Thirza had controlled her racing heartbeat.

'It's my first time back here,' Piers said, glancing around and looking forlorn.

Sometimes she forgot that her father had lost Billy too. Just because he didn't weep or talk, it didn't mean he didn't care.

Her mother wandered into her mind and Thirza saw her standing by Billy's bed, holding her nose.

'What's all this, Billy?' she'd said.

'Acots.'

'Apricots?'

'What I said.'

The apricots he'd hidden under his bed were slowly rotting in secret because he had forgotten them.

'You little tyke! Get me a cloth from the kitchen.'

And then there she was on her hands and knees, scooping up the awful stinking mess and ruining her beautiful linen dress. But when she got back up she just laughed and kissed Billy on the top of his head.

Thirza let the image go and glanced at her father. 'I was wondering when you would come,' she said.

'Your mother wanted me to keep an eye on the place, but I always sent someone else. It was too hard. So many memories.' His voice caught a little and she reached for his hand, feeling closer to him than she had for a long time. He squeezed her hand and then let go.

'You're a good girl,' he said, but he still looked sad and her eyes dampened at the sight of him. He'd always seemed so strong, and it was a shock to see her father's vulnerability for the first time.

They sat in silence for a couple of minutes.

She had been so caught up with her thoughts she hadn't heard someone else coming across to the table and was surprised when she saw Penelope, dripping with multi-coloured glass beads and wearing a blue silk dress swathed in ruffles and flounces. The woman had already pulled up a chair before Thirza managed to dash away her tears. Oh, why had her father brought the woman with him?

'You'll be hot in all that,' Thirza managed to say.

Penelope laughed and looked her up and down. 'I must remember to bring shorts and a frayed old shirt next time.'

Thirza doubted she even owned an old shirt.

'Anyway hello,' Penelope said when she was seated. 'What a wonderful place this is. I hope I haven't interrupted anything.'

Thirza inclined her head but didn't speak.

While she wasn't pleased to see Penelope here, she quickly realised the distraction might work in her favour. If her father was spending his time with Penelope and maybe scurrying from his bedroom to hers, what *she* was doing with Emilio might go unnoticed.

'I'll just pop upstairs,' her father said, once again about to leave her alone with Penelope.

'Must you?' Thirza asked.

Piers smiled. 'Nature calls.'

Thirza shrugged.

'It's so peaceful, isn't it?' the woman said once when they were alone. 'Balm for the soul.'

'Yes, everyone seems to say that.'

'Well, everyone is right. Maybe I could help you here at Merchant's, you know, stay on for a bit when your father goes back to town. There must be so much to do here, especially now that he—'

'He what?' Thirza interjected, frowning.

'Oh nothing. I really shouldn't say. Honestly, me and my big mouth.'

She hated the woman's inference that she knew something that Thirza herself did not, or was Penelope simply asserting her right to affect the balance of power between them?

Either way Penelope seemed genuinely unwilling to answer at first and pulled a doubtful face, but then she quickly changed her mind.

'Ah well. I suppose I've already almost let the cat out of the bag, and I guess you'll know the whole story soon enough. The thing is your father wants a divorce.'

Thirza had been holding her breath and let it out all in a rush.

Her father and Penelope had been for a late afternoon swim and were now 'resting'. Out on the terrace, Ianthe and Walter were doing a crossword together. Thirza had never even seen Ianthe reading a book, let alone doing a crossword, but there she was, and when Thirza frowned in surprise, the girl shrugged and rolled her eyes behind

Walter's back with a *what can you do* look. He was such a serious young man. Did he even know how vapid Ianthe could be? There was neither sight nor sound of Columbine.

Thirza went down early to the boathouse, undressed, and threw on a simple blue-and-green-flowered kimono leaving it open and untied. And then she waited. For him. Nothing else mattered, right now, except for the ache inside her that could not be assuaged by anything or anyone else.

She could not get Penelope's words out of her mind. Divorce. Would her mother agree? It seemed such a sad and hopeless ending.

When Emilio arrived and spotted her naked state beneath the kimono, she saw the desire flare in his eyes. As she undid the white buttons of his blue linen shirt one by one, she could feel his impatience to make love to her, but continued to take her time removing his trousers and underpants as he stood at the foot of the bed. Entirely within her power, she wanted to keep him captive by any means she could.

He turned to look back at the pillows as if indicating they should lie down, and she took in the sight of his firm buttocks. Every part of his body aroused her. Then, when he turned back, she did something she had never done before. Still wearing her open kimono, she knelt before him taking his penis in her mouth, holding him tight by the buttocks, until he grew erect. It took some getting used to, but she enjoyed the mixture of power and submission it gave her and loved it when he began to groan.

It didn't last long, for soon he pushed her away by the shoulders and then lay back on the bed and she realised he wanted her on top of him, so she threw off her kimono and knelt, knees either side of him, and with only a little difficulty she managed to lower herself, moving slowly, circling him at first, then building up while he played with her breasts and pinched her nipples. Quite hard, she thought. But she soon arched her back, twisting her head from side to side, shaking her red hair out like a lion's mane. And then it was over almost as soon as it had begun. And even though she had been desperate to come, within minutes she wanted him all over again.

Her whole life was becoming focused on Emilio in a way that terrified her, but as soon as they made love again and the gold rings around his eyes flared, all that was forgotten.

'Was everything all right?' he said. 'With your employer?'

'What?' she said, not understanding. Then, remembering the assumption she had not corrected, she felt a pang of guilt. It was time to tell the truth.

'He isn't actually my employer,' she said. 'He's my father.'

Emilio turned slowly to look at her.

'What do you mean?' he said.

'That first day, you thought I was just working here and I . . . I didn't put you right. I just wanted to be Thirza, with you – not Theresa Caruthers-Moreland.'

Emilio did not seem reassured by her words, sitting up in bed and looking pale.

'Caruthers?' he said.

'Yes.'

'So, you lied to me.'

'Just a little,' she said. 'I'm sorry, I—'

'A lot,' he corrected. 'You should have told me.'

'When?' she said, smiling a little. She didn't understand why he was taking this so seriously. 'It's not as if we spend much time *talking*.'

Their relationship was almost entirely sexual, and as sensitive as he seemed to her moods, he also rarely talked about himself. She didn't know a thing about the rest of his life, though she knew there must be more to him than he'd shown her – for sometimes there was an air of detachment he didn't try to disguise. An air of trouble that lingered in his voice, and eyes.

'You should have been honest,' he said, and for the first time, she felt conscious of the age gap between them – felt as if she were a little girl, being chastised, and her temper suddenly spiked.

'As *you* have been?' she said. 'I don't know anything about you. You could be married, for all I—'

He tensed visibly.

'*Are* you married?'

'Divorced,' he said. 'Well, separated.'

She reached for her kimono, not looking at him.

'Well, which is it?' she said.

He remained silent for a while.

Then he said, 'As a Catholic divorce is not allowed, even if I want it – but Thirza, there is something more I must—'

'Well, you're not alone,' she said interrupting him. 'Looks like my father wants a divorce too. It feels as if everything is falling apart.'

She thought of her father having an affair behind her mother's back and wondered if he'd told Dulcie about it and now, after all the horrible things she'd been thinking about her father and Penelope, it turned out she was no better herself. Emilio was married.

And without any warning, it all became too much, and she began to cry.

CHAPTER 24

Thirza woke early after a short but welcome sleep, took a deep breath, and wrapping her robe around herself, went over to the window. She opened the ivory silk curtains to see the sky had turned a deep rich coral as the sun rose over the blue mountains of Albania, fading to a dilute blue, with a shimmering lilac sea and dusty pink clouds. She sighed, watching the breeze blow the purple bougainvillea about and lost herself for a moment in the abundant greens of their garden. It was wonderfully cool at this, her favourite time of day, when the air was fresh, and the fragrance of wildflowers still hung in the air, and she felt strangely cleansed after crying so much the evening before. Emilio had been kind to her, scooping her up in his arms as she wept.

A little later she was the first to be seated on the shaded veranda, at their long outdoor table, the scented pelargoniums drifting on the breeze from where they grew close to the orange trees at the side of the house. She kicked off her mules and felt the stone slabs cooling the soles of her feet. The whole family used to always collect together for breakfast, and she couldn't help thinking of Billy. This was where her memories of him were strongest, where she felt his absence every single day. *Oh Billy, why did you have to go back for your damn hat?* All their lives had been turned upside down because Columbine had not stopped him. Thirza realised the woman had barely left her bedroom since she arrived, and wondered if they should call for the doctor. Though the last thing she wanted at the moment was any more drama.

Thirza had not dressed nor eaten yet, choosing only to nurse a strong black coffee. She had a feeling she was going to need it, and before long realised she was right when Penelope appeared at the table on her own, again overdressed and fully made-up. Thirza sighed. Just her luck.

'Good morning,' the woman said with a broad smile and shining eyes.

'I hope you slept well,' Thirza replied, coolly polite.

'Like a log. The air is so clean here and the stars last night! You are so lucky.'

'It's always been my favourite place,' Thirza said. 'Since I was very young. The whole family love it.'

'I hope to be spending much more time here,' Penelope said conspiratorially.

'Really?'

'Well,' she said and she hesitated, looked uncomfortable, then drew a breath and carried on speaking. 'Nothing is decided of course.'

'Of course,' Thirza agreed but she was on her guard, now. What did Penelope mean? Was the woman planning to live here after the divorce?

Her father arrived outside. 'How lovely to see you two getting on so well. Thank you for welcoming Pen.'

Pen! Pen! Could this get any more sickening?

He leant over to give Penelope a kiss on the cheek and Thirza averted her eyes, gazing instead at the garden. Dulcie's garden, bursting with early summer life. She took in the dappled shady spots beneath the trees and the patches of bright white light where the sun broke through, the garden full and glorious, just like her mother had been.

As she pictured Dulcie pruning her favourite pale cream roses while singing to herself, Thirza was also thinking. Planning. Maybe she was being paranoid, maybe Penelope was just happy to be here on such a lovely day. Maybe. But if this ghastly woman had set her sights on Merchant's, then Thirza was going to stop her.

Eleni came out with a tray piled high with pastries and coffee.

'Oh,' Ianthe called out as she slipped into a seat opposite Penelope. 'No hot chocolate?'

Eleni shook her head.

'Where's your mother?' Thirza asked Ianthe.

'Still asleep.'

Walter joined them, dressed with precision in a cream linen suit. He sat beside Ianthe, carefully unfolded his napkin, and placed it neatly on his lap. A tidy man. A very tidy man. Then he greeted them all and gave Ianthe a peck on the cheek. No great passion there, Thirza thought. Not like her and Emilio.

'Well,' Thirza said. 'How jolly.'

Ianthe smiled. 'It's very conscientious of you, Penelope, to accompany your boss here.'

Thirza snorted and said, 'Wasn't there something you wanted to tell us, Father?'

He cleared his throat, a muscle twitching at the edge of his left eye, a sure sign he was trying to control his nerves. 'No, I don't think so.'

Penelope raised her brows at him.

'Ah yes. I understand Pen has already let something slip.'

Penelope giggled. 'Sorry, darling. I just couldn't help it.' She blew him a kiss and Thirza almost gagged. Ianthe simply stared.

'Do we need to now?' Piers said. 'I would have preferred—'

'Anyhow,' Penelope continued, interrupting him. 'It only remains for your father to ask for your blessing.' She glanced around at each one of them, smiling broadly as she did. 'You see Piers has asked me to marry him, just as soon as the divorce is through.'

'Divorce?' Ianthe said, sounding shocked.

'What about my mother?' Thirza said, struggling to keep the note of fury from her voice.

'Your mother?' Penelope said.

'Yes. My father's wife, the woman he promised to be with until death do you part.'

'Really, Thirza, this is the modern age,' Penelope said. 'You can't expect—'

'What I can or can't expect is nothing to do with you. And my name is Theresa.' She turned to her father. 'Have you even spoken to Mother about this?'

He had the grace to look a little sheepish.

'Honestly, you really do take the absolute biscuit.'

'I don't think it will come as a surprise to Dulcie,' he said.

'Perhaps not. But it is a matter of decency that *she* should be the first you discuss this with. Not *your mistress*, or me, or Ianthe, or Walter. Or were you hoping to garner support for your plan, smooth the waters, before they have a chance to grow turbulent? Because they *will* grow turbulent, Father, and you know it. This,' and she pointed at the rest of them. 'This is sneaky and underhand.'

Penelope threw down her napkin. 'Honestly Thirz . . . I mean Theresa, that isn't fair.'

Thirza ignored her. 'You, Father, will conduct a private conversation with me and then my mother, without this ridiculous sideshow. Leaving my mother out of the conversation is an omission that leaves me breathless.'

She rose from the table to hear Walter speaking up. 'I say, Mr Moreland. It is rather steep. Come, Ianthe. Perhaps we should go.'

Penelope pushed back her chair. 'Piers,' she said rather coldly.

He glanced at her and nodded. 'Ah, yes.'

Then Penelope smiled at Thirza and said, 'Everything is going to change. You'll see.'

'Why?'

'I'll go and slip into something cooler,' Penelope said as she stood up. 'Leave you two alone.'

Thirza seethed inside but sat down again. What was going on?

'There's something else,' Piers said.

'Just spit it out, Pa.'

'The thing is—'

'What, for heaven's sake?'

'Well, I know how you love this old place, but I received a letter from Dulcie. I'm afraid she's planning to sell Merchant's.'

'She can't sell Merchant's!'

Shocked by this hammer blow to her heart, tears pricked the backs of her eyelids, and heat burned her cheeks. She simply could not believe it. She was not going to cry. She was not! She forced herself to take a deep breath and exhaled very slowly. 'Why didn't she talk to me?'

Piers shook his head then shrugged.

'Merchant's is our home, Pa. We love it here. It's where Billy . . .'

'I know, but times change, and sometimes we have no choice but to change with them.'

'I don't want to change. I want Merchant's. Surely, she can't mean it.'

'Maybe we can change her mind,' he said. 'But you know your mother.'

Thirza's mind was racing. Her mother could not sell Merchant's!

As Thirza climbed the stairs to her room, she heard Penelope berating her father and then the sound of tears. Moments later her father stood at her own open bedroom door. 'I'm so sorry,' he said. 'I have this for you. It arrived with my letter.'

'What?'

'I don't know why she didn't send it to you here,' her father added.

He handed her an envelope and Thirza instantly recognised her mother's handwriting.

When he had gone, she slit open the blue airmail envelope and pulled out two sheets of pale blue paper. She read the letter twice with a sinking heart.

'No!' she whispered, and even though it was what she had suspected her mother would say, she dropped the letter onto her dressing table.

Dulcie was citing the financial crisis of 1929 as justification for putting Merchant's up for sale.

'No!' Thirza repeated, louder now.

Her mother couldn't sell, especially not now, for her father would be bound to claim a half share of the proceeds in a divorce settlement, or even the house itself if it wasn't sold quickly. And anyway, her mother loved Merchant's as much as she did herself. Dulcie had just forgotten that. *Please prepare the house for sale*, her mother had written. Thirza simply could not bear it, and the sweet warm scents of summer were not enough to assuage her fear of losing the only place that had ever felt like home.

Thirza spent the rest of the morning livid with anger, not even a swim improving her state of mind. She longed to see Emilio and could barely wait until the evening. As she worked on her commission, the series of paintings for the children's story book, she reminded herself the divorce might not happen if Dulcie decided to simply block it. Could she block it? It was all too awful. There would have to be photographs of her father – the guilty party – with Penelope, both of them in a compromising situation and probably in bed. There would be a scandal. Thirza had been vaguely aware of the lack of love in her parents' marriage, but she had never openly acknowledged it, even to herself, and had certainly never spoken of it. Now she wondered how unhappy her mother might really have been. How much she might have needed more and for how long. Her father's insouciance preyed on her mind, the casual way he'd spoken of divorcing her mother, as if it were nothing, and the insolence of Penelope to come here, to her mother's house.

She skipped lunch and then later made herself a cucumber sandwich and grabbed a bottle of wine to take down to the boathouse where she spent the evening.

Most girls she knew were repressed. They were not brought up to respect their own needs, let alone their own desires. It was always about the man. The father. The husband. The brother. The lover. What suited *them*.

Even though Dulcie had not been a typical woman or mother of her time, Thirza had still internalised some of the mores and messages of the status quo. From those school friends who had less emancipated mothers than Dulcie, from the teachers, most of whom were single, and from the literature of the day too. Being with Emilio had thrown all that up in the air and she needed him now because when he wasn't there, she doubted herself, questioning everything and going round in circles. She folded her arms across her chest to protect herself from the growing hollowness inside.

Alone and disconnected, she missed Emilio; her father's news and her mother's letter only serving to imprison her in gloom. It had been an upsetting day and as the hours dragged on, the sadder she grew, listening to the waves gently breaking on the rocks below, hearing the night birds in the garden, and smelling the gorgeous perfume of the tiny night-scented flowers. She used to love the gentle rhythm of life at Merchant's. The way she and her family wandered through the hills and valleys of their days. All gone now. Ripped up. Destroyed. They had lost so much after Billy died. And now this. Her father. Penelope. Dulcie. What was to become of them? She lay on the daybed, drank the entire bottle of wine, and unable to stifle her tears she began to weep. By ten o'clock she had to face it. Emilio wasn't coming.

But then the door opened, and her heart lifted.

'What are you doing down here in the dark?' Ianthe said. 'We've saved you some supper.' Then she shone a torch into the room and Thirza's tears started up all over again.

Ianthe sat on the bed and reached for Thirza's hand. 'He hasn't come, has he?'

'Got a hankie?' Thirza muttered as she wiped her face on the sheet.

'I do. Here you are. Look, Thirza. You can't let yourself get all worked up over Penelope and your father. They'll be gone soon.'

'It isn't just that.'

'Come on darling, I know. But you can't let yourself get all het up over a man either.'

'You know about me and him?'

'You haven't exactly been discreet. I've heard you, too. Sounding quite wild, I might add.'

'Oh no! Really?' Thirza covered her face with her hands. Ianthe gave a little chuckle.

But Thirza gulped back a sob. 'I love him, Ianthe. I'd do anything for him.' There, she'd said it, but she couldn't say that she felt as if she'd shed a skin and was raw now, smarting, and stinging, as if from a terrible burn.

'I know you're lovestruck. I can see it in the way you mope about the place one minute and then seem to be floating on air the next, but does he love you?'

'I . . . I . . . I don't know. I think he loves the sex.'

'Oh God. This isn't like you. As you know I don't believe in sex before marriage and neither does Walter. What if you get pregnant?'

Thirza refused to consider that. She had tried to be careful, as Emilio had too, but by no means every time. 'How can you tell if you'll be compatible with Walter?' she said.

'There's more to marriage than sex.'

'Is there?'

Ianthe laughed. 'Honestly Thirza, you really have got it bad.'

Thirza dabbed at her eyes. 'What do you think of Penelope?' she asked.

Ianthe thought for a moment then said, 'I think she's all right. A bit brash but all right. You don't like her much, do you? But what do we know about her? Nothing at all really.'

Thirza shook her head. 'Nothing I want to know.'

'Come on, Thirza. That's harsh even for you. Columbine saw them together, you know, in Corfu Town, ages ago. Penelope definitely set her sights on him from the start.'

'Does she love him?'

'Honestly Thirza, how would I know? She might need the security, and she might be good for him. Life isn't all about love, you know.'

'So you say.'

'Listen, as soon as she, your father, and my mother leave, why don't we have a wonderful picnic on the beach?'

'Like when we were children?' Thirza asked with a smile.

'Exactly.'

Except it would not be exactly the same, for Billy would not be there. She closed her eyes and heard him calling her:

Thizzy. Thizzy.

Come and play on the rocks with me.

Thizzy. Where are you?

She pictured his gummy little-boy grin, and it made her heart ache. She saw Dulcie cradling him as a baby, a look of absolute devotion on her face, and her father saying, 'Who does he take after?'

'My mother,' Dulcie had said rather tartly. 'Surely you can see it?'

'Of course. You're right.'

CHAPTER 25

Thirza washed at the small hand basin in her bedroom, and despite her headache, she managed to admire the light dusting of gold on her usually pale porcelain skin. She had acquired the colour since arriving back on the island – like her mother, she almost never bathed in the sun. *So bad for the complexion, darling.* But her limbs were smooth, muscular, and she loved that they were glowing now, the result of daily life at her beloved Merchant's. She threw on an old blue cotton dress, sun-dried and softened from countless washings, the smell of it evoking memories of so many lost summers.

Thirza tried to tell herself it was normal for a girl to drink an entire bottle of wine on her own when her heart was breaking. It was normal to feel angry from time to time. Normal to feel rage or disappointment. Normal to feel guilt. And she tried to put Emilio out of her mind. But there were so many expectations about how one ought to behave, how one ought to feel, how one ought to be, that she found it confusing. None of these things had mattered when she was sixteen, now they consumed her days. It was an uncomfortable way to live, and she ached for those innocent moments of joy that had once washed over her, leaving her buoyant and glad to be alive.

A knock at the door interrupted her thoughts and she opened up, surprised to see her father standing there.

'I wonder,' he said. 'Would you accompany me on a walk?'

'Now? Do you mean now?'

He nodded. 'Before anyone else is up.'

By anyone she knew he meant Penelope.

'All right. Just let me grab my plimsolls.'

On their way through the kitchen Thirza ran the tap for a moment, filled a glass then downed the water before following her father into the sparkling early morning.

He didn't speak for the first five minutes, and she felt comforted by the sound of the birds singing in the trees and the gentle rhythm of their feet crunching the dry grass.

'I never know what women want,' her father suddenly said, and her heart started to beat against her ribcage. He'd never said anything so revealing before.

'Especially your mother,' he added. 'I never truly understood *her*.'

Thirza considered that. Her own deepest cravings had lain hidden, secret even from herself, and it had taken Emilio to ignite them. Had her mother been the same?

'Isn't it our job to just love people?' she said. 'Not understand them. Isn't understanding always going to be limited?'

'Yes. But Dulcie – oh, I don't know.'

'Go on.'

'There was always a large part of herself she kept hidden from me.'

And there it was. Just as she had thought.

'Dulcie withdrew entirely after Billy died,' he said. 'Threw herself into her career and completely shut me out. I understood of course but it wasn't easy.'

'Did you try to get through to her?'

'Of course. Many times. I wanted her to come back to Corfu, but she refused point blank.'

Thirza knew how Dulcie could be consumed by her work. 'She shut me out too, you know,' she said, finally telling him how it had been for her.

He looked anguished. 'I'm so sorry. I didn't realise. I thought at least with you . . .'

Thirza shook her head. 'No. It was awful. I wanted to come back here, but didn't feel I could leave her.'

'She's vulnerable underneath.'

'I've come to realise that. So many times I watched her barely able to get through the day, limping, just as much as if she had a broken leg and not a broken heart. Often, I thought she was on the verge of falling, begging for help.'

'But?'

'She never did, and eventually I knew the time had come for me to return to Merchant's without her.'

'I'm sorry you were so alone.'

'It wasn't your fault.'

'Wasn't it? After the trial it seemed there was nothing left for me to do but get on with my work too. I hit the bottle, just at night. It numbed the pain of losing Billy.'

In the silence that followed, Thirza reached for his hand, feeling the warmth and the strength there.

'What about Penelope?' she asked, sensing he was expecting her to speak.

'Ah well, she saved me from myself.'

Thirza nodded.

'She wants a simple life, like me.'

'I think she wants Merchant's.'

Damn! She hadn't meant to say that, but in the peace of the morning she'd stupidly dropped her guard, and it had slipped out. She'd have to be more circumspect because in the night she'd come up with a plan. A plan to keep Merchant's out of Penelope's reach *and* prevent its sale.

Her father stopped walking and frowned as he studied her face. 'Merchant's is your mother's, to keep or to sell.'

'But in a divorce settlement?' she said, noting he did not actually deny it.

He only looked a little guilty and said, 'No.'

'You really must ask Mother for a divorce right away if that's what you want.'

'It is. I love Pen and it would mean a lot if you could try to like her.'

'I don't dislike her,' she muttered, knowing how insincere she sounded, especially when he snorted.

'Come on, Thirza. I'm your father. I know you too well to believe that. Your feelings have always been written all over your face.'

'Really?'

He nodded. 'Look. I know Pen is different from your mother.'

'You can say that again.'

'She's more transparent than your mother, but she isn't stupid. Don't be taken in by blonde curls and baby-blue eyes. And you must remember things were already rocky between Dulcie and me, even before Billy died. I accept that I was not the perfect husband, and she was not, well, you know.'

'I *don't* know.'

'It really isn't for me to say.'

Thirza had wondered if Dulcie was unfaithful too. She'd always suspected her father – from overhearing her mother's heated accusations. Always whispered or hissed, of course, but perhaps he was not the only one. And why was her study door locked? Thirza urgently needed to access the cash now, but also she wanted to find out if her mother had a secret life of her own. Something hidden in there that she'd hoped to keep private.

'Come on,' he said. 'Let's not dwell on it.'

He linked arms with her, and they walked on. But Thirza didn't accept his analysis of Penelope's character. The woman was manipulative and not nearly as transparent as her father suggested. No fool like an old fool, isn't that what they said? But what was she to think about Dulcie?

Back in her room she glanced at the blue envelope containing her mother's letter. It was upside down on the left-hand side of her dressing table. All well and good but something didn't look right. She frowned, pulled out the sheets of paper. They looked a little bit creased, as if they'd been quickly stuffed back inside, whereas she was almost sure she had smoothed down the sheets and slipped them back into the envelope carefully. Perhaps she was mistaken. In any case she decided to write to her mother without wasting another moment.

Dear Ma,

I hope what you are about to read is not a terrible shock and forgive me for being brutal, but Father is going to ask you to agree to a divorce, and I believe we need to take urgent action. I do hope he has already spoken to you by the time you read this letter. He wants to marry this awful woman, Penelope Aston, who can't be much older than me and who, I'm almost certain, is manipulating Father in order to get her hands on Merchant's. I love my father, but you know how he can be, only believing what he wants to believe.

Please don't go ahead with your plan to put Merchant's up for sale.

I don't know if this is possible, but I have an idea. I'm not sure about the exact legalities and I suggest you speak to a lawyer before mentioning any of this to Father. Go to someone new, not our old family solicitor. This is my idea — transfer the deeds to me as soon as you can so that Father cannot claim the house nor the value of the house. Or if you think I'm too young, put Merchant's in a trust for when I'm thirty. A trust that will sit outside any divorce settlement. I believe such things are possible to safeguard family assets.

Please don't reply to our town house. I wouldn't be surprised if Penelope reads his letters. I suspect she may have slipped into my bedroom while I was out and read yours to me. Which is why I think you need to take swift action. As she already knows of your plan to sell, she might try to push for the divorce before you can complete. I don't know. Whatever transpires, we have to prevent her from becoming mistress of

Merchant's. I would be happy to live here all year round and take care of the house, working on my commissions to earn money, maybe even accepting paying guests, anything to keep the house where it belongs. With you and me and Billy's memory.

Remember to address your letter here, not the town house, and the caique will deliver it.

In haste and hoping very much you will make your way here soon. I will be sure the house is ready for you, and Mother, please remember how much you used to love being here.

Your loyal daughter,
Thirza

When she'd finished, she quickly sealed the envelope and hurried down the levels of the garden, spotting a black-and-white swallowtail butterfly hovering above the wild Corfiot sage. She paused further down and gazed at the pink-and-white oleanders, recalling the day her mother had told Billy the legend behind why people believed the flower symbolised love. A young Greek girl had been in love with a boy called Leander. He swam to see her every night until he drowned in a terrible storm. The girl found his dead body washed up on the beach and cried out, 'Oh Leander. Oh Leander.' He was holding a flower in his hand. She treasured it, surprised when it grew and grew, eventually becoming a symbol of everlasting love.

When Thirza reached their little landing stage, she shook off her plimsolls, sat down on the wooden boards and dangled her feet in the cool water as she waited for the caique. She drank in the peace. It was hot now, and she could feel the perspiration blooming beneath her dress. The sea was calm and so blue it didn't even look real. She simply couldn't bear the thought of Merchant's being sold.

Billy was here at Merchant's. Only here could she feel him close by, especially on days when the birds seemed to still in the trees, in the air, everywhere. Waiting.

She saw the light and love within her brother so bright that she felt she would burst with happiness whenever she saw that madcap grin on his face. Only here could she connect to their childhood and the part of her that loved Billy so dearly. The part of her that would always be broken like the wing of a bird, and she knew instinctively that Merchant's would be her only hope of ever really healing her heart and her soul. And her wing. It wasn't rational but she truly felt that if she lost Merchant's she would end up endlessly brooding on dark thoughts and be unable to navigate the difficult parts of life. Merchant's and the island of Corfu itself, all blue and gold, was the antidote to all that despair, both a privilege and a blessing, and she wanted to stay here for the rest of her life. Here you could step out of your ordinary self, be in the world but not of it. Here you really could live your dreams.

Flooded with thoughts of Billy and how much she loved this old place, she didn't at first hear someone crunching on the pebbles but turned just in time to see Penelope.

'Hello,' the woman said, looking immaculate in a lilac sundress and pink straw hat. 'Don't get up. I've just come to say my farewells. Your father is seeing to the horses and Columbine is coming with us.'

'I've barely seen her. Is she all right?'

'Ianthe is looking after her, but she doesn't look well. Anyway, what are you up to, all on your own down here?'

'Just waiting for the caique.'

'Expecting something special?'

'Only household supplies.'

'I would have thought your servants would be the ones to see to that.'

Thirza sighed and gazed out at the water. She didn't want this tedious conversation but for her father's sake she would be polite so said, 'These days we only have Eleni, a stable boy from time to time, plus Spiro, and yes he usually carries everything up with my help.'

'Why so few servants?'

'Oh, you know. Times change.' She shrugged and rose to her feet.

Penelope nodded and fixed her gaze back at the house. 'I suppose it must be awfully costly, the upkeep of a house like this.'

'Indeed.'

'I wonder if this place really will be sold.'

The woman hummed with avarice, or maybe that was too harsh, maybe she just hummed with excitement. Either way Merchant's was Thirza's mother's kingdom, or queendom, more like, and Penelope could hum as much as she liked, she wasn't going to get it.

Thirza managed to reply calmly although she was stewing inside. 'I don't think it will be sold.'

'But then I suppose it isn't your decision.' Penelope smiled and kissed her lightly on the cheek. 'Anyway, cheerio. See you again very soon. Hopefully for longer next time.'

CHAPTER 26

The dawn view across the Corfu Straits was eye-wateringly beautiful. A golden sky, the mountains of Albania in shades of ochre fading to pale lemon in the distance and burnt sienna closer to the sea, the water like rippling turquoise ice. For a moment Thirza considered running down for a swim right away, but later they'd be preparing for the picnic supper on the beach, and she could swim then.

For three weeks Emilio had not turned up and Thirza felt out of sorts as she began work on her final few drawings. He was gone and that was that. Stricken by the possibility he might never return, she could see him clearly in her mind's eye, could picture him turning to her with so much love when she had told him her father wanted to divorce her mother, and how tenderly he'd reached out to comfort her. She shook her head. Had she imagined everything? Whatever else might have been going on, they had seemed so real together. She could still sense the warmth of his hand, his strong clasp as he drew her to him. She threw down her pencil. She treasured what they'd had, but this obsession had to stop. She went for a swim after all.

As she came out of the water, gulping and panting, she shook herself, watching the droplets flying from her hair in a shower of light. She wrapped herself in a towel and, picking her way across the rocks, headed back up through the garden.

Later, on the beach with Ianthe, as the sun set, and the sky turned to glorious shades of purple and pink, Thirza began to imagine Emilio's wife. Her eyes. Her hair. For she was increasingly sure that not only did she exist, as he had told her, but that they were not separated. Why else would he disappear like this? He had shown her some pages of his writing, so that much was true, though she had not yet accompanied him anywhere. Then again, maybe he was travelling in the Ionian Islands on his own. He didn't owe her an explanation.

She began to pile up the sand. 'A castle with a moat, Ianthe. What do you think?'

Ianthe clapped her hands, and they worked in silence but for Thirza humming a tune and the sound of the sea.

'You're off-key,' Ianthe said, startling her out of her thoughts.

'No. I'm not.'

Ianthe laughed. 'Seriously, you are.' Then she paused for a moment and out of the blue said, 'I know you think my mother is mad, and she may be flaky—'

'Flaky!' Thirza interjected, able to think of other less cosy epithets to apply to Columbine.

'Yes, but she's well-meaning, and not mad.'

Thirza watched Walter, huffing and puffing, rather inefficiently attempting to build a fire. He didn't seem to like the sand nor – with his pale freckled complexion – the sun. Thirza didn't really know what he liked, apart from Ianthe. That had been one of Ianthe's hopes for this summer, originally. She wanted Walter to get to know the family, before their wedding – Thirza knew she had not tried very hard. At least she was here, but where was Dulcie?

'Will your mother come back again this summer?' she asked.

'I don't know. She's staying with her friend Lucie in Corfu Town, but she's been so odd ever since we left the island all those years ago.'

'Since Billy.'

Ianthe nodded.

'Dulcie too. She's withdrawn, buries herself in work and refuses to talk.'

'My mother talks to her psychiatrist, but she doesn't talk to me.'

'Strange how they're reacting to Billy's death in such a similar way. Withdrawing, I mean.'

'Yes. I understand why Dulcie's that way. After all, she lost her son. But Mum, I don't know—'

'Has she said anything at all?'

'Not really. She's very low, cries a lot, and blames herself for not looking after Billy.'

Thirza appreciated how Columbine might be suffering from guilt and that it would bring anyone to their knees. She longed for Dulcie to come back to life and felt sure Merchant's would help. Whether it would help Columbine to come back again was less certain. What had happened in 1923 couldn't be changed and she felt sad for the woman.

She reached out and touched Ianthe's hand. 'I'm sorry.'

They sat in silence, Ianthe fiddling with the pile of shells she had collected earlier and Thirza gazing out to sea. Walter's fire had at last taken hold and the flames danced as twilight turned to dusk. Thirza always felt a sense of an ending at this time of day, the permanence of the island and her own impermanence in such deep contrast.

'We've all been odd since then,' she said and paused. 'I see him sometimes, you know. I hear his voice.'

Thizzy. Thizzy. Where are you?

Here, my darling. Here. Always here.

Ianthe reached across, squeezed her shoulder and Thirza's eyes watered. She didn't say that if she had any fears now it was the fear of forgetting him. The fear that one day she would not be able to see the exact colour of his eyes, or the colour of his freckles in summer. This was the fear that kept her awake at night as she searched for his image in her mind's eye. But then he'd be there again, just for an instant, whole and complete, grinning like a Cheshire cat, whirling around.

I'm an eagle, Thizzy.

I can fly.

And the pain she felt was sharp and absolute.

'Coming for a swim?' she said, desperate to change the subject.

'Maybe later.' Ianthe glanced around. 'Anyway, you didn't bring your bathers.'

Thirza laughed. 'I don't need them.'

She undid her blouse, took it off, slid out of her skirt and then, much to Walter's horror, ripped off her underwear, and ran into the water completely naked. She swam until her muscles hurt and all she could do was float on her back kicking her legs from time to time while staring at the starlit sky as night fell. She could float like this forever, float away and away and away.

When she did finally emerge from the sea it was to find Walter stomping up and down the beach with Ianthe following behind him pleading with him not to be so silly.

'Silly, is it?' he shouted over his shoulder.

'Yes.'

He stood still for a moment but didn't turn round. 'I am not accustomed to seeing naked women flaunting themselves so brazenly in public.'

Thirza grabbed a towel to cover herself for she realised she was the cause of his outburst.

'That's just Thirza,' Ianthe was valiantly saying, 'and she isn't flaunting.'

'Oh. And what do you call it?'

'This little beach isn't public. It's just ours.' Ianthe began to cry. 'Nobody can see. Don't be mean, Walter.'

He turned to face her. 'No, my dear. This is the last straw. Your family, Mr and Mrs Moreland's divorce, well it's downright unacceptable.'

'Please Walter,' she pleaded through her tears.

'No Ianthe. This makes me seriously reconsider things between us.'

'But Walter, please. Can't we talk?'

'I don't think there's a lot to say, is there?'

'Come up to the house with me.'

'Very well. We will go up to the house together. But let me tell you, I am not happy.'

After they'd gone Thirza uncorked the wine and drank straight from the bottle. She felt dismayed and anyway there was nobody to see her. Even an innocent beach picnic had been ruined. Nothing was going well and now Walter and Ianthe's future looked in doubt. She'd come back to Merchant's with such hope, dreaming of how glorious it would be once she'd finished the house, and everything was falling apart. She felt her heart might actually break for Merchant's, for her family, for herself. She had so wanted Dulcie to come back to the island. She wanted her mother. The Dulcie of old. And now she couldn't deny how cut off and lonely she'd been without her. More than once she had pictured Dulcie smiling again, but her mother hadn't come and now there was Penelope to contend with too.

She glanced towards the house, frowning, then let her towel drop to the sand. There was nobody to see her nakedness either. She smoothed the towel out and lay back in the warm evening air, closed her eyes and drifted.

She had no idea how long she'd been asleep when she woke to feel fingers gently stroking her brow. Her eyes flew open.

'Hello,' he said. 'My sleeping beauty. What are you doing all alone down here?'

'We were having a picnic.'

He nodded. 'I was waiting for you at the boathouse. I heard the commotion.'

'How long have I been asleep?'

'Just a few minutes. Mind if I join you?'

Emilio removed his shirt, his trousers, his underpants, and in the light from the sky, and despite being Italian, he looked like a Greek god, his skin glowing, his muscles firm. She reached for him, but he shook his head and very gently he kissed every inch of her body until she was shaking. She didn't ask where he had been. She was not going to be that kind of woman. Not ever. Then he made love to her and afterwards they swam in the shining moonlit sea to get rid of the sand that had crept into the folds and crevices of their bodies. And in the ocean when they were treading water and tired, he finally told her he had fought to keep away, that there had been a lot to think about, that there were problems they would need to talk about, but despite everything, he truly loved her.

CHAPTER 27

Thirza had mixed feelings about finishing her task at Merchant's, now that her mother wanted to sell up. Dulcie hadn't yet replied to Thirza's last letter and part of her felt like running away, leaving it all behind, yet despite the turmoil of everything, she was feeling surprisingly happy and knew it was because of Emilio. Whatever the problems he had referred to were, she didn't really care. He would tell her when he was ready.

She chewed on the end of her pencil, frowning at her list. She was sitting at the kitchen table – as had become her habit each morning – and reviewing the list of tasks she needed to get on with. What should she tackle today? She was just considering the order of things, scratching out number four and changing it to number one, when the door opened and then closed with a terrific bang.

'It's all your fault!' Ianthe yelled.

Thirza frowned. Her cousin looked as fresh and pink as ever, though her fair head was untidy, and her baby-blue eyes were blazing. But just short of stamping her feet, she looked more like a furious five-year-old than a grown woman, and Thirza almost laughed, only just managing to control the urge in time.

'What is my fault?' she asked.

'I wasn't worried at first,' Ianthe said. 'I thought he'd come round.'

'Who?'

'Walter, of course. I thought he'd cool down, say he didn't mean it. He's gone Thirza; he's ending our relationship and it's all your fault. My one chance and he's gone.'

'I—'

'Don't make excuses! You shouldn't have done it. Any of it.'

Thirza sighed. 'Darling, Walter will not be your only chance.'

'But people will hear he threw me over. Nobody will want me. And it's your fault.'

'Yes, I already gathered that, though I still don't know what you mean exactly.'

'I mean your affair with that Italian,' Ianthe said, her eyes darkening as she glared at her.

Thirza frowned. 'How's that anything to do with Walter?'

'And swimming naked, and, and, well everything about this family. I wanted to go and live in America and now I can't.'

Thirza held out her hand. 'I'm sorry, Ianthe. Honestly, I am, but we are who we are and if he doesn't approve of me, or of us, well maybe he doesn't belong.'

'You don't get it, do you? I don't belong! I never have! Your mother made sure of that! You owed me this, and now you're ruining my life just like Dulcie ruined Columbine's.'

Thirza's chest tightened. She pushed back her chair noisily and rose to her feet. 'For God's sake, don't be ridiculous. Anyone can see how my mother has done everything she can to help Columbine.'

'Oh yes! Dulcie made sure everyone could *see*.'

'What does that even mean? It's hardly Dulcie's fault that your mother turned to drink.'

'But it is. I know it is, but none of you will listen!' And with that Ianthe gave out a great loud sob and ran from the room.

Thirza stared after her, sweating, far too hot. Yes, she was angry, fed up with the girl's accusations – Columbine had clearly messed up her own life – but she felt dreadful that Ianthe was so upset.

It really wouldn't be Ianthe's only chance at happiness but she, Thirza, should have realized how Walter might react.

Her skin tingled as she felt another burst of anger, this time over the mess *Dulcie* had left behind. Her mother had abandoned everything when they'd left so suddenly, before the intrusive newspaper coverage of the trial could destroy them.

Her mother was complicated, one minute a stickler for tradition, the next a complete free spirit. Thirza had learnt to gauge Dulcie's moods so wasn't often left gasping in stunned silence at the sudden shifts or inconsistencies. This vague promise to come back followed by complete silence, other than the letter saying she intended to sell up, was something else.

At the end of the next day when the shadows were lengthening, and the light changed to a rather mournful mauve, Thirza had just finished clearing up after painting the boathouse floor. She wiped her hands and heard the door open and there he was. Her heart lifted immediately.

'Don't come in, Emilio,' she said. 'The floor is still wet.'

'I can see. And it reeks of paint and turpentine in here.'

She tiptoed around the edge of one side of the floor, knowing it would be almost dry there, and joined him on the stairs.

He wrapped his arms around her and, just as tall as him, she pressed her face into his hair which smelt of oranges.

'I've missed you,' he said. 'There wasn't time to explain the other night.'

'But where did you go when you were away?' she gently asked him, knowing they didn't normally question each other.

'Italy and then I came back to finish my research in Corfu Town. For my book, you know, the one I told you about, the reason I came here in the first place. I met a very interesting man. An artist who invited me to the little island of Paxos, where he has his studio. I know I originally suggested we might go together, but it was too good a chance, so I jumped at it.'

Thirza nodded, aware he was talking quite quickly as if, as if . . . what? As if he were hiding something, she thought. 'And what did you think?'

'Think?'

'Of Paxos.'

'Adorable, totally unspoilt. A fisherman took us across, and I stayed with Thomas, that's the artist's name, in a tiny village called Loggos.'

'Heavenly, isn't it.'

'You know it?'

She nodded, suddenly tongue-tied. She wanted to undress him, kiss him, touch him, feel him making love to her, but the boathouse was unusable. She glanced around, uncertain of what to say. Ianthe's outburst came back to her. She'd believed they had conducted their affair in private – it was such a remote place – but Ianthe had known, Walter too, and her father had almost caught them. Who else might have noticed?

She looked back at him and saw he was gazing at her. 'How about coming to my place tonight?'

'All night?'

He smiled and put a finger to her lips. 'We won't tell anyone.'

She glanced down at herself. 'I'm covered in paint.'

'I have a bathroom.'

She smiled. 'And food?'

'Indeed.'

'Wait here. I won't be a moment.'

And hearing the gulls circling overhead she ran up to the house, grabbed her key to the front door and left a note for Eleni asking her to lock up later as she had her own key and would be back very late. No need to prepare supper. A sudden flash of guilt. She wasn't sure about the last bit as Eleni had probably already made supper.

She and Emilio walked in single file and eventually he threw open the front door of his rented home. In the drawing room she saw a sheepskin rug on the floor in front of the fireplace. A fire was already lit, and food lay on the table.

'The water will be hot,' he said and kissed her hard on the mouth.

'You knew I'd be coming here for a bath?'

'Let's say I spotted what you were doing earlier in the day.'

'You were spying on me?'

He laughed. 'Always.'

He led her upstairs to the bedroom.

'Wait here,' he said, and she could hear him turning on the taps in the bathroom and then he came back to kiss her neck, her breasts, her shoulders, and her wrists.

When the large cast-iron bath was ready, she climbed in and watched as he removed his spectacles and his clothes. And then, in the bathroom lit only by dozens of candles, he joined her.

'How is Bellini's coming along?' she asked.

'You want to talk about that?'

She didn't but something was better than nothing. He nudged her with his toes and her knees fell apart.

'Yes, I do,' she said. 'Let's talk about your hotel.'

'Bellini's it is then,' and he rose onto his knees and began to caress her breasts. She threw back her head and his hands left her breasts to move between her legs. And right then she didn't care if he was hiding something or not; if there were problems or not.

'The hotel is doing fine. It is beautiful. You would like it, I think.'

She groaned.

'You want more about Bellini's? More about the view, the gardens, the restaurant maybe.' His fingers were inside her now, and she groaned again.

'Yes!' she replied. 'More. Much, much more.'

And then he laughed, stopped, and said they'd be far more comfortable downstairs beside the fire in the drawing room.

Wrapped in towels they went down, bringing some of the candles with them, and he opened a window so that they could listen to the sea. Then under the flickering light she lay on the sheepskin rug, and he came to her. She heard the sound of an owl, and gazed up at the ceiling where long shadows were shifting and then she looked at him. He didn't seem able to take his eyes off her.

'You don't know how beautiful you are,' he said as his hand grazed her thigh.

She shivered and smiled. Since being with Emilio she had felt beautiful. She hadn't set out to fall in love, but she had, and no longer scared of her own pleasure she gloried in it. He ran a hand over her smooth stomach and then between her legs. She sighed, long and deep, as if she'd been holding her breath. He called her *amore* and she began to speak, telling him how she felt, but he pressed his lips to her mouth, and she fell quiet. Then he was on top of her, and she felt her body beneath his, the weight of him, the pressure, and she felt him moving inside her, his mouth on her neck. She gasped and not very long after she cried out in a wilder way than before. A way she had not been free to do in the boathouse. He didn't stop but soon he groaned, and it was done.

In air saturated with love and woodsmoke, she felt the softer curves of her body against the firm muscles of his back. It was wonderful, but something was starting to bother her. She listened to the susurration of the sea from the open window and the sound of his breathing. But there was an edge to him tonight and she couldn't put her finger on it. She wanted to know more about his life, his real life, and she decided she would make a start by telling him about *her* life and *her* family. Perhaps it would encourage him.

'I want to tell you about my brother,' she said.

He raised himself up on his elbows and she gazed up at him.

'You have a brother?' he said.

'I *had* a brother. Billy.'

'Older than you?'

'Younger. He died in 1923 when I was sixteen.'

He didn't speak at first, looked away and then he said, 'I'm so very sorry.'

'In my mother's mind he's always associated with Merchant's.'

Emilio went rather quiet.

She didn't know what else to say.

'How old was your brother? Billy. How old was he?'

'Nine.'

'I see,' he said, and then he closed his eyes, and when he looked back at her there was sadness in his eyes. Perhaps he had lost a younger brother too.

He cleared his throat as if to settle himself.

There was a long pause.

'What kind of boy was he?' Emilio asked eventually.

'The best kind.' Thirza smiled. 'You would have adored him every bit as much as we did.'

'I'm sure. How sad for you all.'

'It was the last straw for my parents. Billy had been keeping them together.'

'You loved him very much.'

She nodded, swallowed, and tried to smile but could not.

He took her face between his palms and kissed her forehead, her cheeks, and her lips. She was surprised to realise her cheeks were wet.

'Will your mother be returning to the island?' he asked, his brow furrowing.

'I hope so. I'd like you to meet her but she's busy in London, so may not come.'

He appeared a little more relaxed now, wrapped her in a blanket and brought over bread, cheese, and red wine which they ate and drank sitting cross-legged on the floor.

'There's something I need to tell you,' he said, when they'd finished the wine and he'd brought through another bottle but not yet uncorked it, his tone suddenly serious.

There was silence and the tension made her head pound, her mind running wild. He was back with his wife. Was that what he wanted to say?

'I need to go away,' he added.

'All right. For how long this time?' she asked, keeping her voice light although she knew something about this was different.

'Maybe forever, *amore*.'

Her heart missed a beat, and she sat up startled, needing air. 'What?'

He took her hand, but she pulled it away. She felt a chill run through her and narrowed her eyes in confusion.

'You're telling me this is over? You're just going to walk away?' She waved a hand at the fire, at the rug, at the remnants of their meal. 'And all this was what . . . play-acting?'

'No. Not at all.'

'Then?'

His attempt to deflect her question by smiling at her didn't work, and she raised her brows as if to repeat her question.

'I don't know yet what is going to happen but I'm still here *now*.'

'And then?' she asked him again.

'I will have to go.'

'You said forever. *Forever*, Emilio.'

'Please don't spoil this.'

'Me, spoil it! I think you've managed that all on your own.' She pushed him away from her and rose to her feet, hearing her own voice crack as she said, 'I love you, Emilio, and you . . . you told me . . . you loved me.'

'I do. You will never know how much.'

'Then why?'

He didn't meet her eyes. 'It is complicated. You don't understand.'

'Oh, I understand all right.'

'Thirza, there is something . . .'

'No,' she said. 'I don't want to hear your excuses.' She looked around, found, and then clutched her clothes to her chest.

'Thirza,' he said, his voice pleading. 'Listen to me.'

'No.'

He stood up in his beautiful nakedness watching her, and she wanted to weep, wanted to beg him never to leave her.

'But I will still be here for a while,' he said. 'It does not have to be goodbye. At least not yet.'

She shook her head, dressed quickly, and picking up the uncorked bottle of red wine she threw it against the white wall where it smashed satisfactorily. Then she ran into the pitch-black night, tears streaming down her face now that he couldn't see her, slipping and sliding in the dark as she passed the heavenly scent of jasmine without even noticing and fell over the rocks.

She had been such a fool.

CHAPTER 28

In the bare morning light, Thirza gazed at her bruised, red-rimmed eyes in the mirror on her dressing table. How was she going to bear this? How was she going to find the dignity to bear this and not simply rush back to his house and beg him to stay? 'He might change his mind,' she whispered. *He might. He might.* And she prayed that he would, but she also forced herself to accept she could not, must not, must, must, must not make the first move. She could not go crawling back and that was that. And if he didn't come, then he didn't. People had their hearts broken all the time but oh God, it hurt.

She went down to the boathouse, intending to lose herself in work. Instead, feeling hollow inside, she listened to the trees creaking, the waves softly breaking against the rocks below, the seabirds squawking. But being in the boathouse, where there were so many memories of him, was painful, so she went back up to sit on the veranda, a sour taste in her mouth. Hurt, anger, or just disillusionment. Which tasted worse?

She was surprised when Ianthe threw herself down next to her and said, 'Can we be friends again? Please.'

Thirza turned to gauge her sincerity, then reached out to hold her hand for a moment.

'I've been looking for you everywhere,' Ianthe said. 'Where were you?'

'In the boathouse.'

'Working?'

'Trying to.'

Ianthe frowned and said, 'Darling, you look as if you haven't slept.'

Thirza swallowed the lump in her throat.

'Oh,' she said, as if realising. 'Has he gone? He's gone, hasn't he?'

Thirza bit her lip. 'As good as.'

'For good?'

'I think so,' Thirza said in the smallest voice.

Ianthe put an arm around her. 'So, we've both been abandoned.'

'Looks like it. What a pair we are.'

They sat in silence for a while just holding each other, and to Thirza it felt as if she and Ianthe had come to a better understanding of each other. Or, at the very least, acceptance. She allowed her thoughts to drift.

After some time, Ianthe pulled away and said, 'You know I love it here, but I wanted so much to go to America. Walter said my mother could come too. I thought it would be good for her.'

'I'm so sorry. Swimming like that with Walter on the beach was thoughtless.'

Ianthe sighed. 'Life happens, doesn't it. And maybe if it hadn't been that it might have been something else.'

Thirza sighed. 'Maybe.'

'Look, I brought you out a lemon tea,' Ianthe said, sliding it across to Thirza from where she'd put it on the table. 'Just us now, Thirza. The men are gone, and we have to get on with things on our own. Agreed?'

'Agreed.'

But still the next two weeks passed slowly. Thirza was listless and spent far too much time brooding, walking barefoot on the hot rocks, and when she felt them burning the soles of her feet, she relished the pain. Physical pain was easier to bear. But what was she to do now? Pack up. Go home. Her illustrations were almost finished but she found it hard to get up any enthusiasm to take them to Corfu Town and send them back to England. Eleni gave her mournful looks and tried to engage her in conversation, but Thirza only replied in monosyllables. And in the end Eleni shook her head and let her be.

Late one morning Spiro came across her sitting on a bench in the orchard and handed her an envelope.

Thirza glanced at it. Her mother's writing. What bad news was coming now?

'You didn't hear the caique arriving?' he said.

Thirza shook her head and opened the envelope, read the brief contents. 'Oh,' she muttered as two sentences stood out from the rest.

Darling, I'll be with you by the end of the month. We'll discuss the trust idea then.

No small talk from Dulcie, not even in a letter.

She thanked Spiro then said, 'My mother is coming.'

'That's good. We are almost ready.'

Thirza frowned. Were they ready? Would they ever be ready? Did she even care anymore?

Spiro left her, then she got up and headed to the drawing room to think.

But Ianthe was there standing at the window gazing out with her back to the room.

Thirza was about to tiptoe away, but at that moment Ianthe turned and smiled at her. 'You all right?'

'My mother's coming.'

Ianthe's eyes widened. 'Really?'

Thirza nodded.

'Well, that's marvellous, isn't it? What's left to do?'

'I don't know. This and that, I suppose.'

'Come on, Thirza. This isn't like you. Your whole purpose coming back here was to make Merchant's beautiful again. Remember?'

Thirza pulled a face.

'You can't let your sadness over Emilio ruin all your hard work. I'll help. Tell me what to do and I'll do it.'

Ianthe was corralling her into hopefulness, and it made Thirza smile. She could see how much the girl had changed since they first arrived. Grown up, really.

But the house wasn't finished and, now that Dulcie was probably coming, it was even more important that when her mother stepped through the threshold, she would be assailed by how fresh and beautiful it all was. Too beautiful to sell.

'Spiro will finish the woodwork, and the shutters will be back up soon,' Thirza said. 'And I'll run up some new curtains and revamp the cushions to bring the whole house back to life.'

Ianthe smiled. 'That's better. You'll have to go to Corfu Town to buy fabric. I'll come too if you like.'

CHAPTER 29

The morning had begun overcast during the journey down to Corfu Town but gradually the small white clouds drifted away, the sky turned sapphire blue, and sunshine dusted the land with gold. Thirza loved the town, full of glamorous old-world grandeur, loved too its charm, the hustle and bustle of the narrow streets – the beating heart of the place. The entire town was flooded with a mix of perfume and food, and flowers adorned its balconies along with brightly coloured clothes drying in the warmth.

While Ianthe chattered on, Thirza stood for a moment taking it all in. She usually spent hours wandering the tangle of small alleyways in the historical centre, loved listening to conversations, arguments, laughter, but today the town did not cast its usual bewitching spell.

At least she had finished her illustrations overnight, rushed them she thought, and was now heading across to the post office to send them to London. Then, as she left the building and the images were on their way, she felt anxious, crossed her fingers, took a deep breath, and said, 'God I hope they like them.'

A little later she and Ianthe met her father for lunch at the most exclusive restaurant on the Liston, all snowy-white tablecloths, stiff napkins, discreet waiters, and plenty of people-watching windows. Penelope was at their lunch too, striving to give the impression that this was perfectly normal and looking pretty in pastel pink, her decolletage plump and creamy, with an array of pearls at her neck. If you like that sort of thing, Thirza thought, but didn't say. She decided it was time to play Penelope at her own game. Thirza was in a grump, cross, irritable, mean. So what if she took it out on Penelope? The woman had no business even being there.

'We need to stay overnight,' she said, and her father nodded.

'Plus, I need some money to buy fabric,' she added.

'What for?' Penelope asked, smiling, and fiddling with her pearls. They looked real.

Thirza smiled sweetly back at her. 'To make new curtains and cushion covers of course. You know how worn things become over time and what with the damp while we've been away, well it has rather done for some of them. Maybe you spotted that on your brief visit to us.'

'Oh yes. But I thought I would, well you know. Choose. Your father said I could make ... you know after ...' Her voice trailed away at the look of admonishment on Piers' face.

He swiftly turned to Thirza, but not before his look had told her everything she needed to know. She would contact her mother immediately and tell her she must act quickly to put the estate in Thirza's own name. It was the only way.

'You may have whatever funds you need,' her father said.

Was guilt making him amenable, she wondered.

'Within reason,' Penelope added.

Thirza felt the corners of her mouth twitch but took a breath and managed not to show her annoyance. 'Also, I need to pay Spiro and the men.'

'I can let you have that too. We'll go to the bank after lunch.'

'Thank you, Father. I knew you'd understand.'

Penelope was frowning, as she looked from one to the other.

'Perhaps I might accompany you,' she said. 'Advise. On this shopping trip.'

'Famous idea!' Piers said.

'I'd love that,' Thirza said.

Penelope held her gaze, clearly not in the least bit convinced.

Daggers at dawn it is, Thirza thought.

They ate roasted peppers, followed by a traditional melt-in-the-mouth stew, with an intense garlic and vinegar flavour. Penelope declined a pudding, saying she had to watch her figure, but Thirza was even hungrier than usual and ordered a typical Greek dessert – *melomakarona* made with oil, honey, oranges, and nuts.

'Ice cream too,' she added as an afterthought, knowing she was channelling all her anger, frustration, and hurt following the loss of Emilio towards Penelope instead. 'It's so wonderful to be able to eat what one likes without gaining even a pound. You can't fatten a thoroughbred, can you?'

At the bank after her father had handed over a wad of notes – leaving Penelope with a slight downturn to those cherry-red lips – the three women set off to buy fabric.

Thirza smiled as they strolled past the curious eyes of women, some of them perfectly aware of Penelope's affair with Piers, perfectly aware of Dulcie's absence, and perfectly aware that Thirza, Ianthe and the brazen 'scarlet woman' were walking side by side, apparently the best of friends. *If only they knew*, Thirza thought.

In the first shop Penelope tried to assume the superior role and take charge. 'May I suggest this lovely pale blue fabric for the drawing room?'

Thirza couldn't help laughing. It was awful. *Common*, her mother would have said. Tiny unreal-looking blue flowers competing with spots, best suited to the nursery, and Dulcie would not have cared if she sounded like a snob.

'My mother detests baby blue.'

Penelope maintained her bland expression. 'The pale pink then?'

Thirza pulled a face. 'Even worse.'

To her credit the woman laughed.

Then Thirza asked the assistant to show her some natural palettes and patterns for the draperies and some brighter ones for the cushions.

Without consulting Penelope, she chose a large print of pomegranate flowers in soft green shades complemented with soft blue hues for two pairs of floor-length curtains.

'It will look absolutely gorgeous in my mother's bedroom,' she said and added, 'Oh and look at this lovely neutral-coloured fabric. Mother will adore the delicate design of trailing wisteria.'

'Don't you think it's a bit . . .' Penelope said.

'What?'

'Old-fashioned? And anyway, surely your mother isn't really returning to the island if she's planning to sell up?'

'Of course she's returning, and I want the house shining and smelling of fresh paint when she takes up residence again. This fabric is not at all old-fashioned – fabulous for the drawing room. The chinoiserie and oriental trend is making a comeback. My mother hates ostentation and these soft taupe colours are just right.'

For the dining room she chose a deep rose-pink tree of life design with tiger lilies on a cream background, inspired by the early Persian patterns of the Ottoman Empire.

'My mother loves the natural world. She is something of a gardening expert, you know, as well as being a well-known writer. We Caruthers women know what we want in life, and never fail to get it. *Res ipsa loquitur.*'

Ianthe frowned at her.

Penelope looked confused and Thirza smiled to herself. Truth was, she'd never learnt Latin either, but could remember a few phrases of her mother's. She decided to make matching cushions along with some plain fabric that would contrast well with the curtains. 'For a little splash of additional colour,' she said. 'Nothing overdone.'

The assistant bundled up the packages neatly and she requested them to be delivered to Merchant's.

As they left the shop, Thirza turned to Penelope and held out her hand formally. 'Thank you so much for helping me. I'm going home now.'

'To Merchant's?'

'No, of course not. To our town house. My mother wants me to let her know of any decorating changes we need to make there, too. Hope to see you before I leave in the morning. Why not drop in for breakfast?'

The woman's eyes widened, and she reddened, aware she had been cut down to size.

Thirza knew full well that Penelope was living with her father and couldn't help smiling.

They said their goodbyes and Ianthe hurried Thirza away, hissing in her ear, 'What on earth were you thinking? You were beastly to her, Thirza. What's the matter with you?'

Thirza shrugged.

But Ianthe was right. She'd been very mean to the woman, and now she felt rather bad about it.

Late that afternoon, before her father and Penelope came home, Thirza let herself and Ianthe into the house and, while Ianthe rested, *she* decided to be nosy, whistling when she saw that Penelope had already commandeered an entire wardrobe and two chests of drawers for her clothes. Her mother's dressing table was a muddle of powder, rouge, low slanting sunlight glinting on perfume bottles, discarded jewellery, and lipsticks. Her mother's dressing table!

Next, she wanted to see if anything pertaining to the divorce, or the divorce settlement, might be hidden in her father's study. She had a key for that room and was as silent as possible, not wanting the new housekeeper to catch her snooping. But as she locked the door behind her there was a slight noise in the hall. Penelope? Her father? She glanced at the sun shining in from the courtyard garden and enjoyed the drifting scent of rosemary. But she'd have to be quick.

Screwing up her face, expecting to make a noise but desperately trying not to, she opened the drawers of his enormous mahogany desk. One by one. Nothing. And now she heard voices in the hall and footsteps. She froze, listening carefully. *Going upstairs*, she thought. *He's going upstairs. Good.* She leafed through a pile of papers lying on the desk and was horrified to discover a list of both her mother's and her father's assets including not only Merchant's but the Caruthers publishing house too. So, this was what it had come to. Billy's disappearance and his death had opened up a fracture in their lives and this was where it had delivered them. She felt as if she were going through everything on her own, that no one was telling her the truth, and that she alone was left to defend her home. She needed her mother.

She glanced at the tall cupboard in the corner and in a cardboard box found old newspaper clippings from when Billy had died. She scanned them, trembling with sadness.

Then, glancing at the list of assets again, she saw what she had always suspected but hadn't fully considered. Her mother was so much wealthier than her father. So that was what the little minx was after. Not only Merchant's but the business too. Thirza left the list of assets where she'd found it and seized the chance to telephone the operator and place a call to her mother in London while she had the chance.

There was no reply.

CHAPTER 30

As the late afternoon sun turned everything gold, then pink, then shadowy, a deep dusky twilight took over. Thirza's father invited her to join him for a drink in the courtyard garden, just the two of them. As he uncorked a bottle of white wine and handed her a glassful, she drank it one long gulp and held out her glass for a refill. Anything to soften the dark sharp edges of night when her memories hurt the most. It didn't work of course. Nothing did. Nothing ever would. With the scent of rosemary still strong in the air, Thirza breathed slowly in and out, in and out, but no matter what she did she could not relax. Her shoulders were too tight, her neck muscles too tense.

Love and loss and absence. What else was there? Not romance, though that could be nice, but real love with all its blood and guts and broken bones. Real love with all its angles and confusion. Real love and its terrible agonising ending.

'I miss the old days,' her father said, as if picking up on her thoughts. 'The holiday jollity, you know?'

Thirza nodded. The fun had always been driven by Billy. Had he ever been anything but happy? She screwed up her eyes trying to recall tears, tantrums, rebellions, but could only remember one or two. Minor infringements at that. Why had the perfect child died? Why hadn't it been her?

'You don't look your usual self,' her father said.

'What?' She was surprised he'd noticed.

'You're very pale and you look utterly miserable. Pen noticed straight away. Is it the divorce you're worried about?'

She sighed. 'Maybe. How is it progressing, now you've mentioned it?'

'Slowly.'

'How will everything be divided up?'

'We're not at that stage yet. Now tell me what's really upsetting you.'

She knew he was fobbing her off and said, 'Isn't the divorce enough?'

'It could be, but I don't think it's that alone, is it?'

She shrugged. 'Did Penelope put you up to this little tête-à-tête?'

'No. Am I not allowed to be worried?'

'You don't need to worry. I'm fine.'

He frowned. 'No, Thirza. You aren't.'

'Are you trying to be a parent now? Isn't it a bit late?'

He sighed. 'You girls are living up there unsupervised and could be getting into all kinds of trouble.'

'I've been working, and Pa, I am twenty-three, soon to be twenty-four.'

'And *working* is what's making you look so down in the mouth, is it?'

She shook her head.

'Look, my dear. I'll be frank with you. You need to know that Italian men can be, well, untrustworthy.'

She gasped and covered her mouth, tears instantly burning her eyes. 'How do you know about him?'

'Ianthe told me.'

'The bitch!'

'No. She really didn't want to say. But I knew something was wrong and wrangled it out of her. You're my only daughter, Thirza, and believe it or not I do care.'

As the tears slid down her cheeks and she furiously wiped them away with her fingers, more kept coming.

'Italians have not been good news for our family.'

She took out a hankie, blew her nose, and sniffed. 'What do you mean?'

He shrugged.

'You mean because of the Italian invasion?'

'Maybe.'

'You're being awfully vague.'

'It isn't for me to say.'

'And yet you have said something. What do you mean? Tell me!'

'I've said enough. Just be careful. Italian men are not like us.'

As an image of Emilio's naked body flashed before her eyes, she held back a sob. She wanted to scream at him. Why couldn't he be straightforward? At least with her mother, you usually knew where you were. She missed Dulcie so much and the sooner she came back to Merchant's, the sooner life would feel more normal.

'I'm not saying anything. Just a suspicion, that's all. And Italian men can be smooth talkers. Charmers. I've seen it before, their effect on women. That's all I wanted to say.'

'They aren't all like that. It's like saying all Englishmen are fine upstanding fellows, and they aren't.'

'No.'

Her breath was coming far too fast. She put a hand on her chest to try to calm herself and managed to say, 'I love him, Pa. I do. But you don't need to worry because it's over.'

More tears followed and she swiped them away. God this was embarrassing!

'I'm sorry, darling.' He sighed and reached for her hand. 'I wish you'd told me in the first place, before it came to this. We all go through heartbreak at some point, you know.'

'Did you?'

'Of course.'

She leant into him, and he folded his arms around her, stroking her hair as her breathing calmed.

CHAPTER 31

As she and Ianthe were within yards of the port, Thirza
froze, her heart thumping erratically. Emilio, dressed in
a suit and carrying a briefcase, was there too, standing
at some distance from her. She took a step towards him,
desperate to speak to him. Throw herself at him, wrap her
arms around him, and never let him go.

Ianthe gripped her by the elbow. 'Don't,' she whispered.
'You'll only humiliate yourself.'

Thirza's heart lurched. Ianthe was right, for Emilio was
with somebody, had his arm wrapped around the waist of
a dark-haired woman who was leaning against him. She
had her back to Thirza, so she was unable to see her face.
His wife? Oh God! Was this woman his wife? She must be.
Her heart sank. So, she was right. He was not separated,
and she had been a fool.

'Saunter,' Ianthe whispered.

'What?'

'Saunter. In case he sees you, and smile broadly. Show you don't care.'

Half an hour later, caring far more than she ought, and feeling totally crushed, she and Ianthe took the caique home to Merchant's.

There, day after day, instead of finishing the house, Thirza sat in the boathouse, staring at the changing colours of the sea. She felt exhausted, flattened by how much she missed Emilio, and told herself she simply had to learn to live with the 'what might have been's, the 'what if's, the boundless impossible possibilities. The life that never could be. All the while she'd been with Emilio, she'd known it was not likely to last. That it could never be what she really wanted. They had never said as much, yet it had always been clear, so why was she torturing herself, repeatedly picturing Emilio with that woman, and going over hopeless scenarios in her mind, scenarios it turned out she had secretly longed for? Images of a happy ever after, a marriage of true minds, of children tumbling about the garden, of love. Of family meals, of celebrations. Of the kind of happy, noisy, family life she'd lost when Billy vanished.

'Oh Billy,' she whispered, feeling his absence more than ever. 'What would you say about all this?'

She longed for her brother, longed for the straightforward kind of love that had been theirs. His simple enjoyment of life. His fun and laughter.

Thizzy. Thizzy. Let's play hide and seek.

Gone. All gone. And it felt so wrong.

She wanted to weep over Emilio but refused to allow herself that pleasure, for pleasure it would be just to let go of all this anger and despair. Maybe then she could move on. But if she did that, she'd have to accept it was really over.

Thirza was taking a bath some days after returning from Corfu and knew she needed to shake herself into action, despite her low spirits, despite the way her body longed for her lover, despite the way her heart ached. As she soaped herself all over, she felt her breasts. Larger than they had been. Feeling a little tender too. She climbed out of the bath, dried herself, and dressed.

The time for wallowing was over. The fabric they'd bought in Corfu would be arriving today, on the caique. If Thirza was to make the curtains and cushions she had envisioned, she needed to make sure her mother's old Frister & Rossmann sewing machine was in working order. German-made from before the Great War and with a mother of pearl inlay, it was a beautiful thing – but even after searching her mother's bedroom, the storeroom, and every cupboard inside the house, Thirza could find no trace of it. She stopped outside Dulcie's study, frowning. Could her mother had left it in there? She tried the door again. And again it didn't budge.

This was ridiculous. Why on earth had her mother locked the study? Feeling a sudden surge of anger, Thirza twisted the handle and pushed against the door as hard as she could. She was sick to death of being kept in the dark, sick of secrets, of always wondering. It ended now.

She stalked out of the house to find Spiro, who was whistling as he tended to the garden. He agreed to help her readily enough, and together they approached the beautiful old climbing rose so overgrown it almost covered one of the windows of her mother's study. They began cutting back with secateurs, Thirza scratching her hands and arms and barely caring. The physical pain was good, better than heartache at least. When they finally broke through to the shutters, closed of course, they seemed to have been glued shut, but Spiro fetched a crowbar from the tool shed and managed to force one side open. She'd been expecting to have to break in, smash a brick through the glass or something, but was pleased to see the window had not been fully closed. Spiro helped her and, with their fingers in the gap, they managed to pull the window open just wide enough for her to be able to crawl through.

She stood panting in the study, flushed with success and vindication. At last she was in. She gazed around at the dusty room, cobwebs hanging from every corner and around all the lamps. A dead gull must have fallen down the chimney and it lay on the floor just inside the window, poor thing. She quickly found her mother's spare key in the top drawer of the desk where she always kept it and unlocked the door from the inside.

She left the room, went into the hall, and called Ianthe. Before she looked for the sewing machine, they would have to dispose of the bird and clean the room from top to bottom. Almost as soon as they'd fetched a broom, a feather duster, some rags, a mop, and a bucket of water, Ianthe began complaining about her nails and her hair, though only in a half-hearted way.

'Wash your hair and paint your nails again, silly,' Thirza said, smiling for what felt like the first time in days.

Ianthe pulled a face and squealed as spiders went whizzing around as their webs were destroyed. Thirza laughed at her, not unkindly. The physical exertion was invigorating, addictive. Once Ianthe had gone to have a bath and wash her hair, Thirza began mopping the floor. Soon after that she found the sewing machine. As she lifted it out from one of the cupboards, a memory came back to her.

One afternoon long ago while pretending to be fast asleep on the chaise longue, she had watched her mother from beneath her lashes. Dulcie was rolling up the corner of one of the Persian rugs and lifting a section of loose floorboard.

Once she found the right place, Thirza did the same thing, and kneeling on the floor fished around with her fingers, pulling a face at the black greasy dust and crisp dead insects that had piled up under the floorboards. First, she pulled out a box, which proved to have a stack of letters inside it, all tied up with a grey ribbon. She shook the dirt off them, turned them over in her hand and wondered, before putting them down again, then with one hand in the gap and digging about in the dirt she felt for what else might be there. She extracted a dusty white envelope, a brown package of faded photographs, and finally a tin box containing a great deal of Italian, Greek, and English money. Hurrah!

She put the box to one side as she glanced through the photographs. They were mainly pictures of Dulcie years ago looking beautiful. In one she was holding a man's hand, though the rest of him had been torn out. How odd. It must have been her father, but there was something about the ornate ring on the man's finger, which wasn't a bit like anything her father might wear. Thirza picked up the letters and paused, already aware that she was invading her mother's privacy – and that to read the letters would be wrong. But if the past few weeks had taught her anything, it was that one should not wait to find answers. One had to look for them.

She undid the ribbon and flicked through the envelopes. None were addressed. She slid out a sheet of blue Basildon Bond writing paper and saw it was covered in her mother's distinctive handwriting.

My darling,

It is as if everything has come to an end, and I do not know how to live.

I loved you from the moment I first saw you and I cannot accept that you are gone. You haunt my every day, my every night. You slide into my bed and kiss my lips until I weep. My world is sorrow and shadow, a world where I see nothing, hear nothing. All I can see is you. My heart beats only for you. In your embrace I learnt to live. I hear your laugh, feel your hands on my body, and imagine your eyes smiling at me, your warm skin next to mine.

I do not love Piers. He has no subtlety. No sensitivity. I want you, for without you I am cold. I cannot eat, breathe, or sleep. I can barely function. The wind blows through me, and I become more bitter with each day that passes. Bitter and old. Please tell me it doesn't have to be like this. Please tell me you feel the same way and that you will come back to me.

For what is life without love? What am I without love? Without you.

Your love is all I want,
Your very own, Dulcie

Shocked, Thirza let out her breath, unaware she had been holding it.

She did not recognise her mother at all. The mother whom she had believed to be so in control, so in charge of her own life and everyone else's around her, had not been. Not at all. Here, in these words, she sounded unhinged. Desperate.

Who had the man been? None of her mother's letters had been posted and they were all written by her, with nothing else to give Thirza a clue. The man may have replied to Dulcie, if she had posted any to him, but she might have burned his letters. Did her father know about this? She flicked through the rest and read a few more lines here and there. None of the letters were dated, so Thirza couldn't tell when the affair had taken place. Her mother hadn't mentioned Billy so they had probably been written before he was born. Was it Billy's birth that brought her back to life after this awful devastation?

The last letter she'd found was inside a grimy, much-thumbed, white envelope, with no name or address on it and it had clearly been torn open before. She pulled out a single sheet of yellowing paper, and gasped as she read it.

YoU are GOing TO Pay FOR wHaT YOu did

Thirza's hands trembled. What on earth did the words mean? Was that threat something to do with her mother's love affair? Or was it something to do with what had happened to Billy? Thirza looked around at the study, no longer dust-covered, but more mysterious now to her than ever before. The house had been guarding her mother's secrets for far too long.

CHAPTER 32

Thirza might have sat for hours, in her mother's study, clutching the threatening note, had she not heard someone calling her name. She hurriedly packed the letters and photographs into their hiding place beneath the floorboards and got to her feet – just as the door swung open. She glanced up and blinked in surprise, for her mother's old friend Odel was standing there smiling.

'Hello Thirza. Sorry to interrupt.'

Thirza ran, hurling herself into Odel's arms.

'Darling girl,' Odel said after a few moments, as she pulled back to scrutinise her.

Thirza grinned. 'It's so good to see you, but if it's Dulcie you want, she isn't here.'

'I came to see *you*. I'm sorry I missed you when you were in town.'

'That's all right. I think I was a bit mean to Penelope. In fact, I know I was. Shall I ring for coffee?'

'Lovely. But first I have news that needs to be delivered away from curious ears.' She winked and Thirza laughed at the Machiavellian face her mother's old friend pulled.

'Of course. Let's go to the orchard. It's peaceful and the sound of the leaves rustling in the canopy overhead usually masks our words and keeps our secrets.'

'You have many of those?'

Thirza didn't reply but caught Odel looking at her with a strange expression on her face, as if still scrutinising her.

They went outside, walked around the house, and soon reached the orchard where a carpet of tiny, daisy-like flowers had sprung to life between the trees. There was so much Thirza wanted to talk about that it was hard to focus on just one thing.

'So,' she said as they reached the wooden bench. 'Let's sit here and you can tell me what's going on.'

'Firstly,' Odel said. 'Your mother called me. She said she didn't want to write.'

'She doesn't want to write! She doesn't want to come! Frankly, I'm furious with her. She was meant to come out ages ago. I had the whole thing planned and she just didn't come.'

'She must have had her reasons.'

'Reasons! Huh! What reasons?'

'I don't know. We talked about the divorce, your father, this woman Penelope, but the main thing I want to tell you is that Merchant's will hopefully be safe.'

Thirza reached out to touch Odel's arm. At least Dulcie was sorting that out. 'Thank God,' she said. 'So, Penelope won't be able to get her hands on the house.'

231

'Yes, though it will be a little complicated. And I'm not convinced Penelope is the dangerous woman you've painted her.'

'No?'

Odel put her arm around Thirza's shoulders. 'I don't know for sure, but your mother asked me to do a little digging, and as far as I can tell the young woman appears to truly love your father. Not only has she put up with a lot of town gossip, it also seems she had quite a troubled start in life and had her own family tragedy to deal with.'

Thirza pulled a face, unsure whether to believe her or not. 'Don't tell me you like her.'

'I wouldn't go that far.'

They both laughed.

'Anyway, just to be sure, Dulcie's plan is to go ahead with the idea that the estate should be held in trust until you reach the age of thirty. Until then nobody will be able to sell, mortgage, or pass it on in any way. Your mother and I will both be trustees.'

'I see. That does sound complicated.'

Odel smiled. 'Yes, but you know Dulcie. Anyone would think she doesn't want people looking too closely at the deeds. You're twenty-four now?'

'Nearly.'

'So, a proposed condition of the trust is that for the next six years you'd have to live here. The estate and the house cannot be closed up, or the title immediately reverts to your mother. You would not be able to sell until your thirtieth birthday and—'

'I wouldn't sell Merchant's,' Thirza interjected passionately. 'It's my home. I don't ever want to leave Corfu.'

'Well, you say that now. But I wonder. Have you thought about it?'

Thirza considered it now. Merchant's was where she felt most herself and most at home, even after the emotional turmoil of the past few days. She was not ready to have anything else taken from her.

'Do you want to live here, permanently, Thirza? It's such a big decision!'

Thirza drew back her shoulders. 'If a condition of the trust is that I live here all year round, then that's what I'll do.'

Odel leant away and narrowed her eyes. 'Thirza, may I be frank?'

'Of course.'

'Your father told me about your affair with an Italian man.'

'Emilio.'

'Well . . . Looking at you now, I wonder if the consequences of that liaison might in fact become a reason for you *wanting* to leave Corfu.'

'Consequences?'

'Thirza, don't tell me you do not realise?'

'What?'

'You haven't put on weight generally, but . . .'

The penny dropped and Thirza froze, although she wanted to run. Run and run and never stop. She hadn't wanted to think about this. She had known, of course she had, but if she didn't think about it . . . well . . . she never got any further than that. She stared at the ground, listened to the breeze, and felt as if nothing could be any worse than this.

'I'm expecting a child,' she said numbly, looking up at Odel.

'My dear girl,' Odel said, with nothing but compassion in her eyes. 'It will take enormous courage and stamina if you choose to stay. It's an old-fashioned world here with strict rules. Is there any chance he will marry you?'

She shook her head. 'He's separated from his wife, but he's a Catholic so he can't divorce.'

'Ah. I'm sorry to hear that. It's a great pity. I worry about how hard it will be living here with a child and no husband. After all you and your family have been through . . .'

She had a point and Thirza knew it. Billy's disappearance and subsequent death had made them a focus of attention. Attention that none of the family had wanted. They were already considered strange; how would her pregnancy add to that?

She looked away from Odel and at the orchard. She'd come to Corfu to clean up the house and complete a series of paintings. Nothing more. She had accomplished both and now, if she were to inherit Merchant's, she would have to live here all year round – but she had never even overwintered here before, and how would she manage with a baby? *A baby!* And unmarried. The locals would be scandalised. The British too.

'I'm not leaving Corfu,' Thirza repeated.

'Have you spoken to the father about your condition?'

Thirza shook her head. 'No, and please don't tell my mother. Please.'

Odel sighed. 'Thirza, I feel I must.'

'Please Odel. I'll tell her myself when she comes. Face to face. I promise.'

'I don't know that she definitely is coming.'

'She said she would be, by the end of the month, though that has passed. She's just a little late. Please let me do it myself.'

'Despite what happened to Billy, terrible though it was, she's stronger than you know. I think she might surprise you.'

Thirza, recalling the possible secrets she'd only just stumbled on, said, 'What was my mother like when she was younger?'

'She was very beautiful. Still is. Men have always been fascinated by her.'

'Anyone in particular?'

Odel avoided her eyes. 'Maybe. She didn't tell me everything. You'd have to ask her.'

CHAPTER 33

Although warm, it was a breezy day, and Thirza walked the serpentine cliff path, barely aware of where she was going. Since Odel's visit, and despite the good news about the trust, she'd still been feeling alone and frightened. Something ancient curled its way out of the ground and into the air where it thrummed amid the trees. She thought of her mother. So many mothers suffering over time. So many women suffering. So many children gone. She tried to shake herself out of it, but her maudlin mood clung on. She thought about her own mother, and all her secrets. What had been going on and who was the man in the photograph? Did her father know? She thought about her father, who had only recently begun to act like a parent again. How much happier he seemed now. But what kind of mother would she turn out to be? A mother without a husband. That's what. And the thought scared her. When a figure appeared from around the bend ahead of her, she stared, her heart hammering. Corfu had always been a place to push back real life, a magical place, a place to dream, and she wanted that, but now real life intruded, as it usually ended up doing. Especially since Billy.

Thizzy. Thizzy.

Come and push me on the swing.

Thizzieeee!

She blinked the memory away, staring down at her feet, hearing the gulls shrieking and the insects buzzing angrily as the wind buffeted them about. When she looked up her hair was in her eyes, and they were watering.

'I didn't mean to make you cry,' he said.

'I wasn't. It's the wind.'

'If you say so.'

She looked past him at the path ahead. Neither of them spoke for a few minutes. She chewed the inside of her cheek, tasting blood, wanting to move on, wanting to stay. Unsure.

'Well,' she finally said, still undecided.

'Indeed,' Emilio replied.

'I'd better be—'

He held out a hand to stop her. 'Please.'

She shook her head and wouldn't meet his gaze.

'Won't you let me explain?'

Now she looked at him. 'I saw you in Corfu Town.'

He frowned.

'With a woman.'

'A woman?'

'Yes, you know, dark hair, curves. A womanly woman.'

'Oh, Thirza. That wasn't *a woman*. That was my sister.'

'Why should I believe you?'

She took a long slow breath and exhaled rapidly. Could she believe him? She wanted to. In fact, she wanted to throw herself into his arms and never let go. But she would not. Instead, she glanced down at the gnarled olive trees lower down the hill, their trunks twisted and thick. Trees that had seen so much history, watched so many lives coming and going. People being born and people dying but still those trees went on. She might as well hear him out. Or perhaps she should hang on to her dignity and simply walk away. She turned to retrace her steps and head back home.

'Thirza?' he said, reaching out a hand to touch her arm. 'I have much to tell you. There's something—'

He broke off. She waited.

'Will you come up to the house?'

'You still have it? The house.'

'For now. Will you come?'

She nodded mutely, ignoring the arguments going on in the back of her mind as she followed him along the final stretch of the path, their feet crunching the hard dry ground. Her quest had been clear when she'd first come out to Corfu after seven years' absence and it had not included falling in love with a married man. Had not included falling in love at all. She had tried so hard to tell herself it was just sex, that it had only been about that. But it hadn't been. Not for her anyway. She didn't feel as devastated as her mother had sounded in those letters, but their circumstances were different. Thirza was still free, while her mother had been married with a child. Trapped.

She glanced across at the view of the sea and the sky. She loved the light, the luminescence, even as her spirits grew darker.

They reached his house, where he flung open the door for her.

In the sitting room she sat on a firm-backed chair with wooden arms. She remained stiff and unresponsive as he bustled about in the kitchen, eventually returning with two mugs of hot chocolate.

'Sorry,' he said. 'All out of coffee.'

'It's fine,' she muttered and took a sip. Should she tell him about the baby? Should she?

He settled himself then said, 'For the last two years I have been separated from my wife.'

'And now you're back together.' There it was and now, desperately needing air, she rose from the chair and went to stand by an open window, forcing herself to breathe steadily while gazing out at the shifting sapphire sea.

'No.'

She spun round to face him. 'No?'

'I told you, the woman you saw was my sister.'

She narrowed her eyes. 'So you say.'

'You don't trust me now?'

She shrugged. Had she ever?

'Why was she here? Your *sister*,' she asked and moved back to the chair, her legs shaking with the effort of keeping her emotions so tightly bound up inside her.

'We were meeting with a lawyer.'

'You don't have lawyers in Italy?' She had spoken sarcastically, had felt her own eyebrows shooting up.

He sighed to smother a smile, but she'd seen it all the same. Then he carried on with his explanation. 'Since I met you and we became close so very quickly, I have been trying to seek an annulment of my marriage. My wife wants to separate too, but we have twin daughters, so it is complicated.'

'What?' she gasped, feeling her heart fluttering. 'How old are they?'

'Fourteen. Anyway,' he went on. 'This annulment may take some time to achieve.'

'You should have told me what you were doing.'

'And if it had come to nothing? I didn't want to let you down. I love you, Thirza. Are you listening? I love you.'

Tell him. Tell him. And yet she still could not.

He walked over to the window and when he turned to look at her, she saw the worry lines on his face.

'There's been a huge drama over this back home, various factions of the family taking one side or the other. We are a typical Italian family. Many children, cousins, uncles and aunts, grandparents. The lot.'

'Why did you tell me you might be gone forever?' she asked, and couldn't help reliving the devastation she had felt that night.

'Things were not looking hopeful. If I could not achieve an annulment, there would have been no point in my returning to you. I could not ask you to give up any chance of meeting someone who would be free to love and marry you as you deserve.'

'Tell me about your girls.'

He smiled. 'They are beautiful and clever.'

She nodded, really wanting to kiss him, make everything better between them, but managed to hold back. She had to take a stand. Must not continue being the pushover she had been.

'So, when will you know?' she asked. 'One way or the other?'

He closed his eyes, exhaling slowly, and then he looked at her. 'I don't know. That's the one thing I can't tell you yet. Or . . . maybe not quite the one thing. I do still have to confess to something else.'

'If you don't know, why did you come back?'

'Because I needed to wind up the rental of this house and pack my belongings. I have finished my research here.'

She could not take her eyes from his face. Could not look away. Was afraid of the answer if she asked the question and yet she had to. She swallowed then said, 'Were you going to call on me? If we hadn't met by accident, I mean?'

'Of course.'

She'd been holding her breath but now rose to her feet. 'How old are you, Emilio?'

'You're asking me this now?'

'Yes.'

'Too old for you. Is that what you are thinking? Have I read this all wrong, misunderstood your feelings?'

She couldn't speak. Of course he hadn't. But she didn't want to give him the satisfaction. 'All these days without a single word. I just wish you'd explained all this before.'

'Don't you see that I couldn't?'

Their relationship had existed at a deeper level. She knew it and he had to know it too, which was why he was really back, along with all the practical stuff.

'I couldn't walk away from you, but there is more we need to discuss.'

She didn't want to squander these precious few moments but couldn't help her sharp tone when she blurted out, 'Oh please, save me from your excuses.'

'No, Thirza, seriously. You don't know everything about me.'

'Nor you about me. Can't we just live in the present, Emilio? Your past is your past.'

'I don't think we can.'

'Is it about your brother? Did you lose a brother?'

'Lose a brother?'

'When I told you about Billy, my brother, you looked sad. I thought you might have lost a brother too.'

He shook his head. 'I was sad for you. I do have an older brother. A banker in Rome. We rarely see each other, that's all.'

'I'm sorry.'

'No need.'

'Anyway, aren't things simpler than you think? Aren't we? I love you. You say you love me.'

He didn't reply for a moment, then as if deciding something he said, 'I'm not yet able to ask if you would be prepared to marry me. I didn't want to raise—'

'You didn't want to raise my hopes! Oh, for God's sake, pass me the smelling salts! Honestly Emilio, I am not some simpering Victorian heroine!'

He had the grace to look shamefaced as he said, 'Forgive me. You are a modern woman, and I am a fool. Your fool . . . if you will have me.'

She shook her head, and straightened her back. 'You have just explained why you can't ask me that yet. And now I need to . . . I just need to go. I need . . . I need to think.'

What she really needed was him, for them to pick up the driving rhythm they'd had before, for them to both be lying together naked, his hand between her thighs, his lips on her neck. Her fingers running through his hair and feeling his chest against her . . . against her . . . against her full breasts. No! She couldn't have that, not unless she had decided to tell him about the baby. She opened her mouth to speak, to say the words. *I'm carrying your child.*

'Will I see you again?' he asked, breaking her chain of thought.

'When are you leaving?'

'In one week. The owner is coming back to live in this house then.'

'Right.'

'Maybe we could meet in the boathouse?'

CHAPTER 34

That night Thirza lay in the pitch-black room, eyes wide open, staring into a frightening future. Blinded, dazzled, desolate. Pregnant! Who was she now and what was she going to do about the baby? Should she see Emilio again? Wouldn't it be far better if she chose not to? It was their relationship that had left her in this difficult position. And yet she ought to at least let him know. Truth was, she felt a little thrill just knowing he'd come back. As her mind went round in circles, she heard what sounded like the faintest singing. A gentle soothing sound coming from the old nursery. She'd heard it before and even as she realised it was probably in her own head, she had to check just in case.

Lamp in hand, she crept along the corridor and up the stairs to a room at the back of the house beneath the eaves. The singing gradually stopped but she could hear an odd creaking sound, so she turned the handle and cautiously opened the door just a little. She was completely alone in the house. Ianthe had stayed in town, Eleni lived with Spiro and his bride, Magdalena, in their cottage on the estate, and the cleaner came up daily from a nearby hamlet.

Despite knowing it was crazy, she pushed the door open, fully expecting to see Billy there. The rocking horse was moving slightly as if someone had been rocking there not long before. She glanced at the window and saw it hadn't been properly closed. Was it open wide enough for the breeze to rock their old wooden horse? They'd fought over the name of that horse. She had wanted Giles, but Billy said you couldn't call a horse Giles, and it had to be Nobby, on account of his knees. She smiled to herself and sat in the comfy but faded nursing chair. It was so quiet up here she closed her eyes and imagined she was her mother.

Sometimes she heard her mother's laughter, as if she were still walking with Odel in the garden, both of them young and jaunty. Sometimes she heard Billy calling her.

Thizzy where are you? I've got a badness.

A badness, darling?

A horn. From the rose.

A thorn.

That's what I said. A horn.

As his voice died away, she smiled at the memory.

Come back, come back, she wanted to say, and wished she had a magic wand to wave him home to them, all smiles and gappy teeth, eyes shining with merriment. She wasn't afraid of the voices in her head today. These were happy memories. Cherished moments from a past that had ended too suddenly and had completely ruptured their lives. She wondered if that horror had lain in wait all along, while they went about their lives, thinking of ordinary things, utterly oblivious to what had been coming. Thank God you couldn't see into the future, for if you could it might send you completely insane.

And as she sat in the nursery something altered. Up until then she'd only thought of the unborn child as a limitation, a burden, a potential source of shame. She had feared it. Now with a hand on her belly she felt a buzz of excitement. A little flame. Of hope. Of joy. This was a new start. And she felt sure that whether Emilio was free to marry her or not, it was only right to tell him about the baby. And then if he *were* able to marry her one day, everything would be all right. She would not be outcast from society. She would have her own little baby. Hers and Emilio's.

Yet still she bargained with herself and decided she would only tell him if *he* came looking for her. If she was forced to find him, she would not say a word.

The next day Thirza stayed in the house, twiddling her thumbs, itching to go to him. Nothing happened. He didn't come. The day after, unable to keep idle, she started the job of hanging the curtains, with Spiro's help of course, and when it was done, she would clean and then paint the remaining rooms she had so far ignored. But even before the first pair of curtains was up, she heard Ianthe calling her.

'In here,' she shouted back. 'Dining room.'

'Hello,' Ianthe said as she came into the room, wringing her hands and looking tired. 'Oh Thirza, please help me. I just don't know what to do.'

Thirza climbed down from the ladder, noticing her cousin looked genuinely confused.

'It's Walter. I needed to talk to you, so I came back with the caique.'

Thirza took Ianthe's hand and led her to the shaded terrace while Spiro carried on hanging the curtains alone. They sat down and under dappled light she gazed at Ianthe, surprised by how pleased she was to see her and how much warmth she felt for her.

'So, what happened?' she asked.

'Walter is sorry. He says he made a terrible mistake and I'm the only one for him.'

Thirza smiled. 'That's good, isn't it?'

'Yes. It really, really, is.'

'Then what's the problem?'

Ianthe frowned. 'I don't know. I wanted you to like him.'

'Oh darling, it's you who needs to like him.'

'Well I do.'

Thirza thought about it for a moment then said, 'Look. He was upset when he was here. We can forgive him that, I think, and he won't see much of us, will he? Not if you end up living in America.'

'So, you think I should take him back?'

'Do you want to marry him?'

Ianthe grinned. 'I do. Really, I do. Walter might be my only chance for a decent life. He's awfully well off. I know it isn't done to talk about money, but Columbine and I don't have much of it, so it matters.'

'True.'

'By the way I don't think Penelope is as bad as you thought,' Ianthe said.

Thirza snorted.

Ianthe smiled. 'No. Really. She was kind to me while I was staying in Corfu Town.'

'Hmmm! Ulterior motive?'

'I don't see why.'

'Well maybe you're right,' Thirza conceded. 'Odel said much the same thing. As for Walter, I'm sure you'll be very happy together.'

'Thank you, Thizzy.'

Thizzy! Thizzy!

Oh Billy. He had been the only one who had called her that.

Meanwhile Ianthe was inspecting Thirza's face and then she said, 'Are you all right? You look a bit peaky.'

Thirza hesitated. She longed to talk to Ianthe about the pregnancy, share some of her confusion, but her naked swimming had already disrupted the girl's future happiness once before. It might be the last straw for Walter if Ianthe let slip that she, Thirza, was unmarried and with child. Most of all she longed to talk about things with her mother, but knew she could not.

'Not been sleeping too well,' she said. 'That's all.'

After that Thirza kept busy with curtains, cushions, and cleaning. She felt tired, unsure, and generally weepy. Emilio had not called at the house. For three days he had not, and she felt tears filling her eyes again.

She went outside to her mother's favourite little area of the garden at the side of the house, where a vine-covered pergola gently dappled the light. There, among the grapes and flowers, Thirza leant over, head in hands, and now she couldn't stop the tears from falling. It was all too much. She was too up and down. One minute happy, the next so low and tired she could barely move.

She hardly heard someone coming up close and sitting down next to her, but stopped crying, wiped her eyes, and then she saw it was Eleni. The woman gently took her hand and squeezed it.

'Thirza,' she said. 'You are not the only girl to fall, and you will not be the last.'

She gasped at the woman's perspicacity although she shouldn't have been surprised. Eleni had a way of reading people, seeing into them, but still she asked, 'How could you tell?'

'It is not so hard.'

'I don't know what to do.'

'The best outcome is for the girl to marry the man.'

Thirza shook her head. 'That may not be possible.'

'There is also adoption.'

'No! I couldn't. I just couldn't.' Another sob came and then another.

Eleni patted her back. 'It will all come right. You will see.'

Later that afternoon, Thirza looked out of her bedroom window and spotted Emilio approaching the house. She ran downstairs, opened the front door before he reached it and threw herself into his arms. He had come. He had. Everything would turn out for the best. Eleni had been right. Though what that best might be, she still didn't know.

CHAPTER 35

As she and Emilio walked arm in arm to the boathouse, Thirza felt the magic of the island returning. The magic that had always made anything seem possible. The magic that made the sea sing and the air fill with the scent of jasmine, even when the blooms had died. And when ribbons of light danced on the walls of the boathouse as they entered their little sanctuary, she felt as if the place was welcoming them back. Deliriously happy, she glanced out at the crystal waters of the sea and felt such joy in her heart, but when she turned back to him and tried to say something – anything – they both spoke at the same time.

'Umm, would you like to—'

'I have missed—'

'No, after you.'

She knew she couldn't tell him about the baby just yet for it felt a little as if they were strangers. Never fearful of being alone, she found the degree to which she had wanted him disturbing. What if he were horrified at the thought of a child?

There was a long pause.

'Merchant's is going to be mine,' she eventually said, her voice falling into the silence between them. 'I was worried that my father and Penelope would take it. It would have killed my mother.'

'But she has not been here,' Emilio said, frowning. 'Does she truly love it so? Maybe she will never come.'

'Oh, don't say that.'

'It might be for the best.'

'It's complicated,' Thirza said. 'Because of Billy. This place is full of him, you see.'

'Even now?' he asked.

She nodded. 'Yes, even now.'

There was another moment of silence, then she said, 'It seems likely that Merchant's will be placed in a trust, and I'll have to find a way to live here all year round until I'm thirty. Then it becomes mine.'

'You wouldn't be tempted to sell?'

'No. Haven't you heard a word I've said about this place?'

He laughed quietly. 'I've heard.' And he held out his hand from where he stood at the bottom of the bed. 'Come to me now.'

She took her time, opened a window and watched the curtains blowing in the breeze that carried in the scent of wild sage and pink oleander, then she turned and went to him. He held out his arms and she allowed him to hold her, feeling his heart beating against her own. She thought of the night they'd shared on the beach, how the moon had shone on the water, silvering their world, the sound of the waves – *swish swish swish* – so enchanting she felt as if she might just fly.

But now. Reality was knocking at her door. His too. Though he didn't know it yet.

'Will you lie with me?'

'That's a very old-fashioned expression,' she said.

He laughed and let her go.

'I did just mean lie down.'

'You don't want to rip my clothes off?'

He grinned. 'Well, if you are offering . . .'

She laughed, and took his hand, then pulled him to the bed with her, the ice broken. He removed his clothes just as she removed hers, although she kept on a pretty silk chemise that covered her breasts. Such a giveaway. She didn't want him to work it out. Wanted to surprise him when she told him.

It felt different between them. The difference. She wasn't exactly sure how, but it was there. The hesitation not completely banished. Her fingers tangled in his hair as she brought his head closer to hers and she looked into his beautiful dark eyes with the rings of gold that always filled her with longing. He ran his hands from her shoulder down to her wrist then massaged the palm of her hand, lacing his fingers with hers. She felt her body respond, her pelvis aching.

Beneath her chemise her nipples hardened against his chest, and he smiled.

'I have missed you,' he said.

'How much?' she said.

He turned her over, so she was on her hands and knees. When he slowly pushed inside her, she groaned. He moved slowly at first, effortlessly, gently.

Was he trying to drive her mad? But as they rocked together, building a faster and faster rhythm, she stopped thinking altogether – until he unexpectedly stopped, quickly turning her onto her back.

'I need to see you,' he whispered. 'I must see you.'

Their eyes locked and she felt tears on her cheeks.

'Don't cry,' he said.

'Happy tears,' she whispered.

When it was over, she lay beside him, and they held hands like children. His skin was shiny with sweat, and she was hot and sticky too, so she finally pulled off her damp chemise. They let the breeze waft over them, drying their skin. She breathed in the scent of him – tobacco, limes, spice. Was this the moment to speak? But then she realised his breathing had slowed. He had fallen asleep. She rehearsed the words in her head. *My darling Emilio, I am expecting your child.* Or, *Emilio, I have to tell you . . . something rather important.* No. Not that. Much too formal. Maybe just, *I'm pregnant.*

They were still lying naked on top of the sheets, Thirza drowsy, enjoying her daydream of babies, children, swings in the garden, and her pushing an adorable little girl in a pram. A little girl with Emilio's eyes and her red hair. Emilio laughing as the chubby little girl ran to him and he spun, holding her up in his arms, the air full of the sweet fragrance from the small white flowers of the mock orange.

The vision felt so real, so tangible to her, that she almost didn't hear the door creaking open. There was a loud gasp. Thirza's eyes flew open, and she reached instinctively for Emilio's hand, before freezing, eyes fixed on the figure standing in the doorway. Still half-asleep, Emilio reached for the sheet to cover them.

'Mother?' Thirza gasped.

Dulcie's face was white, her eyes wide with shock. Beside Thirza, she felt Emilio stiffen and heard his sharp intake of breath. He cursed softly in Italian.

'Jesus Christ!' her mother hissed, her lip curling. 'Federico!'

Thirza pulled up the pretty cotton bedspread, trying to calm her racing heart and reddened cheeks. This was not exactly how she would have introduced her mother to Emilio – but there was no going back now.

'No, Mother,' Thirza said as calmly as she could. 'This is Emilio. He's my—'

'No,' her mother said, shaking her head. Her face was contorted with rage as she looked from Thirza to Emilio, and Thirza felt her heart quail. Shock was one thing, but she would never have thought her mother would react this badly. She looked to Emilio for support – and saw his face was utterly drained of colour.

'Dulcie,' Emilio said, his voice gruff. 'I can explain.'

Dulcie. Why was Emilio calling her mother Dulcie?

'My daughter, Federico?' her mother hissed, jabbing an angry finger at Emilio. 'My daughter?'

Thirza turned back to stare at Emilio. He would not return her gaze.

'What's going on?' Thirza whispered.

And now Dulcie came into the room, clasped hold of Thirza's arm and hauled her to her feet.

'Thirza,' Dulcie said, her face grim. 'Meet Billy's father! Federico Emilio Bellini.'

PART THREE

Corfu, seven months later

FEBRUARY 1931

CHAPTER 36

Thirza

Thirza stared at the ceiling, the unnatural shine of the beams glimmering in the candlelight. A roll of thunder ripped the sky apart, the trees creaked in the wind, and the house whispered in the dark. It was the middle of the night. And cold. So, so, cold. She shivered. How had it come to this? *How could I have been so stupid? So gullible.* A searing pain tore through her, twisting her inside. She gasped for air and, like an injured animal, she bellowed at the injustice of this.

'Something is wrong! Eleni,' she wailed. 'This can't be right.'

'You need to stay calm,' the woman replied. 'Breathe, slowly, in and out.'

As the woman repeated the words *in* and *out* again and again, Thirza sank back into her pillows, her whole body slippery with sweat, and thankfully, oh so thankfully, the pain died down. Eleni continued soothing her, calming her, reassuring her that everything was fine.

I need him, Thirza thought. *I need him here and I want my mother, too.* Then she remembered. Remembered that she did not want her mother. Did not want either of them.

You have to forget him. You have to.

The sound of muffled barking reached her from somewhere in the house. Georgie, her new puppy. A lolloping mixed-breed animal with a black patch over one eye, one floppy ear and one pointing upwards, a curly cream-coloured coat with three irregular splodges, and gigantic paws. Spiro guessed he was about four months old, but couldn't be sure because the poor animal had been found abandoned, starving at the side of the track.

Another wave of pain rose up, devouring her from the inside. Terror took over. Without a doctor, without a midwife, without a nurse – without a mother for God's sake – surely this would kill her?

But after the pain relented once again, Eleni gently wiped her brow with a damp cloth. Thank goodness for Eleni. Without her, Thirza didn't think she could survive – nor could she have survived any of the turmoil of the past months. Not the love. The pain. Or the rage.

She gripped the pillow tightly, squeezing it with all her strength, as if by doing so she might squeeze out all her anger.

You have to forget him.

Even now, when she thought of them together – Dulcie and Emilio, her mother and the love of her life – her entire being was flooded with disgust and despair. He had begged her to listen, said that he could explain, said that he hadn't known, not until after he had already fallen in love with her, and she'd eventually told him who she was. He'd said that he had wanted to tell her, had tried, but still could not find the words. She had thrown him out all the same. It was not enough. Every moment that he had known who she was, who Dulcie was, and had not spoken – every moment was a fresh betrayal.

'I never want to see you again,' she'd yelled. 'Get out. Get out!'

He'd looked at her with such sorrow in his eyes she had wanted to weep, but the anger was stronger. She had closed her eyes, so as not to see him walking out of her life forever.

Now the sky roared almost continuously, and rain like marbles began pelting the roof, the terrace, and everything in the garden too. It suited her, this wild noisy night, this opening of the heavens.

'Don't draw the curtains, Eleni,' she pleaded. 'I want to see the storm.'

As Eleni left the curtains alone, a flash of lightning charged the air, turning everything outside the house blue, inside the room too. As the crack of thunder broke the sky apart, pain shot through her again, lasting longer, hurting more intensely, and she swore.

Eleni frowned.

Thirza screamed, pushed to the brink of her endurance. And yet. And yet. In some ways this physical battle was preferable to the emotional agony that had preceded it and had seemed to have no end.

The contractions came faster suddenly, much faster, until she could not breathe, and she knew she really *was* going to die. Desperate to push, she heard Eleni sounding flustered when she held her hand and said, 'Not yet. Not yet.'

Time concertinaed to a tiny pinpoint then seemed to stretch out like the knicker elastic of the enormous green pants they'd been forced to wear at school for gym. Stretch and stretch until it snapped.

And then she heard Eleni urging her to push. 'Now! Push. Push now. Hard as you can.'

Thirza's thoughts ceased completely. She was primal, a visceral being. There was only this and only now, only herself, the lightning, the thunder, and the rain. She howled at the terrible burning, then came a slithering feeling. Something had changed, and immediately after that the world completely drained of sound.

Oh God! Was the baby out? Was something wrong with the baby? No! Please God! No! She heard Eleni muttering and she waited, her heart in her mouth, hardly daring to breathe while her child could not.

Then finally a thin indignant shriek.

Thank you. Thank you.

The baby was alive. And the battle between her body and her soul was over and her body had won.

'You have a daughter,' the older woman said, with so much joy in her voice, Thirza blinked the tears away. She'd known it would be a girl, had named her all those months ago when she hadn't told Emilio she was pregnant. He still didn't know anything.

The wind continued to howl, the rain continued to fall, and both Thirza and her baby cried. The tiny newborn shrieking in shock at her sudden arrival in the world, and the mother weeping for joy. For sorrow. For all that had been lost. For all that remained. For all that lay ahead. For what life was and what life was not. And maybe most of all for her brother's everlasting absence, and the black hole of her own mother's absence at her first grandchild's birth.

All of this was breaking Thirza's heart.

Except now everything had changed – did she even want to see her mother again?

She returned to the present in a rush, for Eleni had wiped the baby clean, and now she brought the child across to her. As Thirza held her daughter in her arms, she felt a surge of emotions suffusing her body, her mind, her soul, so powerful she didn't know what to call them. Pride maybe, euphoria, exhaustion, love. Terror, too, for she alone was responsible for this tiny, beautiful human.

Soon after that Eleni took the baby away again and handed Thirza a glass. 'Drink,' she said. 'It is herbal. For sleep. You have had a hard labour.'

The thunder rumbled on, but Thirza fell fast into darkness and a deep, dreamless sleep.

When she awoke it was to the sound of her baby's cries. Her baby! And it was daylight. She could hear the birds. And though it was a cold February day, the weak wintry sun was streaming in, turning the room pink.

'Let us see if she will feed,' Eleni said, and settled the child at Thirza's breast.

Thirza gazed down at her baby's perfection, her fluttering dark lashes, her flawless pink cheeks. So much heartache was behind them now, and so much hardship lay ahead. But in that moment, Thirza's heart was filled only with love. She let fall her tears, her joyful happy tears, with no room for anything else. Whatever had come before, whatever lay ahead, and however people tried to shame her for being unwed, she was going to hold her head up high and make this work. Somehow.

'Hello, Romi Francesca Caruthers,' she said. 'Hello, my darling girl.'

CHAPTER 37

Two weeks later

Thirza was in the kitchen cradling Romi who was fast asleep, warm, and smelling of Johnson's baby powder. Thirza had not yet decided whether to write to Dulcie with the news that the baby had arrived, but she most certainly was not going to let Emilio know anything about her daughter. He needed to vanish completely from her mind. For she was not alone here at Merchant's, was she? She could cope without Dulcie or Emilio, and the whispering outside the kitchen door reminded her of that. Magdalena was out there with Eleni.

The two women entered the room and hovered near her.

'What?' Thirza said, picking up on their hesitation and feeling irritable. 'What is it?'

Eleni cleared her throat. 'Your father and his, umm, his friend, will be arriving any minute. A message came with the caique.'

'You told my father about the baby being born?'

'You asked me to.'

'Did I?'

Eleni inclined her head and screwed up her face. 'You need to bathe, madam.'

'Please don't call me that.'

Magdalena reached out to take Romi, though Thirza held back, not wanting to let her child go. But she couldn't meet her father and Penelope looking unkempt, so she gingerly passed over her baby and hurried up to her room. She had not been herself, nor even looked like herself since Romi's birth, and much of the time she'd given in to tears for literally no reason. Of course, Eleni and Magdalena knew this, even though she had tried to hide from them, locking the door of the bathroom and running the tap so that no one should hear her sobs. She couldn't understand what was going on. She was happy, wasn't she? She adored her baby. So why this awful panicky, weepy, pathetic nonsense that arose from nowhere?

Thirza glanced in the mirror and shook her head. Dear God! Puffy-eyed, pale, hair unwashed. Eleni was right. She must run a bath right now, adding a good handful of Epsom salts for her aching body and the fragrant oil of jasmine to raise her spirits.

After her bath she towel-dried her hair and then tied it back from her face in a low damp chignon at the nape of her neck, just as her mother used to do. She dressed carefully in a loose grey woollen dress to cover her still rounded belly and wrapped a teal-blue cashmere shawl, which had once been Dulcie's, around her shoulders. Then she pinched her cheeks and added a touch of rouge. But she looked like a clown and quickly rubbed it off with her fingers. She felt lumpy, blotchy, ungainly.

During her pregnancy her father had visited regularly, trying to help out when she grew big and cumbersome, Penelope always in tow. To begin with, Thirza had resented every moment of the woman's presence, but in truth, it had been Penelope who had been most helpful.

'Look Thirza,' she'd said. 'I know how it feels when people stare and gossip behind their hands. I know what it feels like to be labelled a scarlet woman. So, if you want to avoid being seen out and about in Corfu Town at the moment, I can bring you anything you need.'

'You'd do that?'

'Of course,' she'd said, pressing Thirza's hand – and it was almost too kind for Thirza to take in, when she had been so raw, hurt, and angry.

'Just as long as you don't bring me any awful pink spotted fabric to make maternity clothes,' she'd said, sliding her hand out of Penelope's grip.

'Fair enough,' Penelope had replied, laughing and seeming unoffended. 'But I can bring you towelling napkins and baby clothes. Whatever you want. Your father or I can ride up with them. If they come by caique it will be a red flag and everyone will know your business within moments.'

The sound of voices outside, and then inside, alerted Thirza that they had arrived, and she headed down to greet them.

In the hall, Magdalena was still holding Romi, and Penelope was reaching out to take her.

'Oh my God, look Piers! Look how utterly gorgeous she is,' the woman was saying.

Thirza felt tears pricking the backs of her eyelids. She swallowed hard. She must not let them see her cry, but

Penelope glanced up while she was still standing frozen halfway down the stairs, unable to gain control of herself.

'Oh, there you are,' the woman said with a cheery smile. 'I hope you don't mind me holding her.'

Thirza came to her senses. 'Hello Penelope. And of course you may hold the baby.'

'Please call me Penny. Penelope always makes me feel like a maiden aunt.'

Thirza gave her a faint smile.

'How are you?' her father said, reaching a hand towards her.

'I hope it wasn't too awful,' Penny said, cooing at the baby. 'The birth.'

'To be honest I can't remember a thing.'

It wasn't true but she really didn't want to talk about it.

'You were so brave, up here in the wilds,' her father said gruffly.

They had not asked outright why Dulcie did not come and why the baby's father was not present, either. Right from the start, Thirza had made it clear that both subjects were out of bounds.

'I'm sure I'd have been terrified,' Penelope agreed.

'I didn't have much choice.'

How could she ever speak of Emilio's betrayal? He had not told her about his affair with Dulcie, although she could take some of the blame for that. If only she'd told him who she really was from the start, he'd have immediately put two and two together, and that would have been the end of it. By the time she did tell him they were both too deeply in. She realised she had crossed a line, and so had he, but whose line? Eleni's? The social world she herself belonged to, where there was a right way – not that you could always know what that was – and a wrong way, which you absolutely *were* clear about?

But exactly where was the line now, and anyway, how could you possibly know if people had withheld the truth? All the cards had not been on the table for her, but would she have done things differently if she'd known from the start? *Of course I would have*, she told herself. But really? He'd had an affair with her mother. Billy was his child! It was too much to take in. *Of course she would have done things differently*.

Anyway, now that she had Romi, how could she regret what had happened? And yet for the sake of her mother she did. *She did*. Thirza had loved him, and she loved her mother too, and now the mix of emotions was so conflicting she felt as if she were going crazy.

She realised her father and Penny were waiting for her to speak and looking a little worried. 'Sorry. I get a bit distracted. It's lack of sleep. I'll put Romi in her cradle, and then we can have coffee on the terrace.'

Penny shivered. 'Really? Outside? It's still only February.'

'Ah, yes, perhaps you're right.'

'There is a fire in the drawing room,' Eleni said.

Thirza nodded.

They headed to the armchairs already drawn up around the roaring log fire and Thirza settled Romi in her cradle.

It was awkward at first, the silence unnatural, with just the sound of the fire crackling; even Penny was simply gazing at the leaping flames without speaking. Thirza felt immensely relieved when Magdalena came in with a tray.

'I make a cake,' the girl said in a halting, heavily accented voice, for she was still not completely used to the house and its new language.

'That's very kind,' Piers said, and Thirza, hearing Romi gurgle in her cradle, realised he still hadn't really looked at her.

The baby's shock of dark hair was so like Billy's as a toddler it took her breath away. Had her father spotted that? Did he know who Billy's real father was? Before she had thrown Emilio out, he had sworn on his life that he had not known Billy was his child until that very moment. He'd insisted his affair with Dulcie had only been a brief interlude, that he'd just reached his twentieth birthday, that Dulcie had been a glamorous older woman, and he had been flattered by her attention.

'Forgive me. Forgive me, *amore*,' he'd pleaded. 'I was young and foolish. Naïve even.'

He was sorry. So terribly sorry he had not told her. He had tried to tell her again and again but had been terrified of losing her. But she had refused to listen and screamed at him to leave.

'She won't bite, you know,' Thirza said, coming back to the present with a jolt and seeing her father was staring at the baby.

'What?'

'Romi. She won't bite.'

'I'm not a baby sort of person.' He twisted his mouth and paused for a moment then said, 'I don't recall Dulcie keeping a baby downstairs. Don't they usually sleep upstairs in the nursery?'

'I'd never hear her cry. Don't forget it was different back then. Mother had a nursery maid and a nanny. I do everything myself.'

Thirza poured the coffee, cut the cake, and handed the slices out on delicate bone china side plates decorated with roses.

Penny clapped her hands. 'Oh, how lovely, a Victoria sandwich. How did the girl know how to make it?'

'Mother's recipe books. And actually, Magdalena is a sublime cook. I'm very lucky.'

When the small talk was done, the coffee taken, the delicious cake eaten and remarked upon, they lapsed into silence again. Eventually Piers said he wanted to see to the horses and left them alone.

'Are you still doing any illustration work?' Penny asked.

'Oh goodness yes. But not nearly enough. I have an agent in London now, and there are commissions from time to time. But to be honest it's a worry.'

Thirza felt her eyes brimming with tears and turned away. Her father was helping her out for the time being, but the financial crash had left things a bit tight for him too and she didn't want to be a burden. If only she didn't have to worry about how to earn money on top of everything else! She wiped her eyes, tried to smile, and decided to tell Penelope what she'd been thinking about.

'I do have an idea,' she said, hesitantly.

'Go on. Tell me.'

'Do you think I might be able to turn Merchant's into a guest house? Make the place earn its keep.'

There was a moment while Penny appeared to consider this, and Thirza felt the woman might be about to dismiss the idea as a ridiculous one.

But then Penny grinned. 'I think it's a bloody marvellous idea. I'll help if you'll let me. I'm rather good at organising things.'

CHAPTER 38

A couple of days later Piers had taken the dog for a walk and Thirza and Penny were alone again. The room was growing a little too hot and Thirza, exhausted from broken nights and constant feeding, really wanted to lie down and be on her own. She gazed at the fire and realised Penny was studying her.

'What?' she said. 'Have I got egg on my face?'

Penny smiled. 'I was just wondering how you're feeling.'

'Fine thanks,' Thirza snapped.

'But a newborn baby must be so exhausting.'

Thirza nodded. What was the woman getting at?

'You are happy, aren't you?' Penny added.

Thirza gave her a hard stare. How much did she know? How much did any of them know?

'Romi is a darling,' Penny continued. 'But it must be awfully lonely.'

Thirza felt her face crumple. Penny had hit the nail on the head. She had been feeling desperately alone.

Had felt ashamed that she couldn't simply enjoy her beautiful baby.

'I . . . I . . .' But she couldn't speak for the lump in her throat.

Penny reached out a hand and Thirza took it as her tears began to form. After a few moments she managed to control herself.

'I've been finding it really hard,' she said, her voice shaking. 'I feel guilty. I love Romi so much but, well, you know.'

Penny nodded.

'Maybe I can help take some of the burden? I meant it when I said I'd help with your new idea,' the woman was saying. 'It would leave you time to focus on the baby and not have to worry.'

Thirza gazed at her, unsure.

Then Penny said, 'We don't want you going downhill, do we?'

Thirza gulped. 'I think maybe . . . I think maybe I already have.'

'Look, it's none of my business and you don't have to say a thing, but I'm a good listener, so if you ever need to talk, well . . .'

Thirza remained mute. Didn't know how to respond. She wanted someone to talk to, but Penelope?

'You look pale,' Penny said, then squeezed her hand and let go. 'It's really not that unusual, you know, my sister Angela struggled too after my nephew was born.'

'Was she on her own too?'

'No. Her husband was there but she still felt overwhelmed. What I'm trying to say is that from watching my sister I know that women can feel terribly low after childbirth.'

Thirza nodded. 'I do feel very up and down. I've always dealt with things by keeping busy. But even that when you're so tired is too hard.'

'Lots of women suffer in silence. I'm just saying you don't have to.'

The room went quiet for a few minutes

'I know Romi is only a couple of weeks old,' Penny said. 'And I really do want to help in any way I can. You see, my sister did go downhill.'

'What happened in the end?'

There was an uncomfortable pause and Thirza wondered what was coming.

Then Penny quietly said, 'I'm afraid she hanged herself.'

At that Thirza burst into tears and, terribly shocked, leant forward and covered her face with her hands. She heard the crackle of the fire and Romi snuffling.

Penelope remained silent.

'I'm so sorry about your sister,' Thirza whispered, as she wiped her eyes. 'You must have been absolutely devastated.'

'Your father helped me through the aftermath of Angela's death. That's probably why he and I fell in love. I don't know what I'd have done without him.'

They sat in silence for a few moments and Thirza knew she had to say something more but still she couldn't find the right words. It was unimaginable. She had categorised Penny far too cruelly, she realised, and wished she'd known about this tragedy from the start. There was so much more to Penelope's story and character than she had thought. She should have been kinder and must try harder now.

Penny reached over and patted her hand. 'Shall we discuss ideas? Give us both something else to think about and, honestly, I *do* think you could make a go of turning Merchant's into a top-class guest house.'

Thirza smiled at Penny's enthusiasm.

'That's better,' Penny said.

'Thank you for listening and telling me about Angela. You've been so kind. I just need to feed Romi now and change her.'

Upstairs, after laying Romi down on the bed where she gurgled happily for a few moments, Thirza went to gaze out of her bedroom window, relieved to be on her own. The view was blurred, as a wintry sea mist was rising, making it impossible to see the dividing line between sea and sky. The garden too had a dreamy otherworldly feel to it. If the mist broke up, she would take a walk today, wrapping herself and Romi up in woollens. She really needed to stretch her limbs but had been feeling so tired since the birth she'd barely left the house, not even to walk in the garden.

She glanced back at the baby who was now twisting her head from side to side, rooting, her mouth wide open, and kicking her legs angrily. How Thirza longed for her mother to meet the new addition to the family, but in all the months since that terrible night they had not been in contact except for one letter. And you couldn't really call that contact. She had written just that once to tell Dulcie about Romi and had begged her to visit; it had hurt when her mother didn't even reply.

As she sat down to feed Romi, she wondered if Dulcie would ever speak to her again and dreaded the thought that Romi might never know her grandmother.

'Coffee and plentiful pastries for breakfasts,' Penny was saying to Piers as Thirza finally rejoined her. 'Bacon and eggs too.'

Piers beamed at Penny, clearly proud of her. 'Jolly good idea, darling.'

'What do you think, Thirza? Picnic hampers for lunch, and delicious dinners in the evening.'

Penny rose to her feet and began to walk about the room, glancing around now and again as if mulling everything over. 'Magdalena is an extraordinary cook, so you're off to a head start. And what about this . . . Spiro could take people for trips around the island on Dulcie's beautiful boat and you, Thirza, you could offer painting classes.'

'Oh! I'm not sure I can.'

Penny turned to stare at her. 'Of course you can. You'd be an excellent teacher. We'd need to ensure a stay at Merchant's is a heavenly break from the real world. A sanctuary. You know? A place to refresh the spirit.'

Thirza couldn't help grinning, for that was exactly how she'd always thought of Merchant's herself. How clever of Penny and how surprisingly practical she was turning out to be.

'The guests should have best-quality bed linen, constant hot water, different rates for different rooms, and seasonal differences too.'

'Gosh. You're thinking of everything.'

Penny sat down again and leant back in her chair with a satisfied smile.

'How will Thirza attract people to come here?' Piers asked.

Penny dismissed the question with a wave of her hand. 'Oh, that's easy, darling. Discreet adverts in classy English magazines like *The Lady*, *Good Housekeeping*, and *Tatler*. Don't you worry, I'll take care of all that. Thirza, *you* need to make a lovely drawing of Merchant's. Why don't we order writing paper with your drawing at the head of it and on postcards too which we will leave on the guests' pillows along with a little gift? Like chocolates or something. What's still left to finish in the house?'

'Spiro and I continued redecorating while I was pregnant, though not for the last couple of months. He had a building job on, and I was just too big and too lazy.'

'I can't imagine you being lazy. You're like me.'

'Am I?'

'We both like to get things done, don't we?'

Thirza nodded. Penny had a strong practical streak and of course she did too. Yet her own nature was somehow less clear-cut. Penny seemed to always know what she wanted, whereas Thirza was increasingly feeling rather at sea. She sighed deeply.

Penny rose to her feet again and reached for Thirza's hand. 'Don't worry. Come and see,' she said, and drew them both over to the window. 'Look, isn't that lovely?'

The mist was clearing in patches and a weak sun was shining through now. The garden looked newborn, as if emerging out of darkness.

'Out of the mists of Avalon,' Penny murmured. 'It's utterly enchanting.'

Thirza silently agreed.

'*That's* what we want our guests to feel. As if they've escaped to somewhere magical. But now back to practical matters. Spiro still has to see to the second bathroom?'

Thirza nodded. 'Yes. As you know, there's one for me and any personal guests of mine, like you and my father, and currently only one other. It's very basic and calling out for Spiro's attention. I do think we need one more than that as well. Mind you there was a time not that long ago when the toilet was in an outhouse. Mother could not abide it!'

It felt like an awful lot of pressure suddenly, and Thirza still had very mixed feelings about this project, but she had to find a way to make more money if she were to go on living here. Spiro, Eleni, and Magdalena needed paying and the bills were never ending. Along with commissions for her illustrations, she had been asked to produce line drawings for magazine advertisements, but that alone would not be enough, and living so far from London didn't help her to meet with potential clients.

'But it's going to be a country guest house,' Penny added. 'Not The Ritz, and people will not expect the same level of amenities. We must emphasise the charm of Merchant's and especially its stunning location.'

Penny had come up trumps, Thirza had to admit that. It would have once seemed impossible, but it did look as if they would be working together at least some of the time and might just make a good team.

Thirza smiled at her. 'You're practical *and* imaginative.'

'Ah, a woman of many talents, that's me. But Spiro needs to get a move on with the bathrooms if we're to open for the summer.'

Thirza gasped. 'This summer?'

'Of course. You need the money, don't you?'

'I can't afford a new bathroom yet.'

'Let me twist your father's arm just a little bit.'

Thirza laughed. Her father wasn't listening, reading the paper, but she knew he was not as wealthy as her mother. He rarely spoke of money, but she knew he'd lost heavily in the financial crash, his investments tumbling. He wasn't poor, had a good salary, but could ill afford to keep her going forever.

'You are incorrigible. But thank you. It must only be a loan. I know things are tricky for him and I want to support myself.'

Thirza really was grateful, though a stubborn voice inside her head was whispering, *Softly, softly*. She considered whether she ought to be keeping Penelope at arm's length, but then decided against it – whatever had come before, Penny had only shown her kindness from the moment she'd announced her pregnancy. And wasn't all the rage she'd felt on Dulcie's behalf a little tainted now – Dulcie was not wholly innocent either and had been unfaithful to Piers.

Hearing Romi, she took her leave and went upstairs to see if her baby was awake or simply dreaming.

How was it possible that Dulcie had not been in touch at all – Thirza could never imagine cutting out her darling Romi. Also, she had no idea if her mother would even allow the trust to go ahead. Would she still be happy for Thirza to own Merchant's now that she knew about Emilio? It didn't seem likely for it must hurt terribly to find out her daughter had given birth to a baby, by the very man she had once been in love with herself! The man who was Billy's real father.

Billy. Sweet, sweet, Billy.

Thirza had read those long-ago letters and couldn't get her mother's heartbreak and the words she had used out of her mind. *It is as if everything has come to an end, and I do not know how to live.* And the most upsetting thing of all was that she didn't know if her mother would ever forgive her. It felt so unfair for it had not been her fault. She hadn't known anything about the connection between Dulcie and Emilio.

CHAPTER 39

Spring

Life settled into something of a routine. And now the birds were singing, the weather was gentle, the sea a delicate lilac colour, and at nearly three months old, Romi was still sleeping much of the time. Thirza had managed to do some illustration work over the last month and was feeling pleased that she'd finally finished a decent drawing of Merchant's the night before. But her greatest joy, no question, was every moment spent with the most adorable baby who had ever lived.

And yet since giving birth to her daughter, Billy was constantly in Thirza's mind. She remembered the excitement when he was born, her father racing down the stairs beaming, calling to everyone, proud that he finally had a son; her mother sitting up in bed, pale but smiling.

While Romi still slept, she went up to the nursery. She didn't use it herself. It was still too full of Billy, and she wanted to preserve that sense of him, and never change it, so Romi slept in the same room as her.

In the top drawer of a white-painted chest, she fingered soft little jackets friends had knitted for Billy when he was about Romi's age and she felt a rush of new feelings and sadness about his absence from their lives. What part might he have played in Romi's life had he lived, what part would he play now that he had not? From a lower drawer she pulled out a pair of dungarees he'd worn as a toddler. She held them to her nose but the scent of him was long gone. How her mother must have suffered after his death. She couldn't begin to imagine how she would feel if Romi died. Didn't believe she could go on living, and yet women did lose children, and they did go on living. Somehow.

She recalled the look on Billy's face when he had first realised he could walk. Sheer joy! And then he'd wailed when he'd plopped back down on his backside and couldn't get up again.

Eleni kept saying Romi's eyes might change colour but right now they hadn't. Thirza went back to her bedroom, fed and changed her daughter, then placed her in her carrying basket where the little girl kicked her feet in delight, utterly mesmerised by her own toes. Thirza was enchanted, the mere sight of Romi enough to make her feel better.

She picked up the basket and went down to the kitchen to have her breakfast. Magdalena poured her a coffee then reached out for the basket and nodded towards a stack of envelopes on the table. *Yet more bills*, Thirza thought, and her heart sank.

Since she had written that letter telling her mother of Romi's birth, there had still been no reply. But now she spotted a light blue envelope sticking out from the rest. Did she dare hope this might be from Dulcie? For didn't her mother have to learn to accept this? Somehow. Surely, she would forgive Thirza eventually. Dulcie could not be happy never to see her daughter again, especially as she had been in such despair after she lost Billy. Thirza gazed at Romi as Magdalena began to move away. She saw so much of Billy in her little girl that it made her heart ache.

When Magdalena had gone, she turned the envelope over and, as she saw the Italian stamp, her pulse quickened.

Eleni said, 'If you look at it closely you will see it must have been posted a month ago.'

'Delayed somehow, I suppose.'

'Italians!' Eleni muttered in a harrumphing sort of a way. She still hadn't forgiven them for 1923.

Thirza tore the envelope open, though whether in anger or in expectation she couldn't, or wouldn't, even admit to herself. Emilio was pleading to be allowed to come and explain himself in person. She read only the first paragraph and then, boiling over with anger, ripped the paper into shreds. How dare he?! How dare he bloody well even breathe after what he'd done.

She drank her coffee, burnt her tongue, and chewed one mouthful of toast.

'You need to eat more,' Eleni said.

'Not hungry. I'm going out.'

Recently she'd gone for a few long, lonely walks in the countryside, or in the foothills of Mount Pantokrator, or along the beach, and she usually liked to take her sketchbook to draw anything that caught her eye. A tree. A view of the sea. The Albanian mountains.

Today she decided to take Romi, not her sketchbook, knowing the feeling of being out in the gentle spring air, putting one foot in front of the other, would calm her. These extreme sudden bursts of anger still took her by surprise – the incandescent heat of them – but she knew they weren't good for little Romi, or for her own milk supply, so she tried to remain as tranquil as possible. Enforced serenity was hardly a natural state for her, but she had to put someone else before herself. She had to put Romi before her own feelings. Whatever they were.

From the bottom of the garden she glanced at the sea, glassy with only gentle rippling waves, and she took a long slow breath, drawing courage and strength from the everlasting nature of the natural world. It would be there long after she had gone, and her present worries would have become as insignificant as a grain of sand. Looking up at the sky and watching the birds she knew they already were insignificant in the greater scheme of things. Everything was going to be fine. As she thought that she heard Billy's voice.

Thizzy, Thizzy.

Moo. Moo. I'm a cowboy.

She had laughed as he'd run about grinning like a mad thing and holding his fingers on either side of his head so that they looked like horns.

But she had to make a new life now, the beginning of the guest house, and yet, despite looking ahead, she still yearned to see her mother, and to know what had really happened to Billy in 1923.

It was such a tangled mess. The fact that Emilio was Billy's father still shocked her every time she thought of it.

And as for Emilio, he had lost the son he didn't even know he'd had. And what about her father? Did he still not know the truth? Did it matter? Surely it had to matter.

On her way home she saw Emilio ahead of her, instantly knew it was him, recognised the way he walked, how he held himself. Her instinct was to escape. She turned away, intending to run, but as she did, she stumbled and one glance at the ground was enough to stop her going on. The path was far too stony and uneven for running, and she was carrying the baby. Oh God! Her heart was pounding wildly, but she took a long slow breath and drew comfort from Romi pressed close up against her like this, and feeling like she was still a part of her.

You are not alone, she told herself. *You are not alone*.

And then Emilio was right there, standing just a few feet away with his hand over his mouth. He wasn't even looking at her. He was looking at Romi, staring, his eyes wide with shock mixed with something akin to longing. She glimpsed another life, one she could never have, not with Emilio.

'I . . . I had to come,' he said hesitantly. 'But I didn't, I didn't *know*. Why didn't you tell me?'

'This is Romi,' Thirza said, keeping her voice low and cool. 'She was born in February.'

'My daughter?' he asked almost in a whisper.

She gave him a look.

'Can I see her?'

His eyes were intense, dark, pleading, and she could not bear it. She took a step back, pulling the shawl over her baby's head.

'Please.'

She shook her head. 'You have no place in my life.'

'And the baby?'

'Nor in hers.'

He reached out as if to touch her arm and she took another step back.

She had never gone in for lectures on what was right or wrong. If it didn't hurt anyone, how could it be wrong? Yet her relationship with Emilio *had* hurt others. Her mother. The ugly truth was she had hurt her mother terribly and Emilio had allowed her to. Even her own daughter had been hurt, deprived of her father. Thirza had tried to persuade herself that it didn't matter. She would be mother and father. But it did matter.

'Won't you let me explain?' he said. 'You didn't reply to my letter. I sent it a month ago.'

'Well, it was only delivered this morning. But my answer is still the same. Now, please can you get out of the way.'

'The child? I could help support you?'

'No!'

He stood his ground. 'Thirza, I've come back to Corfu because I needed to see you.'

'Please stop.'

'I love my girls, but I was devastated to discover I had a son I never knew anything about. I'm haunted by it. You must see that. Billy was *my* son, and I never knew anything about him. I knew nothing of his life, nor of his death. And I want to know more.'

'For God's sake, Emilio! I'm sorry, but can't you understand, I don't want to talk about this. Not ever.'

'Please.' His voice broke and she could feel his distress.

She squeezed her eyes shut, trying to stop this from reaching her, from touching her where it could still hurt.

'It's no excuse but my marriage had already failed when I met you, and I was missing my daughters.'

'Stop this, Emilio! Stop now!'

'I didn't know Dulcie was your mother. You didn't tell me. I met *you* and I fell in love.'

'No!' She was shouting at him now but then, feeling Romi stirring, she lowered her voice. 'No more! That's enough.'

'I didn't set out to have a brief affair. I love you, Thirza. I want to spend my life with you.'

'And what about my mother? Did you want to spend your life with *her* too?'

'No! I was only just twenty when I met her. A young twenty at that. She was an elegant older woman, twenty-eight I think, and I felt immensely flattered. It was the briefest of affairs. I had no idea it meant anything more to her. I had no idea about Billy.'

'You should have told me about all of that.'

He sighed. 'There was no reason to tell you. It was just something that happened in my past and was long over. Until you explained who *you* really were. Not some worker employed to paint the house, but Dulcie's daughter. At that point I ran away. I'm sorry. I was a coward, and when I came back, I was afraid to tell you the truth. I tried a couple of times but just couldn't say the words.'

'And you told me your name was Emilio.'

'I said my friends called me Emilio. When I met your mother, I wanted to impress her and gave her my full name. She always preferred Federico. Said it sounded jaunty.'

'Well, you're not obligated to me in any way. I have plans of my own now, and I need to get home to feed my daughter.' Thirza knew her voice was shaking but she couldn't help it, and she didn't look at him. If she looked while feeling so vulnerable, she would be lost.

'But Thirza—'

'No buts, Emilio. Please go back to Italy.'

He stood aside without another word, and she walked on and didn't turn back to check if he was still watching her. But she felt his eyes on her back, burning through her clothes, into her skin, into her heart, and she could almost feel herself sinking once more into him. Loving him. Allowing him to love her. She gulped at the air and then straightened her back.

I have to get over him. I have to.

CHAPTER 40

When Thirza finally got back to the house, tears streaming down her cheeks, she heard voices in the drawing room. A quick glance told her Ianthe and Walter must have arrived. Oh, not now! She could just imagine what Walter might be thinking about her being an unmarried mother. The couple had been in London for the last few months, but Ianthe had written to ask if they could come to see the baby. Thirza hadn't known exactly when they would arrive and hoped it might not happen at all, but here they were. With a brief wave of her hand, she raced up the stairs, went straight to her room, and locked the door behind her. She laid Romi in her cradle, grabbed a pillow, and then she dropped to the floor where she lay curled up, her heart aching.

After a few minutes she heard knocking at her door and stiffened.

'Thirza, can I come in? It's Columbine.'

'Just a second,' she called out. Thirza hadn't noticed Columbine downstairs, but she scrambled up off the floor, stretched, pulled her shoulders back, and splashed her face in the small hand basin in her room.

'Dear me,' Columbine said as Thirza opened the door to her. 'You look—'

'Terrible, I know. I feel it too.'

'As if you have been crying, is what I was going to say.'

'I need to feed Romi. She's beginning to snuffle. But you can come in if you don't mind.'

'Shall we sit together over there?' Columbine gestured at the two pale blue armchairs near the window.

Thirza nodded.

Before she sat down, Columbine glanced out of the window. 'Lovely day,' she remarked.

It truly was a glorious sunny day now, with just a few low-lying white clouds, and all the spring flowers coming into bloom, the garden leaping back into life.

As Thirza picked up the baby and then settled her at the breast with a discreet lacy shawl to ensure decency, she took a good look at Columbine. The woman was thinner, looked worn out, but seemed completely sober. Had she finally come to terms with things? Had the treatment with the psychiatrist helped her?

'Have you heard from my mother recently?' Thirza asked.

Columbine shook her head.

'Me neither.'

'I, well yes, actually I did see her once, very briefly at her house.'

The woman had spoken reluctantly, as if she didn't want to think about Dulcie at all.

'Did she say anything?'

'Barely a word. You know . . .' Columbine glanced around as if she wasn't sure if it was safe to speak, but then she continued. 'Between you and me, I always suspected Dulcie's affair meant far more to her than to him.'

'You knew about it?' Thirza couldn't keep the surprise from her voice and stared at her. Was Columbine making this up?

'I guessed.' Columbine heaved a long sigh. 'She was frequently unhappy with your father, as you probably know, though as far as I could tell she was fully reconciled to the marriage. She had a family, and an enviable life which she protected fiercely.'

Thirza needed to know what was going to happen to Merchant's and the question was on the tip of her tongue. But it wasn't something she could discuss with Columbine. 'What made you guess?' she asked instead.

'She changed.'

For a moment Thirza felt like a confused child betrayed by her mother's affair. 'How could she have an affair behind my father's back if her life was so great?'

'I don't know. But for a brief while she became her old self again. Delighted by life. Joyous. Not at all the grave, hard-working woman. Suddenly, her eyes sparkled, the resignation left her face, and she was happy.'

'I remember my mother always at her desk, except when we were here in Corfu. In London only her work mattered.'

'Until Billy was born?'

'I suppose so.'

'Of course, divorce for adultery was unlikely, unless she caused a scandal.'

'There was no salacious gossip?'

'Not that I heard.'

Thirza thought again of those desperate love letters her mother had never sent and felt such a powerful mixture of sadness and disloyalty it almost made her cry again, but she swallowed hard and managed to get a grip.

'Give her time,' Columbine said and reached across to pat her hand. 'She will come round.'

The image of her mother finding her in bed with Emilio flooded her mind, and with it the shame. 'How much do you know about—''

'About you?' Columbine interjected.

'Yes.'

'Not much. Rather unexpectedly, Piers took me into his confidence, but he didn't say much.'

'Luckily my father doesn't know everything.'

Columbine raised one brow and said, 'Always a good thing when it comes to Piers.'

Thirza smiled but then grew serious. 'Romi is Dulcie's granddaughter, but she hasn't even come to see her.'

'That is a shame. Look, I don't know the ins and outs of your rift, but your mother is a proud woman.'

Thirza narrowed her eyes, thinking, then she said, 'I've never thought of her like that.'

Columbine sniffed. 'How well do we ever know our parents? And Dulcie is something of a closed book.'

'Yes . . . but she's my mother and I need her, and it hurts that she's rejecting not only me but Romi too. I would never reject my child like this.'

A strange, unsettled look crossed Columbine's face. The old, haunted, guilty look that had swallowed her after

Billy disappeared. 'We never know of what we are capable until it happens,' she said, sounding almost bitter.

Thirza sighed.

'Build your life here. Let Dulcie do things in her own way. You are still her daughter,' Columbine said.

Thirza didn't say, but wondered if it was just that Dulcie felt betrayed by her, or if, at some unconscious level, she might be punishing her for not being Billy. It seemed ridiculous, but people were complex with complicated motives. And how much of life was a result of conscious choice anyway?

She took a long slow breath. No point going over it again and again.

Only one thing really mattered now. Did Dulcie still intend to go ahead with forming the trust to keep Merchant's safe? She didn't dare ask if Columbine knew, for there had always been bad blood about the ownership of the estate, and although Columbine had changed a lot, she had always been at the heart of that.

CHAPTER 41

The next morning Ianthe and Walter, their heads close together, were deep in conversation and Columbine was nowhere to be seen. Thirza coughed to signal her presence, and they spun round self-consciously.

'Secrets?' Thirza said with rather a forced laugh.

There was an awkward atmosphere as they stared at her. She had last spoken to Ianthe on the phone from her father's house, when the girl had been harshly disapproving of Thirza's pregnancy. Had she seen it as another risk to her relationship with Walter? It would certainly be a bone of contention between the pair.

Ianthe, dressed all in blue silk, recovered first and smiled, her eyes sparkling. 'Look!' she said and held out her hand where, on her ring finger, a large diamond surrounded by sapphires glittered in the sunlight.

Thirza glanced at it, and then turned her attention to Walter. Could Ianthe really be happy with a man as stiff as he? And yet it couldn't be easy for him to come here again. So that had to be something in his favour.

'I have . . . business to attend to,' Walter said, red-faced under Thirza's scrutiny, then added gruffly, 'But I'm sure Ianthe is anxious to see the baby. Congratulations.'

He was wearing a three-piece suit, an overcoat, and a hat. *He must be boiling*, Thirza thought. He certainly looked uncomfortable as he backed away. 'I'll see you later, Ianthe.'

When he'd gone, Ianthe held out her hand again, twisting it this way and that, the diamond changing as it caught the light. 'Isn't it lovely? Walter went down on one knee last night on the beach.'

Thirza nodded, thinking how uncharacteristically romantic that must have been.

Ianthe frowned. 'You don't look very pleased.'

'Sorry. Shall we walk and you can tell me all about it? Beach or orchard?'

'What about Romi?' Ianthe asked.

'She's fallen asleep. I'll just go and ask Magdalena to listen out.'

'Beach. Let's go there.'

As Thirza headed for the kitchen to find Magdalena, she felt a little ashamed to feel a tiny twinge of envy. It was truly embarrassing and didn't make any sense at all. Would she ever want to marry a man like Walter? Absolutely not. And yet there was something seductive about that kind of certainty.

She hoped this marriage would be good for Ianthe. The girl had always longed to be settled – her unpredictable childhood had seen to that – and she'd wanted financial security too. And Walter, whose family were immensely wealthy, was the one who could make her dreams come true. Thirza wondered if Columbine was still invited to go to America with them.

'Are you all right? You seemed out of sorts when we arrived,' Ianthe said when Thirza joined her again.

'Of course,' Thirza replied, though she absolutely could not have been further from *all right*.

'Look, before we go down to the beach, there's something I have to say.'

Thirza's heart sank. 'Go on.'

'I'm sorry for what I said on the phone,' Ianthe continued. 'I really came back here to apologise, to try to put things right. I needed to get it off my chest and I wanted to meet Romi too, of course.'

Surprised by all this, Thirza let out a long slow breath, and it struck her how much Ianthe had grown up.

'Can you forgive me?' Ianthe pleaded. 'Please.'

Did she forgive Ianthe? She didn't really know what to say but decided on the truth. 'I was hurt. All alone, Ianthe, and frightened. I asked you to come for the birth because I needed you.'

'I'm really sorry,' the girl said. 'I know I let you down.'

'I suppose it doesn't matter now,' Thirza said, happy not to talk about this any further and, seeing the relief in Ianthe's eyes, she reached out to hug her.

A few minutes later the two of them headed down the levels of the garden to the little cove, where they sat on the rocks skimming pebbles across the water and laughing at their lack of expertise. In the gentle breeze the air smelt strongly of seaweed, brine, and fish, and the sky was a bright electric blue.

'Penny for them,' Ianthe said, turning to Thirza.

'Oh nothing.'

'You're sure? You looked sad.'

Thirza nodded then asked, 'Is Columbine going with you?'

'I think so.'

'What does that mean?'

'She has a boyfriend.'

Thirza couldn't help laughing. 'Oh my God! I can hardly believe it. How do you feel about it?'

'Relieved. She's ever so much better, though something still bothers her, and I don't know what it is.'

'Probably just life.'

Life was certainly bothering Thirza one way or another. There seemed to be so much to think about or do and she still needed time to come to terms with her mixed feelings about seeing Emilio.

They sat in silence for a while and, to take her mind off everything else, Thirza went over lists in her head once again, though that didn't really help. Even with the cash she'd found in her mother's study, the money was running out now, and she wasn't sure how to prioritise things. Anxiety over bills was consuming her, and with constant dreams of failure, or the loss of Merchant's, waking her every night, heart pounding, sheets drenched in sweat, she was tired. She had racked her brains trying to find savings in her outgoings, but it seemed as if there was no way through and only disaster lay ahead. It was all expense with very little income.

If they were to open for the summer, which she had to do, she still needed to order bed linen, blankets, towels, crockery, cutlery, napkins, tablecloths, soap, and whatever else Penny had in mind. They had quite a collection already of course but most was mismatched, chipped, or had been mended again and again and yet still had holes in it. It had to be new, and it had to be quality.

'You do realise I haven't seen Romi yet,' Ianthe was saying, drawing Thirza back from her worries. 'You didn't bring her downstairs yesterday. Does she look like him? Emilio.'

'A little. It's hard to tell. She looks very much like herself.'

'Just like you then!'

'Am I like that?'

'Of course. You are the most like yourself person I've ever met. And I do love you, Thizzy.'

'Oh Ianthe. Don't make me cry.'

Ianthe laughed. 'Sorry.'

'He came back, you know. Yesterday. That's why I was out of sorts. You were right.'

'Emilio came back?'

Thirza nodded.

'You never told me why he went away in the first place. I heard your father and Penny talking about it when I was staying with them.'

'Well, they don't know either, unless my mother told them.'

Ianthe's eyes widened. 'Your mother!'

Thirza sighed. 'She was here.'

'I didn't know.'

'No one does. It was months ago. She arrived and then left the same day.'

Ianthe looked stunned. 'Well, my goodness. What a strange bunch we all are.'

'Not you though. Not once you are Mrs Walter!'

'Well, our wedding is going to have to be in America so it'll be very small as I don't know a single soul over there. You *would* be invited but Walter doesn't want his parents to know about Romi, or rather he doesn't want them knowing that you aren't married, and if you came everyone would be asking where your husband was. So . . .'

Thirza gave the girl an exasperated look. 'Honestly, Walter does take the biscuit. Won't you find it hard living up to his strict expectations? And his family's too?'

'Maybe, but it's what I'm going to do whether you like it or not.'

'And you're absolutely sure?'

Ianthe nodded.

Thirza laughed. 'Well, it's your funeral, I suppose.'

On the way back up to the house the garden was smelling wonderful, and they took their time, lingering over the roses and watching the birds.

'By the way, Penny asked if I might take the drawing of Merchant's back to Corfu Town with me.'

Thirza hesitated. She would rather deliver it herself for safety's sake. It had taken ages to get right, and she didn't want it to arrive damaged. Maybe she'd go to Corfu Town herself and take Romi with her. People could stare as much as they liked, but she would hold her head up and hide away no more. Romi had been born from love and that was what mattered. She would talk to Spiro about the final bathroom and then go with them all on the boat.

'You've gone quiet,' Ianthe said, interrupting her thoughts.

'Sorry. Do you happen to know where Columbine is?'

'In your mother's study. Apparently, Dulcie asked her to find something.'

'Really? I thought they hadn't spoken?'

Ianthe shrugged.

Thirza couldn't believe Dulcie would ask Columbine to find anything. She left Ianthe sitting on the terrace and hurried to her mother's study. She opened the door and went in but there was no sign of Columbine.

Wandering back outside, she smelt smoke. She ran towards the source of it, spotting Spiro striding away in the opposite direction and Columbine standing alone in front of the bonfire he must have built for her.

'What are you doing?' Thirza asked, as she approached. 'And what the hell were you doing rooting around in my mother's study?'

The woman spun round with a mortified look on her face. 'It's just a small bonfire. I'm burning some bits and pieces. Spiro said it was probably too windy for a bigger fire.'

Right on cue the breeze gusted, and Thirza coughed. She brushed her hair from her eyes and as she moved in closer, she gasped. 'Dear God, those are my mother's letters! How dare you burn them?!'

'You know about them?'

'Give them to me!' Thirza snapped, furious now. She pushed the woman away from the fire and tried to grab the letters, but failed as Columbine held them out of her reach. This was too much. She made another attempt, and this time snatched the remaining few letters.

Her eyes were stinging and watering from the smoke and she had nothing to wipe them with, so had to use the back of her hand. She felt a tight band of tension around her head, and it was only then she spotted that among the letters she also held that awful anonymous note in her hand.

'You know anything about this?' she demanded.

The only sound was the spluttering of the fire.

'No,' Columbine paused, and everything felt extremely odd. Eventually Columbine said, 'I told you I saw her. She asked me to burn all these for her.'

Thirza didn't believe her. Dulcie would not have asked Columbine to do this.

Thirza glanced at the fire, dying down a little now, then back up at the woman. 'Even if that were true, you can't burn this. Isn't it evidence?'

'Of what? Nothing came of it.' Then Columbine spoke more gently. 'Billy's not coming back. You know that.'

Thirza looked away. Even now, she could not quite believe that Billy was gone. It had made no sense then, and it still didn't now. Especially as his body had never been found. Thirza didn't know if that would have helped. If they had been able to bury him, would her doubts have been laid to rest, too? But it was pointless wondering. Most likely poor little Billy had been washed out to sea, or buried somewhere they would never find him. Try and say goodbye once and for all. That's what everyone said. But the truth was, and always had been, that she did not really believe that Billy was dead, or at the very least that he had died in the way they said. Something more was going on.

'Do you know what that note means?'

Columbine looked uncomfortable as she sighed and said, 'No. I think Dulcie knows but I don't.'

'Is it something in the past?'

'Maybe. Do you think your father could have sent it? If he knew about the affair, I mean?'

Thirza was shocked – but thinking back to what Piers had said about Italian men, could it be possible? On reflection it seemed far too childish a thing for a grown man to do, so she dismissed it from her mind.

'Why didn't Dulcie give it to the police?' she asked, angry now. 'It might have helped the investigation.'

'There's no date on it, so we don't know when it arrived. And if *she* knew what it referred to, maybe she just didn't want the police knowing.'

Thirza glanced again at the horrible words on the yellowing paper, and the warning of something she couldn't even begin to grasp. She wiped her stinging eyes again and read the words once more.

YoU are GOing TO Pay FOR wHaT YOu did

But what had her mother done and did it still matter now?

CHAPTER 42

Corfu Town

All the talk at her father's house was about Mussolini. Fascism had arisen in parts of Europe following the end of the Great War, when people were desperate for national unity and longing for strong leadership. It was becoming clearer that in Italy, Benito Mussolini was using his personal magnetism to develop an unassailable fascist state, his rise dizzying and incomprehensible to outsiders.

As she listened to Walter, her father, and Odel's husband, Thaddeus, talking during dinner, the main reason Thirza concerned herself over this was because Emilio was Italian and therefore Romi was half Italian. She had told nobody that she'd declared both herself and Emilio as Romi's parents on the birth certificate. She hadn't wanted to leave the space for *father* blank, but might this become a problem? People were talking about Mussolini as a great leader, who had adopted the title *Il Duce*, or 'The Leader', back in 1925, but nobody knew what he was planning to do next.

'That's populism for you. His speeches are emotional,' Thaddeus said, and Columbine nodded but didn't speak.

'And the crowd roars its support,' he continued. 'I've witnessed it.'

'You have to admire the way he's organising industry,' Walter said. 'Agriculture too, and the trains, all into state-controlled labour unions and employer associations. In my book that has to be good news.'

'Maybe,' Piers said, 'but I don't trust him. Not after 1923 when the Italians bombarded and occupied Corfu. We never knew the exact number, but anything between five thousand to ten thousand troops landed here. Twenty people were killed, mainly refugee children, and over thirty were wounded.'

There was a sudden pause, a silence for a moment, in respect for what was left unsaid here – for Billy went missing in the midst of all that had happened then. Columbine, looking pale, stared down at her plate and Thirza, struck by finding herself on the sidelines of such a masculine conversation, felt a tug to her heart and missed her brother all over again.

Billy covered in mud, and falling about laughing, as he chased her.

Thizzy. Thizzy. I'm coming to get you.

And she'd be hiding in the undergrowth and picking leaves, twigs, and insects from her curly hair for hours afterwards.

She missed Merchant's too, where the women were in charge. This ponderous male conversation made her feel fifteen years old and voiceless. She, Penny and Columbine remained mainly silent – Odel would have spoken up but she was busy elsewhere.

'I guess we will just have to wait and see,' Walter was saying.

'His "Blackshirts" have been very heavy-handed,' Piers added. 'It's a dangerous time, mark my words.'

Odel's husband asked Thirza how everything was going with setting up the hotel. She was grateful to him and smiled. He'd always been kind and was clearly trying to include her.

Walter laughed and she could see by the supercilious look on his face just how preposterous he thought she was. Could imagine exactly what he wanted to say.

An unwed mother planning to run a business? Ridiculous.

At a time when women rarely controlled their own lives, he wouldn't be the only one who'd be thinking that. Did all the men think she was crazy?

In a way they were right, for it was an unusual situation, but she was determined, if a little scared. Well, if she were perfectly honest, very scared at times. But she was doing this for Romi, so it had to succeed no matter what, and at least her father was on her side.

After dinner, while the men smoked outside in the pretty courtyard garden surrounded by lavender, rosemary, and mint, Thirza took Penny aside and away from Columbine's hearing. The woman might have been much improved but there was something about her Thirza still didn't trust and she didn't want her knowing too much of her business.

To Penny she quietly said, 'I know my father can't do any more for me, so I'm going to the bank to see if I can arrange a loan. It's not something I've done before, but I must have cash to pay for the new bathroom.'

She didn't add that when she thought of all the things she still needed to buy, it made her feel physically sick, terrified that she was about to sink into a dark hole from which there would be no escape, the anxiety forming a hard knot in her stomach.

Before Thirza went out the following morning, she called Penny into her bedroom intending to ask for her advice. It might be a wrong move, but she needed help.

'This is the dress I thought I'd wear to go to the bank,' she said. 'What do you think?'

A little nervously she strode up and down in a smart pink-and-green floral dress, drop-waisted, and cut simply in the shape of a shift. She'd expected the dress to be tight as she'd bought it long before she was pregnant, and it had hung in the wardrobe in Piers' house for a couple of years.

Penny frowned. 'It's fine, but maybe add silk stockings, Cuban-heeled shoes, and one of your mother's hats.'

Thirza chose one made by Dulcie's favourite milliner, and Penny found her some shoes and stockings. 'They're your mother's. I'm afraid I packed them away. I hope that's all right.'

'Of course,' she said, though she wasn't really sure.

When she was ready she gave Penny a rather self-conscious little twirl.

'So?' she asked.

'You look lovely.'

'Not too tight on the bust?'

Penny shook her head. 'Actually, you look rather unexpectedly beautiful. I didn't realise you brushed up quite so well. However, I suggest red lipstick and I have the most darling diamanté clips that would look lovely in your hair. And don't be above showing a bit of leg.'

'Honestly, Penny!'

But Thirza was smiling, enjoying their newly improved relationship.

'Don't worry, it will be all right.'

'God, I hope so. I don't know what I'll do if they don't approve a loan.'

'They will. You'll see.'

It was a bright warm day, and Thirza enjoyed the sudden feeling of freedom as she left the house and headed towards the bank. 'Please don't let them refuse,' she whispered to herself as she marched along swinging her arms. If they refused, the guest house might never happen, and she'd have no way to support herself and Romi.

The bank was one her parents had always used and was rather an old-fashioned, gloomy sort of a place, but Thirza had chosen to set up her own account there too.

She was given a comfortable chair and a cup of tea along with a garibaldi biscuit, not her favourite, and she waited anxiously for what seemed an interminably long time, her palms sweating. She kept her eye on the comings and goings of staff and clients and eventually a thin bespectacled young man wished her good morning, then led her through to a wood-panelled room at the back which overlooked a small garden full of climbing roses.

'What may I help you with, Miss Caruthers-Moreland?'

She could feel the sweat prickling the back of her neck now, but she took a breath and just came out with it. 'I want to know how I go about taking out a loan for my new business. I've never done this before.'

'You have recent accounts, showing profits and losses?'

'Oh no. The business isn't open yet. I need to finish the work on the house first. That's why I need a loan, you see, to put in a new bathroom.'

'How much do you need to borrow?'

When she mentioned a sum, he laughed. She was taken aback. Was it so very much?

'With no accounts, and therefore no clear repayment scheme possible, you would have to provide surety. Your home perhaps? Merchant's, isn't it?'

'Yes. I didn't know I needed to do that.'

'Or any other security you could offer? Property or land? Valuable belongings, jewellery, paintings, and so on.'

Her spirits sinking, she shook her head and felt like a fool.

'You may wonder why I smile. Let me explain, Miss Moreland. The thing is you already have a very healthy bank balance, enough for . . . I don't know, maybe twenty bathrooms.'

'What?'

'So, unless you have enormous debts and the loan is essential, I would not recommend taking one out, even if you could provide security.'

'I don't understand.'

'Let me show you.' He went over to his desk, flicked through a file, and then passed her a sheet of paper. 'There, you see.'

She did see but frowned, nevertheless.

'And if you look to the right, you'll see, in the other column, that a large amount was paid in recently from an Italian bank.'

She stared at the spot he indicated and gasped.

'The money was deposited here in your account by a representative of the Bellini Hotel in Naples. You see?'

He sounded as if he were talking to a child, and she gazed up at him, but now he looked a little worried, a line appearing between his brows.

'You seem shocked,' he said. 'Are you aware of the hotel? Could this be an error?'

'I . . . I . . . know the owner,' she stuttered.

'Well, there you are. An unexpected windfall is always a delight. Now I know what you ladies are like. I have a wife myself. Newly married in fact.' And he rubbed his hands together, rather gleefully.

She didn't reply, still unable to take in the amount Emilio had given her.

He smiled. 'So, a little dress shopping, or a new hat perhaps, to celebrate.'

She replied automatically, still stunned, and not really knowing how she felt about all this. 'Actually, I'm going to buy sheets, towels, and cutlery.'

As she left the bank her spirits sank. She would have to return the huge sum to Emilio. Insist on having nothing to do with it. She would give it back. That was all. She didn't want to be beholden to him, and yet Romi was his daughter after all, and running a thriving guest house might be the only chance she had to keep the roof over her daughter's head.

How could she possibly go on without any money? Apart from the new bathroom, she had bills to pay and staff to pay, and right now she could do neither.

She saw her beloved Merchant's slipping away from her. She saw Dulcie selling up. She saw herself having to leave Corfu, her tail between her legs, and having to beg a home with her mother until she found her feet in England. She doubted Dulcie would even have her, and she could hardly live with Piers and Penny. She did have some income, but it wasn't nearly enough. She had prayed for something, something definite to help her set up her new life, and this was what had arrived. Without it, if she were unable to support her daughter, she might even lose her, and that thought brought hot tears burning her eyelids. Dulcie wouldn't let that happen, would she?

Thirza felt lost. Terribly, terribly lost. It was hard to forge your own path in life when so much was stacked against you. Yet she was one of the lucky ones who'd always had a safety net. A loving family. Money. She had never before realised how privileged her life had been.

She glanced at the sky and then at the sea. She'd wanted to pull herself out of the dark place she had been in, but Emilio had done it for her and she had very mixed feelings. But there was nothing for it. She would pay him back. Every single penny. She would pay him back. For now, she *had* to keep the money. And with it she would make life at Merchant's a success. She had wanted to do it on her own but, finally, she raised her arms high and cast her doubts into the blue that surrounded her.

'So be it,' she said to the birds flying overhead. 'So be it.'

And at last, allowing the growing feeling of elation and relief, she went shopping.

She met Ianthe, Columbine, and Penny for lunch and told them what had happened. All gaped in astonishment.

'Well, aren't you the lucky one,' Columbine said rather sourly, earning herself a disapproving look from Ianthe. 'Why has Emilio done that?'

'Mother,' Ianthe whispered. 'You know why.'

Penny stepped in to shut Columbine up too and, with a mock stern look on her face, she narrowed her eyes at Thirza. 'Now don't you go thinking you shouldn't accept it.'

Thirza laughed. 'Well, I did think that for a while, but now that I've already spent some of it, it's too late.'

Penny laughed. 'Good for you! He's doing the right thing, and by the way the baby is with your father.'

'Oh God! Really?'

Penny nodded and looked a little crestfallen. 'He insisted. Told me to go out for lunch. I wanted to look after her myself.'

'Anyway,' Ianthe added. 'Emilio did run off and leave you, so blooming well keep the money.'

'He didn't run off,' Thirza said quietly. 'I threw him out.'

Penny exchanged glances with Ianthe and Columbine then said, 'You are a dark horse. And I don't suppose you're going to tell us why.'

'Correct,' Thirza said and smiled as she thought back over the morning.

She had been balanced on the edge of a precipice, but at least she had plucked up enough courage to visit the bank to ask for a loan. She hadn't taken anyone with her, and she had done it off her own back. But with Emilio's money nothing was going to stop her now. And just as soon as she could do it, all that money was going to go right back to him. With interest! Yes, he had been the one to pull her out of a hole, but *she* would be the one to make sure that she and Romi stayed out of it for good.

CHAPTER 43

The following year, early summer 1932

Mr and Mrs Taylor had booked a month-long stay at Merchant's and Thirza was hovering nervously at her bedroom window as she waited for their arrival. The bookings either came by mail to her here at Merchant's, or to Penny in the town, and both types were delivered by caique. When she received her very first booking late last summer, Thirza had cheered and danced around the kitchen with Romi. Now the little girl was tottering about on her own chubby little legs.

Thirza glanced out of the window and heard the carriage pull up, took a deep breath, and forced herself to walk slowly downstairs holding Romi's hand.

As Edwin Taylor helped his wife Harriet down, Thirza immediately saw the young woman looked far too thin, her face drawn, her eyes only on Romi. *Oh Lord! What has happened to her?* she thought.

While Spiro led Romi away and then dealt with their luggage, Thirza took the couple up to their room.

Mrs Taylor headed straight for the bathroom and Thirza addressed her husband. 'I'll organise some refreshment. I'm sure you must be tired. It's an exhausting journey from England.'

'That is most welcome, but actually,' he paused to lower his voice, 'we've only come from Italy where we spent a week. My wife . . . well my wife has been unwell.'

'I'm sorry to hear that. Let us hope Merchant's can help to restore her.'

He nodded but the look in his eyes was hard to read.

Thirza left them to it and asked Magdalena to take up a pot of tea and sandwiches, along with two slices of a recently baked seed cake. Then she went outside to find Romi, who was 'helping' Spiro in the garden. Romi adored the garden, and Thirza could only think that Dulcie would love to see her granddaughter so keen on the outdoors and sniffing all the different scents, with Georgie the dog at her heels. How could her mother fail to fall in love with her beautiful granddaughter? But Dulcie still had not written, not a single word, and she had not visited. So, there it was, and Thirza felt as if their estrangement might be final and everlasting.

When the Taylors came downstairs Edwin told her he was a journalist with *The Times*, and that he was worried because in 1922 the paper had been bought by John Jacob Astor, son of the first Viscount Astor, who was currently advocating appeasement of Hitler's demands.

'Darling, we said,' Harriet admonished him. 'No politics.'

'Sorry,' Edwin Taylor said. 'My wife loves to swim, sail, and climb, and we don't do enough of it.'

'Because my erudite husband mostly wants to read in peace,' Harriet added in a subdued tone of voice.

They both smiled awkwardly.

Nearly a year had gone by since the first few guests arrived, just five days after Spiro had completed the new bathroom. Although Penny had argued for bright and cheerful colours, Thirza opted for a timeless, elegant look with cool dark green walls offset by white tiles. Spiro had installed a pedestal basin, a large cast-iron, claw-footed, roll-top bathtub, in dark green to match the walls, though obviously with white porcelain inside. The floor tiles, patterned in black and white, were stunning, and delicate lace curtains hung at the window for modesty. Thirza had bought a mixture of towels – linen, waffle, Turkish cotton, and plain cotton – and was immensely proud of the overall result. Merchant's, however, was not yet breaking even.

A little later Thirza found the couple sitting on the terrace and asked if there was anything else they needed.

'Nothing,' Edwin said. 'It's all wonderful.'

'It's our sixth wedding anniversary,' Harriet added.

Thirza beamed at them. 'Many congratulations.'

Harriet nodded but Thirza caught a look of sadness in her eyes.

'How did you hear about Merchant's?' she asked.

'We were in Naples, and a member of the Bellini hotel foundation recommended you.'

'Kind of them,' she said but, feeling herself reddening, quickly made her excuses.

She had to write to Emilio, it was only fair, so she sat down at her mother's desk, drew out a sheet of writing paper and began. She missed him, though she would never admit it.

The physical intimacy of course, but also she missed having someone with whom to share her innermost thoughts and feelings. It was lonely. And she worried about him too. With everything going on in Italy she hoped he would be safe. She could not imagine Emilio ever being a supporter of fascism, yet if her father was right, it seemed that anyone who did not support Il Duce was likely to become a target for harassment at the very least and possibly much worse than that.

Sunlight shone in stripes across the desk distracting her, so she got up and closed the offending shutter. It didn't help much. To Thirza's increasing frustration her first two efforts to write rather predictably ended up in the wastepaper basket, but she tried again, and this time kept it brief.

> Dear Emilio,
> I hope you are well.
> Last year I wrote to thank you for your . . .

She paused, searching for the right word, then continued:

> investment in my business and now I would like to thank you once again. This time for recommending Merchant's to potential guests. Mr and Mrs Taylor arrived today for a month-long stay. It's exactly what I needed at this present time.
>   My second purpose in writing today is to invite you to Merchant's yourself, if you would be interested . . .

be interested? Scrub that. Should she mention Romi? Yes . . .

if you would like to come and meet Romi. You would be welcome.

Yours,
Thirza

She thought about trying again but decided it would have to do, though she couldn't help thinking that such a momentous invitation should not have been suggested in such a cursory manner.

At dinner the Taylors were very quiet, and Harriet barely ate a thing. Thirza wondered what was wrong with her, but she chatted with Edwin and tried to keep up a semblance of normality. When the meal was over Harriet went straight upstairs, and Thirza came across Edwin sitting outside smoking on his own.

'Hello,' she said. 'Fancy an ouzo?'

'You read my thoughts.'

Thirza nipped inside and brought out her best ouzo and two glasses. 'Mind if I join you?'

'I'd be delighted.'

They sat in silence as the cicadas sang and the day bled into night. She lit a candle to deter the mosquitoes. They seemed to be so much worse this year. The garden, however, smelt soothingly of jasmine, roses, and honeysuckle.

'It's so peaceful out here,' he said, 'away from London.'

'How is the paper?' she asked.

'So many owners of our major newspapers are bent only on making money and increasing their audience.

Sometimes I feel that truth has gone out of the window, especially when they try to shape British politics.'

'Do they succeed?'

'Not really, or maybe I should say not yet. I think we may need to leave London anyway. It isn't doing Harriet any good.' He glanced around and gestured at the garden. 'This is what she really needs, but she won't come down.'

Thirza nodded. He was speaking so quietly, almost to himself really, and she didn't want to intrude.

'She lost a child at six months, just when we thought she would go full term. It has rather broken her.'

Thirza's eyes heated up in sympathy. 'I'm so terribly sorry.'

'Her fourth failed pregnancy.'

'You must be devastated.'

'I am, but it's worse for her. She blames herself.'

Thirza's heart twisted in sympathy.

'There's another couple arriving tomorrow,' she said, 'and then at some point a friend of mine. I hope it won't disturb the peace too much, for you.'

'Not at all, and I think a little company will help Harriet, and the solace this beautiful place offers is exactly what she needs.'

Thirza thought back to the day she and Penny had talked about the future, and Penny had emphasised that Merchant's would offer people a sanctuary, and that they would love the peace. She had been right.

When the second couple, Mr and Mrs Cooper, arrived the next day by boat, Thirza saw they were both overdressed for the weather, the wife simply rolling in gold jewellery, and gasping for breath.

'Ouf, my goodness, I have a stitch,' the woman said in a strong Black Country accent, holding her side. 'I hadn't expected such a climb to get here from the sea.'

'Oh, I do apologise, Mrs Cooper,' Thirza said. 'I should have warned you.'

'Not to worry,' the woman said. 'We need the exercise and please call us Brian and Marie. We don't stand on ceremony, do we, love?'

Thirza nodded. 'Well, I hope you'll have a very happy time. Spiro will take your bags and someone will bring refreshments out here.'

As she walked away, she could tell Mr Cooper was happy to divulge everything about himself and his family to anyone, and that included poor Magdalena who could barely make out a single word.

Some days later Thirza left the guests to amuse themselves and dressed Romi in a blue-and-white-striped dress and white summer hat. It was silly really, but she was inordinately proud of her sweet little girl. Even Piers, who had never been a baby person, lit up whenever he saw Romi and was proving to be an adoring grandfather, much more so than he had ever been as a father.

She played with Romi on the rocks, picking up shells, and green sea glass, her daughter giggling and flapping her arms like the cheeky gulls swooping to spot if there was food to snatch. It was a beautiful fresh day with just a gentle breeze and Thirza felt happy.

She watched the caique arriving, took a few steps forward to greet it, and then she stood completely still, narrowing her eyes, her heart racing. For there, climbing out of the boat, completely unmistakable, was Emilio.

CHAPTER 44

The world drained of sound as Emilio climbed out, looking leaner, tired, a little wounded, and wearing different gold-framed spectacles.

'Hello,' Thirza said, as he drew near.

'Hello.'

Romi was hiding behind Thirza's legs.

'Is she shy?' he asked.

'Not really. It's just her game.'

He bent his head and drew something out from his jacket pocket. 'I wonder if Romi would like a fruit jelly.'

Romi immediately ran round, her dark eyes gazing up at Emilio. 'Peese,' she said.

With a swift intake of breath his mouth fell open. She watched him struggle, as he swallowed visibly and blinked, before saying in a low emotional voice, 'For you, little one,' and he gently placed the jelly in her outstretched hand.

Then he turned away and Thirza could see his shoulders heaving. When she went round to look at him, he had silent tears on his cheeks.

She smiled. 'Honestly Emilio, could you be more Italian!'

He wiped his face with a large white handkerchief and then he smiled too. 'I'm so happy.'

'I'm sorry you had to wait so long.'

She felt differently now, less ready to judge. Life was not always tidy, things happened, people did things they maybe shouldn't have. And what was important now was that he was Romi's father.

He shook his head. 'Do not blame yourself. It was my own fault. She is very lovely. Just the sight of her makes me want to cry . . . and when she spoke. Well, you saw the state I was in.' Then he frowned. 'Is she safe on the rocks so close to the sea?'

'Perfectly safe. She's been an outdoors child from the start, a water baby too, and is very wilful, I might add, and rather advanced for her age. She had blue eyes. Eleni said they might change, and they did. Just like yours now with the same ring of gold around the dark iris.'

'I saw that.'

'Shall we go up to the house? There are four guests, I'm afraid, but well . . .' she trailed off.

She led him up to the house and showed him to the nearest guest bedroom.

'As you see it's rather small, but you're opposite me, and we'll be sharing a bathroom.' She felt momentarily embarrassed by the intimacy of that.

'It's a lovely room.'

'It overlooks the orchard at the side of the house. I hope you'll be comfortable. I'll ask Eleni to bring you towels.'

He walked to the window to look.

She had expected to feel unnatural with him, awkward, uncertain, but instead she felt as if she'd come home. It shocked her. In all the scenarios she had played out in her mind, this one had not figured. As Romi ran about laughing and jumping up and down, she watched him as he in turn gazed at his daughter with such reverence on his face it almost stopped her breath.

She found herself instinctively stepping forward, wanting to reach out to him – but then Dulcie's look of disgust when she had found them together flashed in her mind, almost derailing her.

Neither she nor Dulcie would ever get over that. How could anyone? The thought of her mother being in bed with Emilio still made her feel ill. It was insurmountable.

Dulcie remained in Thirza's mind. How *she* must have been with him. This beautiful man and suddenly she couldn't cope. She backed away, grabbed hold of Romi, and hurriedly said, 'Right. I'll see you at lunch.' And then she ran to her room with her daughter howling in her arms.

By lunch time Romi would normally have had her meal in the kitchen and be ready for a nap, but her excitement today was so high that nobody could get her to settle. When Romi's cries reached the guests sitting outside at the dining table beneath the pergola, Thirza pushed her chair back and rose to her feet.

'Oh, do bring her down,' Harriet said, looking more alive than she had done so far.

When Thirza arrived back at the table, the chatter receded as her daughter reached out for Emilio, saying, 'Peese, peese,' over and over.

Thirza smiled and surreptitiously glanced at the wide-eyed guests, each one of them unable to hide their curiosity. Then she smiled at Emilio too. Somehow his daughter instinctively knew who he was, and why should she try to hide it?

CHAPTER 45

They were ambling along the cliffs high above the bright azure sea with a light breeze carrying the scent of salt and seaweed with traces of the wildflowers that grew nearby. It felt so natural, so easy to be with Emilio, walking mainly in silence, and taking turns to carry Romi the moment her little legs grew tired.

'I hope you will allow me to visit again,' he said and stopped to gaze out at the view of the Albanian mountains.

Although worried about going too fast too soon, Thirza wanted him to come again, and said, 'I suppose it would be good for Romi to get to know you.'

He leant down to Romi's level and helped her pick the little yellow flowers that grew all along the path.

'More,' the little girl said, and giggling ran ahead with Emilio following close behind.

As she watched them, she wanted to forgive him, longed to do so, but it was hard accepting that she was in love with someone her mother had been with . . . and who was the father of her brother! She worried, too, that any kind of relationship with Emilio might mean never being able to see Dulcie, who she loved so much. If only she'd told him who she was from the start. She took a breath and feeling his eyes on her exhaled slowly. Was she being a fool? She didn't know right from wrong anymore because there wouldn't have been a relationship if she had told him, especially if *he* had then told her. There would have been no Romi. Was she justifying herself? Him too? The moral ambiguity seemed as clear as mud. And yet Romi had taken root in her heart and Thirza could not recall who she'd even been before her daughter was born. She hadn't known it was possible to love like this, for being a mother was not like anything she'd imagined. It was raw, visceral, heart-stopping. And now she could far better comprehend her mother's bitter anguish at the loss of Billy.

As they walked on, Emilio holding Romi's hand, he glanced across at Thirza.

'Could you tell me a little about Billy?' he said gently. 'If it's not too hard for you. I never had a son.'

She swallowed, remembering how there was something luminous about Billy. 'He shone,' she said. 'So utterly full of beans. Everyone adored him. I didn't know it at the time, of course, but he looked like you. Dulcie must have always known that.'

He nodded then asked, 'Do you have a photograph?'

'Just one that my mother must have accidentally left behind. I'll show it to you.'

'You must miss him.'

Tears sprang to her eyes, but she swiped them away and said, 'Every single day.'

Romi was beginning to grizzle so Thirza picked her up.

There was a long silence until she eventually raised the question she hadn't previously dared to ask.

'Did you love my mother?' she said, and it turned out to be as simple as that.

He seemed to consider for a moment but then said, 'No, it was never love.'

'Then what?'

He sighed, glancing at the ground before looking up at her, his eyes sad. 'Infatuation. She was exciting and fun. I was a little bit thrilled to have her attention, but it was a brief affair. She never told me anything about her life, never mentioned Merchant's, nor her family. Didn't even wear her wedding ring or tell me she was married.'

'How did you find out?'

'I saw her in Corfu Town with your father, in a restaurant. They wore matching wedding rings.'

'And that's when it ended?'

'Of course. She must have already been pregnant then, but she didn't tell me.'

She nodded. 'Do you want to take Romi now? She's getting heavy.'

Then, as they headed for home, Thirza asked, 'What's it like in Italy now?'

He sighed. 'Every day we hear of more brutality. I fear for my girls. I have no idea where this is all going to end. Maybe someday the girls could visit Merchant's with me?'

She didn't answer, but as they reached the lower gardens of Merchant's she said, 'Could you take Romi in for me? I've a few things I need to do.'

He smiled, Romi chattering gibberish to him now. He was *good* with children. She knew it as she watched him reply to her little girl's nonsense with such unwavering seriousness.

But after he had gone Thirza didn't actually *do* anything. What she wanted was time alone to sort out the teeming emotions going on inside her. The push and pull of them. The longing, the fear. She was desperate to sort out her own thoughts but the joy of being with Emilio clashed with confusion over her mother's distance and an uncertain future. Although aware she'd be needed in the house as Merchant's owner, she lingered. Small birds flew overhead from tree to tree, gulls shrieked as they swooped across the water, butterflies hovered over the bushes, and bees sought out nectar from the flowers. The garden was bursting with life and as she passed the oleander and plumbago to reach the first rose bushes their scent soothed her.

Emilio left the next day. 'I will write,' he said and gave her a kiss on both cheeks in the Italian manner, then he swept Romi up and held her close.

'Goodbye, sweet girl. I will see you again soon.'

Romi couldn't understand his words, but she had gathered that he was leaving, and her little face crumpled. He put her down and reached into his pocket, then squatted to hand her a fruit jelly.

'For you,' he said and kissed the top of her head before he straightened up and the little girl smiled through her tears.

'Say *bye bye* to Dada,' Thirza said.

Emilio looked close to tears again hearing this.

Then she listened to the caique, close by now, and stepped back. 'We'll go,' she said. 'Thank you for coming.'

Then she lifted up Romi and headed up the levels of the garden, telling herself her eyes were only watering because of the wind.

When she reached the top terrace, she spotted Harriet sitting on her own so went to join her. The woman's sad expression changed the moment Romi ran up to her.

'Hello darling girl,' Harriet said, and Romi showed her the fruit jelly.

'How lovely.'

'I'll bring lemonade, if you'd like some, Harriet?'

'Thank you,' she said but, still gazing at Romi, she didn't look up.

'Would you mind watching her for a moment?' Thirza asked.

Harriet nodded.

Thirza turfed off her plimsolls and went to the kitchen, amazed at the power of young children to light up a person's eyes, but also thought of the aching loss a woman must feel when she badly wanted her own child and was having to face that it might be too late.

In the kitchen Thirza found that the day's lemonade had not yet been made. Magdalena apologised but Thirza waved her away and said she'd do it herself.

By the time she was carrying a laden tray outside, neither Romi nor Harriet were anywhere to be seen.

Thirza scratched her head and called for her daughter.

'Romi, where are you hiding?' Her daughter loved to hide and then leap out shouting, 'Boo! Boo!'

Thirza made a quick round of the garden in her bare feet. 'Romi. Are you hiding from Mama?'

Nothing. And as she remembered Dulcie's cries, and how awful it had felt as they searched for Billy, her heart pounded wildly.

Magdalena came out and Thirza asked her to look in the orchard. Then Eleni approached wringing her hands. 'It is not good. It is not good,' she said.

Thirza felt another stab of fear. 'Could you hurry down the drive, Eleni, I'll go to the beach.'

'Romi,' she called, then, 'Harriet! Where are you?'

Edwin arrived in the garden now.

'I can't find Romi,' Thirza said, her voice rising. 'I left her with Harriet for a few minutes. I only went to make lemonade.' Her heart pulsing in her throat, she felt the panic rising.

'I'll help look. They can't have gone far.'

'Try the cliff path. Take the dog.'

Thirza was shouting now as she called for her daughter, and cries of 'Harriet, Romi, Harriet, Romi,' were coming from all four corners of the estate. And the echo too, of that other name – *Billy. Billy. Billy.* Oh God. Please don't let history repeat itself. Please!

Thirza called Romi's name all the way down the levels of the garden past the roses and the oleanders and, as she reached the cove, she heard a boat speeding up and was surprised when moments later the caique drew up. Hadn't it left a little while ago? She ran up to Emilio, who was climbing out and pointing. Georgie came bounding up, panting, barking, almost knocking her over, and then the dog tore past her.

'Quickly. They're over there,' Emilio shouted. 'Round the headland. On the rocks. I saw them from the water.'

'Oh, thank God.'

He held out his hand to her. 'Come, we'll get her together.'

And they ran, scrambling and falling over the rocky ground, picking themselves up again and following the dog, Thirza scaping the bare soles of her feet raw on the jagged surfaces. And then in the distance she saw her daughter, standing far too close to the water where it was slapping against the rocks, and Harriet was there too, sitting in the sunshine looking as if she were singing.

With her eyes closed.

With her eyes closed. As Romi teetered further towards the edge.

Georgie reached Romi first, opened his jaw, and caught hold of her dress with his teeth.

'No. Dordie,' Romi was saying, stepping back from him. 'Dordie. No.'

The dog held fast.

Emilio let go of Thirza's hand and hurtled across the rocks, leaping over pools, stumbling, running, and then grabbing Romi only moments before, with one more step, she would have fallen backwards into the sea. Harriet, startled by the commotion, opened her eyes, and looked around vacantly, as if she had no idea where she was. Emilio shouted at her in Italian, anger flaring in his eyes. Thirza had been rigid with fear, everything focused on finding her daughter, but now she wept tears of relief, mixed in with tears of anguish over the loss of the little boy who had not been saved, and would never be coming back to them.

CHAPTER 46

Later, after Thirza had put Romi to bed, she stood with Emilio in Dulcie's favourite secluded part of the garden, the scent of jasmine soporific. In one shaking hand, she held an empty brandy glass as she permitted herself to feel the impact of a tragedy that might so easily have happened. She felt sick. Couldn't bear to think how close she'd come to losing her child, couldn't bear to imagine how her poor mother must have felt when she lost hers. Emilio took the glass from her and the tears came again. He held her close, and she sobbed into his chest.

When she finally stopped, she said, 'I'm sorry. Your shirt is wet.'

He laughed. 'I have another.'

'Do you?'

He frowned. 'Ah, maybe not. The caique has gone, hasn't it?'

'With your luggage.'

He nodded and they both began to laugh, the aftermath of tension and intolerable anxiety, until really it became almost impossible to stop. Thirza choked a little, coughing and spluttering, doubling over while he patted her back, until eventually she straightened up, took a gasping breath, and then was able to breathe normally again.

When she could speak, she said, 'I don't understand why the caique was still close enough for you to be able to see Romi and Harriet. I thought it had left earlier.'

'The engine we heard earlier was not the caique's after all. It was just some boat passing by. I had to wait and the caique arrived later.'

'Thank God.' She swallowed hard. 'If it hadn't—'

'But it did, we found her in time, and Harriet is being cared for by her husband. They'll be leaving tomorrow.'

'I shouldn't have left Romi with her. It was thoughtless.'

'You couldn't have known,' he said, then paused for a moment before saying, 'All right for me to stay the night?'

She smiled. 'There's nowhere else you can go. You're stuck here until the caique comes tomorrow. I'll find one of my father's shirts you can wear and wash the one you're wearing. It'll be dry by morning.'

Later, at the end of the day, when the house was quiet, Thirza lay on her bed still fully dressed. A glass of white Corfiot wine sat on her bedside table but she hadn't drunk any of it, still thinking about Romi and how afraid she had been. Then her thoughts passed to Dulcie and Billy again, and she wished she could speak to her mother. She had been too confused, too angry to really want her mother there, had partly been relieved when Dulcie hadn't replied to her letters. Perhaps she might try to reach out once more. For until now she hadn't fully comprehended how the loss of a child might totally change a person.

She got up from the bed, undressed slowly, then sat at her dressing table and picked up her hairbrush. She brushed and brushed until her hair stood out around her head like an orange halo. Because it was so curly it could be dry and brittle especially in the summer, so Magdalena had made her a special oil, rich with the fragrance of rosemary. She tipped the little glass bottle so that a few drops lay in her warm palm and then she ran her fingers through her hair spreading the oil throughout.

Her fear over what might have happened to Romi was mixed with a sense of release now, but she longed for the comfort of Emilio. How easy it would be to simply walk across the hall. Just those few steps and she would feel the warmth of him. She felt suddenly chilled by what had happened that day and needed him more than ever. The temptation overwhelmed her, energy surging and fizzing through her body. She had missed him so much.

When she opened her bedroom door to go to the bathroom, she noticed the light was still on in Emilio's room, could see it shining through the little gap under his door. She lingered in the corridor without a clear idea and then, on a sudden, it seemed sudden, though when she thought about it afterwards, she realised it was not – so, on a sudden, or not so sudden urge – she did it. She crossed the corridor.

Without any hesitation she reached out as if to turn the handle. To open it. To see him. But just before she did, the door opened inwards, and she stepped back as Emilio, wearing her father's old paisley dressing gown, stood there looking surprised to see her.

'Sorry,' she said. 'Umm. I was just about to use the bathroom. I . . . er . . . wondered if you'd finished in there?'

'Yes,' he said. 'I only opened the door because I heard a noise.'

'Oh.'

He frowned slightly. 'Your smell.'

'I smell?'

'Delicious. Edible.'

'Ah. Right. It's rosemary oil. Well.' Her voice had risen nervously. 'Goodnight then.'

'Goodnight.'

Emilio left in the morning along with Harriet and Edwin. Thirza told herself that everything was fine. Nothing had changed, and nor would it, but after he'd gone, she wanted to run after him. He had waved as she watched the caique disappear into the distance, her heart sinking, and her spirits slumping. She wanted him but how could they ever get back together with Dulcie hovering like a ghost between them?

CHAPTER 47

October 1933

As a perfect, blue-skied day drew to a close and the brightness faded, Thirza sat in the courtyard garden of her father's town house with very mixed feelings. Overwhelmed by too many people, too much small talk, and a great deal of good humour, all of it with a smile fixed on her face that made her cheeks hurt, she kicked off her gold high-heeled sandals. With a deep sigh of relief, she breathed in the delicious scent of honeysuckle. Penny and Piers were married. Some months had gone by, but at last it was done.

Columbine, wearing a navy-blue silk dress, and looking better than she had in ages, came out carrying a glass of champagne.

'Oh,' Thirza said, glancing up at her. 'I thought you didn't anymore.'

Columbine laughed and flopped into a chair. 'I don't. This is for you.'

'Not sure I need another one,' Thirza said, but took the glass all the same.

The divorce absolute had come through more quickly than anyone had expected, and Thirza wondered if that might tempt Dulcie to finally return to Corfu as she had promised. Piers was to keep the town house as expected, Dulcie the business and their London home. For the time being Merchant's remained in her mother's control and Thirza still didn't know if the trust had been finalised or not. It made her feel edgy.

'Lovely service,' Columbine said sounding wistful.

Thirza smiled thinking of Romi as a bridesmaid, dizzy with wonder, and Penny as a bride in the palest pink dress you ever saw, flouncy with ruffles, and embroidered with white daisies.

'Penny looked so happy,' Columbine continued.

Thirza had watched Penny floating down the aisle, beaming, while knowing she herself had never fallen for every young girl's dream and would never wear such a dress, would not even want to.

'You old cynic,' she muttered to herself and then, without even consciously choosing to, pictured herself wearing white and carrying a bouquet. She hid her embarrassed smile and Columbine didn't notice.

'How do you think your mother might be feeling?' Columbine said, voicing one of the thoughts that had been in Thirza's mind all day long.

'About Piers and Penny?'

'Mmm.'

Thirza shrugged. 'Who knows with Dulcie.'

'What about you?'

'I'm fine. Penny has grown on me.'

'Weddings always make me cry,' Columbine said.

'Weddings do that, don't they?'

'Rather like funerals.'

During the service, Thirza had felt moments of sadness wash over her and had missed Emilio more than ever. Also, she couldn't help a prickle of envy over her father's relatively easy divorce, while for a Catholic like Emilio, it was forbidden. As for Piers, he'd been looking pleased with himself, and Thirza couldn't tell if he'd given a thought to either his first wedding or his first wife.

'So, you're all right with things?' Columbine asked. 'You said you were fine.'

'What I meant was,' Thirza continued. 'I have, well, *accepted*, things. I think that's the word. More or less. Life moves on. You either move with it or you get left behind.'

'Has Dulcie been left behind?' Columbine asked.

'I don't know, but I suppose she has in a way.' And that seemed such an awfully sad thing to say about her mother, who'd always been the one to lead the way. The decisive one while others floundered.

She glanced at Columbine. 'You look well. America obviously agrees with you.'

'Thank you. It does.'

'And Ianthe and Walter?'

Columbine's eyes lit up. 'Living in wedded bliss.'

Thirza still could not imagine it and was rather glad that work commitments had prevented Walter from making the long journey himself. 'I'm so glad you two could come back for the wedding. I'm sure it means a lot to Penny. Are you staying for a while?'

'For as long as we're welcome at my friend Lucie's house.'

Ianthe came out carrying Romi, who was now fast asleep and snuggled up against her chest. 'Shall I put her to bed?' she asked.

Thirza reached out a hand to Ianthe. 'No. Sit with us. She'll sleep on your lap if you don't mind.'

Ianthe slid into a chair next to Thirza. 'She's so soft and cosy, I don't mind at all. Don't little children smell gorgeous.'

Thirza laughed. 'Not always!'

They drifted into silence.

Ianthe was softly humming to the sleeping toddler when Penny came out. 'Oooh, it's nice to be out here,' she said, throwing herself into the last remaining seat. 'I love this time of day when everything turns pink.'

The others murmured their agreement.

Thirza couldn't take her eyes off the woman. She looked sun-kissed and deliriously happy in her eye-catching way. She had felt so dubious about Penny in the beginning and yet the woman had shown her nothing but kindness. Thirza had to admit she had been wrong from the start, blinded by a sense of loyalty to her mother, and angry with her father. It had been childish . . . she recognised that now.

'I thought you'd be on the ferry by now,' Ianthe said.

'We decided to go tomorrow morning.'

'Italy?'

'Yes,' Penny said. 'I've seen so little of it and yet here we are just across the water.'

'Will you be safe?' Columbine asked.

'Piers knows what he's doing and we're only going for a few days. So yes, I think so.'

As the others carried on talking in a desultory way, Thirza basked in the simple camaraderie of being outside with these three women who, for all their differences, were relaxing together on this balmy evening.

But her mind kept going back to Emilio and how much she had longed to take those few steps across the hall and fall into his arms. She wanted to be with him. It was that simple and she really couldn't keep on denying it. She wanted Romi to know her father and not just as an occasional visitor; she wanted her to have a loving relationship with both her parents, and not just one.

She rose to her feet. 'Could you look after Romi?' she asked.

'Of course,' Ianthe said.

'Where are you going?' Penny asked.

'To my father's study, if that's all right?'

'Sure,' Penny said, closing her eyes. 'All yours.'

Thirza went indoors and in her father's study she pulled out a sheet of writing paper from the top drawer.

Dear Mother, she wrote, then paused, chewing the end of her fountain pen as she tried to find the right words. She saw herself running towards her mother, arms outstretched. This time she would *beg* Dulcie to come, and really mean it when she told her how much she'd missed her. There could be no possibility of ever being with Emilio if she didn't put things right with her mother first.

It wouldn't hurt in other ways either. For how else would she finally establish whether Dulcie still intended to abide by her decision to go ahead with the trust that would ultimately transfer Merchant's to Thirza?

CHAPTER 48

The air was still warm for late October and there was a softness to the light and to the colour of the sea. Thirza breathed slowly in and out. In and out, attempting to calm her racing heartbeat. She didn't know if she was pleased or terrified that this long-awaited day was finally happening.

She had spent the whole week preparing, laundering anything that could be washed, beating every rug, and polishing everything made of wood until her arms were fit to drop off. This morning, she had paced the house restlessly, moving from room to room checking that everything was faultless, and that Romi hadn't done her usual trick of hiding things and then forgetting where they were. Romi was twenty months old now, and had progressed from, 'all gone,' and 'Dada bye-bye,' and had reached the stage of being able to hold a conversation, admittedly still only in three- or four-word sentences, but with a large vocabulary. She was a quick learner, remembering most of what she saw and heard, could open and squeeze into any cupboard in the house, and had a particular penchant for reckless climbing *and* for throwing off her clothes.

Thirza carried the display of scented late summer roses to the coffee table in the drawing room, surveying everything was in place, and checking that no toys had been left on the floor. She shook her head and moved the vase back to the dining room, almost tripping over Georgie and Romi, who were following at her heels.

'When Gwanmama coming?' Romi asked for the hundredth time.

She'd been asking the question relentlessly ever since Thirza had first explained that Dulcie would, for the first time, be visiting her granddaughter. Romi had taken it in her stride – to her, it seemed rather normal that the caique regularly delivered new family members as well as supplies.

Emilio had been to stay twice more since his first arrival. He came on his own each time, without his elder daughters, and just like the first visit stayed for three days. Thirza missed him after he'd gone but the two of them exchanged letters fairly frequently, and with Merchant's Guest House rushing her off her feet, and her small daughter to look after, she had little time to dwell. Except perhaps during the colder weather when guests were few on the ground, when days grew misty, and she grew melancholy. Then she wondered how Emilio might have handled Romi when she was rebellious, or how he would have soothed the little girl when she cried.

'When Gwanmama coming?' Romi repeated imperiously.

'Today,' Thirza said. 'Soon.'

Thirza had been anxious ever since her mother had replied to the letter she'd written on the evening of her father's marriage to Penny. She had felt Dulcie could not continue to be left out of their lives and when her mother had actually suggested a date, she had jumped at it.

Georgie began to bark furiously. He always alerted them to an arrival before anyone else had a clue and – sure enough – a few moments later, Thirza heard the sound of an engine. The caique!

She grasped Romi's hand in hers, took in a deep breath, and went down to meet the boat, tugging nervously at her dress made of a glassy blue-green georgette fabric that brought out the colour of her eyes.

When Dulcie stepped out of the boat dressed all in white and onto their little landing stage, holding a small case, Thirza couldn't move.

Her mother looked different.

Dulcie took a step towards her. 'Thirza,' she said.

Thirza still could not speak and felt the backs of her eyelids grow hot. She touched her neck nervously, unused to the awkwardness between them. Though how else could it be? A gap had opened up, and she had no idea how to breach it.

But Romi did.

Romi, who was not the least bit shy, ran up to Dulcie with arms stretched out. 'Gwanmama,' Romi said. 'Gwanmama. Pick up.'

As Dulcie hesitated, Thirza felt desperately afraid her daughter would be rejected, just as she had been. But then her mother's eyes glittered, and she reached out to pick up and swing the little girl into the air. After a few moments of this she put her down and, bending over, gazed at her. 'Let me look at you.'

'Me look too,' Romi said and gazed back.

Dulcie, laughing, glanced at Thirza. 'The spitting image of you at that age. Apart from the eyes of course.'

Thirza nodded but she'd seen the tears in her mother's eyes, and knowing how like Emilio's Romi's eyes were, and how like Billy's, she did not speak. Anyway, her breath seemed to be stuck, and she found it hard to take in any air at all. Her chest was tight. Awfully tight.

'Well,' Dulcie said, brisk and businesslike. 'Aren't you going to lead the way up to the house?'

'Of course, and welcome. I . . . I . . .' Her voice faded away.

'Yes. Me too. Least said soonest mended, don't you think?'

Thirza fought a frown. Their stark fallout had seemed insurmountable but how were they to mend it, if they were not going to talk about what had happened?

She carried the suitcase, glancing back at her mother and daughter, as they meandered up through the garden, Romi chattering nonstop, clutching Dulcie's hand. It was wonderful to see and quite ridiculous to feel a tiny bit sidelined, although she did, like a child desperately wanting her mother to love her again.

Thirza had expected Dulcie to look a little older, maybe even thinner than when she'd last seen her, but it appeared that her mother had gone through some kind of reinvention. A few silver threads, but otherwise the lovely strawberry blonde of her hair was much the same and she was, as always, beautifully dressed. If anything she was a little sturdier than before, but that might well be a good thing. Most of all Dulcie still looked incredibly beautiful. Truly beautiful. No wonder Emilio as a twenty-year-old had been flattered when she chose *him*. She could still have any man she wanted.

Inside the hall Dulcie gazed around, sharp-eyed, a look of pleasure suddenly mixing with one of overwhelm, or maybe uncertainty. Her mother's brisk immunity from emotion slipped a little, leaving something vulnerable in its wake. Billy. Of course. What else? She was looking for signs of Billy. Thirza couldn't tell for sure, but this *was* the first time she'd been back since Billy disappeared.

'Well, this is quite something,' Dulcie said, sniffing and recovering herself. 'You've done a wonderful job. I haven't seen the true colour of those tiles for about twenty years.'

Thirza smiled but did not answer. Was it all going to be small talk between them, just as it had been in her letters? Dulcie had neither remarked on Thirza's declaration of peace, nor responded to the white flag she'd held up when she'd begged her mother to come, confessing how dreadfully much she missed her. Yet Dulcie *had* come and that might have to be enough. For now.

'Well done,' her mother was saying, 'and as for this little angel . . .'

She turned to regard Romi again, with slightly narrowed eyes and an odd expression on her face. Curiosity and disbelief, maybe? Despite informing her mother of her pregnancy and then of Romi's birth, there had been no response. Now, it seemed to be really sinking in.

'Well, she's a credit to you,' Dulcie finished, holding out her arms to the little girl again. 'Come here, darling, and let your grandmama give you a present.'

Romi's eyes sparkled as Dulcie squatted down, opened her case, and rummaged for a parcel. She handed it to Romi who ripped the paper open and lifted out a beautiful Victorian doll.

'That used to be mine when I was a little girl like you,' Dulcie said as she straightened up.

Thirza saw the tears in her mother's eyes again and, on a sudden urge, went across to stand by her. So far, they had avoided any physical contact, but now Dulcie reached for her hand and squeezed it. They stood in silence together, Thirza feeling her mother's warmth. Feeling the terrible distance between them shrinking. Guilt fading. Absolution arriving. Like something from a Greek tragedy. This time the gods were on their side. Around them the still world seemed to acknowledge the moment, and Thirza recognised that the loss of one's mother was one of the greatest losses of all. They would be all right now.

'I'm happy to see you,' Dulcie eventually said, with a discreet wipe of her eyes.

Thirza nodded. 'Me too.' And it felt like the culmination of something she had long yearned for.

The lump in her throat stopped her from saying anything more.

They stood together watching Romi dancing around the hall with her new doll and Georgie joining in for good measure. So much was going on inside Thirza, and she felt dizzy with the mixture of relief, hope, sadness, love.

Dulcie, as if acknowledging that, squeezed her hand again and then let go. 'It's strange to be back,' she said.

'It must be quite hard.'

'I suppose it is.'

They fell silent then Dulcie added, 'Romi, will you show me to my bedroom?'

Romi grinned and pointed at the stairs. 'Up! Up! Up!' she cried and began to race up towards the first landing.

Thirza went to the kitchen to speak to Magdalena about lunch, while all the time going over how Dulcie looked and how she seemed. Was she really happy to be back?

CHAPTER 49

Later that evening Dulcie read Romi a bedtime story. *Winnie-the-Pooh* and *The House at Pooh Corner* were Romi's favourites. But instead of those, Dulcie opened a French book she'd brought with her about an elephant called Babar who escapes from a hunter and comes to town. Dulcie translated it as she read – her mother had been French, and she herself was bilingual, as was Thirza to some extent. She left out parts of the story that were too old for Romi and made it all about how Babar would learn such a lot and eventually return to the forest, where he would become king of the elephants.

After that Romi, utterly entranced, allowed herself to be tucked up in bed and kissed on the forehead with no objections, and no demands for more books to be read. Thirza watched, feeling deeply moved at the sight of her mother so obviously falling in love with her granddaughter. And Romi falling in love with her.

At Dulcie's request they ate traditional Corfiot food that evening – *pastitsada*, a dish of chicken cooked with fresh tomatoes, cinnamon, nutmeg, and so on, and served with pasta and grated cheese. And for pudding a baked tart with kumquat marmalade and candied pieces of citrus fruit.

After dinner they settled down with coffee in the drawing room. Thirza left the curtains open – she liked to see the light changing outside the windows. So far, she and her mother had not spoken as two adults with a great deal to settle, because Romi had been a conduit through whom they had communicated. But as night fell it was their turn, minus the little girl's healing presence and her ability to still what might yet become turbulent waters.

Thirza knew that apart from that one very brief visit when Dulcie had found her in bed with Emilio, her mother hadn't been back since the moorings had come loose in their world. Since the news that the police believed Billy had been murdered and they'd thought they had the evidence to prove it. She knew this visit had to be tremendously painful for Dulcie. Thirza herself, with all the time she'd spent here, was used to it – that feeling of loss in the air, that sense of his young ghost never being far away.

As Thirza glanced at Dulcie quietly sipping a coffee, she spotted her mother's hand was shaking. The line between what she knew about her mother's life and who she really was blurred like the sea and the sky when the early morning mist had not lifted. Was Dulcie on the other side of that line now? Or had Thirza put herself on the other side of that line?

'So,' her mother was saying. She swallowed visibly and then continued in a hesitant tone. 'I suppose you had better tell me more about what happened after I left?'

Thirza considered her reply then simply said, 'As you know, I told Emilio to go.' She didn't mention that her entire world had fallen apart, nor how terribly angry she'd been with him.

'That's all?' Dulcie asked, obviously aware there really would have been so much more.

'It *was* all.'

'And now?'

'He has been to see his daughter.'

Dulcie sucked in her breath but then nodded slowly. Thirza didn't know if that was it, or if her mother might raise the topic again. In a way she didn't really want to talk about Emilio, although on the other hand he was all she ever wanted to talk about.

They sat in silence.

She longed to challenge Dulcie about the threatening note, ask her why she hadn't come forward with it, but just as the words were forming, she bit her tongue.

'What shall we do tomorrow?' Dulcie asked.

'Rather depends on how well the weather holds.'

'It's only October. Does Romi walk?'

'In a fashion. I usually end up carrying her.'

'Don't give in too easily. It's not good for children to get too much of their own way.'

Thirza smiled. 'You've changed your tune. You carried Billy all the time.'

Her mother's face fell, contorted, as a spasm of pain and grief visibly washed over her.

Thirza gazed at her, horrified to have been the cause. 'I'm so sorry,' she said.

Dulcie waved her apology away and Thirza, not knowing what else to say, decided just to wait. Billy was everywhere here, and her mother was bound to fall over from time to time.

'So,' Dulcie said when she'd recovered. 'You're happy running Merchant's as a guest house?'

It sounded more like a statement than a question, but Thirza said, 'Yes. I've loved it and we've had some wonderful guests.'

'I admit I was dubious.'

'Me too, if I'm honest.'

'And you're making money?'

'Not a huge amount but enough to keep going.'

They fell into silence again and Thirza wondered what they might talk about that wasn't too heavily charged with an undercurrent. She poured them both more coffee and then out of the blue her mother said, 'You attended your father's wedding?'

'Romi was bridesmaid. I didn't want to deprive her of that. She adored it.'

'It wasn't a criticism,' Dulcie said. 'And he *is* her grandfather.'

'A surprisingly doting one.'

Dulcie laughed but there was an edge to it. 'That's hard to imagine.'

Thirza nodded.

'And Romi's father. Will you deprive her of him?'

Thirza chewed the inside of her cheek. What could she say? In the end she said, 'He has a wife.'

'I know.'

'I suppose you want to know what happened between me and your Emilio, Federico as I used to know him.'

Do I want to know, Thirza wondered. She felt very much on the borderline, balancing between her carefully ordered life and a descent into turmoil. She gave a noncommittal response and Dulcie carried on talking, apparently not noticing Thirza's reluctance.

'He was young, far too young for me,' Dulcie said, still holding it together, though Thirza could hear the tremble in her voice. 'It should never have happened, but some things do just happen.'

'Don't we always have a choice?'

Her mother gave her an odd look. 'Maybe. I feel like I need to apologise, yet if it hadn't happened there would have been no Billy.'

Thirza squeezed her eyes tightly shut. No Billy. No one should ever regret or apologise for a child's existence and Billy had meant the world to all of them.

It was clear they were both remembering him. Missing him. She felt her mother's eyes on her but couldn't look up. She would have wept, and this was not the right time.

Dulcie began to speak again. 'I'm sorry for how long I kept my distance after I . . . after I found . . .' She paused, swallowed, then continued. 'You. With Emilio.'

Thirza stared into the middle distance, still trying not to cry.

'It wasn't love with Federico. It was infatuation.'

That had been what Emilio had said too, but Thirza, remembering her mother's passionate letters, was unwilling to accept this new sanitised version of events, and she wanted to push Dulcie a little more. The trouble was her mother did not know she had seen them, and Thirza was not going to tell her, so whatever version of the truth her mother was going to hold to, Thirza would have to go along with it. It meant she could never question her about the note either, which Thirza still kept in her room.

'The infatuation would have faded away,' her mother said, 'but for Billy.'

Thirza did not believe that was true. She believed her mother would have left Piers if she'd had the chance. Her letters certainly gave that impression.

'Did you ask Columbine to burn some stuff for you?' she asked.

Dulcie gave her an odd look. 'I did.'

'Ah. She said you had. I wasn't sure whether to believe her.'

'It was of no consequence.'

'I see.'

'I would never have left your father,' Dulcie then said, dismissing the topic.

'Or the family?'

'No.'

There was a long silence, each contemplating their own thoughts, neither willing to say more.

'So, that's what happened,' Dulcie eventually said.

Thirza couldn't reply. She forced herself to look at her mother who was sitting very still, eyes downcast. 'Oh, Mum,' she said.

Dulcie nodded and they drifted into silence until Dulcie spoke again in a different tone of voice, as if having decided what she really needed to say. 'Thirza, please forgive me for not coming earlier. You are my daughter, and you needed me. It was unjustifiable of me.'

Tears sprang into Thirza's eyes. She swiped them away, but they kept on coming.

'I'm so sorry,' Dulcie said, rising from her seat and coming over to wrap her arms around her daughter.

'I missed you,' Thirza said. 'I missed you terribly. I thought I might never see you again.' And then she was sobbing like a child with nowhere to hide her heartbreak.

'I missed you too,' Dulcie said. 'I'm your mother and I will always love you.'

And in that moment, it seemed as if everything was already healed, or if not that, it was well on its way.

CHAPTER 50

The next morning, after a breakfast of delicious Corfiot pastries, they went for a walk. The sky was a startling blue and the sea incandescent with rippling silvery sunlight. As Romi skipped alongside her, Dulcie pointed out the boats and the names of the birds and Romi repeated every word as best she could. 'Eagle' was tricky for her, but she was a happy little girl, and nothing daunted her spirits.

Everything about Romi was wholehearted. She approached life with her arms wide open, welcoming everything and everyone, every experience, and every new opportunity that came her way.

'She's like you,' Dulcie said. 'She behaves just as you did. Almost reckless, but not quite reckless.'

'A considered recklessness.'

'Sounds like a contradiction, doesn't it?'

'Maybe,' Thirza said. 'But in any case I always thought I took after you.'

'Did you?'

'All those adventures you went on, those books you wrote, when most women were sitting quietly at home with their embroidery.'

Dulcie laughed. 'I never did learn to embroider.'

'Or knit.'

'Remember that jumper I knitted for you?'

Thirza smiled. 'Absolute nightmare. One arm far too long, one too short, and it felt so tight I couldn't get it over my head. I kept it though.'

'Did you?'

'The cats used to like sleeping on it under my bed.'

Dulcie shook her head, her eyes dancing with amusement. 'I never knew that.'

After a while she said, 'I must have a word with Spiro. Some planting ideas, shrubs that may only be available in Italy. I'd like to discuss it all with him.'

'Will you be here long enough to oversee all that?'

'Maybe. I haven't decided.'

Back at the house Dulcie led the way and, finding Eleni, asked her what they would be having for lunch.

'It's freshly caught fish today, madam.'

'Fish? Oh no, I think not. Maybe a nice salad with chicken. That would be just the ticket. And for pudding?'

'We don't usually have pudding when there are no guests.'

'Am I not a guest?'

Thirza raised her brows. Dulcie was commanding the staff as if she were still running Merchant's and not behaving like a guest at all.

That night Thirza didn't sleep well. So much about the past had been churned up and when she woke far too early, she felt raw as she brushed her teeth, but then, when she dragged a comb through her hair . . . *Oh joy, her mother had come!* She really had come. But also, *her mother had come*, and Thirza didn't know how long she was going to stay.

She braced herself to talk to Dulcie later that day, intending to issue a gentle reminder that it was she, Thirza, who was running Merchant's now, but when she opened her shutters and saw the shimmering lilac sky and misty garden, she only wanted peace between them. At all costs? She wasn't sure. But the sight of Dulcie out there on her own was painful. She was wandering aimlessly in just a nightdress, ill at ease, her posture all wrong. No doubt with memories of Billy teeming around her. Thirza wondered if she should go down to comfort her mother, but would Dulcie feel her private moments had been invaded?

Later, sipping coffee on the terrace, she watched Romi pottering about with Dulcie. It made her heart soar to see them so comfortable together and, grateful that she and her mother were speaking again, she went down to join them.

'Morning. Have you had coffee yet?' she asked with a smile. 'I can take Romi if you'd like to breakfast now.'

'Why don't we all head to the kitchen. I could eat a horse.'

'Must be the sea air.'

'Must be.'

In the kitchen she noticed Dulcie's eyes still had a hollow appearance, except when she looked at Romi. Her mother gazed at Romi in exactly the way she had always gazed upon Billy. Her eyes softened, filling with love and affection; her brow smooth and serene. Dulcie had never looked at *her* that way, Thirza thought, and she felt a stab of . . . what? Jealousy? No. Too strong a word. And she could hardly be jealous of her own darling daughter. This was what she wanted – Dulcie and Romi to know each other. Love each other. It was more like envy, she supposed. An echo of old childhood insecurities.

Dulcie had been a solicitous mother but had not been demonstrably affectionate, except with Billy. She'd mostly been there when Thirza needed her, but not, naturally enough, after Billy died. Thirza had only been sixteen back then, but she clearly recalled how terribly hurt she had been, especially in that awful moment when her mother had blamed her for Billy's disappearance. A moment she'd never been able to forget.

Romi sat in the chair next to Dulcie, who was cutting the child's toast into soldiers.

'Womi do it. Womi do it,' her daughter declared, and Thirza gasped as Dulcie passed her the knife and showed her how.

Dulcie looked up at her and winked.

What did that wink say? *Give your daughter room to grow*, or, *Don't be so controlling*. Or neither?

Thirza watched Romi like a hawk, for her daughter was already aware of the excitement involved in doing something she wasn't supposed to do. But her tiny girl, looking serious, was making a decent fist of cutting the toast and then, when it was done, she beamed with satisfaction. But it still made Thirza uneasy, who only wanted to wrap her in cotton wool, and it brought home yet again how unimaginable it must be to lose a child. How unimaginable for Dulcie who *had* lost a child. Her breath almost stopped at the thought of anything ever happening to Romi.

She understood when, after Billy had gone, meals didn't always happen, and her mother disappeared for days at a time, and there had been no one to talk to. No one to listen. Deprived of a funeral that might have brought people together, they had all ended up alone. She had become self-sufficient, and as soon as she was old enough, she had escaped Dulcie's all-encompassing sadness.

'I'll just have a word with Eleni about the food order,' Thirza said, shaking herself out of the past.

'Oh, I've already done that,' Dulcie breezily replied. 'She and I were both up at a crazy hour.'

Her mother was different now, how could she not be? A bit more brittle, less truly herself, though continuing to behave as if she were still in charge of Merchant's. That hadn't changed. Thirza felt unlike herself too, wasn't quite sure where she stood anymore – the ground fragile and wobbling beneath her, on more than one count. But mainly because the jigsaw of their lives had broken up and all the pieces had been thrown into the air to fall just anywhere. Could she put them back together in a new way all by herself? She smiled at her daughter who'd just finished eating her boiled egg. Romi was the one who grounded her when she felt all at sea, but even Romi couldn't fix this.

'Why don't you both get your bathers on?' Dulcie was saying, smiling now. 'Then we can all go down to the beach, for an early swim, just like we—'

Thirza nodded as her mother's voice faded away. She couldn't look at her, knowing they would both cry. *I love you, Ma*, she wanted to say. *I love you*. But the words wouldn't come. They would eventually, she was sure, but not yet.

As they all went into the hall and Thirza, holding Romi's hand, took the first few steps, it seemed momentous, and she knew the time had come to lay all her cards on the table. She wanted Dulcie in their lives and that was looking very likely now. Just as soon as she was able, she would begin by asking her mother about the trust. And only after that was finally resolved one way or the other, would she tell Dulcie that she was still very much in love with Emilio. She thought back to their most recent letters and how they had discussed the next steps they might take. She had no idea how Dulcie would react, but she would open her heart to her mother, for if there was to be any future for them this had to be faced.

Suddenly Thirza felt a tug as Romi turned back to her grandmother and held out her hand. 'I love you, Gwanmummy,' she said.

Thirza and Dulcie both had tears in their eyes as they exchanged a look that spoke the words they still could not say.

Then as Romi raced on ahead Dulcie said, 'I remember holding Billy when he was sick, burning up with fever, and I thought I would die if anything ever happened to him.'

Silence, as Thirza held her breath.

'And yet, when it did happen, I didn't die. It felt like a betrayal, as if I should have.'

'Died?'

'Yes. But I had two children. I love *you*, too, Thirza. Remember that. I always have done.'

CHAPTER 51

When they came back from the beach, Romi still full of beans, Thirza drew breath slowly and firmly because, right now, she had to get ready. There would be new guests arriving, a family of three who'd booked time away from home and didn't mind the prospect of cooler weather. An Italian family, which was unusual, and Thirza hoped Dulcie wouldn't mind them being here at the same time as she was.

By late morning it had turned into a golden autumnal day. While Romi was sleeping and Dulcie was upstairs resting, or changing for lunch, the noise of a vehicle approaching alerted Thirza, who was cutting back some jasmine at the side of the house. It grew like a weed taking over everything if you weren't careful. She paused to listen. Motor cars were still a novelty up here at Merchant's, but the tracks had improved and there was something of a road from Corfu Town now.

She rose to her feet as excited female voices chattering in Italian reached her. The new guests had arrived a little earlier than expected. She waited for a few moments, then stretched, and went round to the front. Her mouth fell open as Emilio appeared from around the corner where they had left the car. He was followed by two beautiful young women. All of them smiling broadly.

She felt a little shiver and, completely thrown, began to panic. What about Dulcie? How was *she* going to react to this?

'I wanted to surprise you,' Emilio said. 'In your last letter you said you'd like my girls to know Romi.' He frowned, looking visibly uncertain. 'Is it all right?'

Thirza couldn't even smile at him, her heart hammering wildly.

He hadn't noticed and turned to his daughters, indicating that they should step forward. 'Allow me to introduce—'

At that moment Thirza heard a gasp and twisted round to see Dulcie who was coming through the front door carrying Romi in her arms. With a look of horror on her face, and white with shock, she put the child down. For a second Thirza hurtled back to the first time her life fell apart – the moment when the police had declared Billy dead. Her mother, shaking, white, looked exactly as she did now.

Romi immediately ran to Emilio who picked her up and, stepping back, fell backwards over the dog who was leaping and barking. As if in slow motion and with a loud groan of pain, Emilio landed on the paving slabs with a thump, still clutching Romi to his chest. Unhurt, the little girl giggled. In the noise and commotion that followed, his elder daughters, while exclaiming in rapid Italian –

'*Papa*' and '*mannaggia*' repeatedly – managed to help him to his feet. But when Thirza turned to look again at the open door to see how Dulcie was coping, her mother had vanished.

'Just give me a minute please,' Thirza said and touched Emilio's arm. 'If you're all right, I'll organise lemonade. We can do the introductions properly then. Could you look after Romi?'

Emilio nodded and the girls, happy their papa was not seriously hurt, were now repeating '*Che adorabile, che adorabile*' as they reached out to stroke Romi's cheeks and hair while she was still happily held captive in Emilio's arms. The little girl, loving the attention, looked immensely pleased with herself.

Thirza raced up the stairs to her mother's room where Dulcie was already packing a suitcase. It lay open on her bed, a gaping wound of accusation.

'Mother. What are you doing?'

Dulcie spun round, fury in her eyes. 'Isn't it obvious? Why didn't you warn me he was coming?'

'I didn't know.'

'You expect me to believe that? As if I haven't had to live with the shame of it for all this time, the humiliation, and now to have him showing up in my face like this. It's mortifying, Thirza. And a dirty trick. I thought better of you.'

'It wasn't a trick. I truly didn't know. He didn't make the booking himself. He must have wanted to surprise me. I've never even met his daughters before.'

'Well, he certainly surprised *me*. Spiro will take me back to town by boat.'

Conscious of a note of irritation in her own voice, Thirza tried to defend herself. 'Mother. His daughters are Romi's half-sisters.'

'I don't deny that. I just think you have been very underhand.'

'I *promise* you, I didn't know. I'm sorry.'

Dulcie glared at her. 'Oh, don't concern yourself over my feelings. You never have before.'

Crushed by the unfairness of that, her skin prickling with irritation and feeling terribly overheated, Thirza's temper reared, and she raised her voice. 'That is not true or fair.'

'Life isn't, and do not shout at me,' Dulcie said through gritted teeth and turned her back to finish her packing.

'Please don't go.' Thirza could hear the pleading tone of her own voice and despised herself. She ought to stand up to Dulcie.

'I must. Can you ensure *they* are not outside when I come down again. Once is quite enough.'

'Why not just stay for a bit longer, get to know everyone?' On an impulse she reached out a hand, but her mother quickly stepped back.

'If by *everyone* you mean Emilio, or whatever his name is these days, then no thank you, I already know him a little too well.'

Withering beneath Dulcie's glare, Thirza felt another flush of anger herself. 'Mother, you're being childish. This is ridiculous. You know Romi now, and she absolutely adores you. What about her? Isn't it time to move on?'

'And I suppose you expect me to move on from Billy too.'

'I never said that. No one can ask a mother to do that. I don't even know how you would.'

'Quite. Now if you don't mind—'

'Mother!' Thirza interjected. 'I'm young. I have to live my life. Emilio is my daughter's father—'

Her mother snorted. 'Ha! As I thought, you *are* together again.'

'Mother! For pity's sake, I didn't say that. We have not been together. It doesn't mean I stopped caring though.'

'And I suppose you've been laughing at me in your little love nest.'

'Of course not. No one has been laughing! You're overreacting.'

'And the fact that I loved him before you?'

Dulcie sounded bitter and Thirza knew her mother was not listening but still she said, 'Of course that matters, which is why we have not been together all this time. But it's in the past. You were married to my father. That isn't my responsibility. You can't just run away.'

'I think you'll find that I can. And I am far too old to contemplate doing anything I actually do not want to do.'

'But Mother—'

'Desist, Theresa. Desist!'

And with that the subject was closed.

In her bedroom Thirza splashed her face at the hand basin and took several long slow breaths, wishing she had not risen to Dulcie's bait. She had not handled that well, but truly, how else could she have handled it? Everything had happened so quickly.

The timing could not have been worse. This had been a special time for Dulcie and Romi. A time in which an olive branch had been offered *and* accepted, and it had been spoilt. Ruined. Any meeting between her mother and Emilio needed to have been properly choreographed. If only he had warned her, it could all have been avoided. She could only hope that her mother would calm down and change her mind about leaving – but this hope proved futile.

Twenty minutes later, Thirza watched from her bedroom window as Dulcie, carrying her own case, marched Spiro and another workman down to the boathouse. Her mother's stiff lonely figure left Thirza with a lump in her throat. She swallowed repeatedly but raw angry tears formed and fell anyway.

Dulcie was gone.

CHAPTER 52

'I would have been happy to talk to her,' Emilio was saying. 'Apologise for intruding. Apologise for everything. I didn't know she was here. I wouldn't have come. But, as you said in your letter, we needed to talk about the future and I—'

Thirza – sitting beside him on the sofa, staring at the ceiling – gulped back the hurt. 'It wasn't your fault. She was angry. Not in any mood to listen.'

'You look so sad.'

'I am. She's my mother. I love her and she's gone,' Thirza said, trying not to cry again, but still her voice broke. 'After all the effort to get her here. And just like that. Gone.'

Thirza's heart twisted. She'd wanted to fall to her knees, beseech her mother to stay, and now she didn't know which way to turn. It was impossible. Completely impossible. She couldn't have both Emilio and Dulcie in her world and the pain of that, the awful gut-wrenching pain of that, was sucking the life from her. She doubled over. And then it really sank in, the question she couldn't bear to ask herself – did she still want Emilio, at any cost?

'I would have offered to go,' he said.

But I don't want you to go, she thought. It had risen from nowhere, but it was true.

'I know you would have left,' she said, then paused, with no idea how to recover from the crushing defeat of her mother leaving just when things were getting better. Just when they were finally balanced on the edge of a lasting repair.

'Is there anything I can do?' he asked.

'It hurts,' she said and shook her head. 'She wouldn't listen. I feel let down. Angry. Sad. Guilty. All at the same time.'

'My darling, I am so sorry.'

She blinked rapidly and then, sick at heart, she leant against him. He stroked her hair and let her sob.

How much time passed she didn't know but eventually she wiped her eyes and said, 'What about Romi? Is she with Lucia and Valentina?'

'Yes.' He smiled, looking proud of his girls. 'They adore her. I knew they would.'

She held out her hand. 'Shall we go and rescue them?'

He nodded.

'They must be seventeen by now,' she said, trying to rein back the desolation she was feeling.

'Yes. One minute they're toddlers like Romi, five minutes later you're looking at young women.'

She raised a slight smile.

After she'd splashed her face and pinched her pale cheeks, they crossed the landing in silence. But what she wanted was to roar out the depths of this alone. Weep into her pillow. Drink too much wine and fall asleep in the orchard just as she had after Billy died. This was too much. Much too much. But she was a mother herself now, and she had responsibilities.

'Their mother didn't mind them coming?' she managed to ask.

'Their mother has other fish to fry.'

'Mysterious.'

He smiled. 'All will become clear later. I promise.'

'I hate secrets,' she said.

'Not a secret. I'm just biding my time.'

They knocked on his daughters' door and went in. Romi was jumping on one of their twin beds.

'Look, Mama. Look at me!'

'Darling, I'm looking. And what am I going to say?'

Romi frowned and the girls laughed at the serious face she pulled. 'Me not jump.'

Thirza nodded. 'Not on the beds, no.'

Romi stuck out her bottom lip and looked even more comical.

Thirza ignored her and said, 'Lucia, Valentina, I apologise for the rather unusual start to your visit. Shall we all go outside now? It has turned into such a lovely day and lunch will be served shortly.'

She didn't know how she'd got the words out, and made them sound almost normal, but they beamed at her, both of them stunning in the way only Italian girls could be. Flowing chestnut-brown locks, perfect features, full lips, and deep brown eyes. Thirza wondered what their mother must look like for these two to be so beautiful. She watched as Romi held her head high, scooting down the stairs between the big girls, her right hand in Lucia's and her left in Valentina's. And it was clear that having two older sisters would add something special to her daughter's life.

After lunch the girls begged to be allowed to take Romi up for her nap so Thirza smiled and told them it would be fine.

As the day went on, she recovered a vestige of her equilibrium because she had to. She had calmed her pounding heart, but every time Dulcie slipped into her mind glaring at her, eyes blazing in the way they did, she tensed again. It was only during the night that she was truly haunted by the recriminations and accusations she and her mother had thrown at each other, and she felt ashamed.

At dusk the next evening when they were alone, Emilio, sitting opposite Thirza, reached for her hand and said, 'I have news, *cara mia*. It is the main reason I am here.'

'All right.'

'I have finally received my Sacra Rota annulment.'

She gasped. Could it be true?

'From the ecclesiastic Court of the Vatican City.'

They stared at one another, and Thirza realised she was holding her breath.

He let go of her hand and said, 'Shall we walk and then sit on the rocks?'

She still hadn't spoken by the time they were there, knowing this was going to be momentous, but not knowing how to feel. As she slid off her shoes, she glanced upwards. The sea was already darkening, and the sky looked almost purple, but she dangled her feet in the briny water anyway.

'Is it cold?' he asked.

'A little. Are you chicken?'

He grinned. 'Maybe. But not about the water.'

They watched the sea shifting, the birds flying, the remaining clouds drifting, and still she could not trust herself to speak.

He pulled out a small blue box from his shirt pocket, opened it, and showed it to her.

She blinked rapidly. *Please don't let me cry. Please.*

'Diamonds,' she said. 'It's very beautiful.'

He gazed at her, the question already in his eyes. 'Will you marry me, Thirza? Will you be my wife? I'm sorry it has taken so long.'

This *was* what she wanted but, as she searched for the right words, Dulcie strode into her mind again.

Tears began to prickle, though she dashed them away.

Emilio was gazing at her, looking concerned, the question still hanging in the air between them.

This should be the only thing that mattered, and she needed to force herself to close her mind to everything else, but when she tried her heart hammered and a lump began forming in her throat. She didn't want to make things worse than they already were, but was she really expected to put her mother first forever? And could she put Emilio first instead?

'Thirza?' Emilio said.

She saw an anxious look in his eyes now but felt a little distant, a little removed. Surely that couldn't be right, and it wasn't. Yet the loss of her mother. The loss of her mother! If she agreed to marry Emilio, the rupture – the terrible terrible rupture – between her and Dulcie might never heal.

'Darling.' He paused. 'Speak to me.'

She looked at him. She had to think about Romi and wasn't it best to allow some happiness for herself and her own daughter?

I've had enough of pain, she thought. *I'm so sorry, Dulcie. I love you but I have to live my life.*

Emilio, with his dear face, his sparkling eyes, his curly hair, swam before her, waiting, as she took a long slow breath. In and out. Then another – in and out – before speaking again. This joining of one life to another was huge, even without the complications, but she was going to do it.

'Yes,' she said, and took his hand. 'I will marry you.'

And then she did cry, and so did he, for he was Italian after all.

CHAPTER 53

Over dinner, on the candlelit terrace, Thirza and Emilio decided the wedding should be soon, and that it would take place in Corfu Town. When Thirza invited his daughters to be bridesmaids along with Romi, their faces shone, and their smiles were wide.

Later, when she was alone with Emilio in her bedroom, Thirza stood at the window, looking out at the moonlight edging the clouds. Her chest constricted as she said, 'I have to ask. What are we going to do about Dulcie?'

He pulled her to him, kissed her, then he said, 'We must invite her, even if she doesn't come.'

But a heavy, forlorn feeling had taken over. She'd been so carried away in the excitement when they'd told his daughters that momentarily she'd forgotten how much there was still to say. For peace of mind, she had to find an opportunity to talk to Dulcie before the wedding.

'I cared for her,' Emilio was saying. 'But it was a whirlwind fantasy. She had a life here, a marriage. And, as I told you before, she didn't tell me about Billy.'

Thirza wondered if he were seeking something more from her, an assurance perhaps that everything would be all right. She wanted to give him what he wanted, she wanted to give him everything, but she couldn't yet for the road ahead still felt impregnable and her heart ached.

'You said she didn't tell you she was pregnant?'

'No. Though as I said before, she must already have been, that time I saw her with Piers in Corfu, and cottoned on that she was married.'

'I'm sorry you never knew Billy.'

His eyes darkened. 'It breaks my heart. I would have given anything to spend time with him.'

'It's elemental, the love we have for our children,' she said.

'Yes.' He was staring into the middle distance, brooding.

'Come on,' she said. 'I'll find that photograph of him. You still haven't seen it.'

He reached for her and together they went to her dressing table, where she took out the photo, kissed it, and then handed it to him. He gazed at it for the longest time. 'Little scamp,' he whispered, his voice choked, then he looked up at her, eyes swimming with tears.

The air between them thickened with emotion, and she didn't know if she could bear seeing that pain on his face. She bit her lip, not trusting herself to speak, and then began to brush her hair.

After a while she said, 'It will be all right.'

As she stood before him, she felt nervous, raw, as she peeled off her clothes layer by layer. It had been so long since they'd been intimate, it felt as if they were starting over. Well, they *were* starting over. Her body had changed. Of course it had. She'd given birth, had fed Romi herself for nine months, had stretch marks, and was not as lean as she used to be. Not as athletic. Feeling self-conscious and worried that he might mind about the changes, she wanted to cover herself up.

'Close the curtains,' she said.

'I thought you'd like to see the night.'

'I do usually but . . . I don't know.'

He closed the curtains.

She lay on her bed and watched him undress. He looked older too, in ways she couldn't quite identify; after all he must be forty now, fourteen years older than her, but he was still wonderful, and she loved him more than ever.

'I can't believe we've actually reached this point,' she said as he joined her.

He stroked her cheek. 'I'm so glad we have.'

As he touched her, she immediately responded, and desire flared, both hot and mellow. They took their time, despite it having been so long, and she felt with every touch that they were reacquainting themselves with each other. His skin was warm with just that hint of lime and she wanted to breathe the scent of him forever. The sex between them, when it finally happened, felt different. More grown-up somehow, more measured, less wild, less dangerous, but much more loving.

Afterwards Thirza cried happy tears. She surprised herself with how easily she could cry these days. Loving Emilio and loving Romi had changed her. No longer the tough, self-sufficient Thirza she once was, she had discovered that life was all about interdependence and sharing one's self. And not always going it alone. For really what else was there? She was unlikely to lie on her death bed and wish she had earned more money or done better at school. No. She would wish she had loved harder, more completely. She would wish she had not held so much of herself back. Not held herself apart. She would wish she had protected herself less and opened herself more. She would start now and not leave it until her final hour. She wanted no regrets.

A few days after Emilio left, Thirza tied up her hair in a turban and began furiously turning out the cupboards, starting with the nursery. Romi didn't sleep up there, for her daughter had her own little room now, in what had once been Dulcie's dressing room. As the old games, broken dolls, railway tracks, and bald teddy bears piled up in the centre of the room, she wiped her forehead. It was hot, dusty, and she needed water. But even as she rose to her feet from where she'd been squatting to empty the lowest shelves, her mind kept spinning back to her mother. How much of Dulcie's response was grounded in reality? How much was it Dulcie's instinct for drama, which she would always deny, and how much simply the result of habit? She wanted to talk to her mother properly, be open and truthful, and not fight with her.

'One day,' she said. 'Maybe.'

In any case she ought to go to town soon, give her father the good news, and start arranging the wedding, but whenever she thought of it, her mother popped into her mind again, and Thirza could not banish her.

Eventually, as she finished heaping old clothes, towels, and other remnants of her childhood in another pile, she turned her back on it all and went to the kitchen where she poured herself a large glass of water. Then she sat in Dulcie's study looking around at the shelves of books, the pictures, the cluttered desk. As if she could somehow draw in her mother's presence. Make her palpable. It was really her own study now, but Thirza could not think of it like that. It would always be Dulcie's and everything in there attested to that.

She recalled finding Columbine burning those letters of her mother's. Soon she would make changes in this room, but now she chewed the tip of her pen, ordered her thoughts, and finally began to write her own letter.

Dearest Mother,

You must know that I love you deeply and I understand what you have been through as far as I am able, but I must tell you that Emilio has asked me to marry him, and I have agreed. I am so sorry for his sudden unexpected arrival when you were staying, and I hope my news doesn't cause you any more distress, though I fear it might, but please think of this. I didn't fall in love with Emilio with any intention of hurting you. I wasn't looking for a relationship nor was I looking for love.

Mother, please understand, I don't want to bring Romi up on my own. She needs her father and her half-sisters, and she deserves a loving family around her — including you. She needs you and so do I. I long for you to be able to accept this marriage and for you to come to the wedding, since I can't even envisage getting married without you being there.

Please, please, will you come? It means everything to me. I've already lost a brother, I don't want to lose my mother too. Please don't make me choose between you and Emilio.

With my love always,
Thirza

CHAPTER 54

In Corfu Town a couple of weeks later, Thirza sat down at the kitchen table to plan. With her far superior organisational skills Penny rolled out a large sheet of cartridge drawing paper on which she had already pencilled four columns.

'We need to know what we're doing from the start,' Penny said.

'It's only going to be a small wedding.'

'Even a small wedding requires a good plan.'

Thirza knew there was no point arguing. Penny, in chief of operations mode, was unstoppable.

'First you need to tell me your budget.'

'Oh. I don't actually know.'

'Honestly Thirza! You're hopeless. You need to talk to Emilio pronto. I'm sure Piers will chip in too.' She laughed. 'Well, he will if I have anything to do with it.'

Thirza, amused, smiled.

'I know a wonderful seamstress, not too expensive, but she really knows what she's doing. She made *my* wedding dress.'

'And it was lovely.'

'Thank you. I know you'll want something a bit different. Pink, white, and ruffles not being quite your thing.'

Thirza laughed. 'I don't suppose shorts and a paint-splattered linen shirt would cut the mustard.'

Penny reached for her hand and squeezed it.

'Actually,' Thirza continued, 'I've decided I want a deep rose-coloured dress. In silk.'

'Are you sure? How will people know you're getting married?'

Thirza laughed. 'I think being in the church might give the game away.'

'And the bridesmaids?'

'Navy blue.'

Penny began to laugh too. 'Oh my God, Thirza. Only you! Well so be it. It's your funeral.'

Thirza raised her brows. 'I hope not! Anyway, Emilio's daughters are sending over their measurements. Wait till you meet them. They're gorgeous and of course there will be Romi too.'

'Oh, my goodness, she'll look utterly adorable in navy. I suppose you'll allow your father to give you away.'

'I used to think he did that long ago, but we're so much closer now and,' she paused, a little embarrassed, 'and that's down to you.'

Penny beamed. 'I'm glad. He does love you.'

'Yes,' Thirza said, 'I know.'

And so, it went on. Endless discussions about the cake, the flowers, the bouquet, the food, the venue of the wedding breakfast, the photographer, the guest list, and the carriages. Thirza found it all a bit too much and, when she next saw Emilio, muttered that they should have just gone to Gretna Green.

He frowned. 'Where's that?'

'On the Scottish borders.'

He looked bemused and she just laughed.

Dulcie hadn't replied to her letter. Thirza had written again in a similar vein but with no result at all.

Thirza met Odel, looking as elegant as ever, at a café on the Liston. 'I'm sorry to have seen so little of you,' Thirza said as she made herself comfortable. 'It's been hectic.'

Odel smiled. 'For me too. Don't worry, and it's lovely to see you now.'

Thirza gazed out at the wide expanse of grass. No cricket today. 'We're sending out formal invitations soon, but I wanted to invite you myself, in person.'

'So, it's actually happening?'

Thirza nodded. 'I hope you'll be able to come.'

'I hope so too. And you're happy? About everything?'

Thirza sighed. 'Not quite. That's one of the things I wanted to talk to you about.'

'Your mother?'

'I wrote to her pleading with her to come. She didn't reply, so I wrote again.'

'Still nothing?'

'Nothing at all.'

'She'll be licking her wounds.'

'Did she tell you about Emilio arriving when she was staying at Merchant's?'

'She did. It was unfortunate.'

'It couldn't have been worse. She wouldn't even listen to me. It wasn't planned and I had no idea he was coming. We both said terrible things to each other.'

'Give her time. We all say things we don't mean when we're hurt or angry.'

'I know she must have felt hurt and so she hit out and hurt me in return.'

Odel drained the last of her coffee and then rose from the chair. 'Aren't we all so childish, us grown-ups?' she said and laughed.

'Surely not you.'

'Of course me. Just ask my poor long-suffering husband.'

'How is he?'

'Retired, thank God! Now listen, if I know Dulcie at all she won't miss the chance to put on an expensive new outfit and create an eye-watering splash. Just you wait and see.'

'Really?'

'I'll give you a hint. Your mother asked me to find out what colour you and the bridesmaids would be wearing. Cream or white?'

Thirza laughed and felt her heart lift a little. 'Neither. I'll be in dark rose, the bridesmaids in navy blue.'

Was it just idle curiosity, or did her mother actually care? Or, better still, was she planning to come?

Odel bent down, and kissed Thirza on both cheeks. 'Sorry, I must dash. I've got the decorators in, but don't lose heart and do call at the house before you go back to Merchant's if you have a chance. I'll try to speak to your mother.'

CHAPTER 55

April 1934, some months later

In her father's high-walled courtyard garden, alive with flying insects, the orange trees were in blossom, and Thirza almost swooned at their dizzying scent. She was pretending she didn't have a care in the world and was simply enjoying a moment of reflection in the garden before she set off. It was April, just one day before her wedding, and she was watching over Romi, now aged three. Thirza glanced up at the small birds gathering on the rooftops and listened to the swallows chattering and, as the screaming gulls took off and landed around the fishermen's boats, she realised how much she loved to just be there listening to life happening.

Half an hour later, Thirza left Romi with Penny and took a short cut through a small section of garden attached to the Palace of St Michael and St George. The palace, which thankfully had survived the Italian bombardment of Corfu Town in 1923, had been commissioned by the British and was used as the High Commissioner's residence before becoming a Greek royal residence in 1864. The garden overlooking the bay was not really open to the public, so Thirza held her breath until she reached the safety of the local sea baths at the foot of the fortifications.

The Faliraki area, one of the oldest public bathing spots, was tiny but had a wonderful view of the Palaio Frourio, or Old Fortress. So close to her town house, it was where Odel, every day of her life, climbed down one of the wrought-iron ladders that led into the clear water of the Ionian Sea where she swam, though the smell of fish and salty seaweed was strong and not for the faint-hearted.

Thirza was about to enter a small café when she spotted Odel and her mother meandering back along the small stone jetty arm in arm. She stood still and watched them walk, deep in conversation, heads close together, Dulcie now as lean as ever she had been, casually dressed in a spotless cream blouse and elegant black skirt. Hair a little lighter and any sign of the extra weight completely gone.

For a moment she wondered if Dulcie had only come to avoid the tittle-tattle that might have arisen should she have stayed away.

Imagine a mother, not bothering to attend her daughter's wedding.

Well, they were always rather odd, that family.

The mother was a writer, you know.

Odel glanced up first and waved, then Dulcie did the same. Thirza's heart skipped a beat, for until she'd received Odel's note the evening before, she had given up hope of seeing her mother. No communication, no letters, no telegrams. But Dulcie's expression was light as she came towards her and, as Odel stepped away and left them to it, Thirza and her mother exchanged a cautious, curious look. Not a cold look. Nor a warm one either. But something in between. Then they walked back along the jetty to gaze at the incredible blue of the sea.

'I didn't know if—' Thirza said, still feeling wary.

'To be honest neither did I.'

Thirza narrowed her eyes. 'When did you decide?'

'I had an outfit ready a month ago.'

'Really? You didn't say.'

'No.'

'Were you planning to come at that stage?'

Dulcie shook her head. 'Not exactly. I was invited to another wedding, a friend's wedding in Tuscany.'

'Oh.'

'I had to choose. The outfit would have done for either.'

'How very practical,' Thirza teased. 'So how did you make up your mind? Toss a coin?'

'No.'

'Well?'

Her mother's slow sigh signalled surrender rather than defeat. 'The truth is I've been a prize idiot.'

'No,' Thirza said, although her denial didn't really ring true and she had to laugh.

Dulcie laughed too. 'Yes, I have. And we both know it.'

'So?'

Dulcie shrugged. 'I recently had an affair. Not before time, you might say. Anyway, he made me see sense.'

'Oh,' Thirza said, though she wasn't sure if she really did. 'Is *he* coming too? I'll have to check with Penny—'

'Don't be a goose. Of course he isn't. But he made me see how stuck I'd become. Trapped in the past. Frightened to let go. I'm so sorry for that. More than I can say. Truly.'

'I understand.'

'I'm sure you don't, but there it is. I hope you'll let me make up for lost time. Forgive me?'

The question seemed to slip out almost accidentally and Thirza had tears in her eyes as she held out her hand. Dulcie took it and squeezed. Then she put an arm around Thirza's shoulders and said, 'I really am very sorry. I've been such a fool. I've already lost one child, and I'm hanged if I'm prepared to lose another. I'll do better now.'

But Thirza *had* understood perfectly and now, ambushed by the realisation that her mother's relationship with Emilio was all wrapped up with Billy and his death, she swallowed hard and could not speak. Of course Dulcie hadn't been able to let go. Not of Billy. Nor of Emilio. In her mind they had been tied together irrevocably; if she let go of Emilio, then Billy would be gone too.

'I looked for Billy here, you know,' Dulcie said, her voice low. 'Well Piers and I did, in 1923, those first days after . . .'

Thirza nodded, unable to speak for the lump in her throat.

'We looked everywhere.' Dulcie shook her head, lost in thought. 'It was the worst feeling. Like being catapulted right into hell and,' she waved her arm around. 'This is one of the last places I ever saw him alive or dead. I waved goodbye as he went to meet Piers the day before. Billy glanced back at me, grinning, you know, and then he waved too.'

'Oh Mum.'

'I'll never forget that moment but if only I'd known then, I would never have let him out of my sight.'

Thirza's eyes filled with tears as she reached for her mother's hand.

'Are you all right?' Dulcie asked.

'Yes. I'm sorry for not understanding.'

'How could you? Anyway, I'm all the better for seeing you. In the end, one must live in the present.'

The silence felt so full Thirza could hardly breathe.

Then she said, 'I have to get back in a minute. I know Penny's really busy and Romi will be awake. My father is not brilliant at keeping an eye on her.'

Dulcie laughed. 'He never was good at that. But there's one more thing.'

'Oh?'

'I'm meeting Emilio for a drink this evening. We need to clear the air before the wedding.'

'Should I come?'

'No. I think not. Best anyway to keep away from the groom on the eve of your wedding. Don't worry, it'll be fine.'

'All right. I'd better go now.' Thirza gave her mother the closest hug, and feeling the warmth of her, didn't want to ever let go. This was something so vital to her wellbeing and she'd been without it for too long

'Darling,' Dulcie whispered in her ear. 'It really will be all right. I'll call in at the house in a little while. I need to see my granddaughter again.'

Thirza nodded then held her mother away from her so she could gaze into her eyes. Then, fearing more tears, she broke away and quickly headed back to her father's house.

Emilio and his daughters had arrived at their hotel near the Liston promenade the evening before – excited and chatting ten to the dozen. Penny had been in full military mode, absolutely in her element as she checked and rechecked all the arrangements and exclaimed over the beauty of Emilio's daughters. The girls had tried on their dresses with no extra alterations necessary and now Penny was rushing around again, doing goodness knows what.

'Things to do. Things to do,' she repeated whenever Thirza asked.

The buffet wedding breakfast was to be held at her father and Penny's town house and a sit-down family meal was planned for the evening at a hotel. Thirza had insisted on a relaxed gathering straight after the ceremony, not a stiff formal event, and Penny had taken care of organising it.

Now, back in the courtyard garden again, Thirza threw a tennis ball to Romi, who was standing with her arms crossed and insisting she needed Georgie to play ball with her. She had wept to hear the plaintive howl arising from her beloved hound when they'd left him behind at Merchant's, and with a sigh, Thirza repeated once again, 'Darling, I told you, dogs can't be invited to attend a wedding.'

Romi sank to the ground and wailed, 'Unfair on dogs! Unfair!'

Thirza went to squat down beside her, wafted away the flies, took a deep breath of orange-blossom-scented air, and tried to sound encouraging when she said, 'Come on, do you want to try your lovely dress on again?' This was over and beyond requirements as the child had already been paraded fully kitted out in front of Penny, who had nodded her approval.

Romi stopped wailing.

'The flowers might be here too. Do you want to see them?'

Thirza had no idea if their flower crowns, of orange blossom and early creamy-white roses, chosen to match Thirza's bouquet, would have arrived or not. All the flowers were Penny's doing.

Romi stood up and took Thirza's hand. They had only just reached the hall when the door flew open, and Penny marched in, her arms loaded with flowers, their fragrance almost sickly. Romi rushed forward to inspect.

'Sorry darling,' Penny said, bending down. 'The crowns won't be delivered until the morning.'

The little girl's face fell but she didn't cry because at that moment someone else was coming through the open doorway. The air seemed to freeze but Dulcie simply glanced around the hall nodding and smiling as she took in the new decor. She had changed into an elegant silk shift dress with a matching jacket in sage green and looked composed, almost nonchalant. 'Well,' she said. 'It's been a while.'

Thirza felt her heart thump with nerves, at the same time as acknowledging how carefully her mother must have chosen her outfit. She could not have looked more serene, more in control.

Dulcie held out her arms to Romi. Then she added, 'Seems like you have your hands full there, Penelope.'

'Er. Yes,' Penny said, still wearing her kimono, and not even having brushed her hair. She ran a palm across her curls with a look of defiance.

'Well, it's nice to finally meet my successor,' Dulcie said.

Penny gave her a fleeting smile but looked unsure if that had been meant sarcastically or not. Either way, she straightened her shoulders, clearly compelled to signal that this was *her* home now. 'You, too. I'll just take these flowers through to the scullery. They're for the house. We're having a small reception here, you see.'

'Yes. I'm aware. I received the invitation.'

Thirza watched the small exchange, her heart beating way too fast. Then after Penny had gone, she turned to her mother. 'Would you like coffee in the garden?'

'Thank you, no coffee, but I'd love to sit in the garden. I've done so much walking. Now where has Romi run off to?'

A commotion in the scullery gave them a clue.

'What happened?' Thirza said as Piers joined them. She'd expected it to be awkward when he saw Dulcie, but it wasn't. At least not very awkward.

'Hello Dulcie,' he said, sounding relatively natural, then with a guilty look he glanced back at the scullery and added, 'Don't worry. It's nothing. Entirely my fault.'

Shrieks and wails were still reaching them from the back of the house.

Dulcie raised a brow. 'Doesn't sound like nothing.'

At that moment Romi was marched into the hall by Penny. Romi's face was red and tear-stained, but there was something rebellious about the way she glared at everyone.

'You'd best look after this one yourself,' Penny said, pushing Romi forward.

'Why?' Thirza asked. 'What has she done?'

'Only gone and cut off the heads of all the flowers I had left in a bucket of water in the scullery.'

'I'll just pop out,' Piers said, backing away.

'You'll what?' shrieked Penny.

'Er, to buy, you know, more flowers. Maybe?'

'They were a special order,' Penny said, 'and you were the one who left the door open.'

Thirza ordered her face to be serious, but the sight of her mother trying to conceal her laughter at Penny berating her ex-husband with so vehemence was too much. Before long Thirza gave up and gulped back a squeak which turned into a guffaw.

Penny looked at them both askance. 'Has everyone gone stark staring mad around here?'

And then as Romi rolled her eyes in the way that only children can do, they were all laughing, and the ice was broken.

CHAPTER 56

Thirza took her first step down the aisle the following morning, arm in arm with her father, and wearing a long, bias-cut dress in a deep rose colour. The church smelt so heavenly she immediately relinquished her nerves. Felt them fly up into the vaulted ceiling, leaving her grounded and happy. Right up until this moment she'd felt queasy, wondering if she might be able to make a break for it, just run off, her and Emilio. No fuss. Creating an impression had never been how she lived her life. That was Dulcie's stance. Or Penny's. Funny how alike those two were, despite being incredibly different. But for a wedding you had to embrace the display or look a total fool, done up to the nines, feeling like a total fraud inside, and unable to carry the whole thing off.

Holy Trinity was Anglican and housed in a simple light-coloured stone building that had once been part of the Ionian Parliament but had been bestowed on the British community of Kerkyra, or Corfu, to function as a house of worship. Today, thanks to Penny, the austere interior had been transformed and looked gorgeous, and so did Thirza's dress. With floaty elbow-length sleeves, a natural waist, and skirt flaring out slightly at the ankle, Thirza had never before felt so elegant or glamorous.

A sigh of pleasure from the congregation echoed as she processed down the aisle, looking left and right, acknowledging friends with a smile and a nod and, only when her emotions got the better of her, glancing down at the beautifully patterned tiled floor. Despite Thirza's initial objections, she had to admit Penny had worked wonders with her hair, taming the wild auburn curls into neat, well-behaved ringlets.

Followed by her three bridesmaids wearing navy-blue satin, Thirza could scarcely believe the moment had arrived. She and they wore identical orange blossom and rose crowns, echoing the incredible profusion of flowers in the church. She sniffed the air, thrilled to find the rather cold ambiance of the church transformed so thoroughly that she felt she was getting married in a brightly scented garden.

She hadn't needed to worry about how the meeting between Emilio and her mother had gone, for one glance at him as he turned to look at her, his eyes shining with love, told her everything she needed to know. She had expected to cry but his eyes told her he was closer to that than she was. She felt jubilant when she saw her mother's face lit up by the sun and, dared she hope, happiness. Dulcie looked proud as she sat bolt upright in the front pew with Penny. There might be a long way to go before those two became good friends, but this was progress.

A beaming Ianthe, clutching Walter tightly and squeezed next to a lonely-looking Columbine, was sitting in the row behind. Momentarily assailed by a passing uneasy feeling, Thirza wondered what was wrong with Columbine.

She was barely aware of her father and the bridesmaids joining Dulcie in the pew, for now she only had thoughts of Emilio. In high-heeled shoes she was almost as tall as him and her gaze took in his wonderful eyes flaring gold with happiness, his suit of silver grey, the buttonhole that matched her dress, and she felt dizzy with the same kind of delirious joy that had followed Romi's birth.

Romi was sitting between her two half-sisters looking smug and gripping the little posy she had been given as bridesmaid of honour.

Thirza believed it was the marriage that counted, not the wedding, and had not expected to feel so deeply moved by all this. But every emotion she'd ever experienced was intensified, coalescing into this strange, almost out-of-body, once-in-a-lifetime moment. Although of course for Emilio it was the second time around. Still, for just a few seconds she actually felt that she might pass out, so focused only on his eyes.

Given the ceremony was in English, in an Anglican church, the order of service was in English, Italian, and Greek. She had insisted Emilio should choose the music and that it must be Italian. He had hired a wonderful string quartet from Italy, and when the music filled the church, and they all listened with rapt faces, she beamed at him.

Afterwards Thirza could not remember much of the ceremony, apart from the music. She remembered Emilio's warm lips on hers when the chaplain said that they were now man and wife, and he could kiss the bride. She remembered everyone clapping, especially Romi, who was bouncing up and down and calling out, '*Hurrah*,' at which everyone laughed and joined in. She remembered the faces of a few friends of her parents, people *she'd* known too, Emilio's cousin who had been his best man. Eleni, Magdalena, and Spiro, of course, and Odel with her husband.

Dulcie's treat had been to bring out a top London society photographer, Marcus Winfield, to record the happy day. As Thirza and Emilio came out into the sunshine ahead of the congregation, the photographer asked them to stand in the arched doorway beside the climbing bougainvillea. Almost an exact match to the colour of Thirza's dress. She had never before felt so elated, her energy fizzing and bubbling so much that it was impossible to stand still. She held on to Emilio who looked dazed and equally unsteady.

Then, as they walked down the stone steps to stand in the small garden at the front of the church, Thirza looked across to smile at the passers-by who had gathered beyond the railings to watch.

As the guests milled about the little garden, laughing, and chatting, happy to be there on such a lovely spring day, the photographer gathered the entire family to stand beside and around Emilio and Thirza. She was aware of the bridesmaids, her mother too, looking stunning in a crisp navy-blue-and-white-striped suit, with a huge wide-brimmed fuchsia hat that shaded her face. Only Dulcie could dare to get away with that hat. Piers was there too, and Penny wearing a pale pink embroidered organza creation, but also Columbine in lilac and Ianthe with Walter. By this stage Romi was jumping about, giggling and wrapping herself around Thirza's ankles.

Suddenly, Dulcie gasped and moved forward with a jerk. A murmur came from the people closest to her and the air seemed to shake. Then she dropped as if in slow motion. Dropped like a stone. Emilio and Piers rushed towards her to try to break her fall before she reached the hard ground and hurt herself. As Dulcie's hat flew off, Thirza and Penny stared at each other in shock. The fall had not been so much a regular tumble or trip, but more of a crumple, a giving way, as if an electric shock had passed through her and caused her to buckle and bend. Had her mother suffered a heart attack or a stroke? As Thirza knelt by her side, she saw from the corner of her eye a young man striding rapidly towards them, looking terribly worried. Was he a doctor? Closer to her now, the young man paused for a moment to glance at her. A young man with deep hazel eyes. Rooted to the spot she felt an icy shard stabbing at her heart, and she shivered even though the day was warm.

It couldn't be! Surely. It couldn't be!

An expanse of blackness opened up and she trembled there on the edge, balanced precariously between what was possible and what was not, her heart pitching and tilting wildly as she focused in and out of what was actually happening, unaware she was sobbing.

The guests whispered among themselves. Thirza could hear them. *Why was the bride crying? Was her mother dead?*

Then Thirza felt so light-headed from the shock that she couldn't breathe, might never breathe again. The guests fell eerily silent for a moment and Emilio stroked her back, encouraging her to take a breath. Finally, she took a shuddering, slow breath, and leant her whole weight against him, feeling his heart pounding against her back.

Barely suppressed excitement now ran through the crowd, and they nudged each other, eager to know if anyone had any idea what was going on. Thirza glanced around and saw that Piers, along with Odel, was still holding Dulcie. Her mother was visibly trembling now, her face ghostly white. And Thirza knew Dulcie had not suffered a heart attack, she had fainted in fright and disbelief. Glancing over her shoulder, Thirza noticed Penny looking utterly astonished, although she spotted that Columbine did not look surprised.

When the young man began to speak, it was as if the entire world just stopped spinning in its tracks. The whole world waiting to hear what he had to say, waiting to know. Expecting an explanation.

'Hello,' he said, in a soft American drawl.

The accent was almost the strangest thing, though not quite. Thirza's thoughts scattered like frightened hedge sparrows and, although she tried, she couldn't quite catch them. This was crazy. For God's sake! Or might he be an imposter? Alarm bloomed in her mind, spreading her thoughts to fly about even more uncontrollably.

She barely noticed Emilio's arms around her, her heart hammering so loudly it blocked out everything else.

And now the guests grew louder, and Thirza heard their repeated whispers, tears, questions, comments.

'*What's going on?*'

'*No!*'

'*Can it really be?*'

Thirza saw her father's white face, heard her mother's broken strangled cry.

'Billy?'

CHAPTER 57

The Parsonage

Dulcie and Thirza both froze as Piers, looking terribly shaken, told everyone that Penny and Walter would take Romi with them, along with Emilio's daughters, and lead the way. The wedding breakfast would take place at his home exactly as planned, and the rest of the family would follow on shortly.

The room the chaplain offered them in the parsonage, situated just behind the church, was old-fashioned, as if it hadn't seen a lick of paint or new wallpaper for years. Not that anyone cared. It was stuffy, despite the slight breeze from an open window.

Thirza couldn't understand how her brain could still be working, how she could even notice her surroundings, when she'd just experienced the greatest shock of her entire life. Greater than his loss was his return. Was this really Billy, standing there looking nervous, and tentative? Her brother?

This didn't feel real. *He* didn't feel real. Surely he must be an imposter because the dead do not come back from the grave, no matter how hard one might wish it. And she had wished it. Again, and again, and again, she had wished it. In her dreams, with the smell of mown grass and damp earth in her nose, she'd seen him break through the freshly dug ground from where he'd been buried. She'd seen him sit up with dirt in his hair. He had held out his arms to her and she had wanted him to really be there, even though his eyes had been dead, blank, unseeing, and when she woke up, she realised she was screaming. Buried in the earth was not where he belonged. You buried treasure, dogs buried bones.

And now here she was stepping into another reality with no anchor to cling to. For it seemed that here was her brother, her brother who had been dead for over ten years. A jagged pain sliced through her as she looked for the boy she had known but this man, who looked so like Billy might have done, was a stranger. She couldn't make out the boy he once was. Why wasn't she overjoyed? Why so cut adrift and feeling like she was drowning, her thoughts and emotions spinning out of control, because how could he be Billy?

She stared at him, desperate to understand, and he smiled suddenly, so warmly, that her heart skipped a beat, and then another, because there he was. For an instant she could actually see him. There he was. He really was. Billy! Come back from the land of the dead.

Her eyes flooded with unshed tears as she smiled back at him but then, a moment later, he seemed like a stranger again.

She remembered *this* was her wedding day.

She noticed Columbine didn't sit but stood gazing out of the open window, wringing her hands, with Ianthe hovering nearby as if to catch her, in case she too might be about to take a tumble. *More likely really*, Thirza thought, though the woman really didn't seem to be drinking anymore.

Piers was walking up and down, pale, still shaken, glancing at Billy from time to time, but then he clumsily reached out and he and his son embraced.

'Welcome home,' Piers said, his voice trembling.

Thirza realised that her mother had not been breathing normally from the first moment she'd seen Billy standing there in a crumpled linen suit. Now Dulcie was pressing a palm to her chest as if she might encourage her lungs to do their job in the increasingly airless room.

'Won't you sit, Mother?' Billy said, standing just inside the door. 'You too, Thirza.'

Thirza and Dulcie exchanged a confused look, neither of them really understanding any of this, but they did both sit on hard chairs with no armrests, and Emilio chose to stand behind Thirza with his hands gently resting on her shoulders. A solicitous act of love that she sorely needed, because she felt so oddly insecure, now that everything that had seemed so important and permanent had not been, after all. She felt disassociated from herself and from everyone else too. Even Billy. Shock. It had to be shock. Her palms were sweating, her forehead was damp, and her heart was pounding in her ears. She wiped her hands on her beautiful dress. *That will ruin it*, she thought. Silk did not like sweat.

She managed to take a good long breath, straightening her shoulders, her hands completely still in her lap, yet chewing the inside of her cheek and not stopping when she tasted blood. Was she even awake?

She shook herself out of it. And the next minute she was overjoyed all over again for the young man smiled at her once more and she *did* know him. Her Billy, her darling brother, but all grown up into a man. She felt tears pricking her lids again but refused to let them fall.

They were all waiting. Thirza saw her mother couldn't stop staring at him, this tall young man, with hazel eyes and dark curly hair and a smile that was as wide as the world and deep as the sky. Loose-limbed, easy in this new grown-up body, his light American accent lending something foreign, unexpected.

On the day she heard he was dead, her heart had broken into a million different pieces. One for each hour of the life he would never live. One for each hour that his heart would never beat. Over and over, she had mourned him, and it had all been in vain. His heart did beat. His life had been lived. Without her.

'I lost my memory,' Billy said quietly, when it seemed like he might never speak. 'But later kept having odd dreams about the past.' He turned to Columbine. 'Do you want to tell them, or shall I?'

'Shall we both do it?' Columbine said, looking drawn and unable to meet anyone's eyes.

Thirza stared at her and searched for the right words. What was her aunt talking about? How was this in any way connected to her?

Then Columbine added, 'First, I want to say how terribly terribly sorry I am.'

Dulcie exploded. 'Oh, for God's sake, do shut up Columbine. Haven't you caused enough trouble in the family? Everything isn't about you.'

'Hey,' Ianthe said. 'That isn't fair. My mother was ill.'

'But what the hell is she talking about?' Dulcie said, sounding more irritable and upset than shocked now. 'I want to hear from my son.'

'Mother,' Billy said soothingly, slowly, as if speaking to a child. 'I'm telling you what happened. I was abducted by two men who later abandoned me in a cave in Italy.'

Dulcie turned even paler. 'Oh God!' she whispered, a hand at her throat.

Thirza stared at him, opened her mouth to speak, but then closed it again.

'I think they planned to demand a ransom, but then because of the massive hue and cry after I disappeared, or maybe because of the Italian invasion of Corfu, they failed, and it never happened. Of course, I didn't know any of that at the time.'

'I just let him go,' Columbine said in a tremulous voice. 'When Billy asked to go back for his hat, I lied to you all.'

'You lied?' Thirza repeated.

'I didn't tell him not to go. I didn't tell him it was too dangerous with the Italians blasting the island.'

'You what?' Dulcie stammered and two angry spots of red appeared on her cheeks.

'I suppose I was angry with *you*.'

'You suppose?'

Columbine bit her lip and didn't speak.

'But this is madness,' Dulcie insisted, turning to Billy. 'You couldn't have been taken to Italy, your clothes were found here in Corfu.'

'When I was found, I was only wearing a grown man's torn cotton shirt.'

'You were all alone?'

'Yes.'

Opposite Dulcie, Columbine rocked back and forth on her feet then sank into a chair.

Thirza scratched her neck where she felt the tingle of a heat rash beginning. Then she managed to focus on her aunt again and said, 'Why were you angry with my mother?'

Columbine sniffed and wiped the tears from her cheeks with a handkerchief Ianthe passed to her. She gazed at her sister. 'You know? Don't you?'

The stillness in the room thrummed with tension. Even the breeze had died down.

Dulcie stared at Columbine in stunned silence.

'The men must have wanted to put the police off the scent,' Billy eventually said. 'With the clothes, I mean.'

Columbine nodded. 'I knew it was all my fault. I knew I should have stopped Billy going for his hat, made him stay close to me. I put him in danger and I'm sorry. I felt awful, terrible.'

Dulcie gasped and pointed at Columbine and then she whispered, 'Oh my God! It was *you* who sent the threatening note!'

'I wanted to get back at you. It was the only thing I could think of.'

'But why?'

'You know why.'

A long silence followed, the air thick. Thirza searched for something to say but her mind had gone completely blank.

'I wanted to tell you that I lied to the police, to you too,' Columbine continued in a halting voice, 'but I was too scared. I hired a detective to find Billy, or his body, but he had no luck.'

Billy was standing beside Dulcie now and she reached for her son's hand.

'Years later,' Columbine added, 'after I went to live in America with Ianthe and Walter, I heard from the detective again.'

Dulcie shook her head as if unable to comprehend all this.

Then Billy said, 'Back in 1923 an American couple on holiday in Italy found me. I don't remember, but later they told me I was confused, filthy dirty, starving, and wandering alone on the beach. When it became clear I wasn't Italian, speaking only English, and unable to explain what had happened, they were allowed to take me to America and eventually adopt me.'

Dulcie gasped and said, 'But you're *my* son!'

'Mine too,' Piers said, his face contorting, and Thirza felt a flash of horror as she realised her father still didn't know about Emilio.

'I am,' Billy said. 'But *they* brought me up. For more than ten years I've been *their* son. They called me Archie. They're good people and they saved my life.'

Thirza glanced at Dulcie who swallowed visibly, looking much closer to tears now, but she pressed the heels of her palms into her closed eyes, as if rubbing the pain away.

Billy squatted down beside their mother holding both of her hands now.

There was a long silence in the room. Piers went to lean against the wall and began coughing repeatedly.

When Piers finally stopped, Billy continued. 'Last year my new family were the subject of a magazine article in which we pleaded for information about my past.'

After a few moments more, Billy sighed deeply, patted, and then let go of Dulcie's hands. 'I was *beginning* to remember, you see,' he said as he rose to his feet.

Thirza nodded, though she hardly knew why.

'Just parts of the abduction to begin with, but the article was picked up by a radio station who interviewed me on air.'

This couldn't be true, could it? Thirza was picking at her own fingernails while blinking rapidly. How on earth must her mother be feeling?

'The detective found out about it and alerted me, so I listened in,' Columbine said. 'After that, I went to see Billy and told him what had happened that day in 1923. I knew it was him. Straight away, I knew.'

Dulcie doubled over on herself. Thirza pushed back her chair and then knelt, enfolding her mother, comforting her and stroking her cheek, before looking up to say, 'I don't understand why you wanted to hurt my mother, Columbine. Why didn't you tell the police the truth? You saw what losing Billy did to her, to me, to my father. We're your family.'

There was a sharp spiky pause, during which Dulcie straightened up and Thirza slumped onto the floor, barely aware of her gorgeous silk dress, knees drawn up, her arms wrapped around her shins, Emilio kneeling beside her.

'I just felt angry,' Columbine said, her voice quiet and still with tears on her cheeks. 'She was always belittling me. Why should I help look after her child, when she had taken everything?'

Thirza stared at her then glanced at Billy, who was gazing down at the ground and looking lost.

'But you let my brother, who was just a little boy . . . you let him go home on his own right in the middle of the Italian invasion, didn't you?'

Columbine held up a hand to hide her face. 'I know. I know.'

At first Dulcie didn't speak out loud, just muttered to herself before rising to her feet.

Thirza stood up too and held out her hand to her mother. 'Why did Columbine do this?' she asked.

Dulcie shook her head, drew in a long slow breath, then exhaled in a rush. 'I . . . I believe she may think that my father cheated her father out of the deeds to Merchant's.'

Thirza gasped.

'The stakes were always so ridiculously high when they played poker.'

Thirza turned to Columbine. 'So, you believe *you* should have inherited Merchant's?'

Columbine nodded.

Thirza felt her legs beginning to shake and forced herself to stiffen. As she steadied herself, she saw Dulcie's mouth quiver.

'Dulcie admitted the truth. Her father had got hold of Merchant's fraudulently.' Columbine spat the words out, the bitterness in her voice unmistakable.

Dulcie shook her head. 'It was a joke, Columbine. You kept going on and on. Nothing I did to help you was ever enough. I was teasing you. I knew nothing.'

'You said it though, and I believed you. And my father killed himself because he lost Merchant's.'

Thirza stared out of the window at the breeze shimmering the leaves in the small parsonage garden. She felt the blood rushing to her head but managed to speak up and control the crack in her voice. 'Columbine, Merchant's will soon be mine. It's Romi's and my home. And my business.'

Columbine shook her head. 'I don't want it,' she whispered. 'It's tainted.'

There was a short, strained silence.

'After your father died, I asked my father, you know,' Dulcie said. 'He just smiled and told me not to be so silly.'

'He was a liar,' Columbine retorted. 'A liar!'

Dulcie glared at her. 'All of this was in your own head. It wasn't real!'

Nobody spoke.

Then, as if filled with sudden overwhelming rage, Dulcie stormed across and grasped Columbine's hair, dragging her from the chair.

Columbine cringed but Dulcie did not relent and slapped her hard across the face.

'You didn't give a thought to my son's safety,' she hissed. 'You let him go off on his own, when the island was being bombed!'

Billy and Piers held Dulcie back. 'Don't,' Billy said. 'Don't hurt her. She found me in the end.'

Dulcie backed away. 'You let my son go because of a house!'

'No, not just that. For my father's death.'

There was silence.

When Dulcie spoke again her words were like shards of ice. '*That* was not my fault. Your father was a whisky-soaked drunk, just like you! He was out of control, owed money everywhere, and Columbine . . . hear this!'

Columbine pressed her hands against her ears.

Dulcie raised her voice. 'Your father jumped to his death because he was in terrible debt. *My* father had been paying off his excesses for decades. I still have the receipts.'

Columbine's anguished sobs broke the silence that had filled the room.

'Come now, Mother,' Billy said. 'It's over.'

'No. I believed you were dead, Billy. We all did. Can you imagine what that does to a mother? To a father? A child should not die first. She not only stole *you*, who mattered more to me than Merchant's or anything else in the world. She stole my life too. She took a sledgehammer to it. For over ten years the grief wrecked our family. *She* wrecked our family!'

'She didn't know Billy would be abducted,' Thirza said, trying to calm things down, but she could tell Dulcie barely heard her.

The air in the room was completely still. Nobody else spoke, Columbine's weeping the only sound.

Thirza watched Dulcie, incandescent with rage and still staring at her cousin.

When she spoke again, she was growling, a dreadful animal sound. 'Get out, Columbine. Get out now. And I swear if you ever come anywhere near my family again, I will destroy you.'

CHAPTER 58

Merchant's House, a few days later

Thirza opened her eyes and peered into the dark mute night – a night that felt preternaturally silent. A night that might swallow everything she knew about her world. For reality had taken a twist and then a tumble. But gradually she made out the outlines of the familiar furniture, the curtains, the lamps. She got out of bed, and tiptoed across the room, careful not to wake Emilio. He had spent much of the night tossing and turning and she had held him in her arms as he cried. Seeing his grown-up son for the first time had been a shock.

She slid open the curtains, unhooked the shutters, and pushed the window wide, raising her face to feel the cool air blowing in the scent of the sea. Stars blanketed the sky stretching far beyond anywhere her rational mind could take her. She stood in awe for a few minutes, her heart soaring at the magic of it, then the sound of Emilio's breathing brought her down to earth, and she went downstairs to wait for the day.

By the time it had turned into a glorious golden dawn, Thirza was on her way through the garden, running her fingers over the flowering oleanders, and carrying on down to the sea.

'You up for an early swim too?' she asked Billy when she saw him standing on their little beach all alone.

He turned, grinned, hazel eyes sparkling, and he looked just as he had as a child. Images of him rolled through Thirza's mind, Billy as a baby, as a toddler, as a nine-year-old. It took her breath away, for this was the first time she really felt it was him.

All these years, despite the dreadful emptiness of his absence, he had been living another life, and now it was almost as if he had never been gone and was just the same, though clearly he was not. His return still made no rational sense to her.

'Just you and me, Thizzy,' Billy said. 'Like it always was.'

Even though he'd been back at Merchant's for a few days, Thirza still could not quite get her mind around the fact that he walked among them, smiled, laughed, ate food, and joked, just as he always had done. Her living, breathing, brother, only different now.

As they walked closer to the water, she said, 'Your return will give Mother a new lease of life.'

'Really?'

'The light went out for her. She just collapsed inwards.'

Thirza didn't add how shocked and frightened she'd been to witness her mother's defencelessness. Her mother who'd always seemed so fearlessly competent. *Except for the content of those letters*, Thirza thought. She'd been vulnerable back then too.

'So, what will you do?' she asked. 'Now that you're back. You can live here, of course, if you want.'

He shook his head. 'Thanks, but my life is in America, and I need to finish my degree.'

'What do you study, or read, as they say? It seems odd not to know that sort of thing about you.'

'Natural history,' he said.

'And you like America?'

'I do. You must come and meet my American clan. They're longing to know *you*.'

'Do you have other siblings?' she managed to ask and, although she was curious, she didn't really want to know.

Please let him say no. Please.

She held her breath as she waited.

He nodded and now she felt like crying again, just like everyone else had been. It would be no comfort at all if he had another sister. She really couldn't bear that.

'Two brothers,' he said. 'A lot older than me, with families of their own. Not close like you and I.'

She let out her breath in relief and rubbed the back of her neck.

'So, you might stay there?' she asked tentatively. 'Permanently, I mean.'

He gave her his old cheeky grin. 'Maybe. There's a girl, you see.'

'Aha! I do see.'

'Felicity. We all call her Fliss for short. I asked her to come to Corfu with me, but she said this had to be family time. When we both graduate, we'll take a month and come together if that's okay?'

She grinned. 'I'll look forward to that. We all will.'

'She'll adore little Romi. As for me I can't quite believe I'm an uncle.'

'Kind of uncle. You are also Romi's half-brother.'

'Jeez!'

She paused as she saw the golden sun shimmering the sea water just as it always had done before he vanished, and would do after he had gone again.

'Billy, I don't know what to say. It broke our hearts, you know, when we believed you were dead. Just broke us, all of us, even Father. But then he changed, became nicer I suppose, and Penny helped. I don't think he ever knew how to cope with Dulcie.'

'I don't remember everything, but he does seem different.'

'Was it Emilio who spoke to you? Or Dulcie?'

He nodded. 'Dulcie told me in Corfu Town. I'll be honest, finding out Emilio is my biological father, well . . . it did shake me up. I believe she told Piers that day too.'

Thirza swallowed, couldn't speak, just listened to the sea, the birds, the breeze rustling in leaves in the trees.

Billy kicked the sand about. 'I have *three* fathers now, if you include my American father, Don.'

'What's he like?'

Billy smiled. 'Solid. Steady, honest. I love him.' He picked up a pebble and skimmed it professionally across the water.

'You were always better at that than me,' she said. Then, after a pause, 'I'm glad you've been happy.'

'It was tough for them. I was a disturbed, troublesome kid to begin with, but they took me to a psychiatrist who helped me deal with the blanks in my memory.'

'Helped you remember?'

'No. Helped me accept I might never remember who I once was. Oddly it kind of took the pressure off and that gave me permission, I think.'

'To *begin* to remember?'

'Yeah.'

'It hurts to hear that,' Thirza said with a catch in her voice, a lump in her throat.

'Hey,' he said. 'I'm fine now.'

'Honestly?'

'Honestly.'

'I'm so happy you're back. Words don't do it justice. Nothing will ever beat you coming home like this. Nothing more amazing could ever happen. I hope you know that.'

He nodded slowly. 'I do. I missed you, even though I didn't know who or what I was missing most of the time. I had this terrible aching void inside me that I never could fill.'

Thirza closed her eyes and imagined Billy when he was nine, all alone in a new country with none of his family and no recollection of who they even were.

'Now, about Emilio,' he said, interrupting her thoughts. 'We had a good chat. He treat you well?'

'Wonderfully well. We had a bumpy start what with Mother and everything.'

He laughed. 'Oh God. I can imagine. Glad I missed that.'

'But here we are.'

'Here we are indeed,' Billy repeated, raising his arms wide to take in the view. 'Just look at this place.'

Thirza gazed at the glittering, cobalt sea, the shadowy Albanian mountains, and the seamless blue sky.

They sat down cross-legged on the sand.

Billy took a deep breath as if taking it all in to store up for later. *Just swallowing it all up*, she thought. For when he would be gone again. A different kind of gone though. Not a vanishing with no knowing. Not a loss with no resolution. No. The vanishing of Billy Caruthers was a loss that could be mended. He was back, something anyone who had ever lost a beloved child or brother would give their right arm for. And they had him back. For that Thirza would give thanks every day of her life until she died. She only realised tears were pouring unchecked down her cheeks when he shifted closer and wiped them away with his fingers.

They gazed at each other, and he said, 'Remember when I was a kid and you used to wipe away my tears like this?'

She nodded.

'You were my big sister. I loved you so much, Thizzy.'

'And I you,' she managed to say, the lump in her throat back again. 'I used to hear your voice, you know. It comforted me *and* it made me cry.'

There was a long silence that grew into a warm acceptable silence.

'So much to remember, isn't there?' she eventually said and wrapped an arm around his shoulder. 'My little brother.'

'Not so little now.'

There was a slight pause.

'What will happen to Columbine?' he asked. 'Nothing will ever exonerate her for what she did, I know, but she did find me in the end.'

Thirza shook her head, knowing that neither her mother nor her father would want to see Columbine again. And anyway, Dulcie already had enough to come to terms with – having to share Billy with his other mother would be hard.

'Well,' he said. 'Time for that swim?'

She dismissed all the problems that might lie ahead, glanced across at him, then at the water, thought of Romi, Emilio, and all the wonderful people she had in her life. Her heart swelled with love for her tribe.

Then she jumped up, scattering sand everywhere, and ran. 'Race you in!' she shouted back at him. 'Beat you to the water.'

'You're on!' he yelled, easily catching up with her.

And they ran holding hands into the beautiful blue Ionian Sea, splashing and laughing and shrieking with exhilaration. With happiness, with everything that was good and true and meaningful and, most of all, with gratitude. For their lives, for each other, and the sheer relief of his return. The sun danced on the water, the breeze blew their hair, light shone all around them, and the day stretched out forever.

And when they came out giggling, Dulcie was standing on the shore, waiting for them, just as she had when they were children. Her mother whom the whole family had arranged themselves around and who, since 1923, had looked infinitely smaller. Diminished. Thirza could have cried every time she saw her. She often had cried. But now the impenetrable haze of loss, grief, and uncertainty that had hung around her for more than ten years was lifting. Her mother smiled, her face smoothed, and her posture became brave and firm as she took a step towards them.

'Hello, you two,' Dulcie said. 'Been for a swim?'

And Thirza blinked away her tears as she watched her mother fold Billy, wet and dripping, into her arms and then reach out for Thirza too. The life they might have lived was suddenly there before them, solid and real, as if nothing had changed. But it had changed. Everything was different now and always would be.

CHAPTER 59

Thirza was arranging flowers in her father and Penny's room when Magdalena called everyone to lunch or rather *ordered* them to lunch. But Thirza was enjoying the peace, biding her time, loitering really, unsure how lunch might go today, when she heard the door swing open.

'Penny! I'm so pleased to see you,' she exclaimed.

Gone was the aspirational Penny, the social climber, and instead here was a confident woman, a force of nature, and a loyal friend. Thirza had grown very fond of her.

'Likewise,' Penny said and came to kiss her on the cheeks.

'Thank you for holding the fort together at the wedding breakfast.'

'Darling, you already thanked me.'

'Did I? I can hardly remember a thing. I hope I didn't disgrace myself.'

Thirza didn't add how shocked her husband had been at seeing his son for the very first time, and how bravely he'd put his own feelings aside until they returned to

Merchant's. How he'd smiled as he waved his daughters, Lucia and Valentina off, as they boarded the ferry back to Italy. They'd been invited to Merchant's, but they politely made their excuses, insisting they had to get back to their mother in Naples. It was for the best.

'Listen,' Penny said. 'I have something to tell you.'

'Can it wait?'

Penny nodded.

'I think we'd better go down now,' Thirza added.

'That Magdalena is a tyrant.'

Thirza laughed.

Magdalena had grown in self-assurance too, and was not above speaking her mind, especially to Spiro and her mother-in-law, Eleni, which Thirza witnessed with mild astonishment. And lateness to lunch would not be tolerated. Thirza smiled then went downstairs and hurriedly helped everyone to their seat.

'You sit next to Penny, Father, with Ianthe on your other side. Then Walter, Billy, Dulcie, and me and Emilio over here at the end. Is that everyone?'

'What about my darling granddaughter?' Dulcie said.

'Fast asleep. Don't jinx it.'

Thirza hadn't known if Ianthe and Walter would come but they had, leaving Columbine to stay with her friend Lucie in Corfu. There was mild laughter though Ianthe seemed terribly quiet, and Thirza hoped to be able to reassure her later.

Eleni and Magdalena brought out a large meze platter of peppers in red, yellow, and orange, also black and green olives, hummus, tzatziki, warmed pita bread, tiny meatballs, and dolmades.

'What are they?' Billy asked.

'You don't remember?' Dulcie asked him.

He pulled a face. 'Sorry. No.'

'Stuffed vine leaves,' Dulcie said. 'You loved them.'

There was a tense silence.

'What did you eat in America?' Penny asked.

'Fried chicken.'

'Only fried chicken?'

'Mainly fried chicken.'

Everyone smiled though rather self-consciously.

As they ate their first course, Thirza eyed everyone surreptitiously. Her mother was charming and more or less poised, though she saw her watching Billy, hungry for him, unable to tear her eyes from him. Emilio seemed a little nervous, Ianthe was glowing, and, Thirza quickly realised, so was Piers. In fact, he seemed to be knocking back glass after glass of red wine, which might account for the glow.

He suddenly stood up, unnaturally agitated. 'It's no good,' he said. 'I have to . . . well, the thing is, I . . .'

Her father's brow furrowed, his jaw worked furiously, and tears began accumulating in the corners of his eyes. As he gulped and tried desperately to hold them back, Thirza's heart went out to him. Her father was going to cry! He was going to cry in front of them all. And nothing she could do would prevent it. He crumpled, and just as suddenly as he had risen to his feet he sat down again and began to weep.

Thirza stared in shock. What should she do? Everyone was silent, awkward, anxious even. She could not remember ever having seen her father cry like this and had no idea how to handle him. She gazed at her mother, but Dulcie was staring at her plate and shaking her head.

Someone spoke but Thirza wasn't sure who. Maybe Walter or Emilio.

Then Piers stood up abruptly and, hiding his face with his hand, he rushed from the table. Thirza rose to her feet too, ready to go after him, but Billy was ahead of her, and already running.

'Father,' he called out. 'Wait. Wait for me.'

Thirza took her seat again as the two men moved out of earshot. She felt Emilio reach for her hand and squeeze it. The atmosphere was still strained as they got back to their lunch, passing this or that when politely requested, and thanking each other profusely and unnecessarily.

While Magdalena cleared the table and they waited for the following course, Penny was the next person to stand up. Speaking in a voice almost breaking with emotion she said, 'What my darling, extremely overwrought, and I'm sorry but very drunk husband wanted to say . . . was that he's feeling pretty ropey at the moment, and rather as if he has *lost* his son, not gained him.'

Thirza swallowed the lump in her throat.

Thank goodness Billy had been the one to go after her father.

Later, as Thirza lay down for an afternoon nap with Emilio, she recalled the end of the terrible scene in the parsonage. She closed her eyes and was instantly back there in that stuffy room, her skin on fire, the chaplain hurrying around, red-faced, flapping his hands, telling them that guests were arriving for the next wedding, and they could hear the shouting. Billy holding Dulcie in his arms, soothing her.

Then Dulcie, utterly unhinged by Columbine's confession, meekly allowing her son to take her to Odel's where they could talk in private.

And Ianthe tenderly helping Columbine, holding her by the elbow, edging her forward and ushering her from the room.

As Thirza lay on top of the covers now, she couldn't help but look back.

Their lives had tilted when Billy disappeared and then spun wildly out of control and her mother had not stopped spinning since. Had never regained what she'd had before. Who she'd been before. *Was it always so*, she wondered. *Did a cataclysmic event always have such seismic consequences?*

Thirza felt Emilio stirring beside her. 'You're not asleep?' he asked.

'I can't stop worrying.'

'Tell me.'

'Well, everything really. Billy. My mother. And I haven't had a chance to talk to Ianthe. She must be feeling awful, one way or another.'

'Come here, sweetheart,' he said, and drew her close. 'We'll just lie here. We don't have to sleep. You don't need to worry about anything right now. Whatever happens in the future we'll find a way.'

'But I have so many people staying or coming. There's such a lot to do.'

'There's nothing to do, *now*. So, rest.'

Thirza closed her eyes and before long she felt drowsy.

When she awoke Emilio was not in bed with her. She sat up, swung her legs out, and rose to her feet, stretching her arms high above her head. In the late afternoon the house felt busy, alive, so different from the way it had been when she'd first returned here seven years after Billy disappeared. Then the house had been cold, stricken, packed with spiders.

Now she could hear her daughter's laughter and that never failed to make her smile. She crossed to one of the windows and leant out, breathing air bursting with the sweet scent of roses and aromatic herbs. Billy and Dulcie were swinging Romi between them on the first terrace. It seemed such an impossible sight.

She carried on watching and saw Emilio joining the others, saying, 'Afternoon tea is served, everyone.'

Then he swept Romi up and Billy wrapped an arm around Emilio's shoulders. It was such a lovely warm thing to do.

She washed, tied up her hair, hurriedly dressed in a loose blue linen dress, and went down to join the others.

She almost bumped into Ianthe in the hall. 'Oh sorry,' she began, then seeing the girl's stricken eyes, she reached out.

'I don't know what to think,' Ianthe said, as Thirza held her close, feeling the girl's heart thumping.

'Let things settle. I'm always here if you need me. Always.'

Ianthe nodded then whispered, 'I'm sorry, Thirza.'

'You have nothing to be sorry for.'

'Oh, there you are, darling,' Dulcie called out, spotting them. 'Come and sit by me, Thirza, but why are you wearing a sack?'

Thirza smiled. 'It's comfortable, and I happen to like this sack, Mother.'

Dulcie laughed and shook her head.

Magdalena brought out tea and cake.

At that moment Piers came to sit down. He looked sad, diminished even, terribly hurt.

'Hello Pa,' she said. 'You all right?'

Piers shrugged and Thirza ached for her broken-hearted father. First his son returned . . . then he wasn't his son after all.

'You will always be Billy's father,' she whispered.

After that neither of them spoke for a moment and Thirza blinked. She really did not want to cry today and yet she had the feeling that she probably would. Her father got up and wandered away. She inhaled slowly and let out her breath in a puff before speaking to Penny, 'What did you want to tell me? Earlier, I mean.'

Penny gazed at her, and as her eyes crinkled up, sparkling and glittering, the sadness vanished, and her whole face broke into the widest of smiles.

'I'm expecting a baby,' Penny said then burst into tears.

Thirza passed her a lace-edged handkerchief.

'I'm so happy,' Penny whispered.

'And Father?'

'He doesn't know yet. I can't tell him, not while he doesn't know which side is up.'

Thirza sighed. 'Maybe give him a little time, but not *too* long. He'll be overjoyed.'

'You think?'

'I promise. And the thing is that Billy's return is weird for *all* of us.'

'How do you mean?'

'Well . . . he's our Billy, and he's *not* our Billy. You've only got to listen. He's an American!'

'I suppose he is.'

There was a prolonged pause as they watched Piers returning with a rather large brandy.

'Billy belongs to his new family now,' Thirza said, shaking her head as if to ward off the disturbing truth.

Penny took her hand and squeezed it.

They sat in silence but as the reality finally dawned, Thirza couldn't deny it. 'This is what is so terribly hard,' she said, her voice almost failing her. 'You see, Billy belongs to *them* . . . more than to us.'

'Oh, sweetheart.'

Thirza's chest constricted and her eyes grew hot. 'It's very hard.'

'I'm so sorry.'

'You know what,' Thirza said suddenly. 'Tell Father you're expecting. Don't delay. Do it this evening before he drinks too much. It'll change everything.'

And Thirza could suddenly see clearly. She saw their lives moving on as they must. She saw a new baby in the family opening up the future for all of them. That was what mattered now. Not the past. They would come to accept everything that had happened, and they would live their lives, this flawed mixed-up family that she loved. A piercing shriek reached them from an open window upstairs and she grinned at Penny.

'You have all this ahead of you,' she said, pushing back her chair. 'This crazy, crazy, love we have for our children. But for now, that's *my* girl waking up, and I couldn't be prouder or happier.'

CHAPTER 60

One month later

Dulcie

Dulcie stood leaning against the railings, watching the two figures waving at her. She felt an ache in her chest but continued to stand there, lifting her hand, keeping it suspended in the air, even after Billy and Thirza could no longer see her and she could not see them.

She gazed too at the island of Corfu as it receded. Her island, she'd always thought of it, but too much had happened in 1923 – the Italian invasion, the occupation, and Billy's abduction. Nothing had been the same since and, despite his return, nor would it ever be.

Billy was back. And it was wonderful. Wonderful! But he was not the same little boy, and she would never recover the years of his childhood that she'd lost. His disappearance had marked them all, including Billy himself. Scarred them. *Grief always leaves a mark*, she thought, *no matter how hard you try to hide it. And just as it swallows you, it spits you out again, only to flood you another time, and another, until you feel you might drown.*

She recalled the first year after Billy vanished when they'd all believed he was dead. In great waves the grief had come and gone and when, after a long while, it abated a little, and she had smiled at some trivial thing at work, she'd found herself consumed with guilt. How could she forget? Even for a minute. Yet that had been the crux of her recovery. She'd learnt to forget and remember at the same time. For if she hadn't, she would surely have died.

And just as Billy danced and ran, and threw balls for the dog, and swam in the sea, forever in her heart, she'd had to forget him too.

Now, she continued to gaze out at the sea, hearing the seabirds calling, feeling the spray on her cheeks and tasting the salt on her lips. She smiled recalling Billy's wide grin – he still had it. The light in his eyes too. His curly hair.

Back then time had passed slowly. Nights when she'd been lost in the darkness and couldn't sleep. That deep black hole of endless grieving. Nobody knew how she had mourned her boy. Nobody.

And feeling more alone than she'd ever been, she rose in the mornings, dressed, drank her coffee, and went to work, growing thinner and thinner, and living like a machine. She'd left Thirza to her own devices. Been a bad mother, but when all she could do was keep on breathing, it was inevitable. She'd tried to smile, talk to her daughter, but

Thirza saw right through her and withdrew a little more each day.

And so, she was leaving Merchant's in Thirza's capable hands now. It was the only thing she could do to make up for how she had been. To make up for her neglect. It was her daughter's time. Time to be with her husband and Romi. Time to be the owner of a beautiful home.

Dulcie smiled, wanting to do her best for them all, though it had been hard relinquishing Merchant's. The estate and house had been her life, but in truth it was ruined for her. She had been foolish over Federico – Emilio Bellini – deluded. An imagined grief. Billy's loss had been real and visceral. And though he was back, and he walked and breathed and existed in the world, which was all a mother really longed for, she knew her grief for the years she had lost would be never ending.

She sent a prayer into the air for her whole Corfu family and then she turned away and walked towards the front of the ferry, sliding her hand along the railing as she went, picking up salt and licking her fingers. There was no point in looking backwards anymore, though she would always remember. Always.

'*Goodbye, my darlings,*' she whispered. '*Goodbye.*'

Now, at the front of the ferry, she gazed forward. To Italy and to her future in England, and whatever else might lie ahead. As the sun shone down, casting molten diamonds across the surface of the sea, the ache in her chest lifted. She smiled, aware of the seeds of hope that had begun to settle in her heart.

'Goodbye Corfu,' she said. 'Until the next time.'

ACKNOWLEDGEMENTS

The first rough draft of *The Greek House* was completed before I was diagnosed with a systemic autoimmune disease. If you too have been affected by Polymyalgia Rheumatica, you have my sympathies. For me it hasn't been easy, and it isn't over yet. However, the book would never have reached publication without Lynne Drew and Sophie Burks (Irwin), who both went not just the extra mile, but the extra hundred miles to help me knock it into shape. Thank you. Thank you both so much.

I'm excited about this book. Yes, it was a hard birth, but I'm proud of the work we all did and am hugely grateful to the entire team at HarperFiction, who are just marvellous. For nine months I didn't work at all, was often too ill to get out of bed, and I felt that I'd lost so much of myself and who I thought I was. Turns out I'm still a writer! And writing continues to be my happy place.

Thank you to my agent Caroline Hardman who has always had my back. And a very personal thanks to the writer Sinead Moriarty, who told me it would be all right when I first had my diagnosis and could barely move my body for the pain and rigidity I was experiencing. We never know what's round the corner in life, do we?

I'm so lucky to have loyal readers. So, thank you for continuing to buy and read my books. Do let me know what you think of this one. I'm hoping this will be a good year for you and for all of us. Because even in the worst of times, everything does pass, and quite often does also get better.

The first draft of the next book is done – no title yet – but it's where we'll catch up with some of the characters from *The Greek House*. I hope you love them as much as I do.

As a family we've spent many wonderful holidays in the heavenly Greek Ionian Islands, so in a way this book is a love song to Corfu, Paxos, Zakynthos, and the others. If you haven't been there, you'll love them and, if you have, you'll already know what I mean.

Fern Britton *Picks*

Exclusively for TESCO

EXCLUSIVE ADDITIONAL CONTENT

Includes an author Q&A and details
of how to get involved in *Fern's Picks*

Dear lovely readers,

I am so delighted to share this month's pick – *The Greek House* by Dinah Jefferies – with you. Dinah is the bestselling author of *Night Train to Marrakech*, and this emotional and gripping historical novel of family secrets, love and betrayal will have you hooked!

It is 1930 and Thirza Caruthers has returned to Corfu – the location of her family's summer home – for the first time in seven years. Though the island is beautiful, amongst the wild roses and oleander lie terrible memories for Thirza. Seven years ago, her brother Billy disappeared from Corfu Town and has not been seen since. And now she is back, trying to escape these haunting memories by immersing herself in painting – and a passionate affair. But as buried secrets start to surface, Thirza steps closer and closer to discovering the truth about Billy's vanishing . . .

This is a beautifully written and immersive novel that will transport you to the clear blue waters and rugged beauty of Corfu. Full of twists and turns, it will have you guessing right up until the final page – and I can't wait to hear what you think!

With love
Fern x

Fern
Britton
Picks

Exclusively for
TESCO

Look out for more books, coming soon!

For more information on the book club,
exclusive Q&As with the authors and
reading group questions, visit Fern's website
www.fern-britton.com/ferns-picks

We'd love you to join in the conversation,
so don't forget to share your thoughts using
#FernsPicks

A Q&A with
Dinah Jefferies

Warning: contains spoilers

It's such a gripping and moving novel: what was your original inspiration for the idea of *The Greek House*?

Inspiration for me slips in quietly and is almost never a bright, sparkly thing. Here the inspirational seeds were just two names. One – found on an old headstone in a graveyard overlooking the North Devon coast – was *Thirza*, and a more tranquil resting place I could not imagine. Later I found out Thirza was short for Theresa. The other name was *Dulcie*. When I was studying fashion at art college back in the 1960s, my research project was to follow the wardrobe mistress at a local repertory theatre. As I watched the cast rehearse, I was mesmerised by the star Dulcie Gray. I never met another Dulcie after that, and nor have I ever met a Thirza. *The Greek House* is theirs. For me, they are my most heart-felt characters ever and I couldn't wait to develop their story.

How did you conduct your research about the period and the setting?

The research is where the next element of the inspiration kicked in. I read everything I could find. At that stage, I only knew I wanted to write a moving story about a mother and daughter, and I wanted to set the book on one of the Ionian Islands. We regularly spent family holidays on Paxos, and I'd also been to Corfu and Zakynthos. I love stories set in big old houses full of secrets and mysteries and I needed one for this novel. I find that when I focus on an idea, the more my story reveals itself, so I thought about Thirza and Dulcie endlessly. And when I couldn't sleep one night, I created Merchant's Estate (*The Greek House*) for them, overlooking the bright blue loveliness of the Ionian Sea. It is Thirza's home, her joy and her sanctuary, and she will do almost anything to keep it. But it also becomes the place where the love, passion and betrayal that runs through her story could ruin everything.

I did not want to write about World War Two but when I found out Italy had invaded Corfu in 1923 during a time of peace – the Corfu Incident – and had occupied the island for one month, it gave me the dramatic hook I needed for the beginning. That became the day *he* vanishes and gave me the time period I needed to focus on. It became the day the family's lives are turned upside down and they become desperate for the truth.

The book is written from two perspectives, Dulcie and Thirza – did you find one or the other easier? Are there any challenges when it comes to writing a novel that has a dual point of view narrative?

You want your readers to engage with both characters equally and that's the biggest challenge, although it's only natural that different readers will have different perspectives and sympathies. Sometimes one character comes into being more easily than the other. In this case we only have Dulcie's – the mother's – point of view in Part One and also for just one chapter at the end. Most of the book is Thirza's story but I loved writing both equally.

You often write about strong women; how would describe your novels to others?

I aim to write page-turning dramas and mysteries about unforgettable characters in gorgeous settings. Their stories are packed with emotion and long held secrets, with shocking revelations and, most importantly, redemption. How do we cope when life upends us – when what we thought was forever turns out not to be? How do we find the strength, resilience, love, and forgiveness, when nostalgia is not enough? Some readers have suggested there is a lot of me in this novel and I have to admit this book is very close to my heart. There is grief, and the darkness of the past is never far away, but there is also great love, and that's what I hope readers will take away with them. I always think of the poem *Wild Geese* by Mary Oliver. It reminds us that while we all despair at times, there is still joy and beauty in the world.

Did you always plan to end the book the way you did?

I planned both the big surprises and when they would happen. The second one was very hard to write. After my son died, we went to Crete with my mum and stayed in very simple 'rooms' and yet that awfully dark time was the start of my love affair with Greece. It was late September at the end of the season and a little bit mournful with heavy skies and a backdrop of gloomy mountains. Five chairs at the taverna dinner table instead of six was hard to bear, but so many mothers had suffered there in the island's checkered past that I felt less alone. So, I suppose the answer is yes, I did plan the ending. It had lived in my dreams for decades just waiting to come out.

Do you have any recommendations for anybody visiting Corfu, or any other Greek islands?

Paxos is wonderful for peace and quiet, especially the village of Loggos, but over the 27 years since my husband Richard and I first went there on honeymoon, it has become busier. Back in the day, Paxos was a little dusty, overrun with cats, and you would never have found a cappuccino! It's smarter now but still retains its charm. Corfu has the most wonderful coastline and scenery. Corfu Town is glorious too, packed with Venetian heritage, and the northeast of the island is gorgeous. I'm not surprised it's where the English used to flock. For your taste of paradise go to the Ionian Islands in early June or October. Or go anywhere in Greece if, like me, you have many islands still to discover.

Can you give us any hints regarding your next novel?

I can. We meet Thirza again in the next book. The first part is set on Merchant's Estate in Corfu, but then the story of mystery and intrigue moves to a stunning Chartreuse Manor in France for a few months.

Once again it explores issues of home and belonging, of family and identity. Thirza has been having a terribly challenging time with one of her stepdaughters and leaving for France to look after an elderly relative is a means of escape. I'm loving writing it. When the first draft is almost done, you can begin to live in your story. It's a fabulous feeling as the story becomes more and more real. The house is real. The characters are real and at any moment I expect to answer the phone to one of them. Is that madness? Yes. But it's also how you know you've created living, breathing characters. Thank you so much for reading. My books only properly exist when they are in the heads and hearts of my wonderful readers.

Questions for your Book Club

Warning: contains spoilers

- How did the setting of *The Greek House* influence your experience of reading the novel?

- Which character do you think is most affected by the themes of envy, love and betrayal in the novel? Why?

- As the story unfolds, Thirza uncovers more about her family's past. How do the revelations about her family's history impact her relationships with other characters in the novel?

- What do you think the novel suggests about the themes of family loyalty and forgiveness?

- Thirza attempts to cope with her grief and confusion by immersing herself in painting. How does this artistic outlet serve as both a means of escape and a path to self-discovery?

- How did you feel about Thirza's relationship with Emilio? How does it impact her time in Corfu?

- What were your main takeaways from Thirza's relationship with her mother?

- Did you enjoy the ending of the book? Where were you left in terms of your feelings?

An exclusive extract from Fern's new novel

A Cornish Legacy

CHAPTER ONE

North Cornwall, April, present day

Delia squinted through the windscreen, the sun ahead dazzling her. 'You'll see the turning on the right in a minute,' she said. 'Keep an eye out. I might miss it.'

Sammi tipped the last of the crisps into his mouth and sat up a little straighter. 'My eyes are peeled.' He pulled the sunglasses down from his head. 'Will there be some kind of landmark?'

'There's a big metal sign swinging on a post above the gates. Remember? You said it looked like a gibbet.'

Sammi chuckled. 'The gibbet! Yes, of course! Such a welcome.' He sat up straighter, alert. 'There!'

Delia saw the emerging gap amongst the tangled hedge of rhododendrons, with the rusted sign hanging from the post.

'Is that it?' asked Sammi. 'Can't read the name.'

Delia slowed, changing down through the gears. She wasn't smiling. 'Yep. This is it. Wilder Hoo.' The sight of the tatty sign that she had never wanted or expected to see again forced her stomach into a tight knot. Turning, she slowed the car and braked to a halt. 'I really don't want to be here.'

Sammi reached over for her knee and tapped it briskly. 'You're not on your own. I'm here, and those horrible people are gone. Come on.'

Delia put a hand to her chest and took a deep breath to control the old anxiety welling within. 'It's quite late. Let's go and find somewhere to stay tonight and come back tomorrow.'

'It's only half past four!'

'But it'll be getting dark soon.'

'Darling, it's April, not December.' Sammi's voice became soft and sympathetic. 'I know this is hard. But you can do it, and you will do it.'

'I don't want to do it.'

'The past is past. Dead and buried.'

Sighing heavily, Delia put the car in gear and slowly drove the winding tarmacked drive. 'Dead people can still haunt us.'

Stiff clumps of grass and dandelions had forced themselves between the cracked pitch, and in other places, huge potholes housed red, muddied puddles.

'It'll cost thousands just to repair the drive,' she said. 'Look at it.'

She knew that Sammi saw through different eyes. For him, this was an adventure. When Delia had first told him that the house had been gifted to her, he had been ready to celebrate, despite her horror of the whole thing. He seemed to feel only the thrill of an escapade.

Looking out of his side window at the ancient, rolling parkland with great oaks dotted across the scene he said, 'Delia, this is utterly captivating. Please tell me there's a lake. I'm expecting Colin Firth to stride forth in his wet breeches and shirt.'

Delia was scornful. 'If only. No lake, I'm afraid. Just a beach and all these acres of parkland. Do you know, it takes four men with a tractor each an entire week to cut all that grass? When they get to the end, they have to start again. It's a bloody money pit.' Her eyes flicked to the avenue of ivy-clad beech trees ahead, the bare branches forming a tunnel over sodden leaves. 'That ivy needs cutting back too. Argh. Who can afford all this, I ask you!'

Sammi was not listening. 'How long is this drive again?'

'It's 1.2 miles.'

'Very specific.'

Delia sighed. 'My father-in-law preferred to tell everyone it was two kilometres because that sounded longer.'

'And all this land belongs to the house?'

'Yup.'

Sammi was grinning. 'I'd love to jump on a tractor and spend a whole summer mowing all this.'

'You really wouldn't. Back in the day, there were sheep and deer to crop it.'

'Sheep and deer! Delia.' Sammi laughed. 'And all this is actually yours!'

She shrugged. She was weary and wretched. 'Not for long, I hope.'

They rattled over a cattle grid and onto a sparsely gravelled drive.

'OK. Here we go.' Delia swallowed hard. 'Round this bend, you'll see the house.' She took a nervous breath and added, 'I couldn't do this without you.'

Sammi tutted, 'I wouldn't let you come on your own, would I?'

Delia steered the last curve – and there, suddenly, was Wilder Hoo.

Coming soon!

The No.1 Sunday Times bestselling author returns

A lifetime of secrets. One chance to finally find home.

Cordelia Jago has lost everything. All she has left is a legacy
she never expected – and would never have wanted.

Wilder Hoo – The Wild House – is a crumbling Cornish Manor
House which she hates, full of unhappy memories.
It is falling down to the brink of ruin.

Determined to sell-up and forget the past, Cordelia begins to spruce
up its echoing rooms – but the house seems to exert a pull on her
and awakens a connection she thought she had buried forever.

With the help of the locals, Cordelia breathes new life into
the home, but will she find a way to heal her heart too?

COMING SOON!

Our next book club title

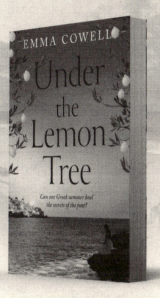

EMMA COWELL

Under the Lemon Tree

*Can one Greek summer heal
the secrets of the past?*

Could discovering a family secret encourage Kat to follow her heart?

Shattered by the sudden loss of her twin, Nik, Kat is lost in grief.
The comfort of family feels both soothing and suffocating, but
everything changes when she inherits a house on the breathtaking
Greek island of Agistri from a mysterious uncle she's never met.

Arriving on Agistri, Kat is mesmerized by its crystalline waters, lush pine
forests, and the citrus-scented air. Among the white-washed houses and
warm, welcoming locals, she begins to feel her heart heal. The island
offers more than solace, sparking courage in Kat to face her loss – and
maybe even embrace the spark of unexpected love…

But as she unearths her family's buried past, Kat must also confront
her own fears of belonging, forgiveness — and the possibility of
rediscovering happiness in the shadow of heartbreak…